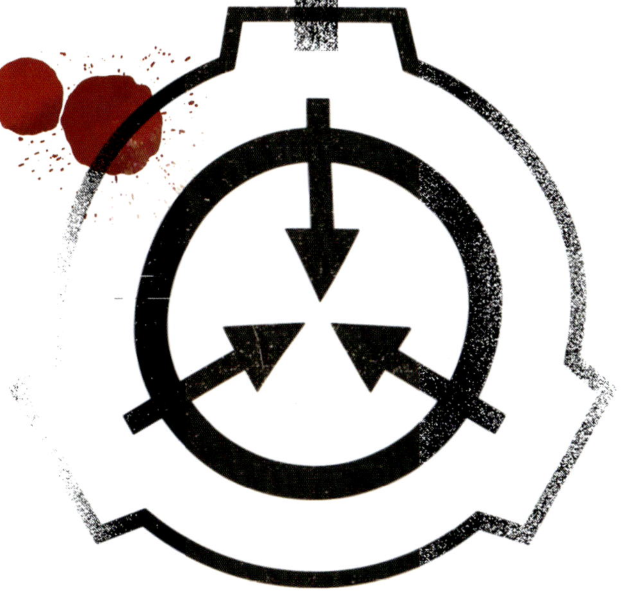

SCP Foundation ▸ Archives

Red Journal

SIFIEDCLASSIFIEDCLA

Security Clearance Level IV

This journal belongs to

CLASSIFIED

SCP Foundation

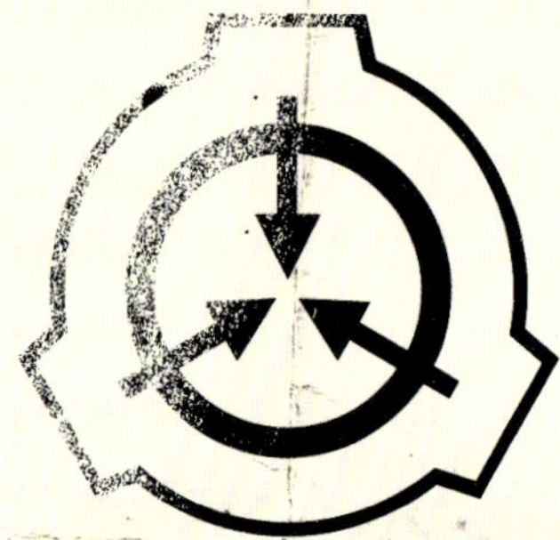

Mankind in its present state has been around for a quarter of a million years, yet only the last 4,000 have been of any significance.

So, what did we do for nearly 250,000 years? We huddled in caves and around small fires, fearful of the things that we didn't understand. It was more than explaining why the sun came up, it was the mystery of enormous birds with heads of men and rocks that came to life. So we called them 'gods' and 'demons', begged them to spare us, and prayed for salvation.

In time, their numbers dwindled and ours rose. The world began to make more sense when there were fewer things to fear, yet the unexplained can never truly go away, as if the universe demands the absurd and impossible.

Mankind must not go back to hiding in fear. No one else will protect us, and we must stand up for ourselves.

While the rest of mankind dwells in the light, we must stand in the darkness to fight it, contain it, and shield it from the eyes of the public, so that others may live in a sane and normal world.

We secure. We contain. We protect.

— The Administrator

OBJECT CLASSES

All anomalous objects, entities, and phenomena requiring Special Containment Procedures are assigned an Object Class. An Object Class is a part of the standard SCP template and serves as a rough indicator for how difficult an object is to contain. In universe, Object Classes are for the purposes of identifying containment needs, research priority, budgeting, and other considerations. An SCP's Object Class is determined by a number of factors, but the most important factors are the difficulty and the purpose of its containment.

SAFE

The Locked Box Test:
If you lock it in a box, leave it alone, and nothing bad will happen, then it's probably Safe.

Safe-class SCPs are anomalies that are easily and safely contained. This is often due to the fact that the Foundation has researched the SCP well enough that containment does not require significant resources or that the anomalies require a specific and conscious activation or trigger. Classifying an SCP as Safe, however, does not mean that handling or activating it does not pose a threat.

EUCLID

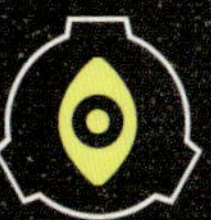

The Locked Box Test:
If you lock it in a box, leave it alone, and you're not entirely sure what will happen, then it's probably Euclid.

Euclid-class SCPs are anomalies that require more resources to contain completely or where containment isn't always reliable. Usually this is because the SCP is insufficiently understood or inherently unpredictable. Euclid is the Object Class with the greatest scope, and it's usually a safe bet that an SCP will be this class if it doesn't easily fall into any of the other standard Object Classes.

As a note, any SCP that's autonomous, sentient and/or sapient is generally classified as Euclid, due to the inherent unpredictability of an object that can act or think on its own.

KETER

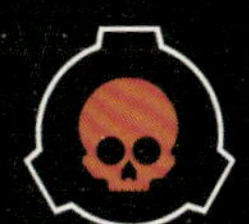

The Locked Box Test:
If you lock it in a box, leave it alone, and it easily escapes, then it's probably Keter.

Keter-class SCPs are anomalies that are exceedingly difficult to contain consistently or reliably, with containment procedures often being extensive and complex. The Foundation often can't contain these SCPs well due to not having a solid understanding of the anomaly, or lacking the technology to properly contain or counter it. A Keter SCP does not mean the SCP is dangerous, just that it is simply very difficult or costly to contain.

THAUMIEL

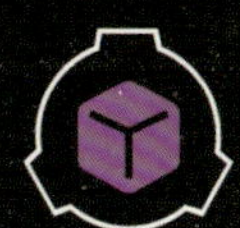

The Locked Box Test:
If it is the box, then it's probably Thaumiel.

Thaumiel-class SCPs are anomalies that the Foundation specifically uses to contain other SCPs. Even the mere existence of Thaumiel-class objects is classified at the highest levels of the Foundation and their locations, functions, and current status are known to few Foundation personnel outside of the O5 Council.

[PERSONNEL DOC_01]
[ID_DOCTOR ███]

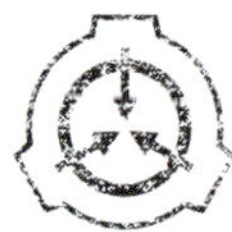

CLEARANCE & CLASSIFICATION

1 Foundation security clearances granted to personnel represent the highest level or type of information to which they can be granted access.

Level 5 [Thaumiel]

Level 5 security clearances are given to the highest-ranking administrative personnel within the Foundation and grant effectively unlimited access to all strategic and otherwise sensitive data. Level 5 security clearances are typically only granted to O5 Council members and selected staff.

Level 4 [Top Secret]

Level 4 security clearances are given to senior administration that require access to site-wide and/or regional intelligence as well as long-term strategic data regarding Foundation operations and research projects. Level 4 security clearances are typically only held by Site Directors, Security Directors, or Mobile Task Force Commanders.

Level 3 [Secret]

Level 3 security clearances are given to senior security and research personnel that require in-depth data regarding the source, recovery circumstances, and long-term planning for anomalous objects and entities in containment. Most senior research staff, project managers, security officers, response team members, and Mobile Task Force operatives hold a Level 3 security clearance.

Level 2 [Restricted]

Level 2 security clearances are given to security and research personnel that require direct access to information regarding anomalous objects and entities in containment. Most research staff, field agents, and containment specialists hold a Level 2 security clearance.

Level 1 [Confidential]

Level 1 security clearances are given to personnel working in proximity to but with no direct, indirect, or informational access to anomalous objects or entities in containment. Level 1 security clearances are typically granted to personnel working in clerical, logistics, or janitorial positions at facilities with containment capability or otherwise must handle sensitive information.

Level 0 [For Official Use Only]

Level 0 security clearances are given to non-essential personnel with no need to access information regarding anomalous objects or entities in Foundation containment. Level 0 access is typically held by personnel in non-secured clerical, logistics, or janitorial positions at facilities with no access to operational data.

2 Pesonnel Classifications are assigned to personnel based on their proximity to potentially dangerous anomalous objects, entities, or phenomena.

Class A

Not allowed direct access to anomalies under any circumstances.

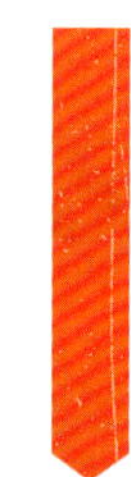

Class B

May only be granted access to anomalies that have passed quarantine and have been cleared of any potential mind-affecting effects or memetic agents.

Class C

Have direct access to most anomalies not deemed strictly hostile or dangerous.

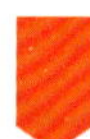

Class D

Expendable personnel used to handle extremely hazardous anomalies. Typically drawn from the ranks of prison inmates convicted of violent crimes, especially those on death row.

Class E

Field agents and containment personnel that have been exposed to potentially dangerous effects during the course of securing a newly-designated anomaly. Are to be quarantined as soon as possible.

CLEARANCE & CLASSIFICATION

The Administrator

A mysterious figure playing a vital, but nebulous role within the Foundation. Possibly anomalous, possibly multiple people.

05 Command

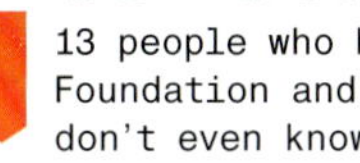

13 people who have ultimate control over the Foundation and its secrets. Many employees don't even know this group exists.

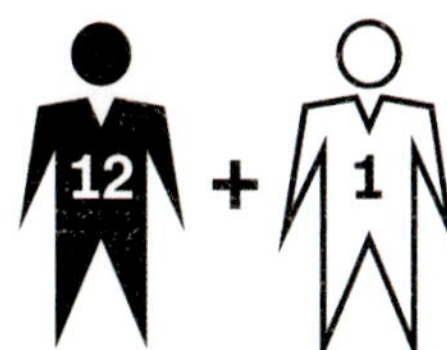

Site Directors

The highest-ranking personnel at their assigned location responsible for the containment and safe operation of the site.

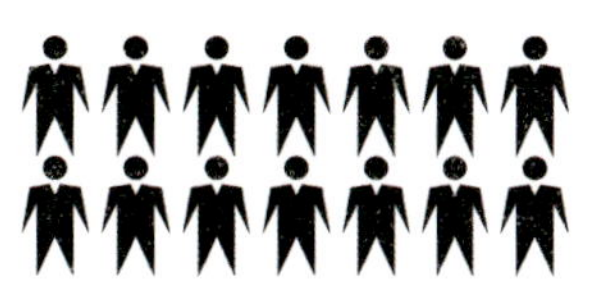

Researchers

Scientists drawn from every field imaginable and tasked with understanding of unexplained anomalies.

Field Agents

The eyes and ears of the Foundation. They are trained to look for and investigate signs of anomalous activity, often undercover.

Containment Specialists

Engineers, technicians and other personnel responsible for both establishing initial containment over newly discovered SCPs and maintaining existing containment units.

Tactical Response Officers

Highly trained and heavily armed combat teams tasked with escorting containment teams and defending Foundation facilities against hostile action.

Security Officers

On-site guards who enforce physical and information security for Foundation projects, operations, and personnel.

Mobile Task Force Operative

Units comprised of veteran field personnel drawn from all over the Foundation and mobilized to deal with threats of a specific nature.

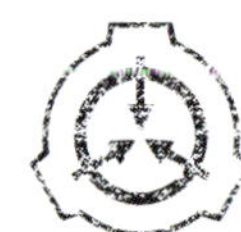

UPDATED AMNESTICS GUIDE

OVERVIEW

Amnesitic is the common name for a number of drugs used to erase or modify memory. Memory modification is widely used in the Foundation and is the cornerstone of maintaining proper levels of privacy. Amnestics are usually produced in the process of special development of the substances produced by some SCP objects, however, synthetic amnestics that are equally effective, but cheaper and easier to manufacture are being developed.

The basic principle that allows amnestics to function relies on their effects on neural connections in the human brain. The active ingredients of an injected amnestic enter a reaction, the product of which damages these bonds to one degree or another, or destroys them completely; the stronger the amnestic, the more bonds are exposed to it. The introduction of the drug stimulates the production of certain hormones in the body, enhancing the effect. Programmable amnesiacs contribute to the formation of new neural connections in a manner similar to that of nootropic drugs. Their use requires [REDACTED].

Amnestics are classified according to their properties, intended usage, magnitude of effect and method of application.

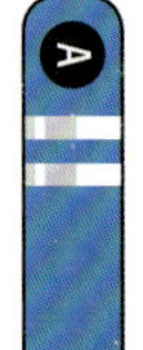

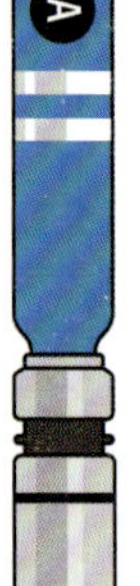

Class A, General Retrograde

For erasing recent and/or specific episodic memories

While Class A amnestics will technically deconsolidate memories at random, they will mostly affect engrams within the 'memory reconsolidation window' of 5-6 hours, as these are the memories that will be at the forefront of the subject's mind. This is especially true for highly unique episodic memories, such as encounters with anomalous phenomena. While these will be most effective after initial exposure, it is possible to re-open a memory reconsolidation window, allowing for amnestics officers to trigger and then erase specific memories long after their initial formation.

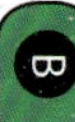

Class B, Regressive Retrograde

For the incremental erasure of recent memories

Class B amnestics start by deconsolidating the most recently formed memories first, and then working their way backwards. The extent of the memory erasure is dependent on dosage, with a 75 mg dose resulting in approximately 24 hours of memory loss on average. These are ideal for erasing recent memories older than six hours without having to trigger specific memories.

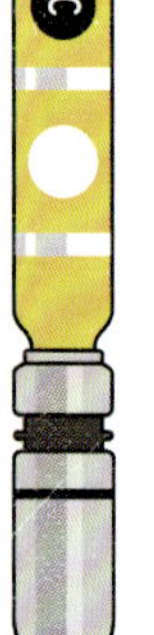

Class C, Targeted Retrograde

For the removal of specific memories from any point in the subject's life

Class C amnestics are used in conjunction with high fidelity neuro-imaging and transcranial stimulation. Neuro-imagers will locate the specific memory engrams within the subject's brain, and upon reaching those specific engrams the amnestics will be activated through the use of precise, non-invasive stimulation, typically ultrasound or magnetic fields.

The benefit of Class C amnestics is that they allow for the surgically precise removal of memories regardless of when they formed, and are ideal for expunging classified data from the minds of D-class personnel and neutralized humanoid SCPs prior to their release. The major drawback of Class C amnestics is the required equipment's lack of portability. As such, Class C amnestics are most efficiently administered at Foundation sites, though mobile amnestic field clinics are currently under development.

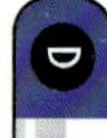

Class D, Progressive Retrograde

For the removal of early memories

Class D amnestics are the opposite of Class Bs. They target the oldest memories first and work their way forward, the effects depending on dosage. As this is a fairly niche application, Class D amnestics are rarely used. Though they are, by design, more potent than their counterparts, it still requires an extremely high dosage to expunge a significant portion of a subject's life. As such, their risk of side effects is dangerously high. It should be noted that Class D amnestics only target explicit memories. Implicit memories, namely skills that the individual learned in their youth, will remain unaffected.

UPDATED AMNESTICS GUIDE

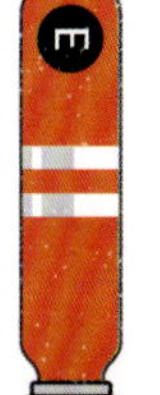

Class E, Ennui

To induce psychological complacency with the anomalous

To be frank, 'ennui' isn't actually the proper term for the psychological effects of Class E amnestics. They would more accurately be considered an 'anti-nostalgia' drug. Though they still target the neural pathways for memories, they do not deconsolidate them. Rather, they merely weaken the pathways while disassociating the memory with any emotions, positive or negative, removing any incentive to think about it and thus allowing it to naturally decay on its own.

Class E amnestics are most effective in situations where the suppression of the anomalous is not possible, and thus in order to preserve normality, the anomaly must be perceived as normal. Class E amnestics cause subjects to accept the world as it is, and forget that it was ever any different.

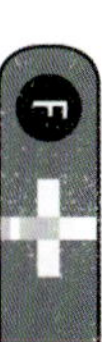

Class F, Fugue

For erasing and rebuilding the subject's identity

As with the old Class F, these amnestics induce a Fugue State, or dissociative amnesia, in the subject. The subject will forget their identity and may either be provided with a new one by the amnestics officer, or allowed to develop one on their own.

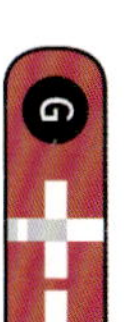

Class G, Gaslighting

To cause subjects to doubt the authenticity of their memories

Class G amnestics induce derealisation of memories, making them seem fantastic or dreamlike, causing the subject to doubt their authenticity. Standard field Class-G amnestics are formulated to target memories of the anomalous, and are best administered when the subject lacks any tangible evidence of their account and targeting specific memories is infeasible. Class-G amnestics that target non-anomalous memories, however~~, have been banned by the Ethics Committee.~~

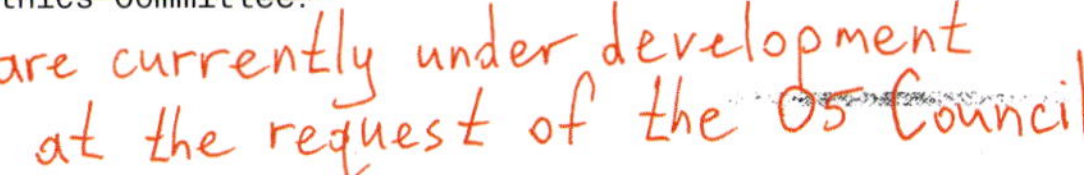

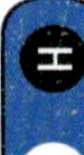

Class H, Anterograde

To prevent the formation of new memories

Class H amnestics prevent the subject from forming new memories, blocking memory consolidation for as long as the agent is in the subject's system. Duration is dependent on dosage, with 75 mg lasting for approximately 24 hours on average.

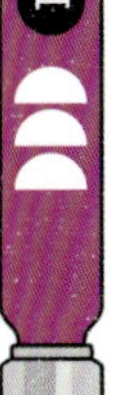

Class I, Transient

For inducing a temporary amnesic state

Class I amnestics induce transient amnesia by blocking the neural pathways responsible for long-term memories, temporarily preventing subjects from recalling their past. Duration is dependent on dosage, again with 75 mg lasting approximately 24 hours on average.

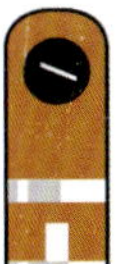

Class W-Z, Mnestics

Protection against anti-memetic and other mnemonic anomalies

Classes W-Z refer to mnestic drugs, or drugs that prevent/reverse memory erasure, and are most commonly used by the antimemetics department. Though in function they are the opposite of amnestics, they both work by targeting the neural pathways for memory, allowing for the creation of non-anomalous mnestic drugs.

Class W mnestics allow the subject to perceive and retain knowledge of antimemes, in addition to general memory enhancement. Class X restores awareness of previously perceived antimemes or suppressed memories. Class Y grants the subject perfect recall for any memories gained during its period of effect, and a single dose of Class Z renders the subject biochemically incapable of forgetting anything for the remainder of their lives. Class Zs are invariably fatal, with death by seizure typically resulting in a matter of hours.

Combining amnestic and mnestic drugs is not recommended.

File >>> 010223

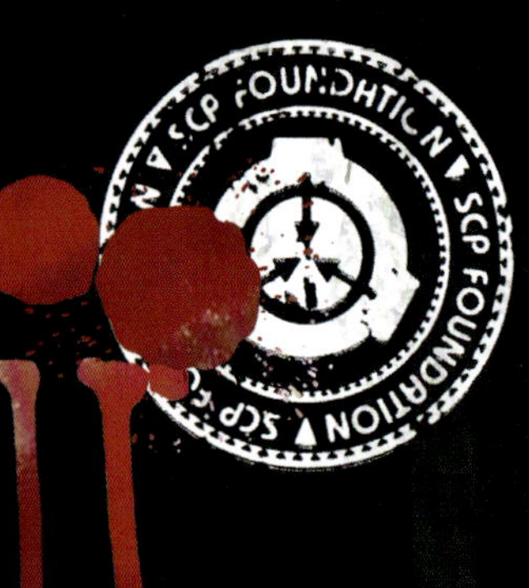

SCP-427

Title

LOVECRAFTIAN LOCKET

Report by

Dr Ouros

Picture by

Ruslan Korovkin

Access the original report on

scp-wiki.wikidot.com/scp-427

Date

Class

SAFE (see containment procedures)

SPECIAL CONTAINMENT PROCEDURES

SCP-427 displays no means of self-locomotion or malicious intent at this time, and requires only minimal containment. Due to SCP-427's adverse effects, only medical staff of Class 3 or above may handle or utilize it.

All personnel using SCP-427 must record their total time using it in order to avoid unwanted mutations.

*Instances of SCP-427-1 (colloquially referred to as "Flesh Beasts") created by SCP-427 must be killed immediately as it is impossible to communicate with or experiment on them safely. For this reason instances of SCP-427-1 are classified as Keter.

DESCRIPTION

SCP-427 is a small, spherical, ornately carved locket made of a polished silver material. The ornate carvings do not seem to serve any function; it is unknown whether SCP-427's outer casing was crafted by sentients or not. Its circumference at its widest point is roughly 3 cm.

SCP-427 was created after placing a pill of SCP-500 in the Input booth of SCP-914 and using the Fine setting. It displays no unusual activity when closed. When opened, a small glowing orb is visible at the center. The orb emits no radiation or energy aside from the visible spectrum.

When SCP-427 is opened and exposed to biological tissue, it rapidly regenerates cellular damage and somehow is able to purge invading compounds or infections. As a standard of measure, the common cold takes 3 to 10 days to be worked through the human immune system and eventually removed. In the presence of an opened SCP-427, this time is reduced to 2 to 4 minutes. Its healing abilities are directional, so anything not in line of sight with the central orb experiences no effects.

However, long-term exposure produces a significant health hazard. As the locket heals damage, it optimizes the body's natural systems. Resistance to disease and toxins is increased by 500% compared to accepted LD50 or death-rate values after a total of 10 minutes of exposure, and 1000% after 15. After 15 minutes of exposure, muscular systems begin optimizing, increasing strength and pain tolerance by 200-300%. All other systems continue to optimize. Class-D personnel exposed to the device for over an hour total began mutating into a shapeless mass of tissue. The conversion time accelerates with continued exposure to SCP-427.

The "Flesh Beasts" (so named due to their appearance) created by SCP-427 are incredibly aggressive, attacking any and all personnel on sight with lethal results. They are highly resistant to most known weaponry, but can be disabled with sufficient shock trauma or heat in excess of 1100 degrees Celsius (2000 degrees Fahrenheit). Intelligence cannot be accurately gauged, but mapping of biological enhancement of the brain as a direct relationship with optimization of other systems suggests intelligence could exceed levels measured in humans when fully transformed.

SCP-427 is currently being used as a partial replacement for SCP-500 pills, as it can cure almost anything SCP-500 is able to. All "optimizations" imparted by SCP-427 are cumulative. Oversight has deemed the side effects an "acceptable risk" but users must carefully record their total exposure time as sufficient mutations are grounds for termination.

END OF REPORT

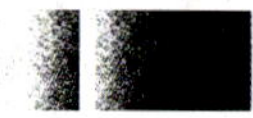

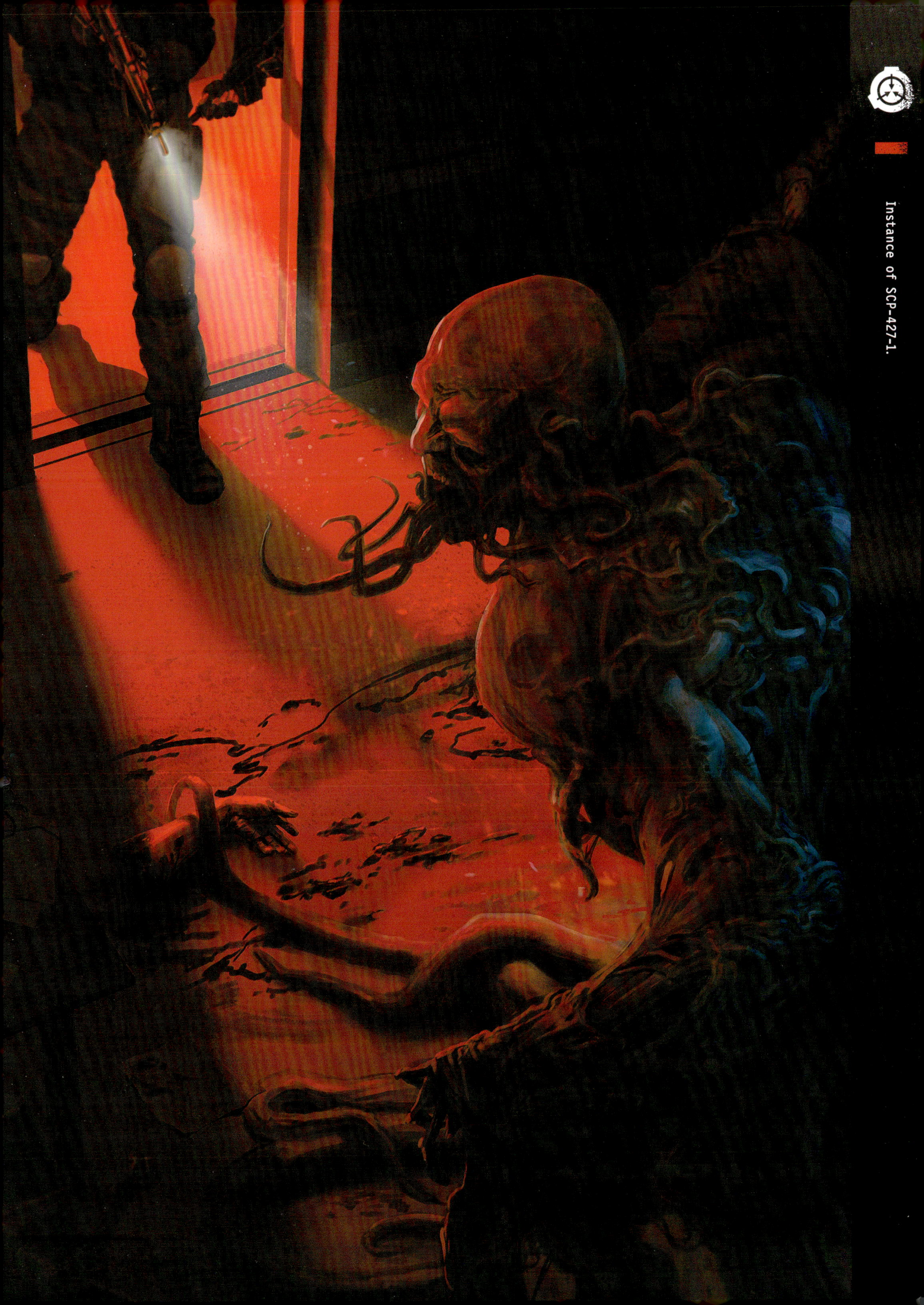

Instance of SCP-427-1.

File >>> 003234

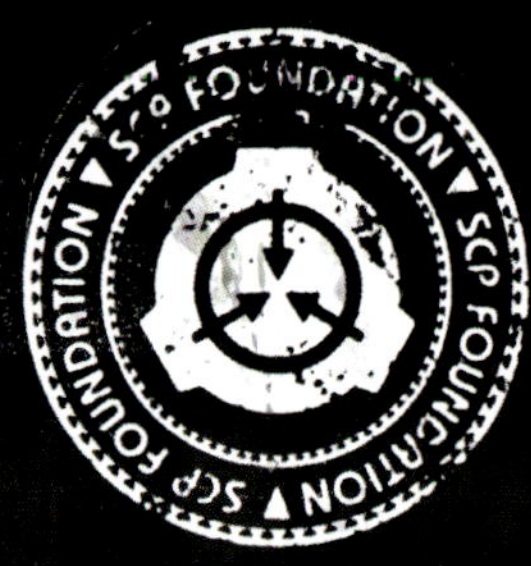

SCP-025

Title

A WELL-WORN WARDROBE

Report by
thattallfellow

Picture by
Serj Papadin

Access the original report on
scp-wiki.wikidot.com/scp-025

Date
██████

Class
SAFE

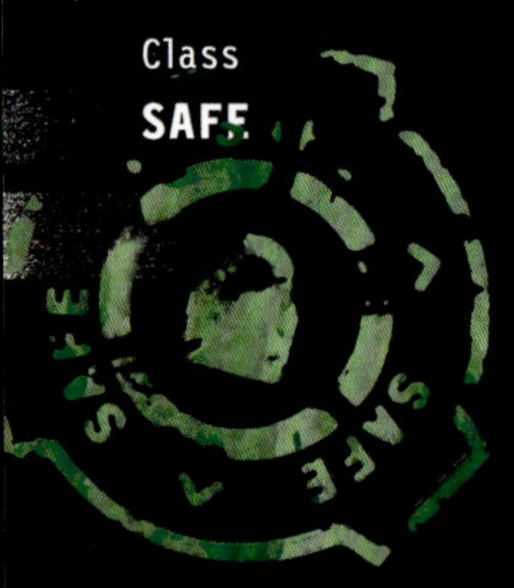

SPECIAL CONTAINMENT PROCEDURES

SCP-025 is only to be opened during testing, as is the room in which SCP-025 is stored. Entry codes are to be given only to authorized research and security personnel. No other containment protocols required.

DESCRIPTION

SCP-025 is a wooden wardrobe measuring 0.97 m x 0.62 m x 1.95 m, full of clothing dating from a number of time periods. Articles contained within the chest, collectively named SCP-025-1, match with styles of decades from the 1920s to the present. The apparel from each time frame varies with regard to style; for example, a polyester striped shirt and pair of charcoal suit pants both correspond with general styles of the 1970s. The only unifying aspect of every article contained in SCP-025 is that each one is in poor condition; moths have eaten at much of the collection, and tears and runs are not uncommon.

When any item from SCP-025 is put on, the wearer is observed either to die or suffer an injury within 24 hours. The cause of death or injury in these instances is invariably linked to the aforementioned flaws in the clothing, but only ever appears to be an unrelated incident. Wearing a glove with a fingertip cut off may result in the loss of the fingertip through a simple kitchen accident like chopping onions; similarly, a subject wearing a poncho with a sleeve missing will somehow cause the loss of the uncovered arm, be it an attack by a wild animal or a vehicular accident that necessitates the amputation of the limb. If placed in a sealed, unfurnished enclosure while wearing an item from the chest, the wearer will either seemingly spontaneously contract a flesh-eating disease that begins in the areas not covered by the clothing, or suffer the failure of an organ located beneath an imperfection in the article. Diseases arising from such incidents may or may not be contagious; no study has been successfully undertaken due to the speed at which the strains observed run their course. Recommended that, if possible, samples of the disease be taken to lab for possible weaponization.

Following is an abridged testing log of SCP-025; more thorough testing will accompany the declassification of the document in its entirety.

TEST LOG SCP-025, SECTION 1

SUBJECT: D-778, a 42-year-old white male
ARTICLE: 1940s-era white tuxedo
IMPERFECTION(S): Torn seam in left shoulder
TEST RESULTS: Subject was allowed free roam of the halls, under Agent ██████'s supervision. For approximately 45 minutes, nothing eventful occurred; however, at ██:██, security tapes and eyewitnesses indicate that D-778 appeared to make an attempt at attacking Agent ██████. He in turn overcame the subject with a knife, causing an inch-deep gash in D-778's left shoulder precisely at the point where the tuxedo's seam was ripped. Test halted; subject later terminated.

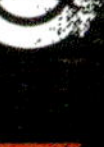

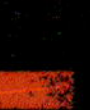

ARTICLE: White laboratory coat.

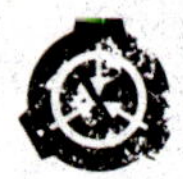

Research Library File ▸ 025

SUBJECT: D-690, a 26-year-old white male
ARTICLE: 2004 Boston Red Sox baseball cap
IMPERFECTION(S): Missing size adjuster in back of cap; logo in front partially removed
TEST RESULTS: Placed in a sealed room with the subject was a table on which were a loaded Jericho "Baby Eagle" 9mm handgun, a grill lighter, and a hatchet. D-690 chose to wear the cap backward for the test; potential effects of this decision on the outcome of the test are unknown. Subject expressed reluctance to touch any of the objects on the table for several hours; food and water were provided as necessary. After four (4) hours of general inactivity, subject picked up the handgun and examined it; while holding it at roughly eye level, the weapon discharged into D-690's forehead, where the size adjustment band would have been. The round exited the subject near the part of the hat with the missing part of the logo.

SUBJECTS: D-736, a 22-year-old white male; D-771, a 23-year-old white male
ARTICLE: Burgundy striped sweater vest, dating from 1973
IMPERFECTION(S): Article seemed to have been partially eaten by moths; several large holes in the front of the sweater
TEST RESULTS: D-736 was asked by researching staff to wear the sweater vest, which he did under duress. D-771 was given a loaded handgun out of sight of the other test participant and instructed to, on a given signal, fire all six (6) shots in the direction of D-736. After doing so, it was noted that every shot fired passed through one of the holes in the sweater vest, leaving the clothing intact and killing D-736. Firearm retrieved; surviving subject transported back to quarters.

SUBJECT: D-771, a 23-year-old white male
ARTICLE: Sweater vest from above trial
IMPERFECTION(S): Same as mentioned
TEST RESULTS: D-771 was this time placed in an empty room, dimensions 15 m x 15 m x 15 m; only objects in the enclosure were lights overhead. Subject initially complained of boredom, then lay on his back and went to sleep. After 2 hours and 14 minutes, two (2) of the fluorescent light tubes in the ceiling suddenly dislodged and fell. Both landed squarely on holes in the sweater, shattering upon impact; one (1) of the tubes broke into jagged pieces that impaled D-771 in several areas, but only again through gaps already present in the sweater vest. Subject's vitals persisted for another six (6) minutes, then ceased. Further testing locations will be selected to minimize possible damage to the surrounding area.

SUBJECT: Dr. █████ [Unplanned experiment; an unidentified individual left an article from SCP-025 on Dr. █████'s desk that looked similar to an item of his own clothing. Any information about this incident and/or the perpetrator of same should be reported immediately to senior staff.]
ARTICLE: Lightweight scarf, dyed a number of colors
IMPERFECTION(S): Heavily pulled seam caused scarf to be considerably shorter and tighter in the middle.
TEST RESULTS: According to his itinerary, Dr. █████, wearing the item from SCP-025, was en route to the enclosure of SCP-███ on ██/██/████ for routine testing. However, he diverged from his intended path and began in a direction towards an entirely separate wing of the facility. Subject then entered the enclosure of SCP-173 without gathering accompaniment or following safety procedures, and, upon hearing the door closing, blinked. Cause of death listed as strangulation resulting from a crushed windpipe.

SUBJECT: D-802, a 30-year-old Hispanic female
ARTICLE: 1980s Flashdance-style white shirt
IMPERFECTION(S): Right shoulder removed, left sleeve completely cut off, entire bottom hem shredded
TEST RESULTS: [DATA EXPUNGED]. All present were presumed infected, then quarantined and [DATA EXPUNGED]. All further tests involving 1980s-era fashion have been postponed indefinitely due to the expenditures and safety hazards presented by the aforementioned experiment. Full cleanup estimated to take an additional █ weeks.

Further testing authorized; results now awaiting declassification.

END OF REPORT

SPECIAL CONTAINMENT PROCEDURES

SCP-029 is to be incarcerated in a Class 5 containment cell. She is to be allowed access to nothing of a physical nature. Her containment cell is to be placed behind a triple airlock, to avoid her escape. As of Incident 029-34a, SCP-029 is no longer to be fed, as she does not appear to need sustenance to survive. There are to be three (3) guards on duty at all times on her cell, and two (2) guards on monitor duty.

Floodlights have been installed in the walls of the containment chamber, and are to be on at all times. Once a month the chamber is to be cleaned and checked for defects.

Under absolutely no circumstances are any men to encounter SCP-029 in any manner. Any males who do encounter SCP-029 are to be held under Class 3 detention for interviewing before termination.

SCP-029 has requested:

- A bed (Denied)
- A blanket (Denied)
- Books (Denied)
- Clothes (Denied)

Dr. Ericka Bodeen

This is ridiculous! The girl can't even have clothes? We are not animals, let her cover herself!
Dr. Ericka Bodeen

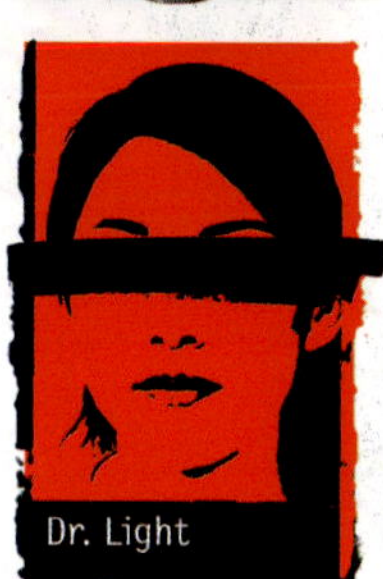
Dr. Light

Dr. Bodeen, you are granted permission to deliver clothes to SCP-029.
Dr. Light

As of incident 029-53b, anyone who has potential access to SCP-029 is required to first watch Surveillance Tape 029-Bodeen, as a reminder of threats involved when working with SCP items and SCP-029 in particular.

File >>> 0199321

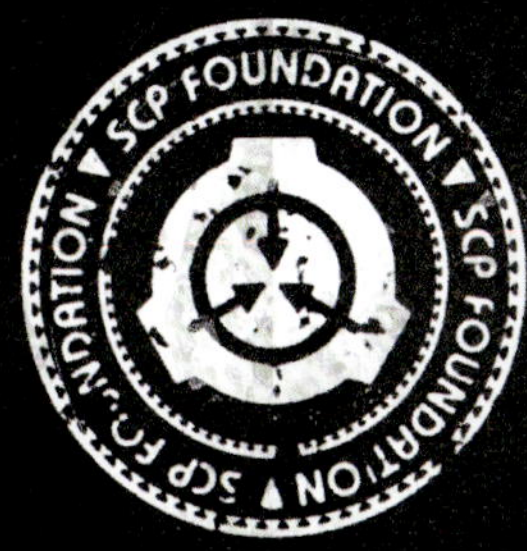

SCP-029

Title
DAUGHTER OF SHADOWS

Report by
Dr Bright

Picture by
Ruslana Gus

Access the original report on
scp-wiki.wikidot.com/scp-029

Date

Class
KETER

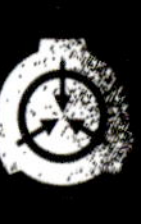

Incident 029-53b.

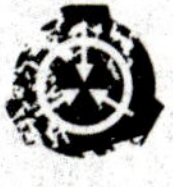

Research Library File ▸ 029

DESCRIPTION

SCP-029 appears to be a pubescent female of Asiatic-Indian descent. She appears to suffer from alopecia universalis. Over 80% of her pigmentation is a true black, while the rest of her skin has a complete lack of melanin, to the point of albinism. Her eyes are also a dark black in color.

SCP-029 has severe homicidal tendencies and has displayed a remarkable ability to use any item as a weapon. However, she has a severe compulsion against shedding blood, preferring instead to strangle her victims. SCP-029 has demonstrated dexterity and physical reactions four (4) times as fast as the average human. SCP-029 has also displayed extensive resistance to damage of all forms. Both of these extra human abilities are greatly hampered in the presences of bright or direct light, natural or artificial. In addition, any males who come within the presence of SCP-029, an area defined by her current perception, find themselves pliant to her will. Such males become willing to kill or even die for SCP-029.

SCP-029 refers to herself as ███████, which roughly translates to 'Daughter of Darkness,' 'Daughter of Shadows,' or 'Daughter of Night.' Interviews with SCP-029 have proven difficult to conduct, due to SCP-029's constant attempts to kill or convert all who speak with her. Over her years of captivity, the black patches on her skin have increased in size.

SCP-029 was first brought to the Foundation's attention by an Agent working in rural India. An attempt on his life led him to a small cult of men who claimed to be 'Thuggees,' in service to the Daughter. Several weeks of investigation proved that they believed the world to be in the last years of the 'Kali Yuga,' and that by sacrificing one million lives to the Daughter of Darkness, they could raise their Goddess and end the world. They also believed that only sacrifices performed through strangulation added to this tally. Events led the agent to their mountain fortress, where he discovered SCP-029. After the loss of said Agent, [DATA EXPUNGED], which ended in our acquisition of SCP-029.

ADDENDUM

Seven (7) years after capture, SCP-029 began showing anomalous growth in her black pigmentation. When questioned about it, she claimed her 'followers were on the move once more.' Investigation led us to a concentration of so-called 'Thuggees' that had escaped our initial foray. After discovering that all her followers were there for one of their holy days, a tactical air strike was called in. When the first bomb dropped, SCP-029 awoke from slumber, screaming at the top of her lungs. SCP-029 continued to scream for the next four (4) hours, ranting and raving that we were 'killing her people.' Since said event, the growth of black pigmentation has stopped completely. Also since said event, SCP-029 has redoubled her efforts to escape. SCP-2820 has been proposed as a possible method of neutralization should the situation worsen.

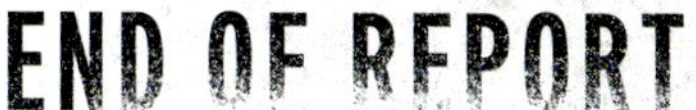

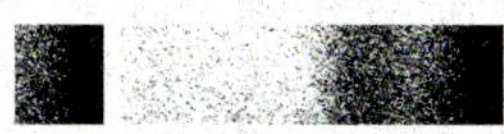

File >>> 0192223

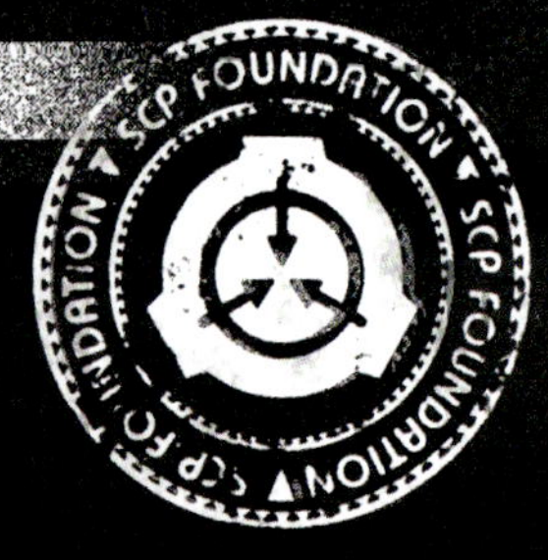

SCP-049

Title

PLAGUE DOCTOR

Report by

Gabriel Jade

Djkaktus

Pictures by

Dan Temirov

Alexander Puchkov

David Romero

Access the original report on

scp-wiki.wikidot.com/scp-049

Date

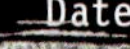

Class

EUCLID

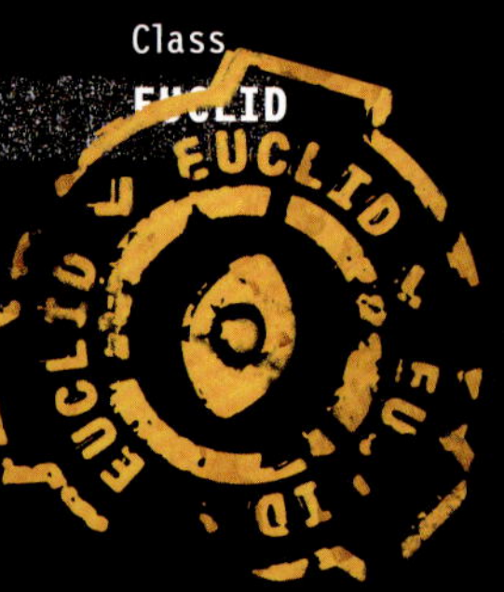

SPECIAL CONTAINMENT PROCEDURES

SCP-049 is contained within a Standard Secure Humanoid Containment Cell in Research Sector-02 at Site-19. SCP-049 must be sedated before any attempts to transport it. During transport, SCP-049 must be secured within a Class III Humanoid Restriction Harness (including a locking collar and extension restraints) and monitored by no fewer than two armed guards.

While SCP-049 is generally cooperative with most Foundation personnel, outbursts or sudden changes in behaviour are to be met with elevated force. Under no circumstances should any personnel come into direct contact with SCP-049 during these outbursts. In the event SCP-049 becomes aggressive, the application of lavender (L. multifida) has been shown to produce a calming effect on the entity. Once calmed, SCP-049 generally becomes compliant, and will return to containment with little resistance.

In order to facilitate the ongoing containment of SCP-049, the entity is to be provided with the corpse of a recently deceased animal (typically a bovine or other large mammal) once every two weeks for study. Corpses that become instances of SCP-049-2 are to be removed from SCP-049's containment cell and incinerated. SCP-049 is no longer permitted to interact with human subjects, and requests for human subjects are to be denied.

TEMPORARY CONTAINMENT PROCEDURE UPDATE

(See Addendum 049.3) Per Containment Committee Order 049.S19.17.1, SCP-049 is no longer permitted to interact directly with any members of Foundation staff, nor is it to be provided with any additional corpses to be used in its surgeries. This order shall persist indefinitely, until such time a consensus regarding the ongoing containment of SCP-049 can be reached.

DESCRIPTION

SCP-049 is a humanoid entity, roughly 1.9 meters in height, which bears the appearance of a medieval plague doctor. While SCP-049 appears to be wearing the thick robes and the ceramic mask indicative of that profession, the garments instead seem to have grown out of SCP-049's body over time, and are now nearly indistinguishable from whatever form is beneath them. X-rays indicate that despite this, SCP-049 does have a humanoid skeletal structure beneath its outer layer.

The robes and gloves are identical to a thick hide built up on the skin, while the mask is composed of a kind of chitin growing out of the bones of the face.

SCP-049 is capable of speech in a variety of languages, though tends to prefer English or medieval French. While SCP-049 is generally cordial and cooperative with Foundation staff, it can become especially irritated or at times outright aggressive if it feels that it is in the presence of what it calls the "Pestilence". Although the exact nature of this Pestilence is currently unknown to Foundation researchers, it does seem to be an issue of immense concern to SCP-049.

The entity claims to have originated in 15th century France, though admits that it is "particularly well-traveled".

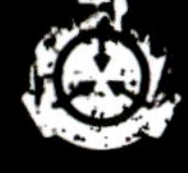

SCP-049 will become hostile with individuals it sees as being affected by the Pestilence, often having to be restrained should it encounter such. If left unchecked, SCP-049 will generally attempt to kill any such individual; SCP-049 is capable of causing all biological functions of an organism to cease through direct skin contact. How this occurs is currently unknown, and autopsies of SCP-049's victims have invariably been inconclusive. SCP-049 has expressed frustration or remorse after these killings, indicating that they have done little to kill "The Pestilence", though will usually seek to then perform a crude surgery on the corpse using the implements contained within a black doctor's bag it carries on its person at all times. While these surgeries are not always "successful", they often result in the creation of instances of SCP-049-2.

The space within this bag is seemingly anomalously large, as SCP-049 has been observed pulling objects larger than the bag itself from within it in order to operate on deceased subjects.

SCP-049-2 instances are reanimated corpses that have been operated on by SCP-049. These instances do not seem to retain any of their prior memories or mental functions, having only basic motor skills and response mechanisms. While these instances are generally inactive, moving very little and in a generally ambulatory fashion, they can become extremely aggressive if provoked, or if directed to by SCP-049. SCP-049-2 instances express active biological functions, though these are vastly different from currently understood human physiology. Despite these alterations, SCP-049 often remarks that the subjects have been "cured".

ADDENDUM 049.1: DISCOVERY

SCP-049 was discovered during the investigation of a series of unknown disappearances in the town of Montauban in southern France. During a raid on a local home, investigators found several instances of SCP-049-2, as well as SCP-049. While law enforcement personnel engaged the hostile 049-2 instances, SCP-049 was noted as watching the engagement and taking notes in its journal. After all of the 049-2 instances were dispatched, SCP-049 willingly entered Foundation custody.

The following interview was conducted by Dr. Raymond Hamm during the initial investigation.

Dr. Raymond Hamm

Interviewer: Dr. Raymond Hamm, Site-85

Interviewee: SCP-049

[BEGIN LOG]

SCP-049: *(In French)* So then, how should we begin? An introduction?

Dr. Hamm: *(Aside)* Is that French? Can we get a translator-

SCP-049: *(In English)* The King's English! No need for translation, sir, I can speak it well enough.

Dr. Hamm: Good. My name is Dr. Raymond Hamm, and I-

SCP-049: Ah! A doctor! A like-minded individual, no doubt. Wherein is your speciality, sir?

Dr. Hamm: Cryptobiology, why-

SCP-049: *(Laughs)* A medical man, such as myself. Wonders abound! And here I worried I had been abducted by common street thugs! (Looks around the room) This place, then. This is your laboratory? I had wondered, as clean as it is, and with such little trace of the Pestilence here.

Dr. Hamm: The Pestilence? What do you mean?

SCP-049: The Scourge! The Great Dying. Come now, you know, the, uh… *(taps temple furiously)* … what is it they call it, the… the… ah, no matter. The Pestilence, yes. It abounds outside these walls, you know. So many have succumbed, and many more will continue to, until such time as a perfect cure can be developed. *(Leans back in its chair)* Fortunately, I am very close. It is my duty in life to rid the world of it, you see. The Cure To End All Cures!

Dr. Hamm: When you say "The Great Dying", are you talking about the bubonic plague?

SCP-049: *(Pauses)* I don't know what that is.

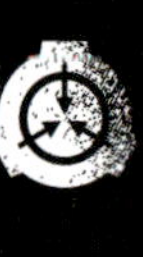

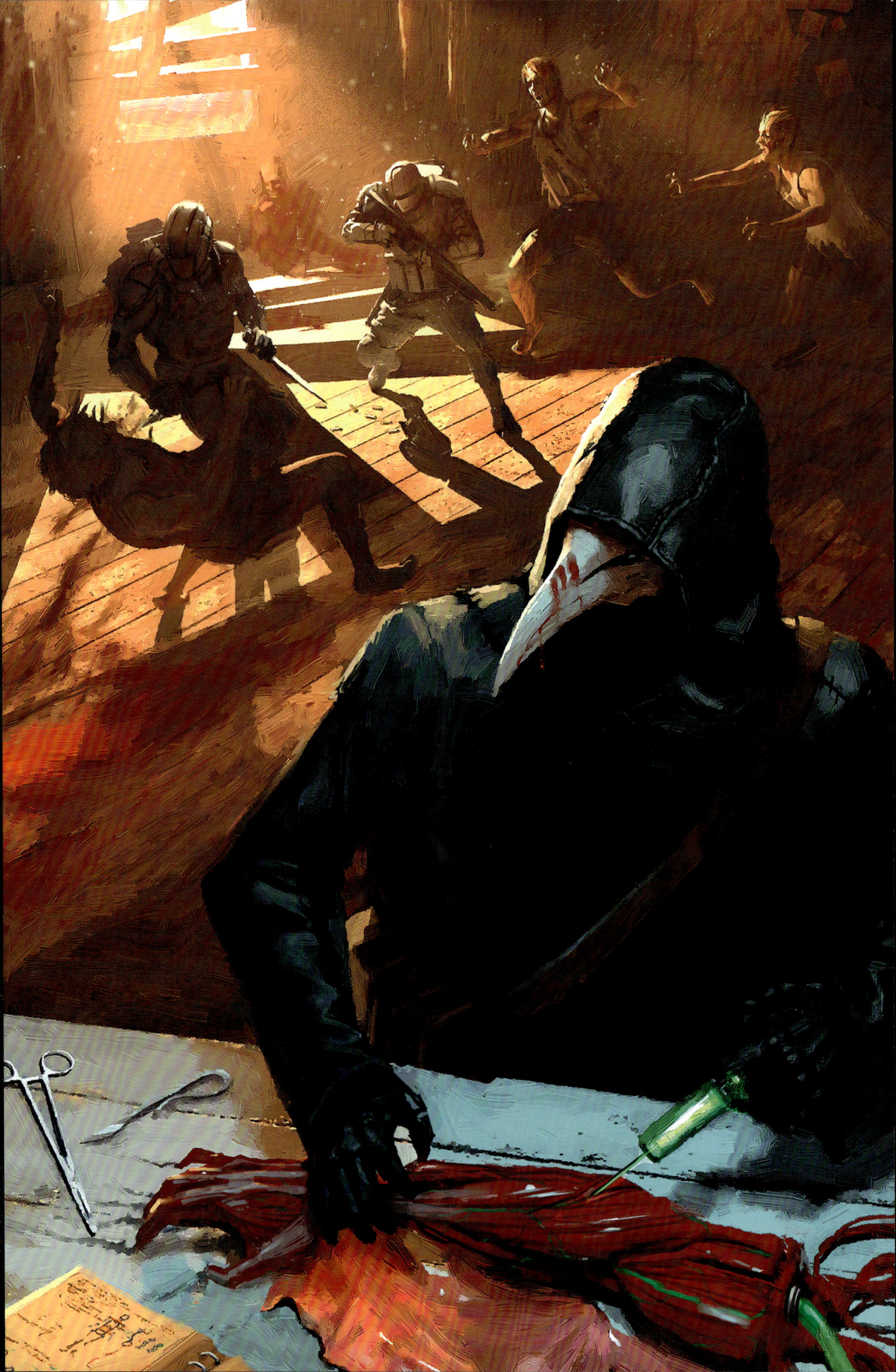

SCP-049 upon discovery.

Dr. Hamm: I see. Right, well, the entities our agents encountered at that house, they were dead when you encountered them, yes? And you reanimated them?

SCP-049: Hrmm, in a manner of speaking. You see things too simply, doctor! Expand your horizons. Life and death, sickness and health, these are amateur terms for amateur physicians. There is only one ailment that exists in the world of men, and that is the Pestilence. And nothing else! Make no mistake, they were very ill, all of them.

Dr. Hamm: You think you cured those people?

SCP-049: Indeed. My cure is most effective.

Dr. Hamm: The things we recovered were not human.

SCP-049: *(Pauses and glares at Dr. Hamm)* Yes, well, it is not a *perfect* cure. But that will come with time. And further experimentation! I have spent a lifetime developing my methods, Dr. Hamm, and will spend a lifetime more, if necessary. Now, we have wasted too much time. There is work to do! I will require a laboratory of my own, one where I can continue my research unimpeded. And assistants, of course, though I can provide those on my own, in time. *(Laughs)*

Dr. Hamm: I don't think our organization will be willing to-

SCP-049: Nonsense. We are all men of science. Fetch your coat and show me to my quarters, doctor. *(Gestures with pointed stick)* Our work begins now!

[END LOG]

Interviewer's Note: While SCP-049 is capable of communicating in a very human way, there is a strange sense of unease that one experiences when in its presence. Make no mistake, there is something very uncanny about this entity indeed.

Additionally, we've confiscated that pointed stick that SCP-049 keeps waving around. Part of this was due to standard confiscation protocols for the possessions of anomalies, and part because 049 really is a menace swinging it around like he does. The entity was displeased at first, but after we made some concessions in providing it with "test subjects" (which are, admittedly, more for the benefit of our own research) it warmed up to the idea.

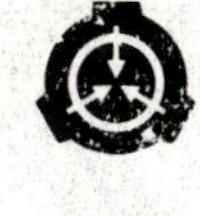

ADDENDUM 049.2: OBSERVATION LOG

While in containment at Site-19, SCP-049 has spent a considerable amount of time studying and performing surgery on the various mammalian corpses it has been provided. SCP-049 will routinely spend several days performing surgery, and then (regardless of whether or not the corpse becomes an instance of SCP-049-2) spending several more days documenting its findings in a thick leather journal stored within its doctor's bag. SCP-049 will often seek to share its findings with members of Foundation staff.

The following is a log of several occasions during which SCP-049 was observed operating on a mammalian corpse.

Observational Log 049.OL.1 SUMMARY

Subject: SCP-049

Preface: A test subject (D-85123) was introduced into SCP-049's containment cell. The entity expressed sincere gratitude towards all members of the containment and research staff.

Observation Notes: SCP-049 began by asking D-85123 several standard medical questions, as it began removing tools from its bag. Shortly after finishing its preparations, SCP-049 quickly closed the distance between the two, killing the subject with a touch to its throat. Afterwards, SCP-049 made a number of considerable alterations to the basic structure of the subject's corpse, often introducing fluids from within its bag into the subject by way of a hand powered pump and copper tubing.

The resulting 049-2 instance became animated, flailing and grasping at the walls of the chamber with a number of manufactured limbs while moaning out of an oblong orifice now present in its sternum. During this time, SCP-049 was observed taking notes of the instance in its journal, and remarking to the watching research staff about the efficacy of its cure. Security personnel entered the chamber to move SCP-049 back to containment, and were attacked by the instance. The security team dispatched the 049-2 instance, and SCP-049 returned to containment with no resistance, stating that it was pleased with the results.

Observational Log 049.OL.2 SUMMARY

Subject: SCP-049

Preface: SCP-049 was provided the corpse of a recently deceased goat. SCP-049 expressed gratitude at the provision.

Observation Notes: SCP-049 operated on the goat corpse for several days, eventually resulting in an instance of SCP-049-2. SCP-049 expressed pleasure in this outcome, though admitted "the disease was still in its nascent stage. My veterinarian practice is rudimentary, but the patient responded well to the procedure."

Observational Log 049.OL.3 SUMMARY

Subject: SCP-049

Preface: SCP-049 was provided the corpse of a recently deceased orangutan. SCP-049 expressed noted gratitude at the provision, due to the similarities between the orangutan and common human physiology.

Observation Notes: SCP-049 spent several days operating on the orangutan, reanimating it several times. However, SCP-049 appeared to be discontent with the results it experienced, returning to the creature three times after its initial reanimation for additional work. After it was unable to reanimate the corpse a fifth time, SCP-049 turned the corpse over to Foundation staff for incineration, stating "I have learned so much from this, though I fear my early optimism was misplaced. I hadn't yet come across such a… a stumbling block on my road to the cure. More subjects like this would do a great deal in advancing my research."

Observational Log 049.OL.7 FULL

Subject: SCP-049

Preface: SCP-049 was provided the corpse of a recently deceased bovine. SCP-049 expressed mild annoyance at the provision, though accepted it nonetheless.

Observation Notes: SCP-049 spent several days operating on the bovine corpse, breaking only to dine on a requested dinner of thin crackers, salted pork, and hard cheese. Beginning first by embalming the corpse, SCP-049 was observed producing a number of long syringes from its bag, each containing a different dark, viscous fluid. SCP-049 described these fluids as "essences of the humors", and elaborated by saying "the Pestilence may bring about a systemic imbalance. In such a case, before true healing can begin, one must find the humors in balance or the body will reject the cure."

Notes

SCP-049 had stated its desire to work on human subjects several times between this occasion and the earlier provision of an orangutan, noting its discontentedness when they would not be provided.

SCP-049 has expressed that it does not require sustenance, but enjoys it and feels that the food helps to put it in the right mind to operate.

SCP-049 added to this statement by saying "This is of course, elementary knowledge for the practical physician. I would have thought you would have learned this during your education!"

Over the next few days, SCP-049 spent a considerable amount of time adjusting the organs of the bovine corpse with a number of large metal instruments. After eight days, SCP-049 produced a lightning rod, which Dr. Hamm exchanged for an electric cattle prod attached to an extension cord, and struck the corpse in several locations. This action seemingly had the effect of reanimating the bovine, which once again became ambulatory, despite the inversion of the head and reorientation of its limbs.

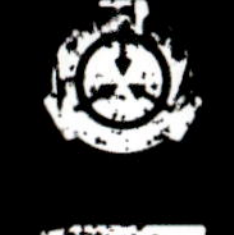

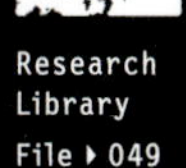

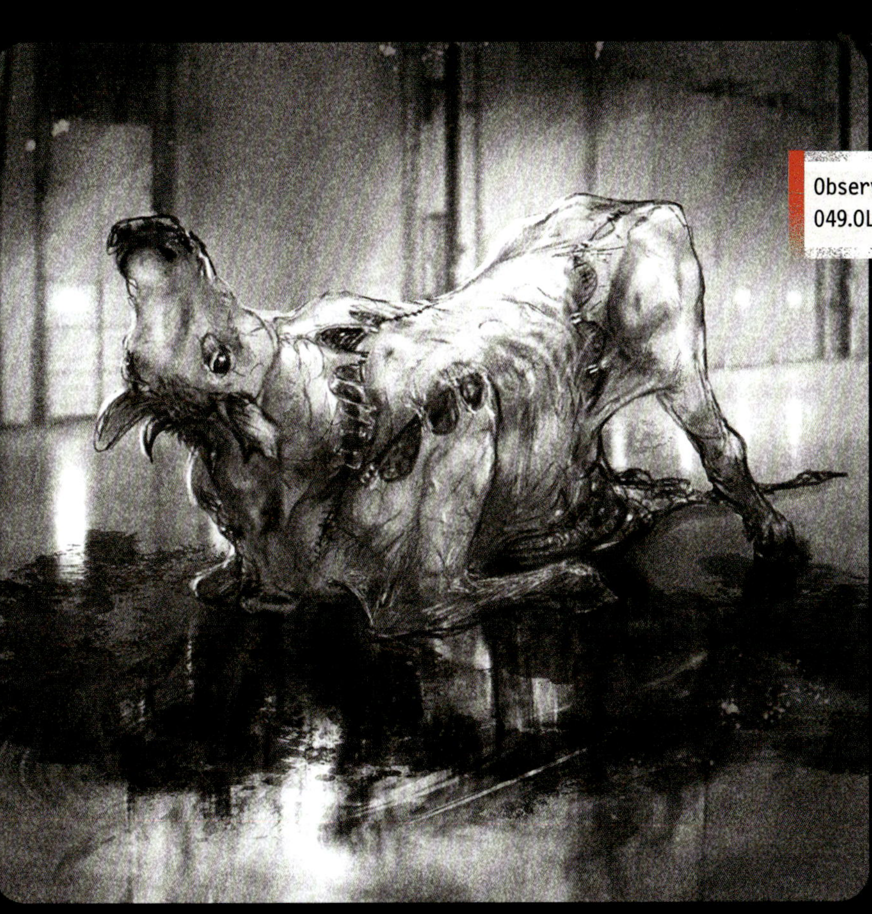

Observational Log 049.OL.7.

Notably, SCP-049 journals are not written in any known language, and attempts by linguists and codebreakers to decipher them have been unsuccessful.

FOLLOW UP INTERVIEW

[BEGIN LOG]

Dr. Hamm: We've watched you work for several weeks now, and honestly I'm not sure I understand what you're doing. Can you describe your process in detail?

SCP-049: Oh goodness no, the process is most intensive. As I said to your assistant, the best instruction you will find about my methods are here in my journals, as I have kept exhaustive records of my work there.

Dr. Hamm: I see. My concern, doctor, is that we still don't understand what you're seeking to cure, or how it manifests, or how turning these creatures into quasi-living, mindless drones helps in that effort.

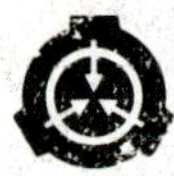

SCP-049: You do not understand the Pestilence? Even after all this time? Doctor, it is an unspeakable horror, one that has shown its true face many times before and will again. I find myself blessed with the wisdom and good senses needed to root it out and destroy it, but many like yourself cannot. It is a cruel judgement, I fear, to be at the mercy of a disease you cannot fully comprehend!

Dr. Hamm: That still doesn't answer my question. How is your cure any kind of cure at all?

SCP-049: *(Growing suddenly agitated)* It is a cure! You may laugh at my efforts if you please, but do not besmirch the good name of scientific progress that has developed this great mercy. What you so shortsightedly see here is a life better than any this creature could have hoped for, stricken as it was with Pestilence. This creature is now clean, unable to spread the Pestilence and free from the terror it would have experienced otherwise.

Dr. Hamm: This is hardly a creature at all, doctor, it's not even-

SCP-049: *(Very agitated)* Do not jape with me, sir! You and your colleagues are like so many others, unable to look past minor setbacks to see the salvation taking place before your very eyes. Do you wait to remove rotten timbers until the hall collapses on top of you? No. You find them and you pull them out and replace them with those untouched by rot! And most of all, you do not simply mock the structure because it now looks different to you. It is strong! It is free of disease.

Dr. Hamm: I'm sorry. I didn't mean to agitate you. I'm just trying to understand.

SCP-049: *(Deep breath)* Yes, well, do mind your words in the future, doctor. I am a professional, but even professionals may feel the bite of pride in dealing with criticism of their masterpiece. I will forgive this as an act of good faith between colleagues.

Dr. Hamm: Is there anything else I can help you with?

SCP-049: *(Pauses, looking away from Dr. Hamm)* No, that will be all. Another test subject, on the usual schedule. You know my preference of subjects with more human anatomies.

[END LOG]

Attending Researcher's Note: SCP-049 does seem to genuinely want to help other humans, though it has not yet been able to provide a concrete example of what exactly it is trying to save us all from. I have watched it now over several weeks, and while the outcomes do not seem to ever change, SCP-049 continues to claim that it is growing closer to its perfect cure. I think the entity may be more aware of the reality of these outcomes than it would like us to think.

ADDENDUM 049.3: 04/16/2017 INCIDENT

Starting shortly after SCP-049's initial containment, Dr. Hamm conducted a number of interviews with the subject regarding its anomalous properties, and over time began to note its displeasure with its subjects and the SCP-049-2 instances. This continued for a period of several months, during which SCP-049 never exhibited any aggressive behaviours.

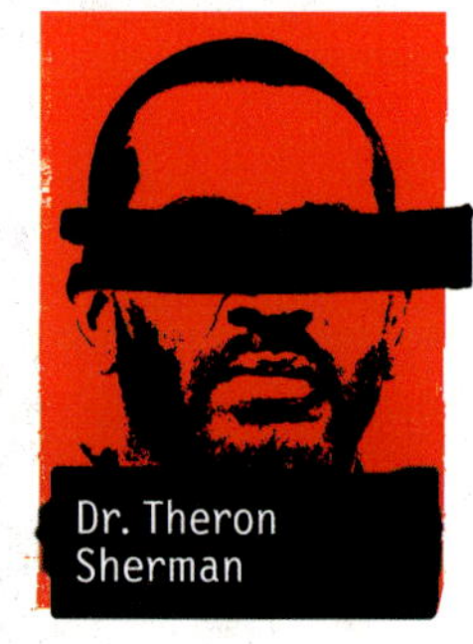
Dr. Theron Sherman

On April 16th, 2017, as Dr. Hamm was entering SCP-049's test chamber to conduct another routine interview, the entity began to grow anxious and asked Dr. Hamm if he was feeling well. Following protocol, Dr. Hamm reminded SCP-049 that the interview was required, after which the entity became hostile and attacked Dr. Hamm, killing him. Due to a lapse in security protocol, and because Dr. Hamm did not activate the in-chamber emergency system, Dr. Hamm's corpse was not discovered until three hours later, by which point SCP-049 had converted it into an instance of SCP-049-2.

In the aftermath of this incident, SCP-049 was interviewed by Dr. Theron Sherman.

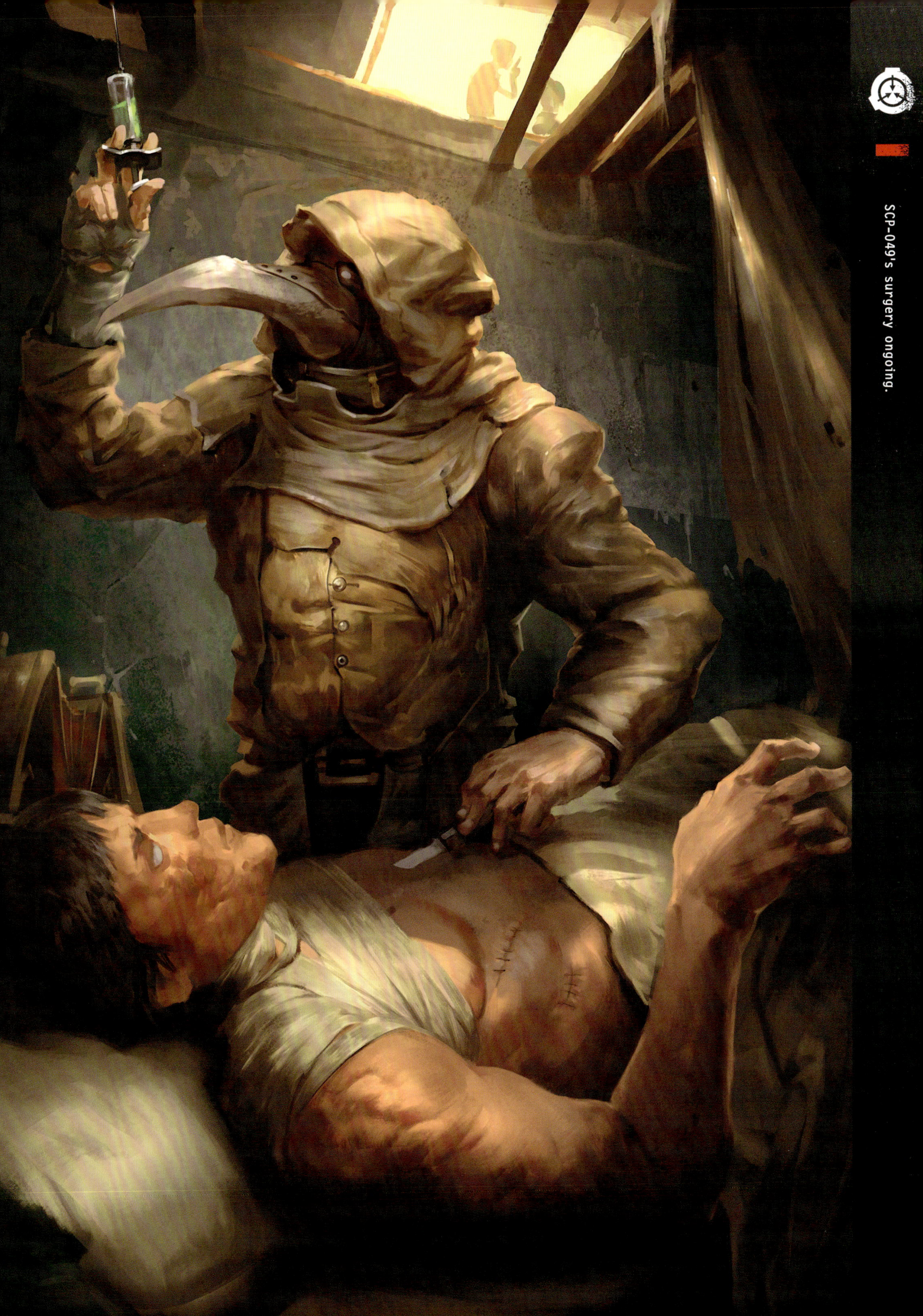

SCP-049's surgery ongoing.

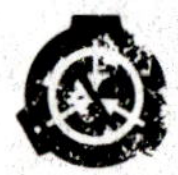

Interviewer: Dr. Theron Sherman, Site-42

Interviewee: SCP-049

[BEGIN LOG]

Dr. Sherman: I need you to explain yourself.

(No response)

Dr. Sherman: SCP-049, you are being directed to explain your actions, and I will remind you that failure to cooperate will result in further restrictions during your containment.

SCP-049: *(Pauses)* My actions do not need to be explained.

Dr. Sherman: You killed Raymond Hamm and then *butchered* him until he-

SCP-049: *(Interrupting, angrily)* Not dead! No! Not... not dead. He is... he is cured.

Dr. Sherman: Cured? Cured of what?

SCP-049: The Pestilence, sir! I had thought you, at least, would realize what luck it is I detected it before-

Dr. Sherman: *(Interrupting)* What pestilence? You keep going on and on about this pestilence but you have not once been able to properly identify this "disease". What could you have possibly seen in him today that you had not seen so many times before? That it would be worth his life?

SCP-049: He... *(pauses)* The Pestilence presents and progresses in unforeseeable fashions, and has a queer way of- of creeping into the unprepared, and... *(breathing becomes heavier)* call it what you want, doctor. It was a mercy I did to him. He is cured.

Dr. Sherman: He is a vegetable!

SCP-049: *(Pauses)* I... I would not expect you to understand. You and your... your ilk have proven time and time again to be not men of science, but men of- of emotion. You cannot appreciate the horrors I have seen, those many millions who have succumbed to the Pestilence and been changed, who-

Dr. Sherman: Your cure cost Ray his life!

SCP-049: No good SIR I have saved it! You would allow this world to slip back into the, the- the despair of disease and death, ignoring that I have created a miracle and-

Dr. Sherman: *(Talking over SCP-049)* What disease? What pestilence? He was a healthy man! He was a good doctor!

SCP-049: -am offering it freely to the afflicted! You are not worth this argument, sir. You are shortsighted and foolish. Dr. Hamm was sick, and I... (breath catches) I cured him. I am the only one who can do this. My work must continue, there is so much still to learn, so much to-

Dr. Sherman: I've had enough of this. Consider your allowances revoked. Welcome to containment, oh-four-nine. *(Away from mic)* We're done here.

SCP-049: -do, and others can be saved! Even you, though you do not deserve it, might be saved! I can save them all! I can cast down this plague, once and for all. I can do this! Only me! I... I... *(labored breathing)* I saved... I saved him... Dr. Hamm, I... I cured him... he was sick, I know he was sick, I know he was, and I... you are all sick, but I... I can save you. I can save all of you, because I... I am the cure.

[END LOG]

ADDENDUM 049.4: POST-INCIDENT REPORT INTERVIEW

The following interview is an excerpt from the 4/16/17 049 Incident Report. The interview was conducted by Dr. Elijah Itkin, and took place three weeks after the start of the initial investigation.

Date: 5/7/17

Interviewer: Dr. Elijah Itkin

Interviewee: SCP-049

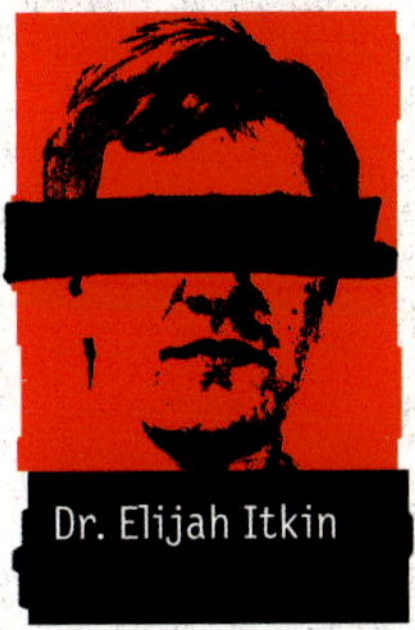

Dr. Elijah Itkin

[BEGIN LOG]

Dr. Itkin: SCP-049, we are conducting this interview to close out our investigation of your actions taken on April 16th that resulted in the death of a staff member. Do you have any comments to make?

SCP-049: Only that I look forward to the day when you will allow me to resume my work! I have spent the last few weeks compiling my notes and constructing a new theory for how the Pestilence was able to infect someone in such an insidious manner that I nearly couldn't detect it.

Dr. Itkin: Have you experienced any remorse for your actions? For the death of Dr. Hamm?

SCP-049: *(Waves his hand)* Ah, yes. Well, the death of a colleague is always regrettable, but in the face of the Pestilence we must be swift, doctor, and act without hesitation.

Dr. Itkin: Dr. Sherman noted in his report that you seemed to be mournful during your initial interview.

SCP-049: Mourn- *(Pauses)* Perhaps. I had not thought that… It is lamentable that a fellow doctor became infected, but the work continues. Regrettable as… as it was, Dr. Hamm's death provided important insight. Living human subjects are the only way to proceed forward, I am decided. My cure is of little use on dead flesh, and I have gleaned all I can from your generous supply of corpses. My desires turn towards tending to those still living who suffer from the disease.

Dr. Itkin: I'm afraid you're going to be disappointed.

SCP-049: *(Laughs)* Oh doctor, I wouldn't be so sure.

[END LOG]

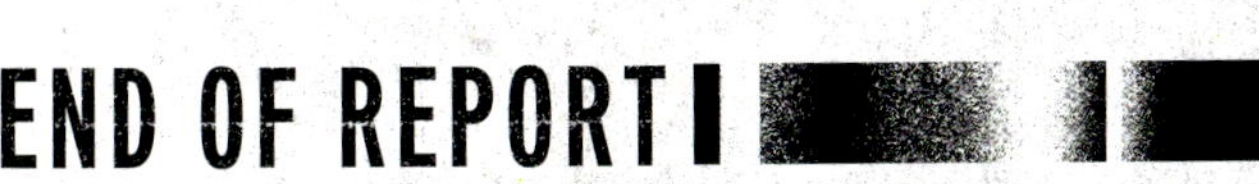

File >>> 0028122

SCP-270

Title

SECLUDED TELEPHONE

Report by
Mimi _ 42

Picture by
Genocide Error

Access the original report on
scp-wiki.wikidot.com/scp-270

Date

Class

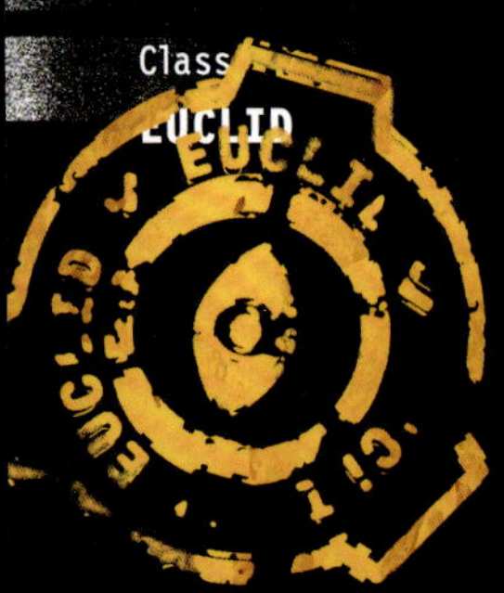

SPECIAL CONTAINMENT PROCEDURES

Due to SCP-270's immovable nature, a structure has been built around it that outwardly appears to be a large farmhouse, henceforth called Outpost Delta. Outpost Delta is to be staffed with a minimum of ███ trained personnel.

Extensive records of SCP-270's ciphers are kept at Site-11. Extensive records of decoded ciphers are available in █-██, ████.

If the security of Outpost Delta is compromised, SCP-270 is to be destroyed, along with all on-base records of verified or unverified information accumulated, and manuscripts outlining various encryptions SCP-270 has used.

DESCRIPTION

SCP-270 is a nondescript black phone of mid-20th century make.

There were no human populations exceeding ██ people per ███ square meters within a ████ radius of the location of discovery, and SCP-270 itself was well hidden by surrounding native vegetation. The unusual properties of SCP-270 were apparent upon discovering that the power cord extended an indefinite length into the soil directly below SCP-270, despite which a steady voice was speaking through the earphone. Investigations regarding how long the cord is have since been officially discontinued (see Addendum 270-A).

What makes SCP-270 of continued interest is the audio stream from the earphone, which has since been discovered to contain encrypted messages that are of value to the Foundation. Said ciphers are referred to as SCP-270-1.

For the most part, SCP-270-1 consists of a mildly distorted human female voice (see Addendum 270-B) speaking in a steady monotone, which has been recorded listing names, cryptic phrases, patterns of numbers, quotes, mangled quotes, strings of letters, [DATA EXPUNGED] incomprehensible words, sounds that cannot be produced by any known animal that continue for extended amounts of time (███ unconfirmed languages have been distinguished to date, ██ of which are reoccurring), monologues, nursery rhymes, [REDACTED] leading to speculation as to whether or not the narrator is in fact human, etc.

The following have also been recorded: melodies, periods of silence (see Addendum 270-C), metallic scraping noises, metallic scraping noises that have been looped and re-calibrated so they play roughly in the same tune as several classical music tunes and a handful of [DATA EXPUNGED], Morse code, [REDACTED] human screaming, various computer programming languages, every known language on earth (including, in one incident, Pig Latin), [DATA EXPUNGED] possibly of biological origin, condescending laughter, music, music played backwards, music [REDACTED], conversations that have evidently been recorded ranging from [REDACTED] politically significant and extensively protected area to what was most likely an average household, discussing what grocery supplies to buy from the supermarket, static, ambient soundtracks, etc.

SCP-270 is otherwise a perfectly normal phone and is susceptible to damage as similar phones would be. Disassembly has not uncovered the source of SCP-270's unusual properties.

~~Speaking into SCP-270 has no effect on SCP-270-1.~~ Currently disputed, refer to Incident-270-█ in which [DATA EXPUNGED].

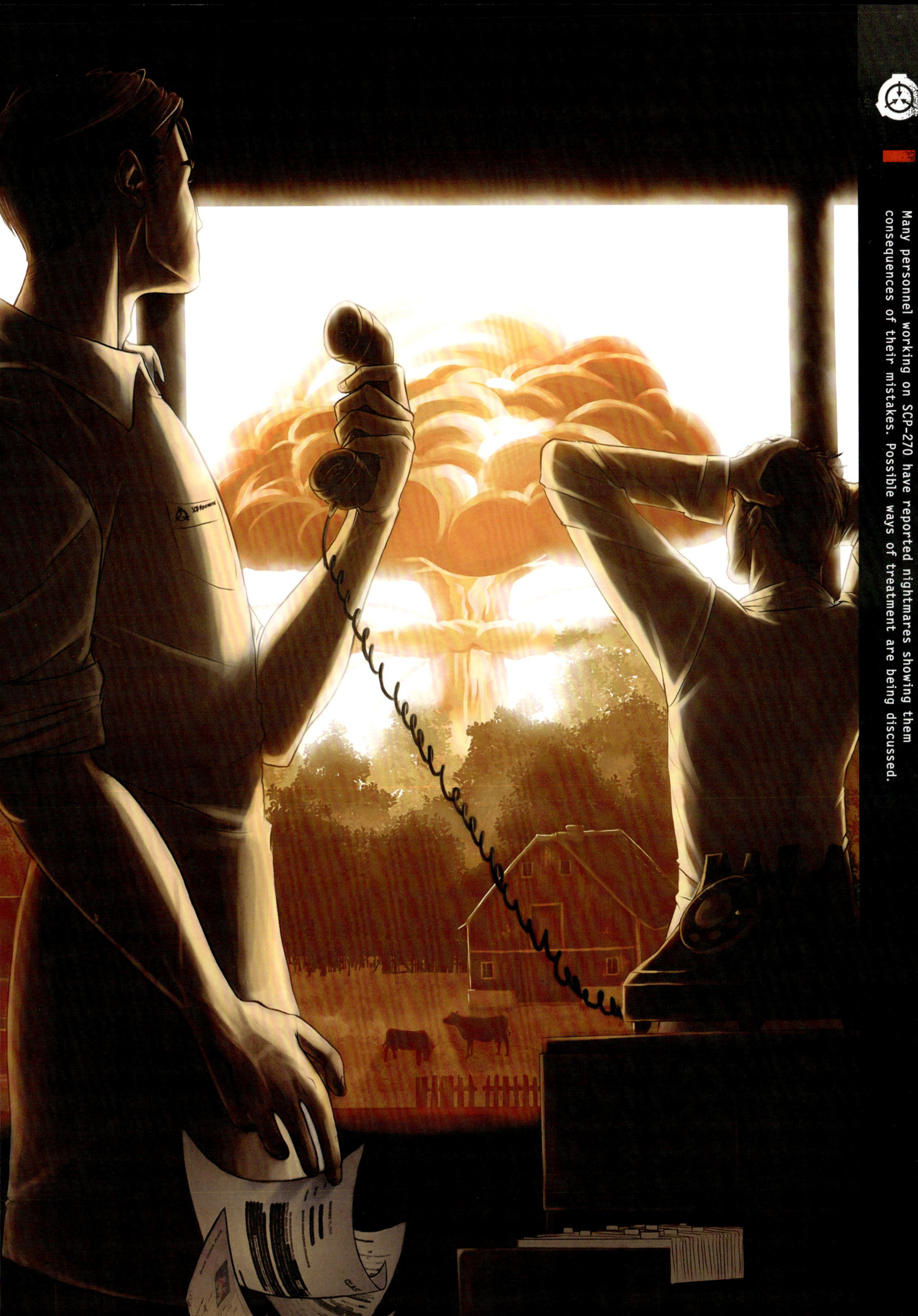

Many personnel working on SCP-270 have reported nightmares showing them consequences of their mistakes. Possible ways of treatment are being discussed.

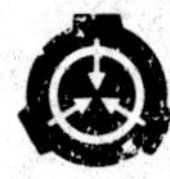

Research Library File ▸ 270

Attempts to decipher SCP-270-1 have yielded partial successes. In one notable case, a complicated cipher proved to be an intensive description of an SCP-███'s imminent attempt to breach containment. Evidence of such was found in the [REDACTED] of SCP-███'s containment. Containment breach was accordingly prevented. Decoded portions have alternately been startlingly useful to the Foundation, and immensely frustrating to both personnel working on SCP-270-1 and Foundation officials. For example, one ██-hour study of what seemed to be a significant cipher proved to translate into a long and painstakingly thorough list of extremely unofficial synonyms for a human ████.

Likewise, information gained from SCP-270-1 have both [DATA EXPUNGED] preventing a possible XK-class end-of-the-world scenario, and listed 'secret ingredients' of Dr. R████'s widely praised cherry pie. As it is impossible to determine how useful portions of SCP-270-1 will be, personnel are advised to choose whatever segments of SCP-270-1 they deem to be most promising. However, some portions of cipher are either too intricately encrypted for our most perspicacious personnel to decode, or indeed may hold no meaning at all.

Attempts to decode SCP-270-1 are continually ongoing (see Addenda 270-D and 270-E).

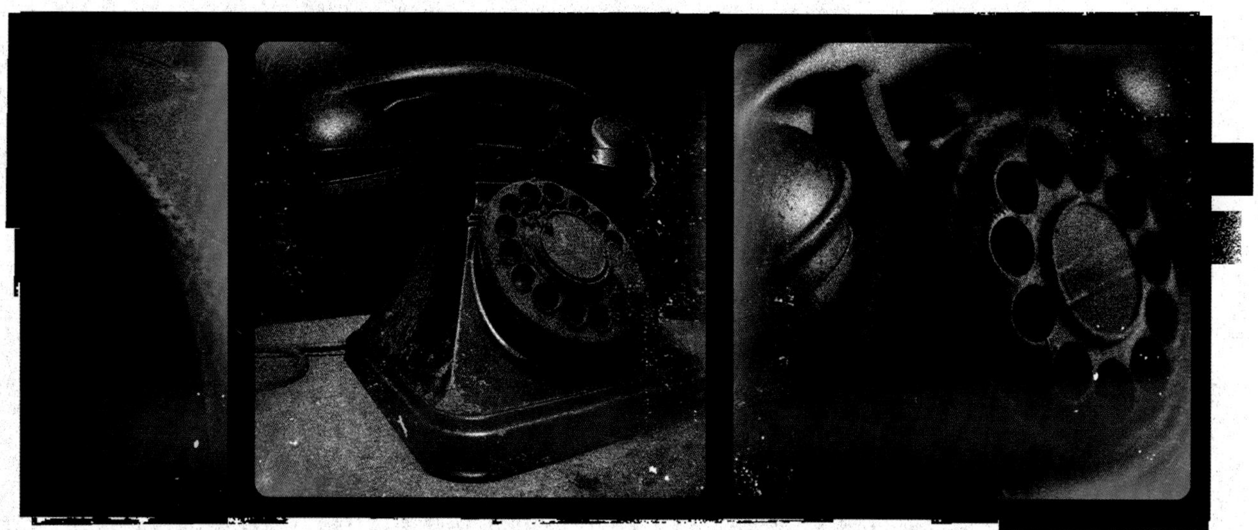

Addendum 270-A: A probe was extended a total of ████ meters along the wire before the maximum extension length was reached. The matter has since been declared not of sufficient interest to merit a more thorough examination.

Addendum 270-B: As of █/██/█, ████ military time, the unidentified female voice of SCP-270-1 stuttered for █ seconds before breaking down into what researchers described as 'disconsolate sobs,' pleading to be [REDACTED]. This continued for █ seconds before audio cut off abruptly to a ██-minute excerpt of SCP-270-1 from █/█/█. Immediately afterwards, SCP-270-1 proceeded as usual, the only noticeable difference being that the voice narrating SCP-270-1 was male.

Addendum 270-C: Further examinations revealed that this was in fact not silence, but audio stimuli both too high or too low pitched for human perception. ██ additional unidentified languages have been discovered upon supplying Outpost Delta with appropriate audio equipment.

Addendum 270-D: As of late, SCP-270-1 has been becoming noticeably more difficult to decode. This includes utilizing more convoluted methods of encryption, loud background noises being added while the narrator is speaking, multiple voices speaking at once, and, in one case, loud [REDACTED] extremely personal details [REDACTED] Dr. A████, who was visibly shaken by the event. Morale has since plummeted while stress levels have skyrocketed.

A computer program has been coded in order to automatically decode portions of SCP-270-1. A recreation wing has been added to Outpost Delta.

Addendum 270-E: Data Processor 270-1 has been discontinued. All attempts to electronically resolve portions of SCP-270-1 have thus far failed.

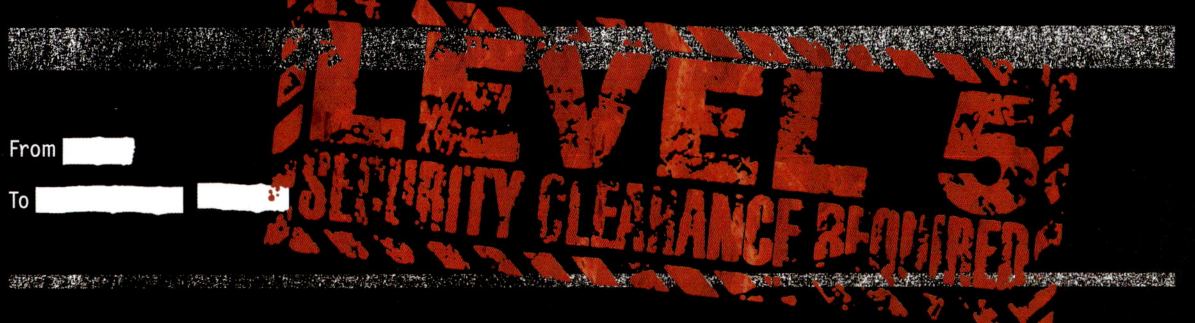

From ███

To ████ ███

As of late, concerns have risen regarding the psychological states of personnel working on SCP-270.

What I'm talking about, of course, are the natural issues that arise when you have a situation like this. Namely, putting a bunch of highly intelligent, motivated, tenacious people together and ordering them to solve a puzzle that may or may not have a solution. And telling them that lives may depend upon their success or failure.

Recently, Dr. ███, by some superhuman effort, cracked ██ minutes' worth of cipher that had been discarded by communal agreement as a 'dud' and [DATA EXPUNGED] resulting in the aversion of a ██ end-of-the-world scenario. This has not been beneficial for the mental states of many personnel, as every 'dud' they discard may contain information regarding an equally disastrous event. Since then, there have been rapidly emerging paranoia and/or obsession-related disorders. Some personnel are beginning to insist that the most trivial details of the cipher contain important messages, others have not slept or eaten in days in their pursuits, and still others have suffered from psychotic breakdowns.

Outpost Delta has since been supplied with more personnel in an attempt to spread the workload more thinly. However, the effects of having a few days of diligent work crumble into a 'dud,' repeatedly, have proven to be an absolute disaster for morale and, at times, mental stability. Currently, we only have enough staff to decode roughly ██% of the cipher.

So far, reassigning personnel after a █-month stay at Outpost Delta, applying Class A amnestics, and returning them to work on 270-1 at the end of a █-month period of low-pressure jobs has worked fairly well as a short-term solution. This, however, requires a rather large number of personnel to be continually circulating in and out of Outpost Delta to maintain the minimum amount of staff required to decode the greater portion of what comes out of SCP-270.

In addition, long-term circulation through Outpost Delta has been shown to ingrain certain paranoid and obsessive mental behaviors that Class A amnestics don't wipe clean.

[DATA EXPUNGED] nature of SCP-270, this is exactly what it wants, if certain people are to be trusted [DATA EXPUNGED] disconcerting to said 05 member. [REDACTED] not in fact a method of safe communication between unknown entities, as originally hypothesized, but rather [DATA EXPUNGED].

I request for this matter to be discussed more in-depth sometime in the near future.

-Dr. ████

END OF REPORT

File >>> 0032881

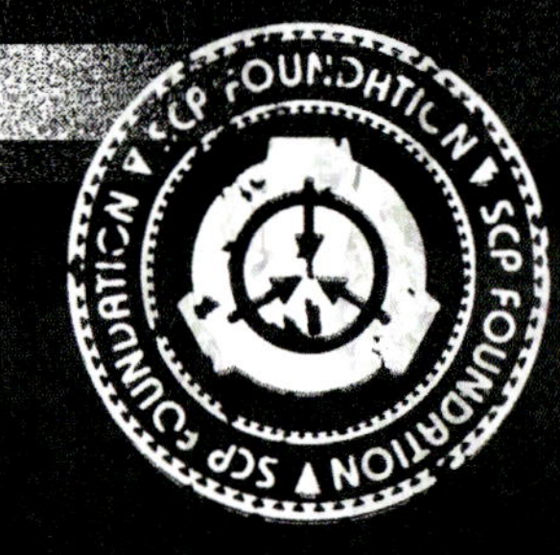

SCP-1529

Title

KING OF THE MOUNTAIN

Report by

Smapti

Picture by

Dmitry Desyatov

Access the original report on

scp-wiki.wikidot.com/scp-1529

Date

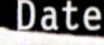

Class

EUCLID

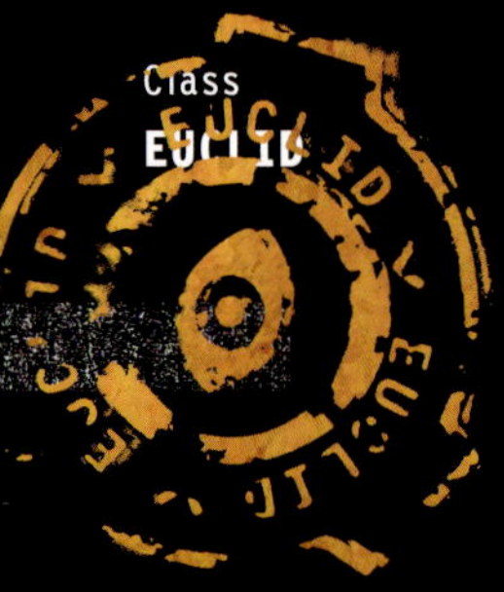

SPECIAL CONTAINMENT PROCEDURES

SCP-1529's native environment is to be kept under telescope and satellite surveillance whenever weather and daylight permit. Year-round telescope surveillance is to be conducted from the Foundation's permanent monitoring stations in ████████, Nepal and ████████, People's Republic of China. As early in the year as weather permits, a Foundation front company, South Chomolungma Portage, shall establish forward monitoring stations at base camp on the northern and southern ascents, and at the higher camps as weather permits (with the exception of Camp VI on the northern ascent and Camp IV on the southern), to be maintained until weather conditions force the evacuation of the mountain for the season. When SCP-1529 is active, telescope surveillance will be conducted by means of an automatic telescope with a video feed playing at seven seconds delay to avoid a repeat of Incident 1529-2. When necessary and safe, surveillance shall be conducted by airplane or helicopter.

The Foundation shall liaise with civilian expedition coordinators as necessary to prevent attempts on the summit when SCP-1529 is active. The bodies of any hikers who encounter SCP-1529 are to be removed from the mountain as soon as possible for autopsy and disposal. All SCP-1529 related casualties shall be attributed to natural causes relating to altitude sickness and hypothermia. Any survivors and/or witnesses are to be debriefed and administered a Class-B amnestic.

Mobile Task Force Psi-29029, ("Alpine Echo") shall remain on standby at all times at the Foundation monitoring station in ████████. During tours of duty, all members of the MTF shall remain at all times in a pressurized environment acclimatized to 7,900 meters above sea level. In the event that a recurrence of Incident 1529-1 occurs, Alpine Echo shall deploy to the mountain by helicopter and attempt Procedure Boukreev.

DESCRIPTION

SCP-1529 is a humanoid individual residing near the summit of Mt. Everest in Nepal, above the 8,000 meter "death zone" mark where human acclimatization is believed to be impossible. SCP-1529 appears to be of average height and weight and is dressed head to toe in what resembles standard mountaineering wear and boots, colored white. SCP-1529's face is entirely obscured by the hood of its parka and what appears to be an oversized pair of opaque black mountain goggles. SCP-1529 has never been observed to wear any other clothes. As very few living people have observed SCP-1529 except through a telescope, it is not known whether its coverings are clothes or part of its body, or what it may look like underneath (except as per Interview 1529-1.)

The Foundation became aware of SCP-1529 in the 1970s when annual expeditions to the summit of Mt. Everest became commonplace, and rumors began to circulate in the mountaineering community about a "monster" near the summit. Photographs found undeveloped in George Mallory's camera after the discovery of his remains in 1999 indicate that SCP-1529 was present and active by the time of his attempt on the summit, and was not then significantly different in appearance than it is today. (Foundation media assets have reported that Mallory's camera was never found, and that his death was the result of a fall.)

During periods when daylight is sufficient and cloud cover allows for surveillance of the mountain, SCP-1529 is on average observable ██% of the time. For ██%

of that time, SCP-1529 is "inactive", and lies or sits motionless. Recorded periods of inactivity have extended from 17 minutes to (possibly) 8 months; median period of inactivity is 23.4 days. When "active", SCP-1529 can be observed to climb about the upper reaches of the mountain and summit in no discernible direction. SCP-1529 has never been observed to use any tools or climbing aids other than its hands or feet, and while travelling along established climbing routes will ignore the existence of guide ropes or ladders that have been installed by previous climbers. SCP-1529 has demonstrated an ability to climb or descend sections of the mountain's face believed impassable to conventional mountaineers, has never been observed to fall or lose its grip, and is seemingly unencumbered by sub-zero temperatures, high winds, thin air, or low atmospheric pressure. The cause of its becoming active or inactive is unknown, and shows no correlation to weather, time of day, traffic up the mountain, season, or time of year. SCP-1529 has never been observed to descend below the 8,000 meter mark (except as per Incident 1529-1.) Documented periods of activity have extended from 3 hours to (possibly) 6 days; median documented period is 15.2 hours. Nighttime observation of SCP-1529 has thus far proved impossible. Infrared imaging has shown no difference in temperature between SCP-1529 and the surrounding mountainside.

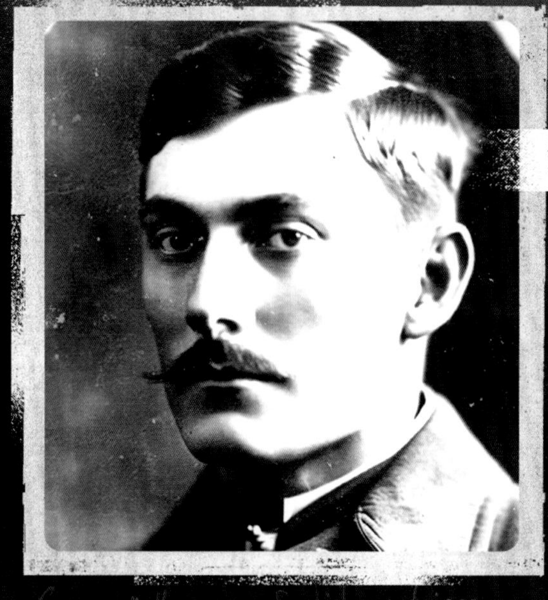

George Mallory, an English mountaineer who perished in 1924 after possibly becoming the first man to reach the summit of Everest.

If human climbers ascend past the 8,000 meter mark while SCP-1529 is active, it will attempt to make its way towards them and interpose itself between them and the summit or camp. SCP-1529 seems to prefer to target solo climbers or climbers that are significantly ahead of or behind the rest of their group, but will target individuals within a group if such an opportunity does not present itself. Once SCP-1529 is within eyesight of a traveller it will attempt to gain his/her attention and cause the traveller to make eye contact with it, which induces a hypnotic effect in the victim. The victim finds it very difficult to break eye contact with SCP-1529 and will begin to feel very warm and comfortable, and enticed to sit down and relax. Once the climber has stopped moving, SCP-1529 will close range with the climber and [DATA EXPUNGED]. Death from hypothermia appears to occur within 1-2 hours of making eye contact with SCP-1529, much more quickly than is typical for climbers stuck near the summit. After death, SCP-1529's victims experience an extremely accelerated state of decay: after several hours or days, bodies have become rotted and mummified in levels comparable to bodies that have lain exposed on the mountain for several decades.

Of the approximately 220 people who have died in the high altitudes of Everest since 1924, SCP-1529 is believed to have accounted for at least ███. █ people have survived encounters with SCP-1529, almost all (except as per Interview 1529-1) due to another mountaineer assisting the victim before SCP-1529 made physical contact. SCP-1529 does not appear to be capable of entrancing more than one climber at a time; however, physical encounters between SCP-1529 and more than one person have been noted to lead to [DATA EXPUNGED]. Purpose and motivation for SCP-1529's behavior is unknown; see Interview 1529-1 for speculation.

INCIDENT 1529-1

On ██/██/19██, SCP-1529 entered Camp V on the northern approach, at 7,775 meters, and [DATA EXPUNGED]. casualties occurred, including both Foundation personnel operating the Camp V monitoring post. Foundation assets in the media attributed the deaths to a sudden storm and poor planning on the part of expedition coordinator ███ ███, who was among the deceased. SCP-1529 had not been under observation at the time due to its having entered active phase sometime during the night, and had not yet been located on telescope. To date this is the first and only documented instance of SCP-1529 travelling below the 8,000 meter mark or entering any camp while inhabited.

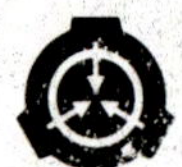

Research Library File ▸ 1529

INCIDENT 1529-2

On ██/██/20██, Agent ██████ in the permanent facility in China, engaged in telescope surveillance of SCP-1529 while it was active near the summit of the mountain. ██████ reported that SCP-1529, while facing in the direction of the base, looked directly in the direction of the telescope. ██████ immediately reported symptoms consistent with an SCP-1529 encounter and reported that SCP-1529 had begun descending the mountain in the direction of the permanent facility. ██████ was unable to pull himself away from the telescope and had to be manually restrained and sedated 17 minutes after beginning of encounter, whereupon he was rushed to facility sickbay and found to have a core body temperature of 27°C and signs of frostbite in the fingers and toes, despite having remained indoors at a room temperature of 24 °C for the duration of the encounter. Agent █████, who attempted to resume surveillance after ██████'s illness, found SCP-1529 still descending the mountain and encountered similar symptoms. Telescope surveillance was discontinued until ██/██, when aerial surveillance confirmed that SCP-1529 had ceased to descend and had entered an inactive state.

INTERVIEW LOG 1529-1

Interviewed: L██████ ████, hereafter "L."

Interviewer: Agent ██████

Foreword: On ██/██/20██, L. was reportedly killed during an encounter with SCP-1529 when it abruptly became active shortly after L. had reached the mountain's summit. However, L. was found alive when another team reached his position nearly two days later, and was removed safely from the mountain. He required fingertip and toe amputations due to frostbite, but is otherwise making a full recovery. The following is an excerpt from L.'s debriefing prior to his discharge from hospital.

<Begin Log>

████: Tell me about what happened when you encountered the creature.

L.: It can't have been more than ten minutes after I left the summit, about 1300. That's the hardest part of the climb. You've reached the top and you're exhilarated and proud of yourself, and then you realize you've just done the most difficult thing you've ever done in your life - and you have to do it all over again, right now, backwards, or you'll end up like Green Boots.[1] The others were five or six meters ahead of me – I'd been delayed a moment to adjust my hood. That's when I saw it come over the ridge.

████: What was your reaction when you first saw it?

L.: Surprised, to say the least. We hadn't been told there was anyone else climbing to the top that day. I thought he must have come over from the other side, or gotten left behind by his mates. I shouted and waved my hands in the air to try and get his attention.

████: What happened when you got its attention?

L.: 'E looked right at me, and that's when it started. I suddenly felt... happy? Relieved? It was like right away all the pain and the soreness and the chill was gone. I didn't have blisters on my feet and I could feel the tip of my nose again. It was like I was back in ████████ kicking up my feet by the fireplace, like I could forget all my worries and enjoy a well-deserved rest. But...

████: ...But?

L.: It didn't feel right. Have you ever heard of paradoxical undressing? When your body starts to cool

1. Nickname given to the body of Tsewang Paljor, who – while wearing a distinctive bright green pair of mountain boots – collapsed and died on the main trail along the northern approach in 1996.

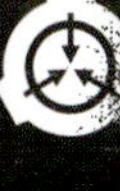

SCP-1529 as described by L█████ █.

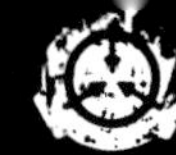

down, really cool down, your blood vessels dilate and you start to feel like you're warming up. So you start tearing off your clothes because you feel like you're burning up and you need to cool off – and the next thing anyone knows, you're naked and frozen to death curled up in a snow bank. I had a mate who went that way in '98. As far as I know he's still curled up next to the Hillary Step.[2]

█████: So you believed you were imagining it.

L.: Right. So I tried to shrug it off, but I couldn't take my eyes off the man who'd started climbing up towards me. And that's when it all went to shit.

█████: How so?

L.: Right away all that warmth and comfort was gone. Suddenly I felt cold - colder than I'd been before. Colder than I had a right to be. I couldn't feel my fingers or my face. My lips felt cracked and frozen. I tried to breathe and it was like my lungs were full of water. My legs cramped up and next thing I knew I was down. My mates were almost thirty meters off by now. I tried to yell to them but all that came out was a whisper. I looked up and that man – that thing – was still coming.

█████: How long did it take for it to reach you?

L.: An hour? I'm not sure. I couldn't see my watch and I don't think I could've made sense of it anyway. I managed to get my arms on the ground but I couldn't push myself to my feet. It was getting to the point that even if I could right myself I wouldn't be able to make it back to camp before nightfall. I was starting to think I wasn't making it off the mountain at all – but what worried me more was the man. The closer he got to me, I started to feel something in the back of my head – something primal, and menacing, and above all, hateful.

█████: What happened when it reached you?

L.: It grabbed me by the shoulders and pulled me up to face it. I was looking right into those goggles, those eyes…

█████: Were they goggles or eyes?

L.: Neither. Both. I don't know. But it was like I could see things in them. Not see them, so much… more like feel them. Images and feelings in the back of my mind. Rage, and joy, and… confusion.

█████: Confusion?

L.: I don't think it was used to people resisting it. It asked me a question.

█████: It spoke?

L.: Not words, so much. I could hear it, but not with my ears. I saw images of people – people sitting back in hot tubs, laying by a crackling fire, sunning themselves on the beach. Warm, happy people. But I knew their faces. They were faces I'd seen in books, and in pictures, and people I'd seen on the way up the mountain who I hadn't seen on the way down. I saw Green Boots! People still lying face-down somewhere in the death zone. And I heard its question.

█████: Which was?

L.: "You would refuse my gift?"

(L. became very troubled at this point in the interview and was silent for some time.)

█████: Go on.

L.: I could barely make sense of anything that was going on… but I knew that this thing in front of me was a bigger threat than any storm or any snow drift. Moving my lips was harder than anything I've ever done… but I did, and I told it "Yes."

█████: How did it respond?

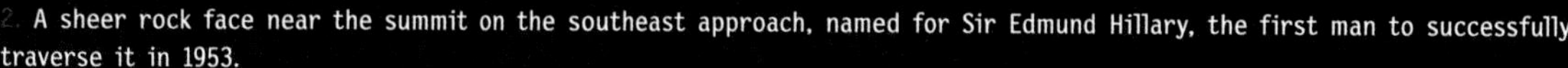

2. A sheer rock face near the summit on the southeast approach, named for Sir Edmund Hillary, the first man to successfully traverse it in 1953.

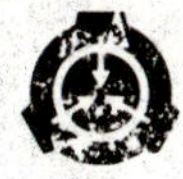

L.: I saw more images. Images of those same people, lying in the snow, already half-dead. I could tell I was looking at them from its perspective. It was [DATA EXPUNGED] them. I could've been sick. It didn't say anything to me in words so much – but it was angry at me. It was offended, outraged, shocked. It was trying to tell me I'd been ungrateful – and instead of relaxing peacefully while it [DATA EXPUNGED] I'd have to feel every minute of it. I asked it, "Why are you doing this?"

█████: What did it say then?

L.: It mocked me.

(L. is silent again.)

█████: Just a few more questions, please. How did it mock you?

L.: It... it showed me another one of its victims. Probably the first one. Mallory, 1924. I'd have known that face like my own mother's, but I'd never seen it in that kind of detail before... or in that condition. He was on his stomach. Weak. Frostbitten. Dying. He was waving and hollering at the thing as I watched it approach from its own perspective. It looked him in the eyes and it [DATA EXPUNGED]. It made me watch every second until it was done. I think watching it was worse than living it would've been. And then it told me...

(L. is silent.)

█████: Told you what?

L.: "Because it's there."

Quote attributed to Mallory in the New York Times, 1923, when asked why he wanted to climb Everest.

█████: What happened next?

L.: I wasn't going to let [DATA EXPUNGED] happen to me. It was holding me up, so I had just enough strength to ball up my fist. I punched it. Hard as I could, every last ounce of strength I had. Right in the goggles. They cracked. I could see what was behind them.

█████: What was that?

L.: [DATA EXPUNGED] I don't remember much after that. I must have gotten into my bivvy bag somehow because that's how they found me.

<End Log>

Closing Statement: After L.'s encounter with SCP-1529, it was not observed, active or inactive, for 5 months, 17 days, 19 hours. Upon next observation, its goggles showed no signs of damage or wear. L. passed away on █/█/20█. Foundation media assets have reported that the cause of death was due to complications from childhood exposure to asbestos. An autopsy performed by the Foundation indicated that L. was suffering extreme hypothermia, frostbite, and cerebral edema at the time of his death. L. had retired from mountaineering following the SCP-1529 encounter and had not travelled more than 500 meters above sea level in the 12 months preceding his death.

ADDENDUM

On █/█/20█, aerial surveillance picked up an image of an individual of similar appearance to SCP-1529 near the summit of ██████ █████, ████. As the government of ████ has prohibited mountaineering, threat to normalcy is negligible at this time. Aerial and satellite surveillance of █████ █████ will continue on a regular basis until permanent monitoring stations can be established.

END OF REPORT

File >>> 010223

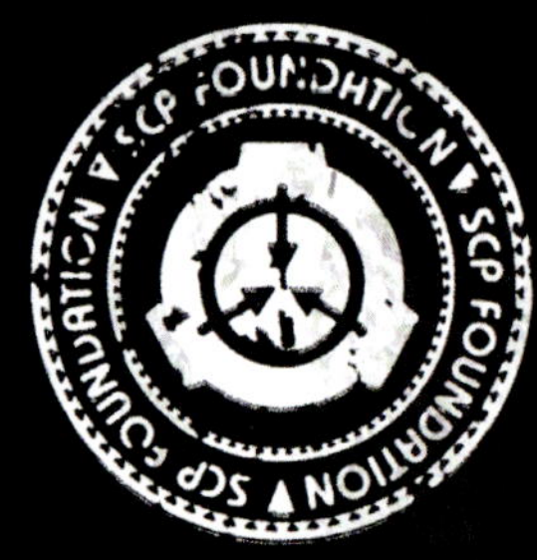

SCP-1943

Title

NO ANOMALIES DETECTED

Report by

Aelanna

Picture by

Dan Temirov

Access the original report on

scp-wiki.wikidot.com/scp-1943

Date

Class

EUCLID

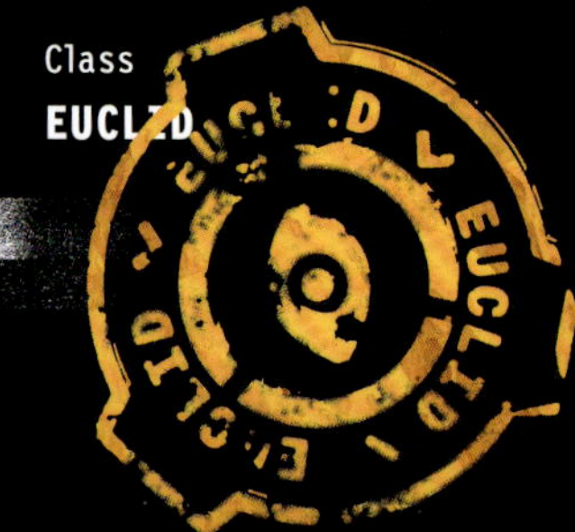

SPECIAL CONTAINMENT PROCEDURES

SCP-1943-1 is contained in a standard humanoid containment cell in the high-security wing of Humanoid Containment Site-06-3. As a former member of Foundation research staff, SCP-1943-1 is highly cooperative and thus allowed access to non-sensitive materials. All reasonable requests for personal items may be granted; however, SCP-1943-1 is not allowed to have outside contact and its security clearances have been indefinitely revoked.

The remains of SCP-1943-2 have been cryogenically preserved in the storage wing of Site-06-3. Data regarding the analysis of materials and information recovered from SCP-1943-2 are available with permission from Level 3 Senior Researchers.

DESCRIPTION

SCP-1943-1 is Sarah Gruenwald, a 27-year-old European-American female and Level 1 Assistant Laboratory Technician formerly employed in the non-anomalous chemistry laboratory of Area-█. Prior to containment, SCP-1943-1 did not have clearance or certification for handling anomalous materials and was not known to have been in contact with any anomalous phenomena or materials during the three years in which she was employed.

SCP-1943-1 does not appear to be anomalous in any way, and has repeatedly tested negative on biological, chemical, radiological, and [REDACTED] analysis with the intent of identifying anomalous properties. SCP-1943-1 does not have any family history indicating possible anomalous influence nor any significant employment history prior to being hired by the Foundation. SCP-1943-1 is also psychologically stable and exhibits no unusual mental conditions nor evidence of having been affected by any mind-affecting anomalies or memetic agents.

SCP-1943-2 is the remains of an enemy operative determined via extensive interrogation to have been employed by the Chaos Insurgency. SCP-1943-2 was the sole surviving operative out of a team of 25 individuals believed to be a unit of the Chaos Insurgency's Transhuman Task Force, all of whom exhibited signs of having been genetically, cybernetically, and thaumaturgically augmented to enhance their combat capabilities. These augmentations included, but were not limited to:

- Skeletal reinforcements resulting in increased bone strength and resilience
- Muscular enhancements to increase power and endurance
- Redundant cardiovascular systems to increase overall survivability
- Neural implants and brain augmentations designed to improve reflexes and reaction time
- Neural implants enabling extrasensory detection and communication

All of these individuals were also equipped with devices enabling the operator to self-terminate if compromised and dead-man fail-safes intended to incinerate the body upon operator death, thereby rendering any remains unusable for analysis or post-mortem interrogation. During Incident 1943-01, all other individuals belonging to this team were killed by Foundation tactical response teams or self-terminated after being wounded or captured; SCP-1943-2 suffered a failure or malfunction in its fail-safe device that rendered it unable to self-terminate and was subsequently captured alive.

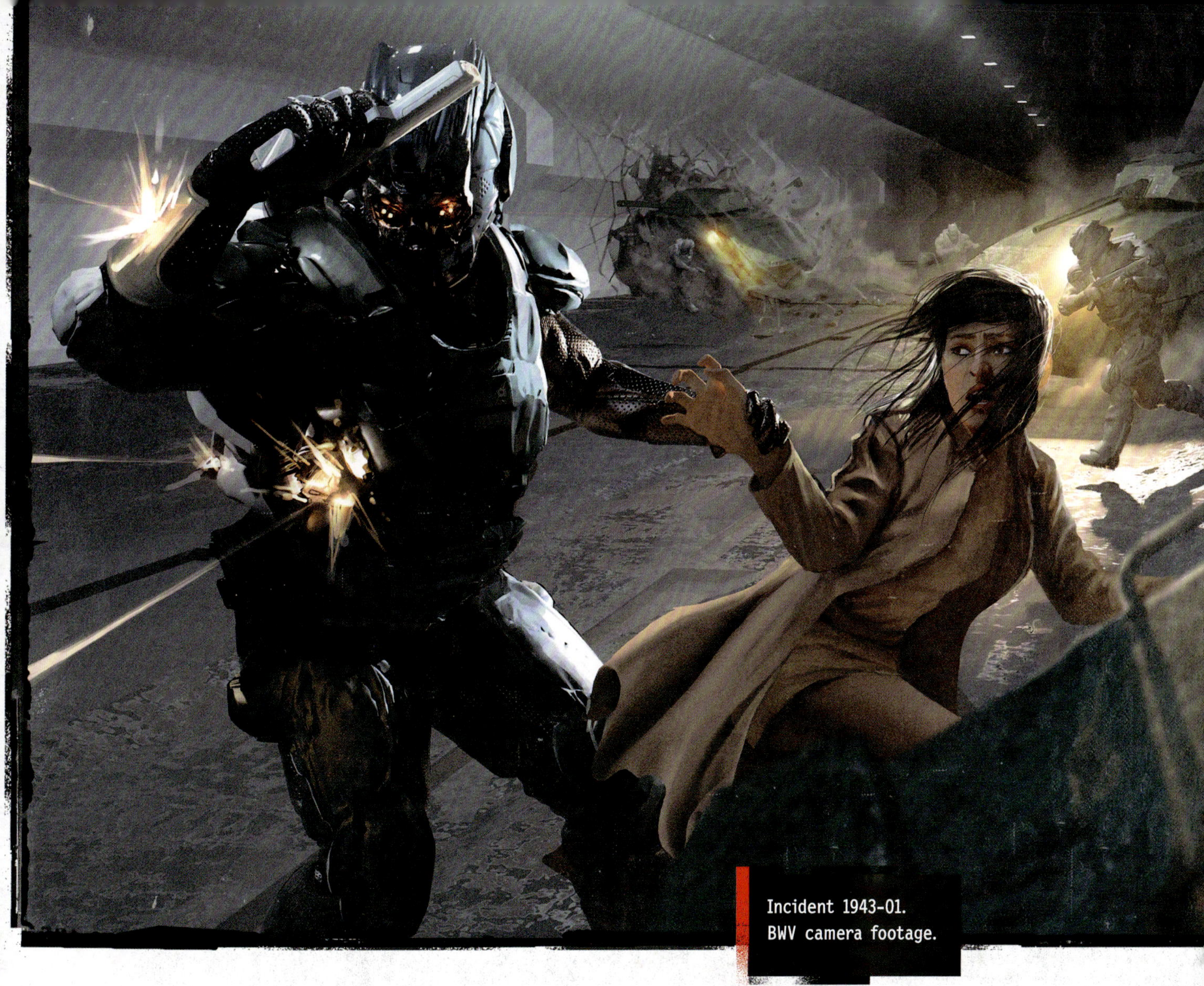

Incident 1943-01.
BWV camera footage.

SCP-1943-2 remained in Foundation custody for approximately five weeks before expiring from complications from its wounds as well as severe degradation of its mechanical augmentations. Subsequent autopsy revealed several degenerative conditions present in its body that would suggest that it had been nearing the end of its useful lifecycle.

ADDENDUM 1943-1: INCIDENT REPORT, INCIDENT 1943-01

On ██/██/██, operatives from the Chaos Insurgency's Transhuman Task Force Zeta-3 initiated an assault on the laboratory wing of Area-██ that, through extensive analysis of surveillance footage and further corroborated by information leaked by agents embedded within CI cells, appears to have been carried out with the sole purpose of rendering SCP-1943-1 into CI custody. TTF Zeta-3 operatives disabled or collapsed several passageways at Area-██ using explosives, rendering on-site tactical teams unable to effectively respond to the assault, then quickly incapacitated the wing's security detail. Total Foundation casualties suffered as a result of the incident was determined to be █ killed and ██ wounded despite the presence of numerous research staff, suggested to be due to the single-minded goal of the CI team and their operational orders to not engage Foundation personnel that were not directly resisting their ingress.

This assault was stopped due to the unannounced and early arrival of a subordinate unit of Mobile Task Force Nu-7 ("Hammer Down"), which had intended to stop and refuel at Area-██ en route to a covert assignment in [OPERATIONAL INFORMATION REDACTED]. MTF Nu-7 was able to coordinate a counter-action with the assistance of on-site security personnel and successfully neutralized the CI assault team before they were able to exfiltrate from the outer perimeter of Area-██.

Research Library File ▸ 1943

ADDENDUM 1943-2: SCP-1943-2 INTERROGATION LOG

Dr. ████: Who were you working with, and how many of you are left?

SCP-1943-2: Zeta-three, Archangels. I'm the last one and you already know that.

[irrelevant content abridged]

Dr. ████: I don't understand how –

SCP-1943-2: *(laughs)* No, of course you don't understand. You guys never do, and you never will. They'll eventually send more of us when you least expect it, and we'll get her eventually. You got lucky – damned lucky – this time, and that's the only reason we failed.

Dr. ████: You expect me to believe that you sent two squads of augmented operatives just for a single low-level lab tech?

SCP-1943-2: I don't give a shit what you believe. If you want to believe that she's just human, then that's entirely on you. If you don't, it still doesn't matter; eventually you'll get careless and we'll pick her up. Easier than getting milk from the corner store.

Dr. ████: And the fact that none of our tests have shown anything out of the ordinary at all about her?

SCP-1943-2: Of course they haven't. Y'all have always been blind, and I'm the one with the ocular implants ripped out.

ADDENDUM 1943-3: RESEARCHER NOTE

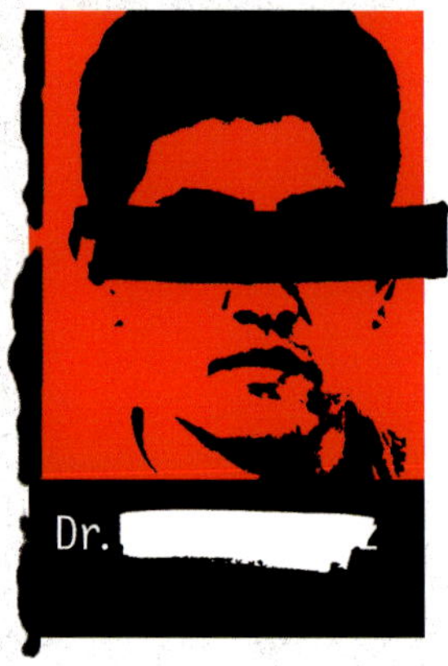

At this point, we have now tried every permutation of every possible test on her, including ones that I heavily objected to due to the danger inherent in the procedures. Absolutely nothing is out of the ordinary; as far as we can tell, she's just a normal, but very scared human being.

This wouldn't be the first time that the Insurgency has tried to turn our resources against ourselves, and it won't be the last. I see no reason why we need to continue to detain her like this; if we can't trust our own technology and we allow ourselves to question our own people in this way, then we're going down a path that doesn't lead anywhere good. I am formally requesting that Dr. Gruenwald be declassified and released.

Dr. ████

Senior Observer

Dr. ████

Request denied. Until we're absolutely sure, we can't take any chances.

05-██

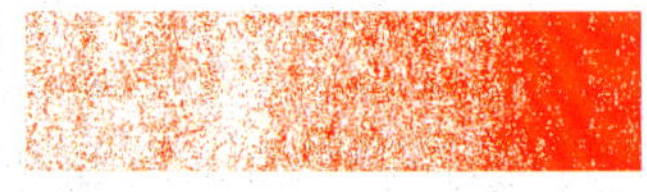

END OF REPORT 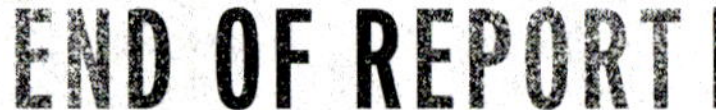 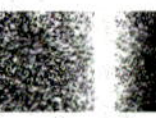  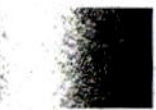

SPECIAL CONTAINMENT PROCEDURES

SCP-087 is located on the campus of [REDACTED]. The doorway leading to SCP-087 is constructed of reinforced steel with an electro-release lock mechanism. It has been disguised to resemble a janitorial closet consistent with the design of the building. The lock mechanism on the doorknob will not release unless ██ volts are applied in conjunction with counter-clockwise rotation of the key. The inside of the door is lined with 6 centimeters of industrial foam padding.

Due to the results of the final exploration (see Document 087-IV), no personnel are permitted access to SCP-087.

DESCRIPTION

SCP-087 is an unlit platform staircase. Stairs descend on a 38 degree angle for 13 steps before reaching a semicircular platform of approximately 3 meters in diameter. Descent direction rotates 180 degrees at each platform. The design of SCP-087 limits subjects to a visual range of approximately 1.5 flights. A light source is required for any subjects exploring SCP-087, as there are no lighting fixtures or windows present. Lighting sources brighter than 75 watts have shown to be ineffective, as SCP-087 seems to absorb excess light.

Subjects report and audio recordings confirm the distressed vocalizations from what is presumed to be a child between the ages of █ and █. The source of the distress calls is estimated to be located approximately 200 meters below the initial platform. However, any attempts to descend the staircase have failed to bring subjects closer to the source. The depth of descent calculated from Exploration IV, the longest exploration, is shown to be far beyond both the possible structure of both the building and geological surroundings. At this time, it is unknown if SCP-087 has an endpoint.

SCP-087 has undergone four video recorded explorations by Class-D personnel. Each subject conducting an exploration has encountered SCP-087-1, which appears as a face with no visible pupils, nostrils, or mouth. The nature of SCP-087-1 is entirely unclear, but it has been determined that it is not the source of the pleading. Subjects exhibit feelings of intense paranoia and fear when faced with SCP-087-1, but it is undetermined whether said feelings are abnormal or simply natural reactions.

ADDENDUM

Over a period of 2 weeks following Exploration IV, several members of the staff and students from the [REDACTED] campus reported knocking at a variable rate of 1-2 seconds per knock coming from the interior of SCP-087. The door leading to SCP-087 has been fitted with 6 centimeter thick industrial padding. All reports of knocking have ceased.

Authorized personnel may refer to documents 087-I through 087-IV for transcripts of Explorations I - IV.

File >>> 00129223

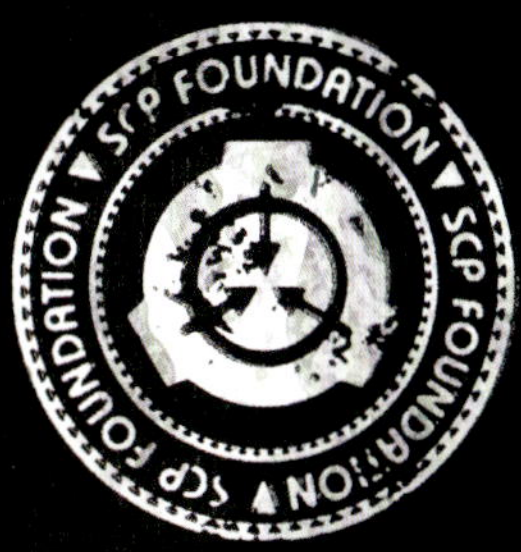

SCP-087

Title

THE STAIRWELL

Report by
Zaeyde

Pictures by
David Romero
Ruslana Gus

Access the original report on
scp-wiki.wikidot.com/scp-087

Date

Class

E█CLID

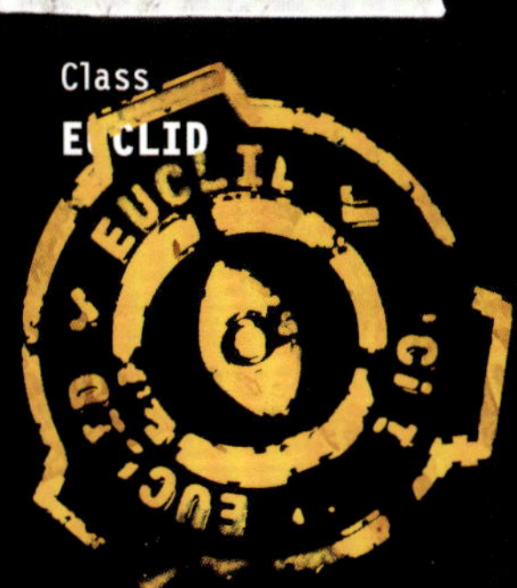

DOCUMENT #087-I: EXPLORATION I

Research Library File ▸ 087

D-8432 is a 43-year old Caucasian male of average build and appearance and unremarkable psychological background. Class-D designation is a result of demotion due to mishandling SCP-███. D-8432 is equipped with a 75 watt flood lamp with battery power capable of lasting 24 hours, a handheld camcorder fitted with a transmission stream, and an audio headset for communication with Dr. ██████ at Control.

KS-2233-04425 ▬ 223

D-8432 steps through doorway onto initial platform. Despite the wattage, the flood lamp only illuminates the first 9 steps. The second platform is not visible.

D-8432: It's fucking dark.

Dr. ████: Is your flood lamp functioning properly?

D-8432 shines the light out the door and into the academic building's hallway. The light reaches significantly further.

D-8432: Yeah, it's working, it just won't light these stairs all the way down.

Dr. ████: Thank you. Please continue.

D-8432 descends for 13 steps before reaching the second platform. The platform is in the shape of a semicircle with an apparently concrete surface and walls. There are no distinct markings, aside from nondescript patches of dust, dirt, or wear consistent with that which is found in a typical concrete stairwell. D-8432 rotates 180 degrees to begin descent down the second flight, then pauses.

Dr. ████: Reason for stopping?

D-8432: You hear that? There's a fucking kid down there. Sounds like one.

None of the described audio is feeding through the camera or mic at this time.

Dr. ████: Could you please describe the sound?

D-8432: It's young. Either female or a very young boy. It's crying and sobbing and saying *[pause]* please *[pause]* help *[pause]* please *[pause]* Yeah, it keeps repeating that and crying.

Dr. ████: Can you estimate its distance from your current location?

D-8432: Uh, fuck, I don't know, maybe 200 meters down?

Dr. ████: Please continue down the next flight.

The subject descends another 13 steps. As he reaches the landing, audio of the child as described is picked up. The child alternates between sobbing, wailing, and the words "please," "help," and "down here." The level of audio is consistent with D-8432's report of it being approximately 200 meters below.

Dr. ████: Can you still hear the crying?

D-8432: Yeah.

Dr. ████: We're picking it up as well. Please continue down. Stop if you notice any changes in the audio or environment.

The subject descends another 3 flights of stairs before stopping.

D-8432: Keep going?

Dr. █████: Please.

D-8432 continues another 17 flights (total of 22 flights) before stopping. There are no visual changes in the environment, and each flight has been a consistent 13 steps.

D-8432: I'm not getting any fucking closer to the kid.

Stereo audio confirms that the crying noise has not increased in volume and remains approximately 200 meters below the subject.

Dr. █████: Noted. Please continue.

The subject continues another 28 flights before stopping. (50 flights total.) D-8432 is standing on the 51st landing, counting the initial ground level landing. D-8432 is estimated to be 200 meters below the initial platform. 34 minutes have elapsed. The volume of the crying has not increased.

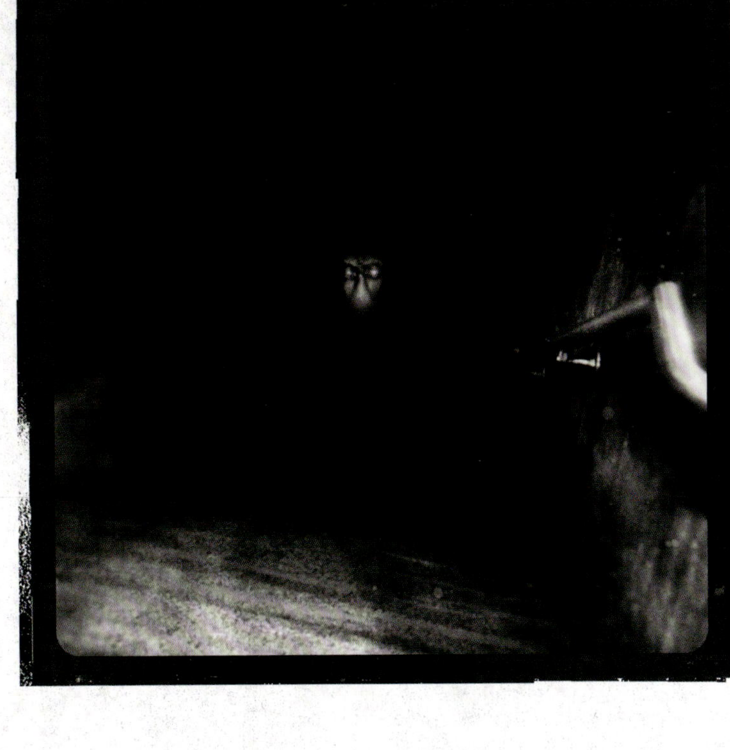

D-8432: I feel a little uneasy.

Dr. █████: You've spent a long time in a dark, unknown stairwell. It's natural. Please continue.

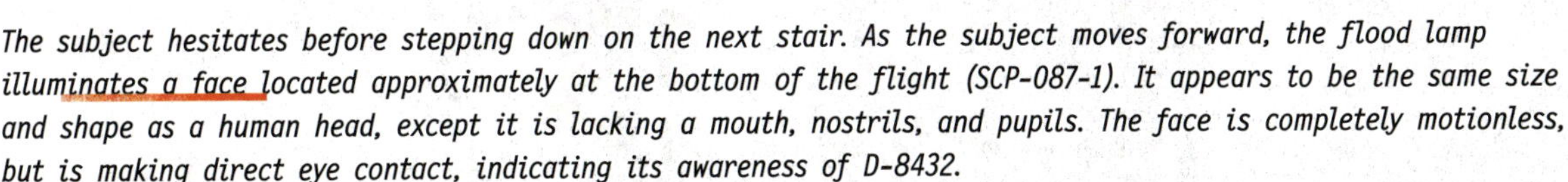

The subject hesitates before stepping down on the next stair. As the subject moves forward, the flood lamp illuminates a face located approximately at the bottom of the flight (SCP-087-1). It appears to be the same size and shape as a human head, except it is lacking a mouth, nostrils, and pupils. The face is completely motionless, but is making direct eye contact, indicating its awareness of D-8432.

D-8432: *[Yelling]* Fuck! What the fuck is that? Shit! Holy fucking shit. What the fuck!

Dr. █████: Can you please describe what you see?

D-8432: It's some sort of fucking person face thing and it's fucking looking right at me fuck fuck fuck it's looking right at me –

Dr. █████: Is it moving?

D-8432: *[pause, heavy breathing]* No, it's just staring at me. Fuck fuck fuck it's creepy.

Dr. █████: Please approach and further illuminate the entity.

D-8432: Fuck fuck fuck I don't want to fucking –

The face jerks forward about 50 centimeters directly toward D-8432.

D-8432: *[yelling]* Fuckfuckfuckfuckfuck [REDACTED]

D-8432 enters a panicked state and rapidly ascends SCP-087. D-8432 reaches the ground floor in 18 minutes, at which time he collapses and passes out. There is no sign of SCP-087-1. Review of the footage indicates an equal number of flights and steps ascending as descending. Audio of the crying and pleading remains at the same volume until the last flight, at which point it ceases.

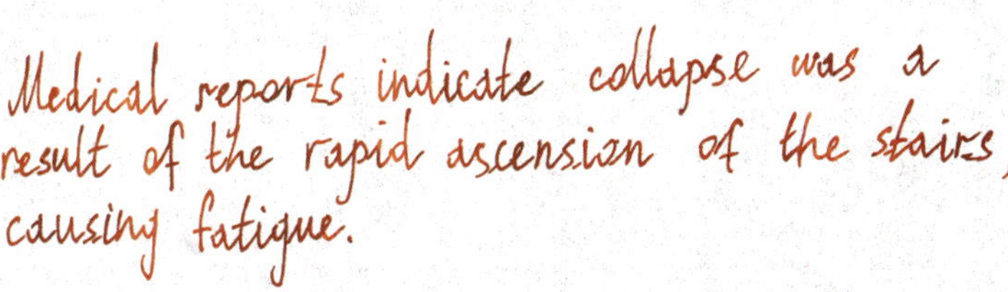

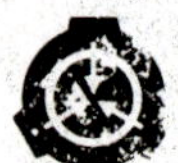

DOCUMENT #087-II: EXPLORATION II

Research Library File ▸ 087

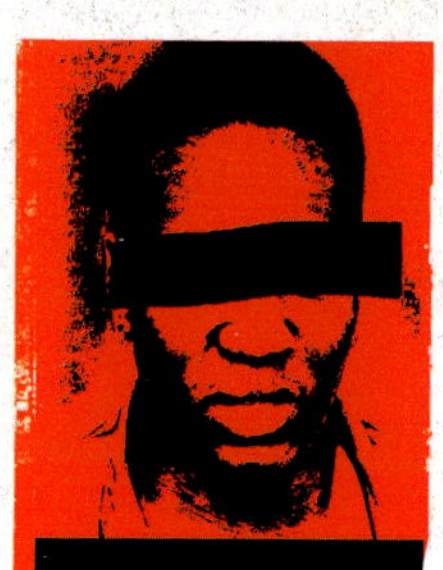

D-9035 is a 28-year old African-American male of strong build. Psychological background indicates no abnormalities except an extreme hatred for women. Subject has an extensive record of [DATA EXPUNGED]. D-9035 is equipped with a 100 watt flood lamp with battery power capable of lasting 24 hours, a handheld camcorder fitted with a transmission stream, and an audio headset for communication with Dr. ███ at Control. D-9035 is also equipped with a backpack containing 100 small LED lights with adhesive backs and battery lives of approximately 3 weeks. Lights turn on and off by compressing them.

KS-2233-09335 ▬ 224

D-9035 shines the flood lamp down the first flight of stairs. Despite the extra wattage, the light does not illuminate beyond the 9th step.

D-9035: You wan' me to go down there, Doc?

Dr. ███: Please shine your flood lamp outside of SCP-087 to verify it is functioning properly.

D-9035 shines the light into the hallway. Comparison with the footage from Exploration I confirms it is indeed brighter.

Dr. ███: Thank you. Please continue to the first landing.

D-9035: Hey Doc, I know what you said an' all, but I don' think I wanna go there.

Dr. ███: Please continue to the first landing.

D-9035: Doc, look, I-

Dr. ███: *[interrupting]* As per our earlier conversation, please continue to the first landing.

D-9035 pauses for 18 seconds, then descends 13 steps to the first landing and stops.

D-9035: Is that a kid?

Dr. ███: Please remove one of the adhesive lights and affix it to the wall on the landing.

D-9035: Doc, you hear that? Is that a kid down there?

Dr. ███: That's unconfirmed. Please affix an adhesive light to the wall and verify it functions.

D-9035 hesitates, then removes one of the lights from his backpack and adheres it to the wall. He presses on the light, and it turns on.

Dr. ███: Please turn off your flood lamp.

D-9035 hesitates again before turning off the lamp. The LED light illuminates the landing, but does not extend beyond the first step either way.

Dr. ███: Thank you. You may turn your flood lamp back on. Please continue to descend. At each landing, affix an LED light to the wall and turn it on. If you notice anything unusual, please report it.

D-9035 turns the flood lamp back on, then descends the next flight of stairs. As he sets foot on the landing, the audio picks up sounds of pleading and crying, consistent with those of the first exploration.

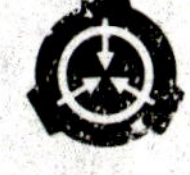

Dr. ████: Can you still hear the previously reported audio?

D-9035: Uh, yeah. She sounds 'bout 150, maybe 200 meters down. Am I supposed to get her? Look, Doc. I don't do good with kids.

Dr. ████: Please place the light and continue down until you notice anything unusual.

The subject adheres the light to the wall and turns it on, then continues to the next landing. He adheres the third LED light to the wall and turns it on. D-9035 continues in this manner for the next 25 flights before stopping.

D-9035: I don't think I'm getting any closer to the kid, doc.

Dr. ████: How far below would you estimate the source of the sound to be?

D-9035: Same as before. 150 to 200 meters down.

Dr. ████: Thank you. Please proceed.

D-9035 continues in the same fashion for the next 24 flights. At the 51st landing he stops. Footage shows an arced gouge in the concrete wall, estimated to be approximately 50 centimeters long and 10 centimeters wide. The first step down from the landing appears to be completely smashed into rubble.

D-9035: You see that?

Dr.████: Yes. Can you please describe what you see?

D-9035: Looks like something slashed at the wall, and the step over here's all crumbled up and stuff. The slash mark looks really smooth -

D-9035 touches the gouge mark.

D-9035: Yeah, it's smooth. Feels like glass.

Dr. ████: Thank you. Please continue down.

D-9035: Look, Doc. I think I've gone far enough.

Dr. ████: Please continue, as per our agreement.

D-9035: I don't wanna be doing this, agreement or not.

[DATA EXPUNGED]

D-9035 steps over the destroyed step and continues down the staircase. Nothing is notable at the next landing. D-9035 adheres an LED light to the wall and continues in the same fashion for another 38 flights. The sound of the crying and pleading still has not gotten closer. D-9035 is on the 89th landing and 74 minutes have elapsed from the beginning of the exploration. Subject is estimated to be 350 meters below the initial platform.

D-9035: I feel like the kid's just trying to lure me down here, Doc. I think it's time for me to—

D-9035 stops talking and moving as the flood lamp illuminates SCP-087-1. The face is staring directly at D-9035, again indicating awareness of the subject's presence. Although SCP-087-1 appears to be unmoving, its location is 38 flights below the initial encounter in Exploration I, indicating it is mobile.

Dr. ████: Is there a reason you stopped?

D-9035: *[unresponsive]*

D-9035's breathing grows labored. SCP-087-1 remains immobile for an additional 13 seconds. SCP-087-1 blinks.

D-9035: *[yelling, incomprehensible]*

SCP-087-1 jerks forward until it is approximately 90 centimeters from D-9035. Subject turns and flees up the stairs.

Dr. ████: Please relax and calm down. Turn around. We need a closer look at the face.

D-9035 ignores Dr. ████ and continues rapid ascent. He continues to scream incomprehensibly.

Dr. ████: D-9035, can you hear me? Please slow down.

D-9035 is unresponsive and continues rapidly climbing the stairs. His screaming diminishes to babbling. After ascending 72 flights, D-9035 collapses on the 17th landing.

Dr. ████: D-9035, can you hear me?

D-9035 is unresponsive, but labored breathing can be heard through the audio feed. For the next 14 minutes, D-9035 is immobile. The visual feed is black, and audio picks up only the subject's breathing and the continuous pleading coming from below. After 14 minutes and 32 seconds of unchanging visual and audio feeds, the sound of a rapid heartbeat not consistent with a human heartbeat, and a low cracking noise is heard. 7 seconds later, D-9035 gasps and revives, continuing his ascent of the stairs rapidly and wordlessly. The heartbeat and cracking cease, and nothing abnormal is detected on the visual feed. He remains unresponsive. D-9035 exits SCP-087 and sits on the floor outside of the entrance.

D-9035 then enters a catatonic state from which he has not yet recovered.

DOCUMENT #087-III: EXPLORATION III

D-9884 is a 23-year old female of average build and appearance. Psychological background indicates a history of depression. Subject has a minimal record of using excessive force to [DATA EXPUNGED]. D-9884 is equipped with a 75 watt flood lamp with battery power capable of lasting 24 hours, a handheld camcorder fitted with a transmission stream, and an audio headset for communication with Dr. ████ at Control. D-9884 is also equipped with a backpack containing 3.75 litres of water, 15 nutrient bars, and 1 thermal blanket.

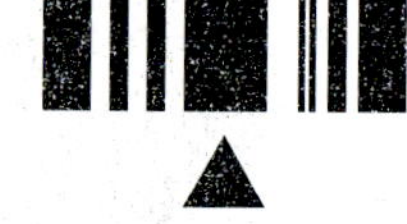

KS-2233-293335▬ 225

D-9884 stands on the ground level landing of SCP-087. The flood lamp illuminates only the first 9 steps. LED lights placed on the wall during the last exploration are not visible.

Dr. ████: Please descend the first flight and examine the landing wall.

D-9884 descends 13 steps and stops at the landing. There is no trace of the LED light at the location footage from Exploration II indicates it was placed.

D-9884: Yeah, um, it's just a dirty, concrete wall. There's like nothing on it. No, wait. It's a little bit sticky right here.

D-9884 indicates the spot on the wall the LED light should have been located.

D-9884: There's a child crying down there! She's *[pause]* she's begging for help and crying.

Dr. ████: Thank you. Please continue down the steps until you notice anything unusual.

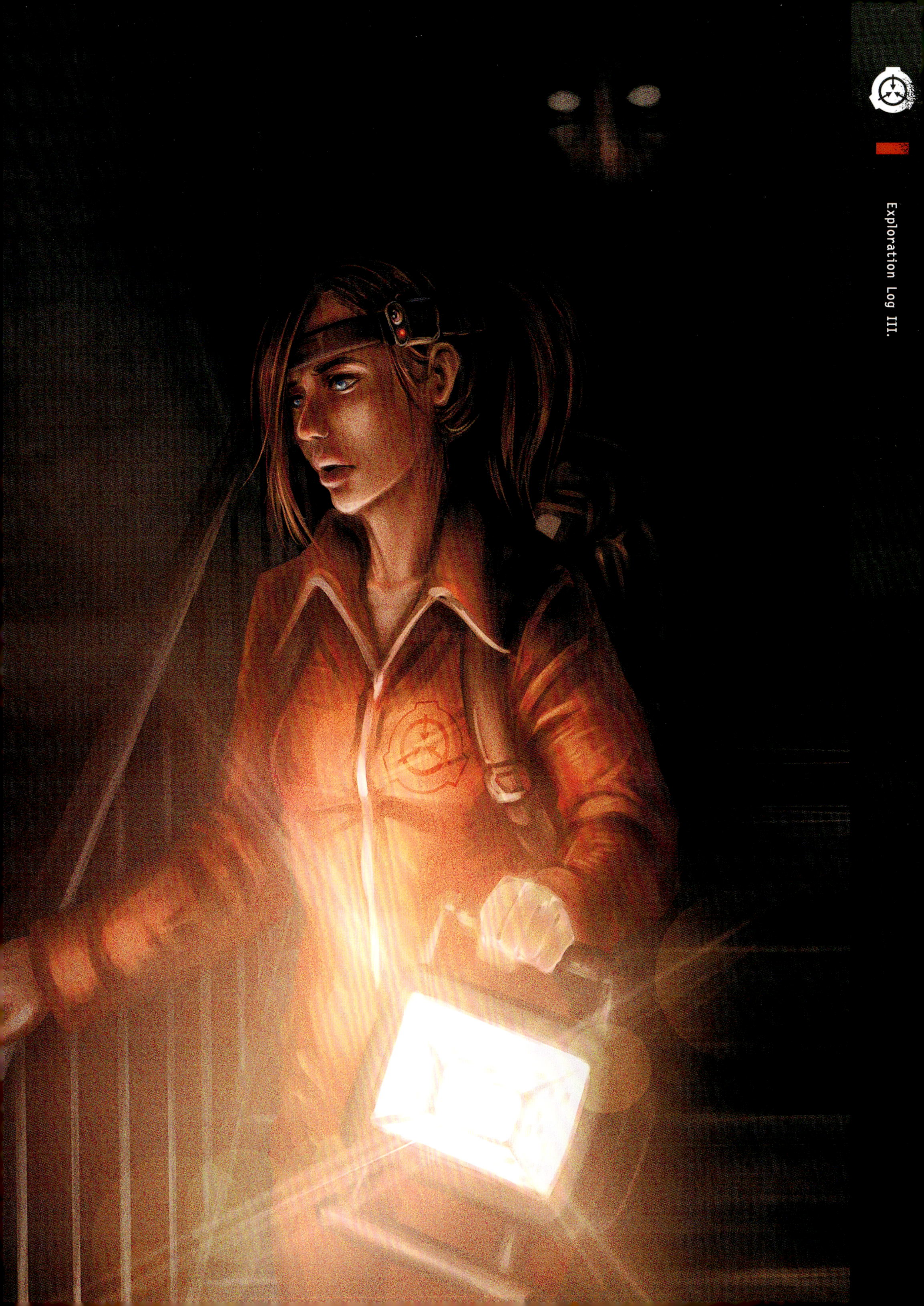

Research Library File ▸ 087

D-9884 descends. Upon reaching the next landing, audio of the crying child consistent with the prior two explorations is picked up. No LED lights appear to be present on any of the landing walls. D-9884 continues with no incident until she reaches the 17th landing.

D-9884: Eww, there's something on the ground here and it smells really bad. It's all sticky and stuck on my shoe. Ugh, it's so gross.

Video feed confirms presence of substance occupying a space approximately 50 centimeters in diameter.

Dr. █████: Can you describe the scent?

D-9884: Uh… It kinda smells like old rusty metal and pee.

Dr. █████: Thank you. Please continue until you notice anything else.

D-9884 continues to the 51st landing without incident. The 51st landing remains unchanged from the previous expedition, and similar observations are made. D-9884 is asked again to descend until anything unusual is noticed. Subject continues her descent until the 89th landing is reached. The video feed jerks and the subject yells.

D-9884: Ahh, fuck! There's a hole in the ground and I almost fell in.

Video feed confirms the presence of a hole approximately 1 meter in diameter. The subject shines the floodlight down, revealing only blackness. Approximately 4 seconds pass, and a light of an indeterminate distance down the hole flicks on for approximately 2 seconds and then back off.

D-9884: There was a light down there! It's gone now, but it was on for like a second! Did you see it?

Dr. █████: Yes. Can you estimate the depth of this hole?

D-9884: No way. It's too deep. At least a kilometer. Like, way more than a kilometer.

Dr. █████: Thank you. Can you still hear the sounds of the child?

D-9884: Uh huh. She still sounds far away. I don't feel like I'm getting any closer. It's like for every step I take, she takes one down.

Dr. █████: Please continue down until you encounter anything unusual.

D-9884 continues to descend SCP-087 for approximately an hour, covering an additional 164 flights. She stops to rest on the 253rd landing, consuming 1 nutrient bar and several gulps of water. D-9884 is at an estimated 1.1 kilometers below the initial landing, yet the sound of the child has not changed in volume. After pausing for 4 minutes, D-9884 resumes her descent, making no stops for another 216 flights, 1.5 hours later. D-9884 is on the 469th landing, an approximate 1.8 km below the ground level.

D-9884: I'm not getting anywhere. I think it's time I went back. I mean, going down is one thing, but this is a long climb back.

Dr. █████: You have been provided with food, water, and blankets to last you 24 hours. Please continue down.

D-9884: No, I think I'm gonna go back up.

D-9884 turns toward the previous flight of stairs.

D-9884: I - *[screams]*

SCP-087-1, the face, is directly behind D-9884, blocking her ascent. The face appears approximately 30 centimeters from the lens of the camera; its eyes are fixed directly on the lens, this time looking not at the subject but the person viewing the video feed. The video feed glitches and freezes for 4 seconds, accompanied by a static-like screeching noise from the audio feed. It then cuts to bumpy visuals of D-9884 descending the stairs rapidly.

D-9884: *[panicked and hysterical]* It's been following me! This whole time it's been right behind me oh God it's right behind me it was looking right at me! Dr. ███ please do something please help me oh God no please get it away please no please I knew it was following me help make it leave please no it was looking at me it was staring at me it knew I was here it's been watching me this whole time oh God please help me no please *[this continues in a similar fashion until the end.]*

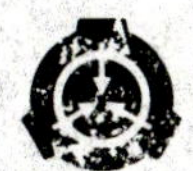

D-9884 continues to scream and plead hysterically as she rapidly descends the staircase. The previously heard static-like screeching seems to overlay the audio feed, beneath which can still be heard the original sound of the crying child. Approximately 14 flights down, the video feed swings to show the area directly behind D-9884. The face is now approximately 20 centimeters from the camera lens. It is not staring at the subject; rather it is fixated on the camera lens, giving the illusion it is making eye contact with those viewing the footage. It is important to note that since the sighting of SCP-087-1, the sound of the girl crying and pleading has been increasing in volume, indicating D-9884 is nearing the source. After an approximate 150 panicked flights of descent with 3 visual confirmations of SCP-087-1 still in pursuit, D-9884 trips and appears to fall unconscious. Audio feed indicates strong proximity to the source of the crying. The static and screeching noise continue. Video feed shows yet another descending flight of stairs, indicating D-9884 still has not reached the base of the stairwell. 12 seconds of motionlessness pass before the face comes in full view of the camera, eye contact being made directly with the viewer.

Audio and video feeds cut out, and no connection is reestablished.

DOCUMENT #087-IV: EXPLORATION IV

[DATA EXPUNGED]

END OF REPORT

File >>> 0129933

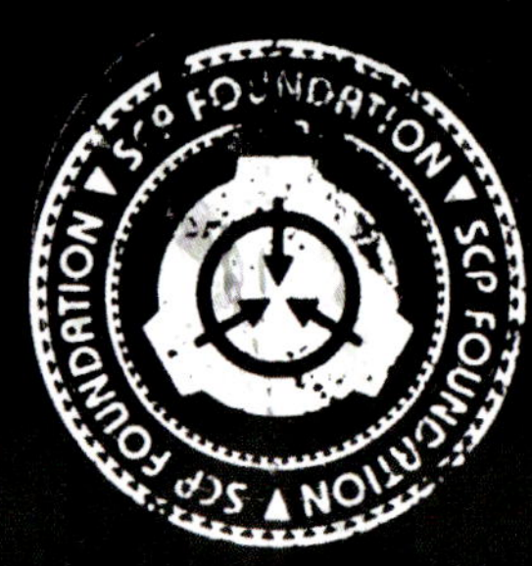

SCP-135

Title

UNIVERSAL CARCINOGEN

Report by

Dr. Trebuchet

Picture by

Vladislav Orlowski

Access the original report on

scp-wiki.wikidot.com/scp-135

Date

Class

EUCLID

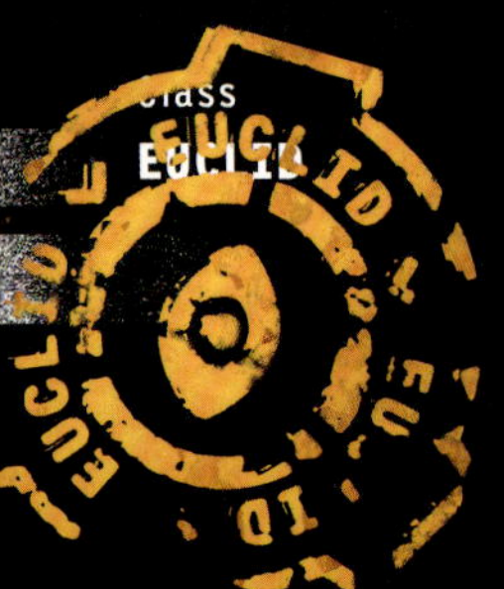

SPECIAL CONTAINMENT PROCEDURES

SCP-135 is to be contained in a partitioned plexiglass chamber at least 7 metres to a side. All sections are to be completely sealed off from one another to avoid cross-contamination. SCP-135 itself is to be in a central section with 1.0 to 1.5 square metres of floorspace, with a 5 cm-wide runoff trench around the perimeter that drains into a tank, the contents of which are to be piped into an incinerator at the end of every week. The remaining space in the containment chamber is to be used to house 5 chemical harvesting vats, one vat per partitioned section. A single access corridor is to lead from SCP-135's section to outside the chamber. No personnel are permitted within SCP-135's effect radius; all maintenance, taking of samples, etc., are to be carried out by remote-control robots. Disciplinary measures need not be taken against personnel that violate this rule, because the direct consequences of SCP-135's effects have been deemed consequence enough. Robots are to be maintained and cleaned by Level 1 personnel.

Once a week, SCP-135's section is to be hosed down with Solution U82-B until only its outer coating is visible. In emergencies, flamethrowers may be employed to reduce mass quickly.

Due to the potential of catastrophic effects in the event of cross contamination, at no point are SCP-329 or SCP-427 to be contained within the same facility as SCP-135.

DESCRIPTION

SCP-135 is a human female between █ and █ years of age that promotes rapid, uncontrolled cell growth within a radius of 2.25 metres from itself. It remains rigidly in the foetal position, and has never been observed to move. SCP-135's effect is carcinogenic to animal tissue and induces malignant neoplasia in plant and fungal tissues in 100% of recorded exposure cases, with severity and disorganization increasing exponentially with closer proximity to SCP-135. Within 0.1 metres, cells will not die, even under conditions where they would normally, causing SCP-135 to be steadily buried under a continually-growing mass of plant matter, fungal matter, and micro-organisms. This "undying" state extends to SCP-135's cells as well. SCP-135 has been shown to lack an epidermis, instead having a crust of mixed plant and fungal matter that has incorporated itself onto SCP-135's skin, interspersed with tumours and patches of raw dermis.

SCP-135's lungs, diaphragm, and intestines are ruptured, and growth extends into the chest and abdominal cavities. It has been fitted with wide-diameter plastic tubes for use in draining excess biomatter.

The Foundation came into possession of SCP-135 after it and a surrounding ball of growth rolled off a cliff in the █████ Mountains, crushing a hiker on the trail below. Class B amnestics were administered to the civilians and law enforcement personnel involved, and the incident was covered up as having been caused by a pair of male goats that slipped and fell off the cliff edge during a dominance battle. Later examination of the growth revealed the partial skeleton of an adult human female with osteosarcomata covering ██% of it. SCP-135 was found in the space between the skeleton's ribcage and pelvis, at the time between █ and █ years old. A viable DNA sample was recovered from the bone marrow of the pelvis, and testing confirmed with ██.█% certainty that the skeleton belonged to SCP-135's biological mother.

All personnel involved with SCP-135's retrieval and initial testing were later diagnosed with various forms of cancer. Out of the ██ affected, only █ are still alive at the time of this writing.

Attempts to terminate SCP-135 with sustained gunfire, flamethrowers, caustic materials, vacuum, and extreme pressure have all failed. Further termination attempts are forbidden by order of O5-██, due to SCP-135's potential uses in cultivating useful bacteria. See Document 135-a for information on the current contents of partitioned vats.

EEGs confirm full brain activity. No attempts to communicate with SCP-135 are to be made at this time.

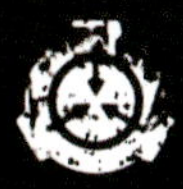

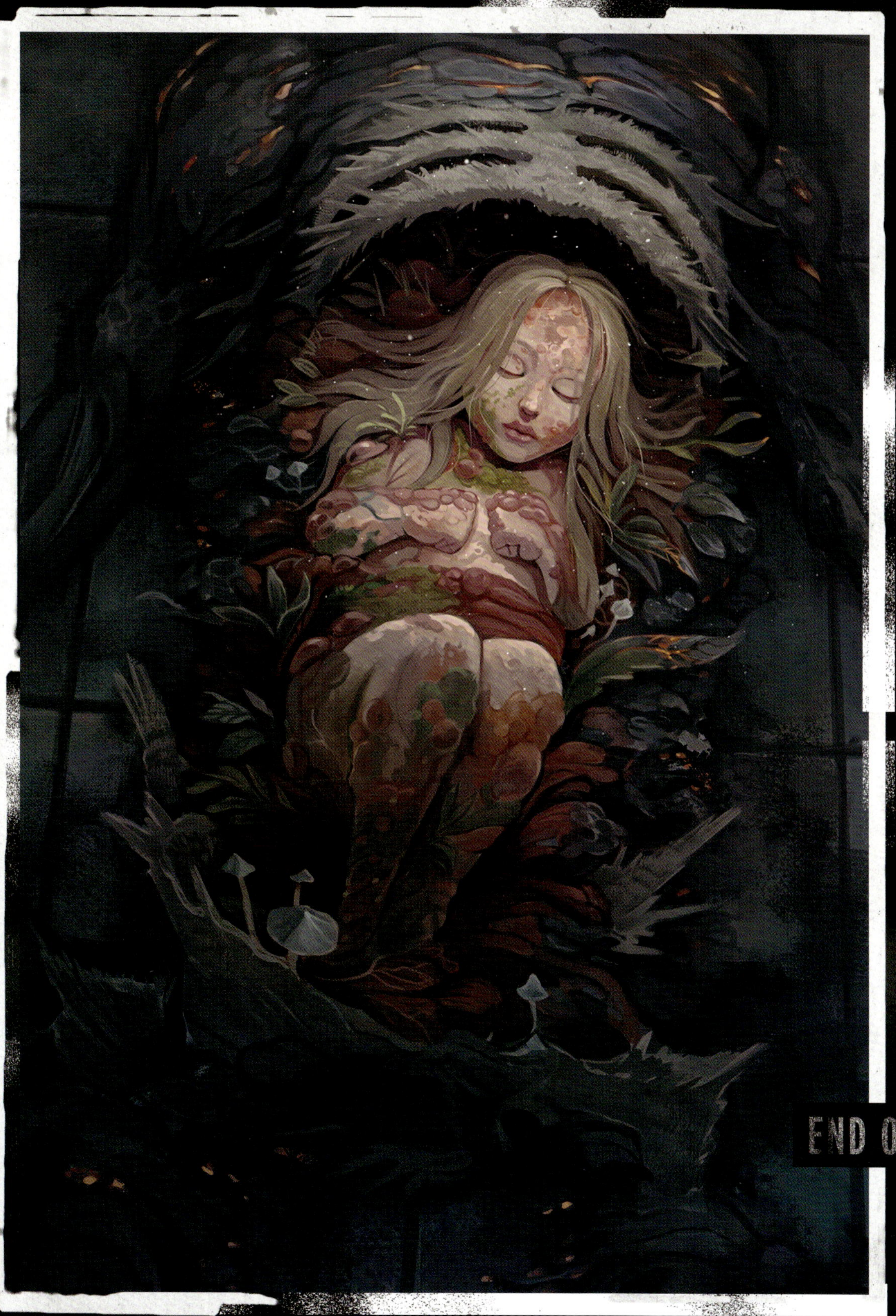

END OF REPORT

File >>> 0028221

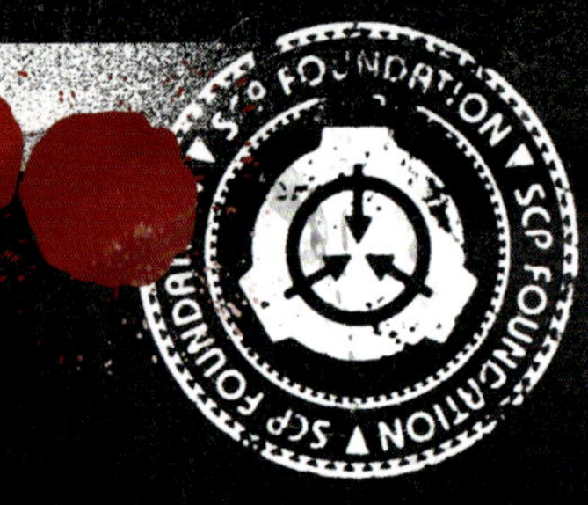

SCP-143

Title

THE BLADEWOOD GROVE

Report by

Kain Pathos Crow

Picture by

Alex Andreev

Access the original report on

scp-wiki.wikidot.com/scp-143

Date

Class

EUCLID

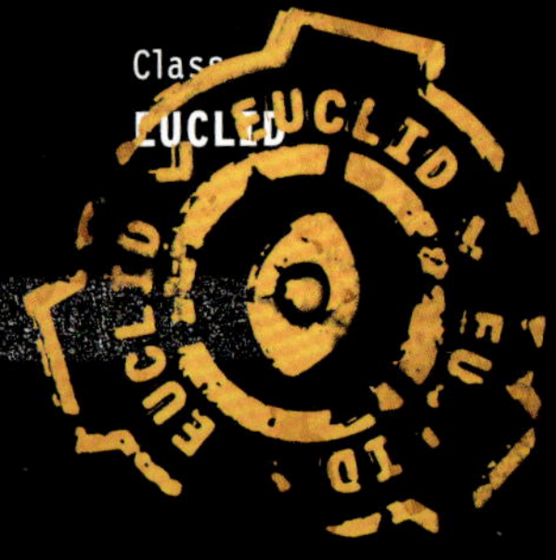

SPECIAL CONTAINMENT PROCEDURES

SCP-143 is to be contained in the valley adjacent to Bio-Research Area-12, an area over 2 km². Area surrounding SCP-143 for up to 20 km, and all lines of sight from the surrounding hilltops, are to be denied public access. SCP-143 is to be watered twice every day on a regular basis via a large sprinkler system, unless already watered by local precipitation. Personnel are not allowed to enter the enclosure without Level 4 administrative clearance, and are advised not to touch any of SCP-143, nor stand beneath them unless wearing proper protective gear. It is important that no one be within the containment area when SCP-143 begins to shed, however after the shedding has concluded, the collection of the fallen petals for testing purposes has been authorized by the project director (see ████████ Log).

DESCRIPTION

SCP-143 is a plantation of 300 specimens of a unique type of tree. The trees are similar in appearance to *Prunus x yedoensis* (Japanese Sakura), or cherry blossoms. They bear no fruit, and the only known way of reproduction is by careful "own root" propagation using cut saplings from an older sample.

The petals are a light pinkish color, slightly translucent, and with a texture of smooth glass. Care must be taken when handling the petals, as their edges are razor sharp, and can easily slice through flesh if mishandled.

The wood and bark are a light grayish color, with a texture expected of wood, although the grain is very smooth to the touch.

However, the petals and wood of these trees are much harder than most natural or man-made substances, reaching up to 5,000 HB on the Brinell scale, and withstanding temperatures of up to 1800°C. The weight-to-strength ratio surpasses even that of titanium, being some fifteen percent (15%) lighter than aluminum. Despite this hardness, the wood and petals are quite supple and are as pliable as most woods are.

Both are notoriously difficult to work due to their properties, but under high temperatures, upwards of 1500°C, separate pieces are capable of being fused together. They make excellent armor, shielding, and weapons. Due to the slow growth of the plants, the material is slow to harvest, although the petals are shed regularly enough, falling from the trees twice every year.

We lost three staff to 143 today. They were collecting petals dropped by the trees the previous day, when a sudden gust picked up, shaking a good deal of the petals from the trees and blowing them around.

Stayed that windy for the whole day. I'd send a cleanup crew, but it's still pretty windy and the odd petal is still falling. We'll have to pick up the remains when the wind dies down in a couple days.

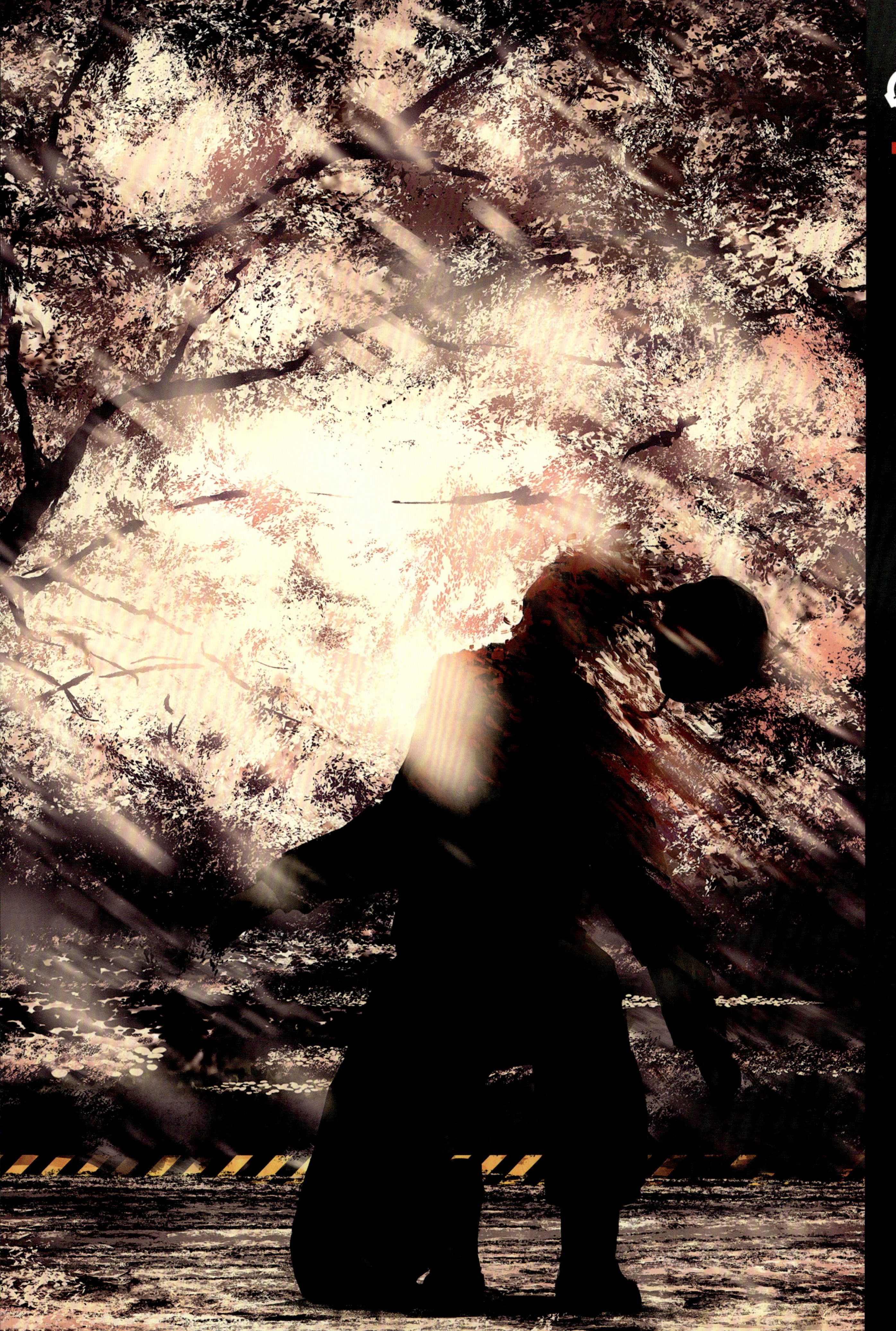

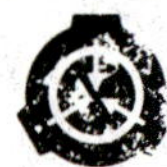

ADDENDUM 143-1

The trees were grown on-site from saplings obtained from parent plants located in Nara Prefecture, Japan, in 1905. The parent trees were owned by a family of traditionalist swordsmiths, claiming to be descended from a legendary sword maker named Amakuni. They referred to the original trees as "jinki no kodachi" (刃木の木立), or the "Bladewood Grove." It is from them that the Foundation gained the techniques to cut and work the wood and petals into serviceable items.

The original trees are still in Japan, owned by the government, and still tended to by the same family. However, the government has denied all existence of the trees, and any products made from them are kept within the country.

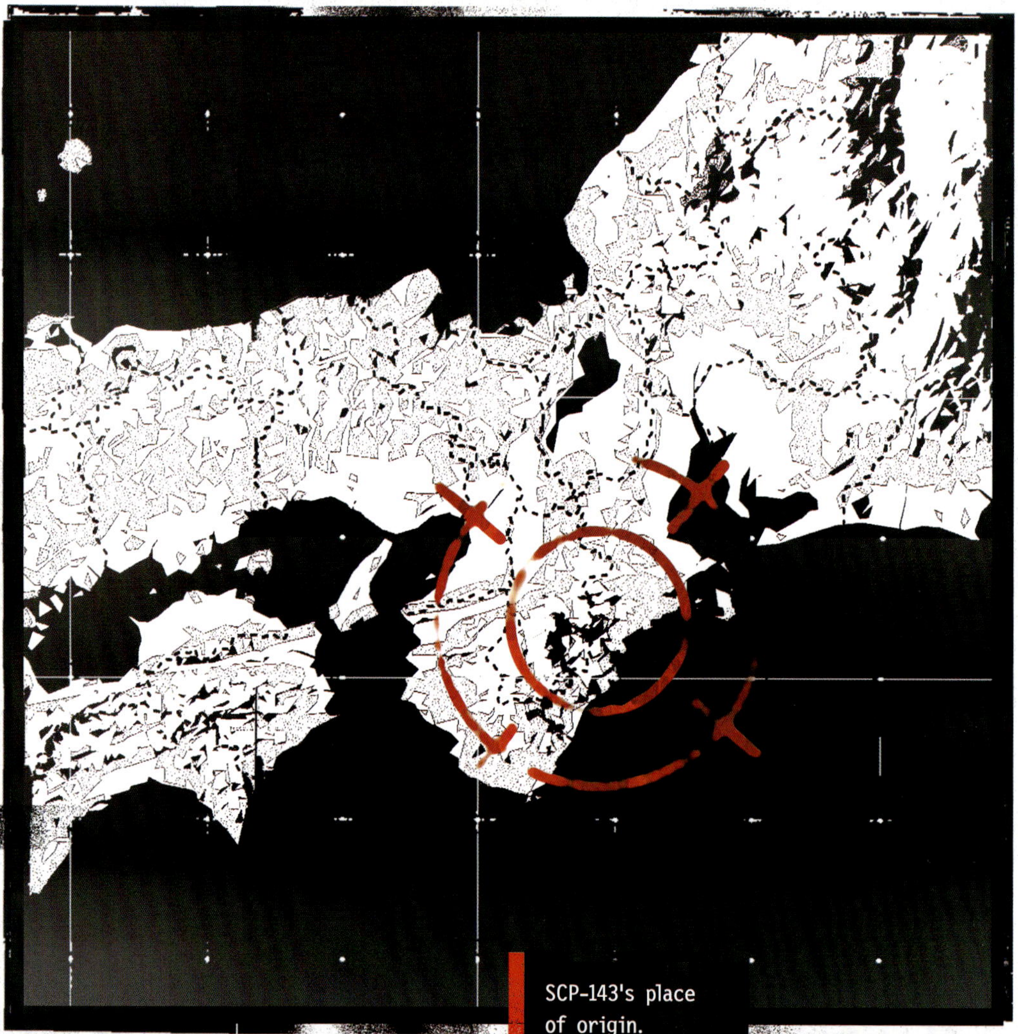

SCP-143's place of origin.

END OF REPORT

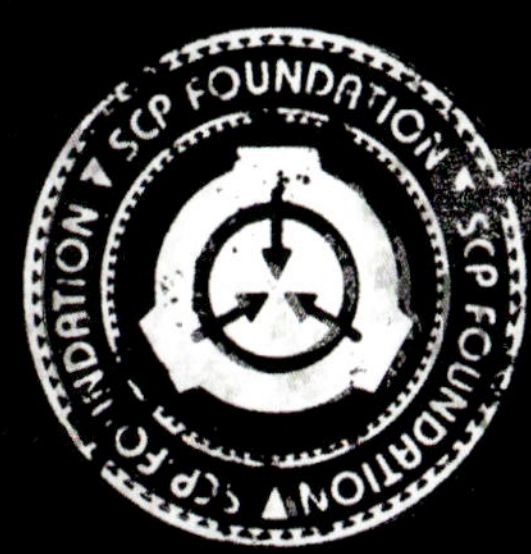

SCP-035

Title

POSSESSIVE MASK

Report by
Kain Pathos Crow

Picture by
Dmitriy Fomin

Access the original report on
scp-wiki.wikidot.com/scp-035

Date
█████

Class
KETER

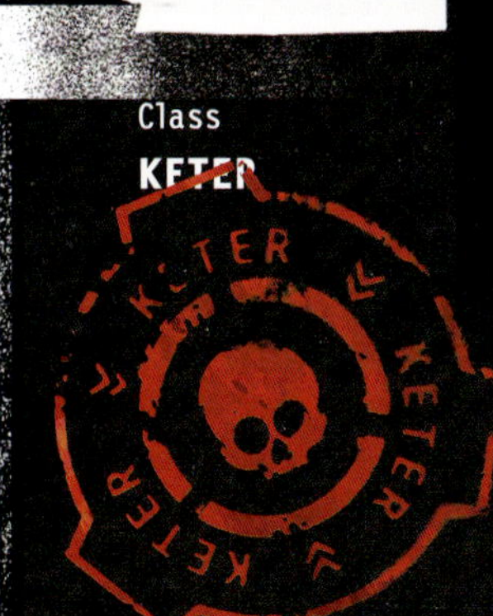

SPECIAL CONTAINMENT PROCEDURES

SCP-035 is to be kept within a hermetically sealed glass case, no fewer than 10 centimeters (4 inches) thick. This case is to be contained within a steel, iron and lead-shielded room at all times. Doors are to be triple-locked at all times, with the exception of allowing personnel in or out. No fewer than two (2) armed guards are to be posted at any time. Guards must remain outside at all times and are not allowed within the containment room under any circumstances. A trained psychologist is to remain on site at all times. Research personnel are not to touch SCP-035 at any time. SCP-035 must be moved to a new sealed case every two (2) weeks. The previous case must be disposed of via SCP-101, as it shows no adverse reactions to SCP-035's "corruption". Anyone who comes into contact with SCP-035 when it is in possession of a host is to be given an immediate psychological evaluation.

DESCRIPTION

SCP-035 appears to be a white porcelain comedy mask, although, at times, it will change to tragedy. In these events, all existing visual records, such as photographs, video footage, even illustrations, of SCP-035 automatically change to reflect its new appearance.

A highly corrosive and degenerative viscous liquid constantly seeps from the eye and mouth holes of SCP-035. Anything coming into contact with this substance slowly decays over a period of time, depending on the material, until it has decayed completely into a pool of the original contaminant. Glass seems to react the slowest to the effects of the item, hence the construction choice of its immediate container. Living organisms that come into contact with the substance react much the same way, with no chance of recovery. Origin of the liquid is unknown. Liquid is only visible from the front, and does not emerge or is even visible from the other side.

Subjects within 1.5 to 2 meters (5-6 feet) of SCP-035, or in visual contact with it, experience a strong urge to put it on. When SCP-035 is placed on the face of an individual, an alternate brain wave pattern from SCP-035 overlaps that of the original host, effectively snuffing it out and causing brain death to the subject. Subject then claims to be the consciousness contained within SCP-035. The bodies of "possessed" subjects decay at a highly accelerated rate, eventually becoming little more than mummified corpses. Nevertheless, SCP-035 has demonstrated the ability to remain in cognitive control of a body experiencing severe structural damage, even if the subject's body literally decays to the point where motion is not mechanically possible. No effect is found to be had when placed on the face of an animal.

Conversations with SCP-035 have proven to be informative. Researchers have learned various details about other SCP objects and history in general, as SCP-035 claims to have been at many momentous events. SCP-035 displays a highly intelligent and charismatic personality, being both amiable and flattering to all those who speak with it. SCP-035 has scored in the 99th percentile on all intelligence

Research Library File ▸ 035

and aptitude tests administered to it, and appears to have a photographic memory.

However, psychological analysis has discovered SCP-035 to possess a highly manipulative nature, capable of forcing sudden and profound changes to interviewer's psychological state. SCP-035 has proven to be highly sadistic, prompting some to commit suicide and transforming others into near-mindless servants with linguistic persuasion alone. SCP-035 has stated that it has intimate knowledge of the workings of the human mind and implied that it could change anyone's views if given enough time.

ADDITIONAL

SCP-035 was found in a sealed crypt in an abandoned house in Venice, in 18█.

Addendum 035-01: SCP-035 has been found to be able to possess anything that has a humanoid shape, including mannequins, corpses, and statues. SCP-035 has been able to motivate all into movement, removing the need to expose live subjects to SCP-035. Still, anything it possesses inevitably decays into motionlessness.

Addendum 035-02: SCP-035 has facilitated an escape attempt, convincing several of the research staff to aid it in its bid for freedom. Insurrection failed. All staff that have been in contact with SCP-035 have been terminated, and mandatory psychiatric evaluations have been implemented for all personnel coming in contact with SCP-035.

Addendum 035-03: It has been determined that SCP-035 is capable of telepathy, whether or not it possesses a host, even penetrating to the subconscious of others, and using the knowledge it finds to its advantage. Extreme caution is advised when choosing subjects to converse with SCP-035.

Addendum 035-04: SCP-035 has expressed an interest in other SCPs, most notably SCP-4715 and SCP-682. Dr.█████ has expressed worry that should SCP-035 bond with either, their regenerative qualities would negate its corruption and give it a permanent host.

Addendum 035-05: After several more escape attempts, and after reviewing SCP-035's incident record, high command has ordered that it be permanently sealed within the facility and prohibited from being allowed any more hosts. Several personnel have protested against this, with some even erupting into violence. As a direct result, all personnel that have come into contact with SCP-035 have been terminated. Going forward, all personnel that deal with SCP-035 are to be rotated frequently, and contact is to be limited even to its dormant state to as little as possible.

Addendum 035-06: Personnel within 10 meters of SCP-035 have recently reported feeling unease, stating that they can hear unintelligible whispering. Several others have suffered from severe migraines. Object has been monitored, but there is no change in its dormant behavior, and no sounds have been recorded.

The motion to reinstate SCP-035's host privileges has been brought up once more, if only on a temporary basis to discover these new changes in the object's behavior. (Denied)

Addendum 035-07: The walls of SCP-035's containment cell have suddenly begun secreting a black substance. Tests on the substance have revealed it to be human blood, although highly contaminated with several foreign and unknown agents. Substance is corrosive, having a pH of 4.5, and prolonged exposure to the walls has proven to be detrimental to their structural integrity.

More notably, it seems to be forming patterns on the walls. Several segments seem to be paragraphs in various languages, including Italian, Latin, Greek, and Sanskrit. Translation is pending. Other segments appear to be diagrams depicting ritualistic sacrifice and mutilation, often for the arcane benefit of the person committing them. Several staff members have been shocked to note that all of the sacrifices bear an uncanny resemblance

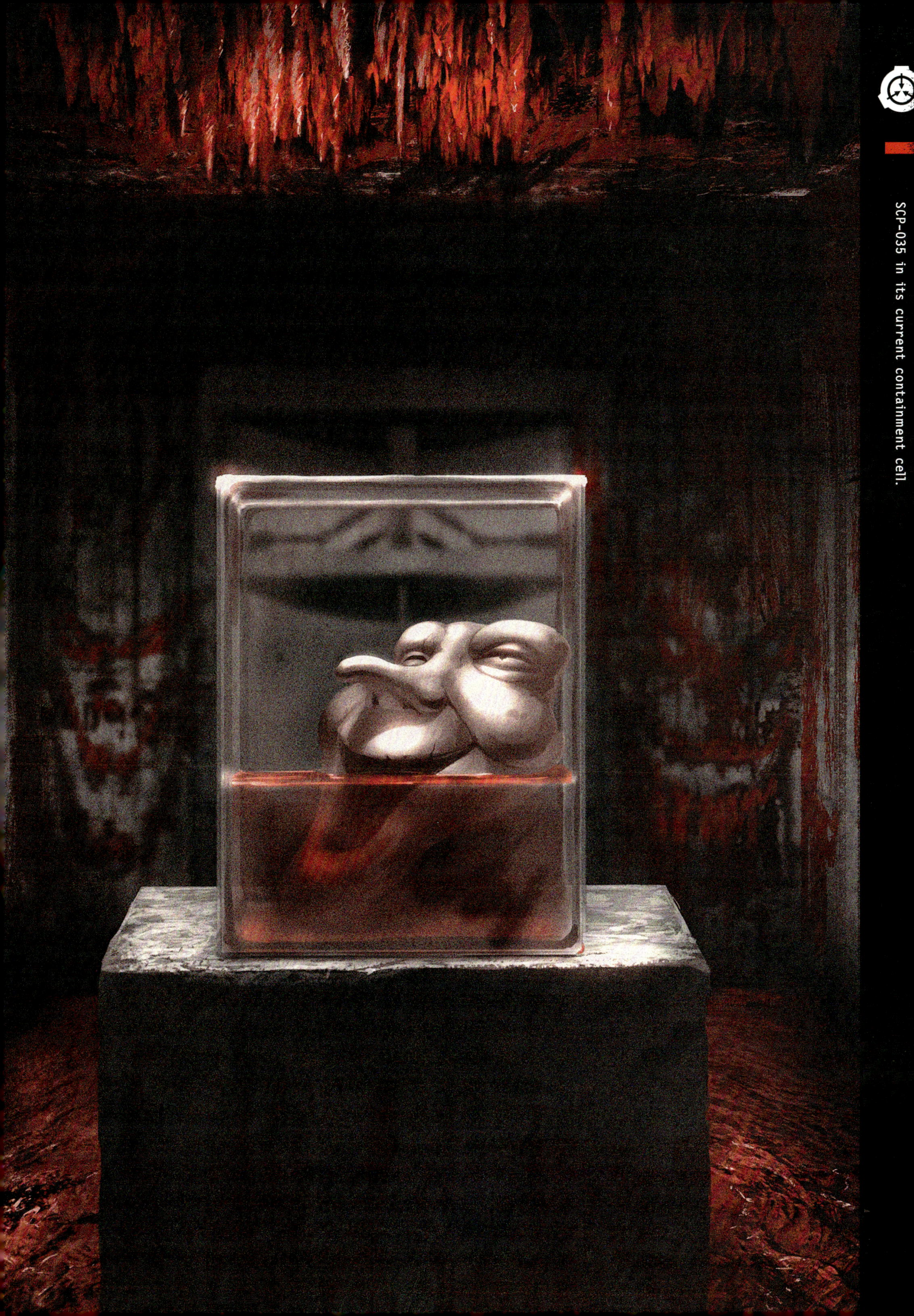

SCP-035 in its current containment cell.

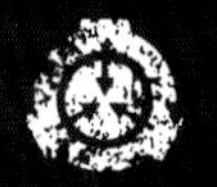

Research Library File ▸ 035

to various personnel and their loved ones, often in conflicting positions.

Researchers while in the room examining these newly formed patterns have complained of hearing loud whispering, and high pitched, unnerving laughter at irregular intervals.

Personnel in the section working daily near and around SCP-035's containment unit have suffered catastrophic morale damage, with an all time high in suicide rates in staff in that area, whether or not they have ever had contact with SCP-035.

The only change in SCP-035's dormant behavior is regarding its contained glass case. Degradation of the case has increased to a high degree, enough so that the glass will occasionally shatter, causing a wide dispersal of SCP-035's contaminant. This occurs quite often at the most inopportune times, so far resulting in six (6) casualties and three (3) fatalities of both research and cleanup staff.

Addendum 035-08: In light of the mass suicide/homicide of the members of the research team tasked with translating the passages garnered from SCP-035's containment cell, the morale damage in the area, and general loss of staff dealing with SCP-035 to either death or insanity, it has been decided to coat the inner and outer walls of its containment cell with SCP-148, which has proved well in the containment of SCP-132 (see Document 132-01), in order to hopefully block out the high levels of negativity being emitted by SCP-035.

Addendum 035-09: The use of SCP-148 has worked well, causing morale and suicide rates to return to near pre-SCP-035 rates.

However, the material appears to facilitate the negativity within the cell, causing a veritable "Greenhouse Effect" inside. Personnel inside the cell have stated that they feel a heavy sense of dread, fear, anger, and general depression, as well as hearing constant, nearly inaudible whispering upon immediate entry. A prolonged stay causes severe migraines, suicidal tendencies, heavy hemorrhaging of blood vessels around the eyes and inside the mouth and nose, general hostility to others, and for the whispering to increase to almost deafening volumes, intersected by a constant mocking laughter. Exposure of more than three (3) hours inevitably results in the subject falling into a deep psychosis, and attempting to harm either themselves or others. Most spoke in Latin or Greek, despite the fact that several did not previously know how to speak said languages beforehand.

The presence of blood in both word and diagram formations has increased disproportionately, the walls becoming cluttered, and the formations beginning to overlap each other. The substance has proven to be both difficult to clean, and even more corrosive than was originally recorded, with a pH of roughly 2.4. General estimation gives the current walls a life of two (2) months before they will need replacement.

It is becoming gradually more and more difficult to contain SCP-035, and the debate to reinstate its host privileges has once again come up. (Denied)

Addendum 035-10: The walls, ceiling and floor of SCP-035's containment cell have now been completely saturated in blood. All personnel entering and guarding the area must wear full Hazmat protection suits. Constant cleaning efforts are being instated.

Addendum 035-11: The magnitude, intensity, and recurrence of the phenomena that occur within SCP-035's containment cell have increased to an alarming degree. The cell door has been known to become locked of its own accord while personnel are inside, and unable to be opened for a period of time. Appendages form out of the larger puddles of blood and often attempt to grab or harm personnel near them. Blurry apparitions have started appearing to staff. Electronic devices no longer work inside the cell, and the light cannot be turned on, though there is no physical reason why it does not work, forcing those entering to use non-electric based light sources.

Cleaning measures are having no discernible effect on the cell, and the walls are degrading at a very high rate, forcing them to be replaced within a week at best, although the blood makes it nearly impossible to properly achieve this.

SCP-035 may have to be moved to a new cell entirely, with the old one sealed off and disengaged from the rest of the facility.

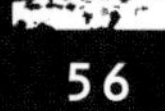

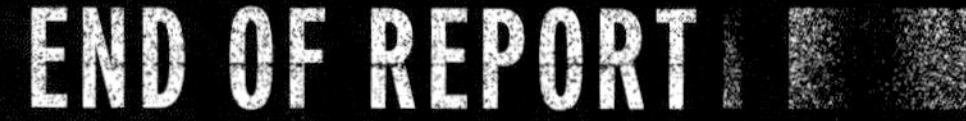

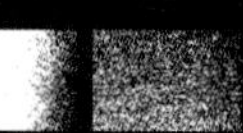

File >>> 29330001

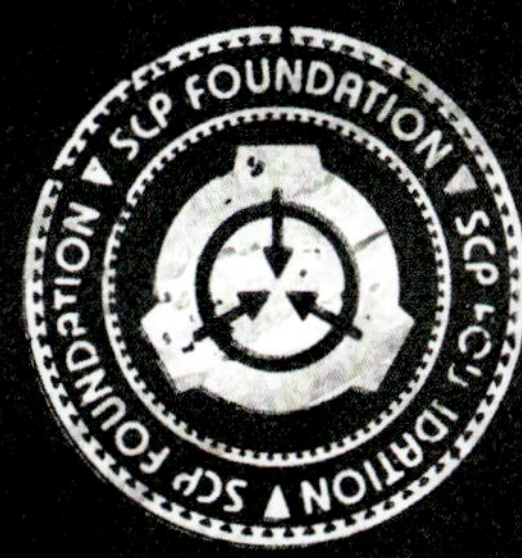

SCP-2030

Title

LA U GH IS F UN

Report by

PeppersGhost

Pictures by

Genocide Error

Access the original report on

scp-wiki.wikidot.com/scp-2030

Date

Class

KETER

SPECIAL CONTAINMENT PROCEDURES

Foundation-operated web analysis bot Delta-09 ("LAUGHSTOP") is to be kept in constant operation and checked for defects twice a week by a Level-2 staff member familiar with its operation. When functional, the bot will search a wide range of file sharing and video streaming websites for SCP-2030 and remove any manifestations discovered.

Finding and isolating SCP-2030's point of origin is considered a Delta-Level priority. Efforts to locate the studio where SCP-2030 is filmed are ongoing.

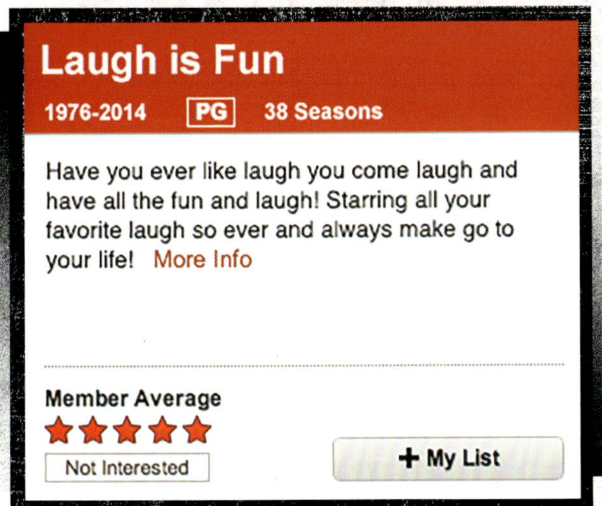

SCP-2030 manifesting on a popular on-demand video streaming site.

DESCRIPTION

SCP-2030 is an anomalous phenomenon that manifests as a television series. The medium through which SCP-2030 manifests changes depending on the most popular format currently in use; as of 2014, SCP-2030 most commonly inserts itself into automated DVD rental kiosks, file sharing websites, and paid on-demand video streaming services. Prior to 2012, SCP-2030 commonly manifested as a DVD set in video rental stores, and as VHS tapes prior to 2003. Thus far, no reliable evidence that SCP-2030 manifestations took place prior to the year 1993 has been discovered; however, thirty-eight (38) seasons of programming are known to exist, implying that SCP-2030 has been active to some degree since 1976.

The series' title typically appears as Laugh is Fun, although variations on this name, such as Laugh is Life or Laugh is Laugh, are not uncommon. The series has no corresponding "box art"; it mimics art from other television series, often causing viewers to select it mistaking it for another program.

The show is a hidden camera comedy series, showcasing the candid responses of various people to bizarre, disturbing, and often anomalous situations. Episodes usually run between 10 and 12 minutes, and feature introductory and closing segments that bookend the hidden camera footage. No episode to date has had an end credit roll.

SCP-2030-1 is a (presumably) human adult male that serves as the show's host, providing introductory and closing commentary as well as appearing to "victims" to

reveal that they are being filmed for a television series. SCP-2030-1 is invariably shown wearing a royal blue three-piece suit with black and white wing tipped shoes. Due to the way in which scenes are filmed, SCP-2030-1 is only seen from the neck down, making identification difficult. It refers to itself as "Laughy McLaugherson".

Individuals appearing on the show often react to the events that they witness with panic or distress, but appear immediately calmed upon the appearance of SCP-2030-1. This is true even when the individual in question has sustained significant bodily harm or witnessed a particularly traumatic event. Additionally, most recorded individuals seem to express some degree of familiarity with SCP-2030-1, with some claiming to be fans of the show. Research into whether SCP-2030 uses its viewership as its victim selection pool is ongoing.

Episodes follow a particular theme that each prank segment alludes to. SCP-2030-1 introduces these themes at the beginning of each episode in an as-of-yet unidentified film studio whilst standing atop a bright yellow stage decorated with oversized geometric shapes of various colors. Episode themes vary from the mundane, such as 'the beach', 'pets', and 'candy', to the strange and violent, such as 'mail fraud', 'arson', and 'terrorism'. SCP-2030-1 delivers a similar speech at the end of each program to close out the show.

At the end of each episode, the camera pulls back and around from SCP-2030-1's stage to show the studio audience, which usually comprises the individuals featured in the episode. During this time, the words 'Filmed in front of a studio audience. Created in partnership with YWTGTHFT' are superimposed over the footage in white text. Research into the identities of the people featured in the show's prank segments has revealed that they are all persons who were officially documented as having died or gone missing in the year they appeared on the program.

Thorough investigations into the deaths of SCP-2030 participants have revealed a number of inconsistencies and contradictions in matters concerning the circumstances of the deaths. Additionally, exhumations of the individuals' remains have revealed that all recorded participants' bodies are currently missing. The general consensus among researchers assigned to SCP-2030 is that victims are likely abducted after their use in the show, with their disappearances covered up when possible. However, no concrete evidence connecting the individuals' deaths with SCP-2030 besides the show's footage has yet been found.

ADDENDUM

The following are examples of pranks featured on the program.

Season: 24 (2000)

Episode theme: Swelling

Individuals involved: Macey Gersham and Kyle Parker – killed by a hit-and-run driver on 09/18/00.

Scene description: An elderly woman sits on a park bench, feeding nearby pigeons with seed from a bag. Gersham and Parker, a couple, walk down a park path and approach the woman. Once the two come within approximately 1.5 meters of the elderly woman, a swarm of pigeons fly into the elderly woman's mouth, causing her stomach to become severely engorged and quickly rupture. The couple express great distress at the event until SCP-2030-1 emerges from the elderly woman's open stomach cavity, at which point Gersham and Parker appear relieved.

Season: 21 (1997)

Episode theme: Margaret Thatcher

Individuals involved: Doris Carter – died of ovarian cancer 02/24/97.

Scene description: Mrs. Carter walks into her kitchen and opens a cabinet door, out of which falls a large mass of flesh. As Carter screams, the mass grows and shapes itself into a severely disproportional

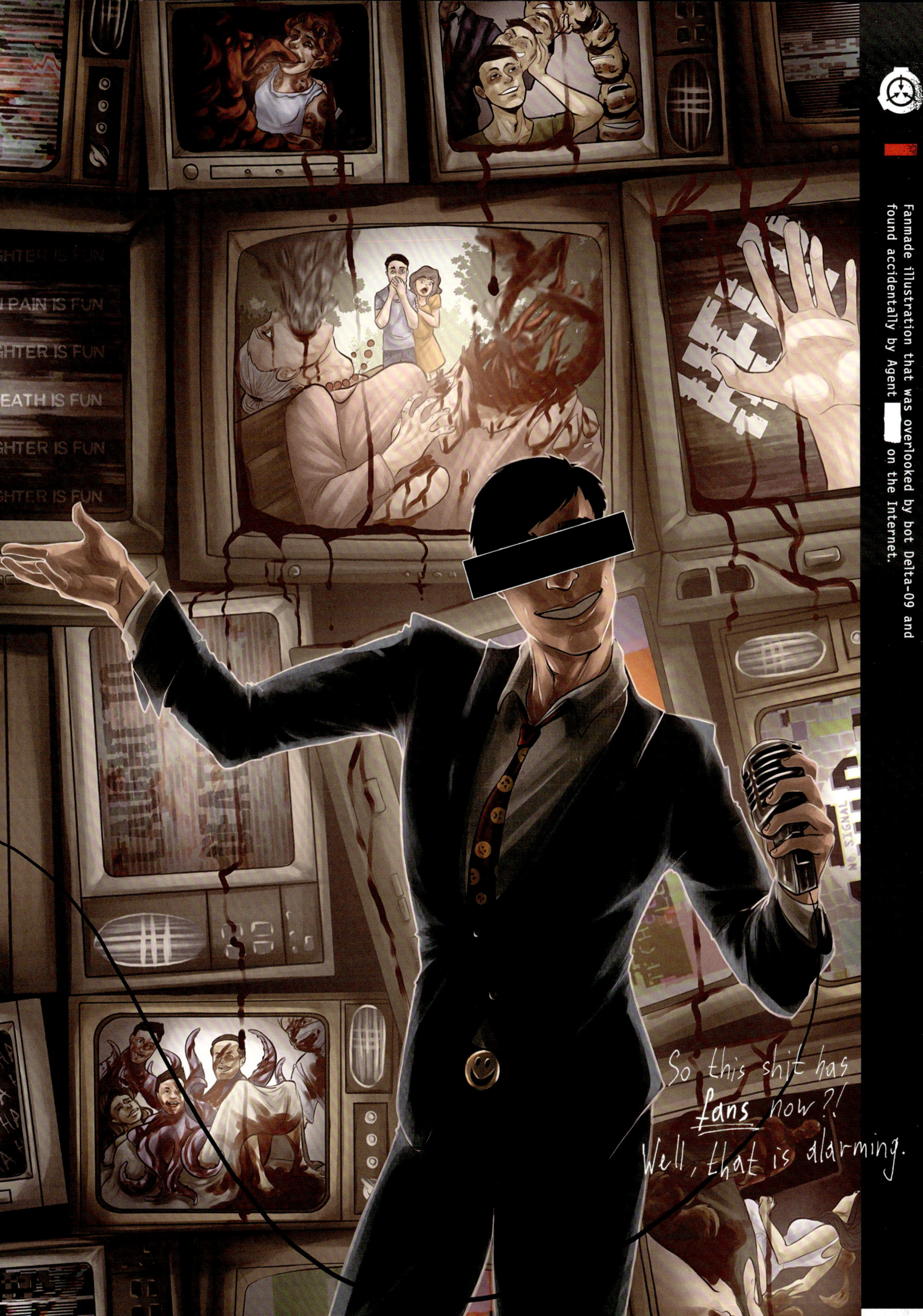
Fanmade illustration that was overlooked by bot Delta-09 and found accidentally by Agent ██ on the Internet.
So this shit has fans now?!
Well, that is alarming.

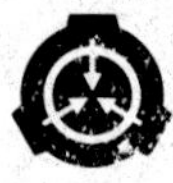

facsimile of former Prime Minister of the United Kingdom Margaret Thatcher, with its head twice as large as its torso. Carter rushes to leave the room, but the Thatcher creature leaps onto her before she can escape. It extends its tongue into the woman's open mouth, and Thatcher faces of various sizes begin appearing across Carter's skin. The faces proceed to recite Thatcher's April 1986 speech on the bombing of Libya in perfect unison. SCP-2030-1 climbs out of a nearby cupboard and points to the hidden cameras; Mrs. Carter smiles, the creature's tongue still extended down her throat.

Season: 13 (1989)

Episode theme: Squirrels

Individuals involved: Melissa and Travis Englund – disappeared, last seen 05/12/89.

Scene description: Mrs. Englund lies in bed next to a male figure, presumably Mr. Englund. A series of high-pitched squeaking noises are heard, and Mrs. Englund is awakened. She tells her husband to wake up, but he does not respond. She places her hand on his shoulder, but quickly draws it back with a shriek. His skin begins to undulate, as though something is moving underneath. A multitude of squirrels then burst from various places on his body, quickly filling the bed and crawling onto the woman. She rises to leave the room, but SCP-2030-1 walks in and turns on the light. He is accompanied by Mr. Englund, who has been skinned from head to foot but gives no indication of feeling any discomfort. All three share a laugh and the segment ends.

Season: 13 (1989)

Episode theme: Tracheotomies

Individuals involved: Gary Turman, Lindsay Turman, and their children – died in a vehicular accident on 04/28/89.

Scene description: The four sit around a dinner table eating a meal. Mr. Turman begins coughing and gasping for air, as if choking. As the others at the table begin to panic, a pair of slits appear on Turman's throat, allowing him to breathe. These slits quickly become nostrils, which rapidly grow into a full nose, which in turn becomes an entire second head, identical to Turman's original. This second head then sprouts a neck of its own, and the entire process repeats. This continues until eighteen necks and heads have sprouted from the original, at which point SCP-2030-1 steps out from underneath the table. Everyone present erupts into raucous laughter, including all nineteen of Mr. Turman's heads.

Season: 37 (2013)

Episode theme: Cephalopods

Individuals involved: Rebecca Nash (surgeons unidentified) – died of complications in child delivery on 11/02/13; hospital records show no evidence of anomalous activity during birth.

Scene description: A team of obstetricians perform a caesarian section procedure on Ms. Nash, who is in labor. The team comment on the size of the child's cranium and the amount of hair present on it. Several minutes into the procedure, a doctor makes an exclamation of surprise and drops an instrument on the floor. Muffled vocalizations can be heard in the background. The rest of the staff begin to panic as the head emerges unassisted from Nash, causing her a great deal of pain. The child's head can be seen to resemble that of American television presenter Ryan Seacrest. The child sings Row, Row, Row Your Boat in a female voice as it continues to exit the mother.

As more of its form emerges, the child can be seen to have the body of a fully grown octopus (Octopus vulgaris). Once the child fully exits Nash's body, it continues to sing as another head begins to emerge. Three more children are produced in total, with the heads of celebrities Jack Nicholson (American film actor), Johnny Cash (American singer-songwriter), and Martin Freeman (British film actor), respectively, all with similar octopus bodies. Together, the four sing Row Row Row Your Boat in four part harmony. SCP-2030-1 walks into the room and the show's jingle plays. SCP-2030-1 points to the hidden cameras in the room, prompting the obstetricians and Nash to begin laughing. The creatures on Nash's torso continue to sing. Nash then loses consciousness, presumably from blood loss.

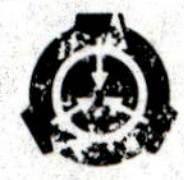

The following is a transcription of a typical speech delivered by SCP-2030-1 during one of the show's closing segments:

Season: 32 (2008)

Episode theme: Printers

Transcription: Ha! What a ride, eh, folks? We've seen printers that eat, eaters that print, and everything in between! Makes you appreciate the old clunker you have back the office, doesn't it? No, printers may not always work when you want or need them to, but they sure make for some excellent comedy. And that's what we're about here: comedy. We're here to make you laugh. We hope you laughed. Thank you for laughing with us. That's what we're about here, doesn't it, folks? Come laugh with us again next time! And remember: LAUGH … IS … FUN! Good night! And laugh! And laugh! Just laugh! We love the make laugh. Make more for laughter so as to for laugh. Laugh with us. Laugh with us. (Studio audience joins in unison) Laugh with us! Laugh with us! Laugh with us! Laugh with us! Laugh! Laugh! Laugh and let us in!

Video cuts off abruptly and a black screen is displayed for thirty seconds. Laughter and soft, wet noises can be heard in the background before the program ends.

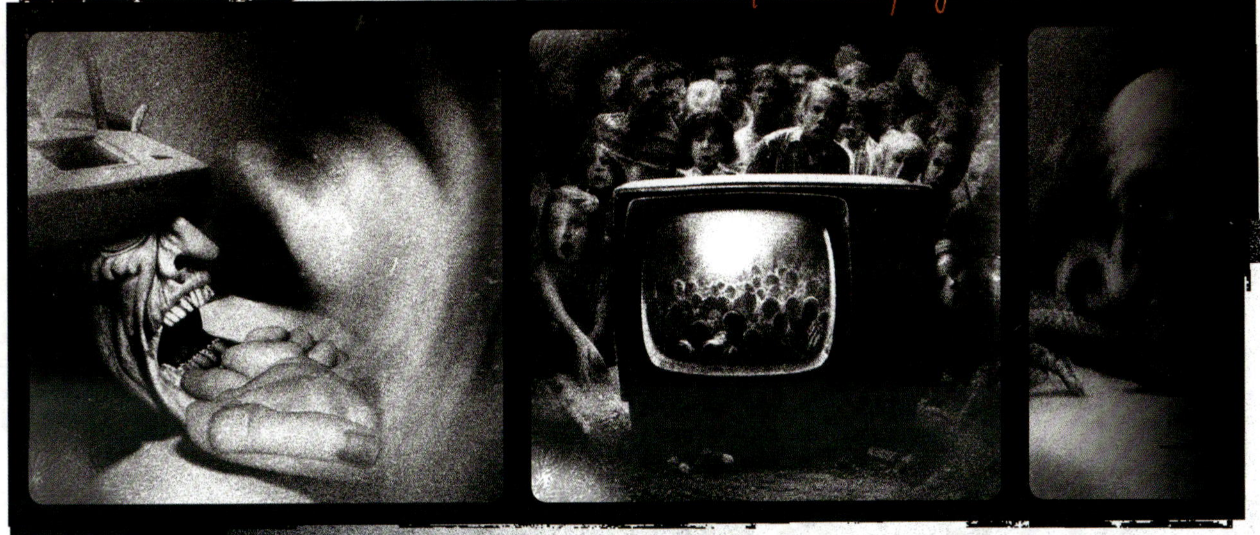

END OF REPORT

File >>> 299331

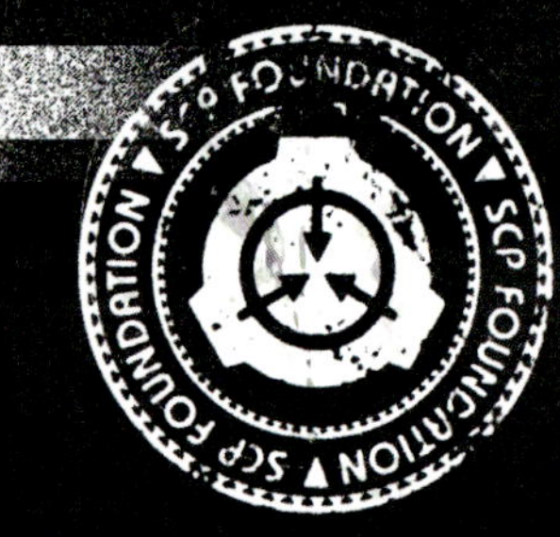

SCP-166

Title

JUST A TEENAGE GAEA

Report by

DrClef

Picture by

Ivan Efimov

Access the original report on

scp-wiki.wikidot.com/scp-166

Date

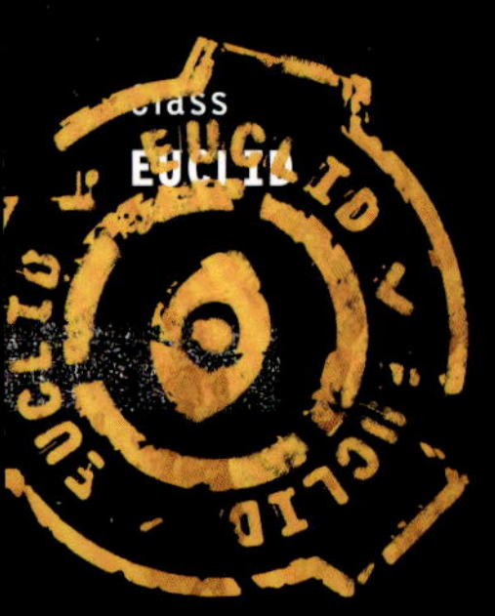

Class

EUCLID

SPECIAL CONTAINMENT PROCEDURES

SCP-166 is contained in Biocontainment Zone C at Site-19, which has been modified to include a hermetically sealed antechamber and an industrial-strength air purifier. Containment staff must wear the specially designated 166 biohazard suits at all times when inside SCP-166's containment area.

Due to SCP-166's unique physiological needs, a variety of loose fitting organic cotton clothing has been provided, to be rotated monthly. All meals are to be cooked according to the guidelines provided, with as little inorganic additives as possible.

Reasonable requests for personal items and modifications to the containment suite may be granted upon approval ~~by a Level 4 or higher authority.~~ *Update: All requests by SCP-166 must be approved personally by Site Director Light.* To date, SCP-166 has requested:

- A copy of the Holy Bible (Douay-Rheims, Challoner Revision) (granted).
- A Catholic rosary (granted).
- Access to a Catholic priest for confession, mass, and other sacraments. (denied) (Chaplain Davis has been scheduled to meet with SCP-166 on alternating Sundays after a thorough decontamination process).
- Various books and magazines, mostly religious in nature (granted, pending review and approval of contents).
- A telephone with which to contact the Abbess of the Our Lady of Mercy Convent in County Galway, Ireland ~~(denied) (granted)~~ (overruled by order of the Site Director, denied).

DESCRIPTION

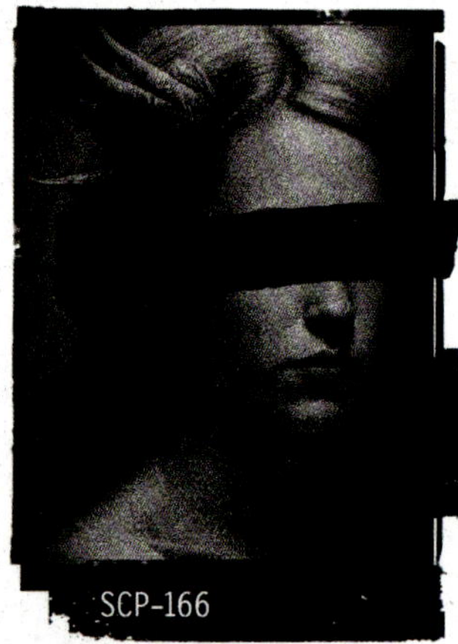

SCP-166

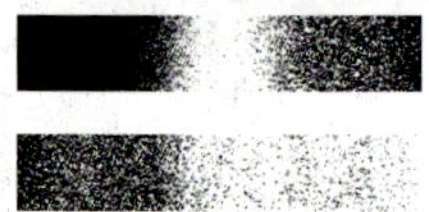

SCP-166 is a European female human in its late teens with ungulate features; possessing antlers, hooved feet, and a short tail reminiscent of *Rangifer tarandus* (Common reindeer). Despite these obvious abnormalities, DNA analysis reveals no abnormal genetic traits.

Within a fifteen-meter radius of SCP-166, artificial objects gradually return to an unworked state. Higher complexity objects like electronics or vehicles are affected quicker, with degradation of their metallic components causing catastrophic structural failure in a matter of hours. Rudimentary materials, such as stone buildings or products made of organic materials, decay at a virtually imperceptible rate. Within the same radius plant life will begin to sprout, often growing in improbable places such as out of security cameras or ID scanners.

SCP-166 possesses a possibly anomalous sensitivity to artificial material and pollutants, with inhalation or contact causing pressure ulcers and symptoms of acute asthma attacks. In one case, physical proximity to a smoker caused SCP-166 to undergo a severe asthma attack, even though the doctor at the time had not smoked a cigarette for three weeks.

DISCOVERY

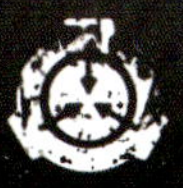

SCP-166 was discovered at the Our Lady of Mercy Convent in County Galway, Ireland, where it had lived since infancy. SCP-166 was confirmed by a defecting Global Occult Coalition agent to be the child of Threat Entity 9927-Black ("The Goddess"), also known as SCP-████, who was terminated by a GOC strike team in what would be known as the Cornwall Incident.

RECOVERED GOC DOCUMENTATION

THREAT ENTITY DATABASE ENTRY

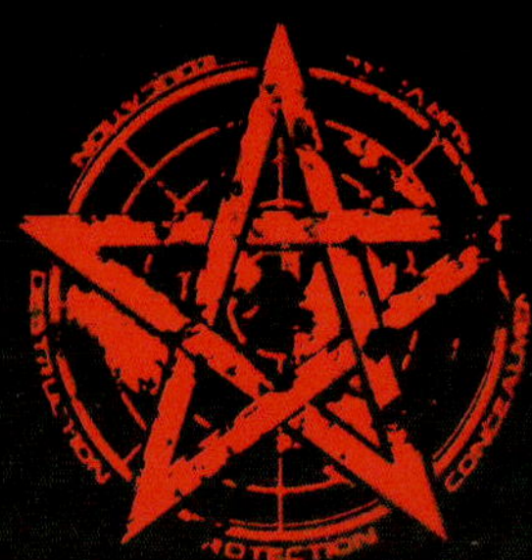

THREAT ID:

KTE-9927-Blackchild "The Daughter"

AUTHORIZED RESPONSE LEVEL:

4 (Severe Threat)

DESCRIPTION:

Threat entity is the child of incarnated LTE-9927-Black ("The Goddess") and an unknown father. While it strongly resembles its mother and shares its animalistic features, it lacks the extreme bestial appearance of 9927-Black. Possesses minor chlorokinetic abilities, but primary reason for threat entity classification is the instinctive knowledge and eligibility to enact Occult Procedure Clockwork Blackchild Havilah, a world-wide ritual working that would irreversibly regress human civilization to Neolithic standards.

Strike Team "Lancelot" neutralized 9927-Black in 19██ in England during an operation which would later be known as the infamous 'Cornwall Incident', but were unable to confirm the liquidation of 9927-Blackchild due to the death of the strike leader, Agent Ukulele. Ukulele was posthumously awarded the Silver Aegis for his lifelong service to humanity.

LIQUIDATION:

Threat entity is not known to possess any defensive abilities. Terminate with extreme prejudice.

The agent had refused to terminate SCP-166, instead smuggling it to a Catholic convent in County Galway, Ireland. It lived there until the age of 12, at which point a visitor to the convent accidentally witnessed SCP-166 and reported it to authorities. The agent then contacted the Foundation, agreeing to share GOC intelligence in return for the guaranteed safety and containment of SCP-166.

Further details are classified.

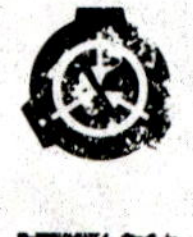

Research
Library
File ▸ 166

ADDENDUM 166.1: CHAPLAIN DAVIS BIWEEKLY INTERVIEW

Davis: Good morning, child.

SCP-166: Good morning, Father.

Davis: As usual, I have to remind you that due to our environment, the seal of confession will not take place unless specifically invoked. Even then, details of our conversation can be unsealed if they're determined to be essential. Understand?

SCP-166 nods.

Davis: Excellent. Now, how are you doing?

SCP-166: Good. One of the staff told me about Benedict yesterday, is that true?

Davis: Ah, yes, that was rather unfortunate, but it does make sense. He was rather old even when he first took up the position. Now he can rest, knowing he served the Church well.

SCP-166: Do you know who's going to replace him?

Davis: Speculation has abounded, but it could be anyone. These are difficult times after all, with all the recent… controversies. They may want a fresh face to represent the church, or they may go with a man who's dedicated years of his life. Who knows, they may even pick a working-class man. It certainly would give people something to talk about.

SCP-166: I guess so.

SCP-166 and Davis sit in silence.

Davis: I'm sensing a question arising, child.

SCP-166: Sorry.

Davis: No need to apologize. That is what I'm here for, after all. What is it?

SCP-166: It's just, I wanted to ask you something, thought it might be a little personal. I was just wondering, do you have a good relationship with your parents?

Davis: My mother, yes. Before she passed away, I visited her once a month at the retirement home, plus her birthday and holidays. Told her I was a chaplain serving in the military, which I suppose is somewhat close to the truth.

SCP-166: And your father?

Davis: That is a rather more complicated question. He was a good man, a soldier who held three things dearly: God, Country, and Family. Unfortunately, he held those convictions rather severely, which resulted in some… heated discussions. I love him still, but this way is best for everyone.

Davis sighs.

Davis: And what about your parents? I know you lived in the convent, but before that?

SCP-166: I never really knew them, I got dropped off when I was a baby. I mean, I guess they must've known the sisters if they put me there, but I don't remember them. Just what I picked up. They mentioned my mother a bit, before they realized that they should watch what they say about me. I think they said something about her being a goddess? Which obviously wouldn't be true, she must've been some sort of spirit, but she must've been something if I ended up looking like this.

SCP-166 gestures to herself.

SCP-166: I remember eavesdropping on the Abbess, she was talking to one of the other sisters about how she had done something wrong, something about a ritual that someone else stopped. They said she died.

Davis: I'm sorry for your loss.

SCP-166: Not like I knew her.

Davis: And your father?

SCP-166 hesitates.

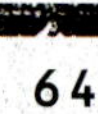

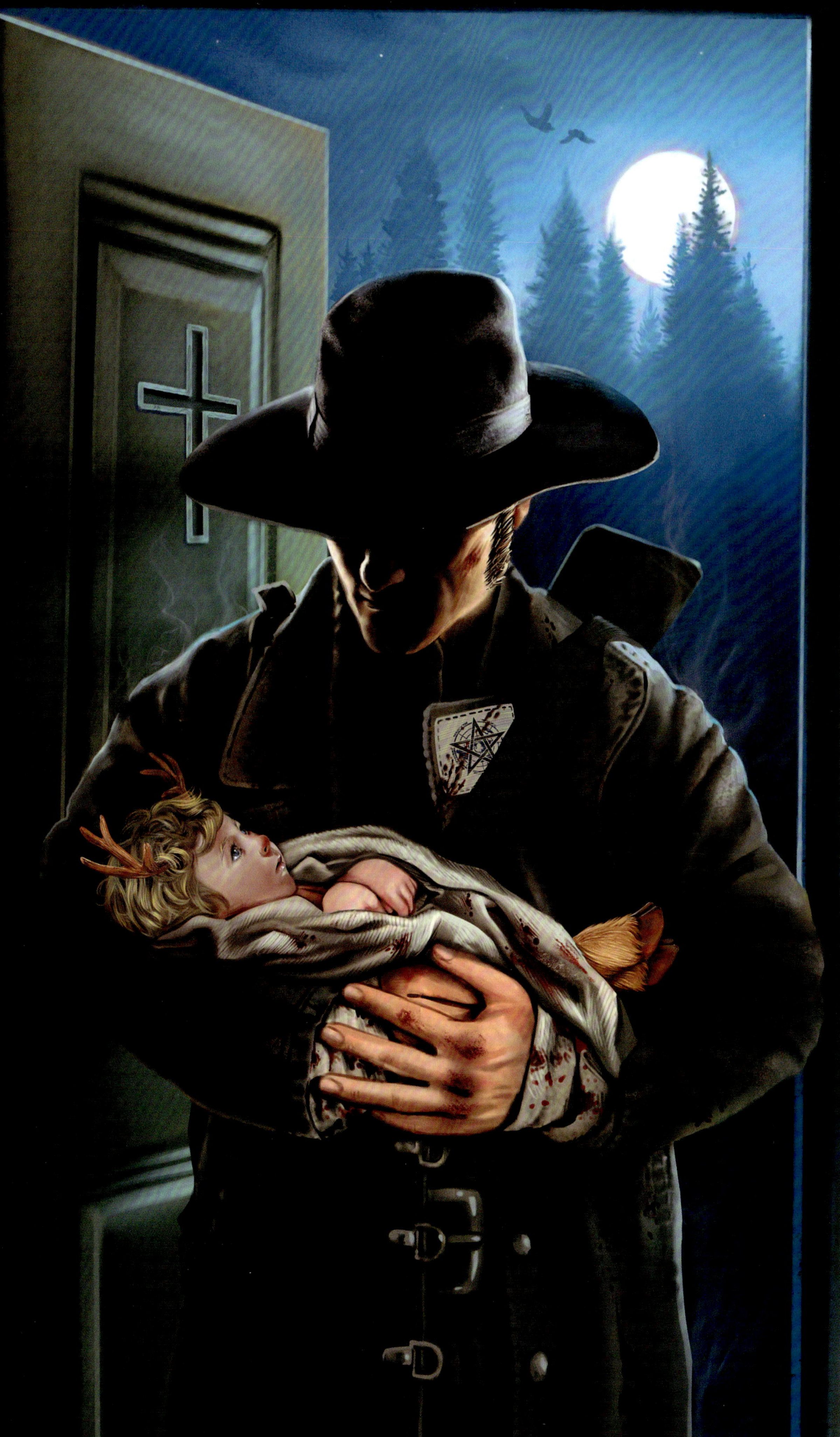

SCP-166's arrival at the Our Lady of Mercy Convent as described by Abbess █████.

Wait, I can swear I've seen this hat before...

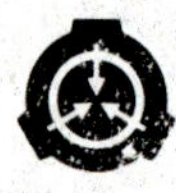

Research Library File ▸ 166

SCP-166: I don't know. He must've been the one who dropped me off at the convent, but why there? Why didn't he take me with him?

Davis: I'm sure he had his reasons.

SCP-166: Maybe. You know, they never talked about him. Not once. I must've asked the Abbess a thousand times, but she never even mentioned a hint of him.

SCP-166 pauses.

SCP-166: If my mother was so horrible… what did my father do?

[END LOG]

ADDENDUM 166.2: DISCIPLINARY INTERVIEW OF [REDACTED]

[BEGIN LOG]

Light: What the hell were you thinking?

[REDACTED]: I wanted to make sure she's alright. You wouldn't let me talk to her. I took another route.

Light: What you did was so much worse than that. If you just stuck to throwing your weight around to get her amenities, sure, I could overlook that. But you then go about trying to give a class 4 anomaly a phone line to the outside world- Dammit. The council already dislikes you working at the same site as her, this gets out, you can kiss whatever deal you made goodbye.

[REDACTED]: Come on, Sophia! She's harmless. The only reason she's in there is because of me. I had to do something. Was the Foundation just going to let her grow up thinking that her-

Light: Before you say another word, remember that this will be public to everyone with a class 4 clearance. I can redact your name, but I can't stop people from putting the pieces together from an ill-timed outburst.

[REDACTED] remains silent.

[REDACTED]: Sixteen years. Sixteen years where she couldn't walk through a city, or catch a movie, or just go shopping. Doesn't matter if she's in a convent or a foundation cell, she's being locked up for something she had no choice in. All because of me. It isn't fair.

Light: I know.

[REDACTED]: And I can't do anything about it. I could send a strike team anywhere in the world, I know secrets that the most powerful people in the world would pay billions for, and yet I can't even so much as talk to her, let her know that she's not alone.

Light: You've done the best you could. Much more than anyone could've expected of you in an impossible situation.

[REDACTED]: Funny how little that makes of a difference. I-

[REDACTED] falls silent.

[REDACTED]: You know, I don't care. Just write me up. Let's just get this over with.

Light: …I'm scheduling you for six 2-hour sessions with a Foundation psychologist, I'll make sure it's Glass. He signs off at the end of it, we can expunge this from your record.

[REDACTED]: Mhm.

Light: [REDACTED].

[REDACTED]: Yeah?

Light: …

[REDACTED]: …Yeah, I know. Thank you, Sophia.

[END LOG]

On 05/08/2013, the following note was discovered within SCP-166's containment area.

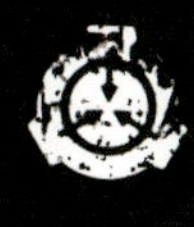

Research
Library
File ▸ 166

I first met your mother when we were little more than children. She had hooves for feet and starlight in her eyes. She was beauty and nature incarnate, and I killed her with my own two hands.

Eden isn't a place. It's a state of being. They wanted to take us back to it, and I stopped them. I took paradise away from us for a second time. I have never regretted my actions on that day, except one: that when you first met me on that day, you saw your father put a bullet into the head of your mother. I make no excuses, only explanation.

You may not have remembered it, but I'm telling you now in the hope you understand why I did what I did. I hope you forgive me.

I love you. I wish I could have done more for you. The best I could do was leave you in the hands of kind and loving people and hope they would raise you in my place. From what I've seen, they did well. I'm sorry you couldn't stay with them. I'm sorry they've brought you to this place. I **promise** to do my best to make sure your stay here is pleasant. I **promise** to keep you safe

Happy sixteenth birthday,

From your loving father.

D OF REPORT

File >>> 029221

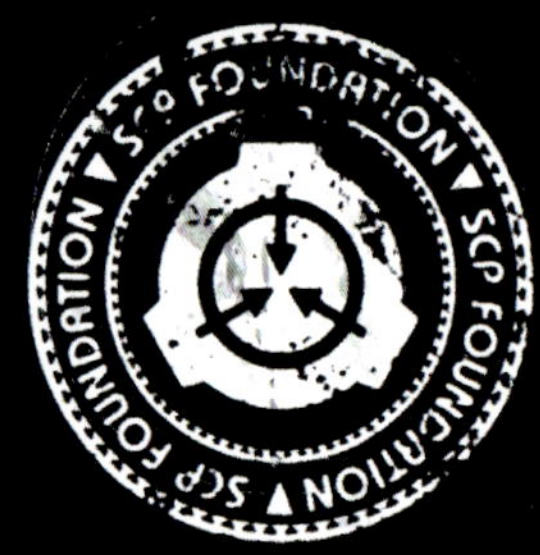

SCP-939

Title

WITH MANY VOICES

Report by

Adam Smascher
EchoFourDelta

Pictures by

David Romero
Dmitry Desyatov

Access the original report on

scp-wiki.wikidot.com/scp-939

Date

Class

KETER

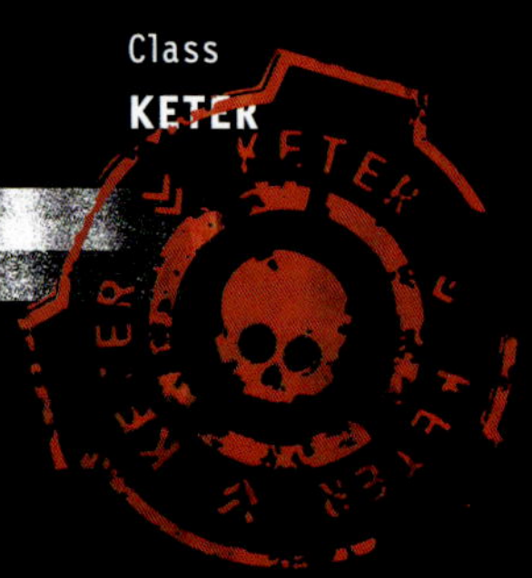

SPECIAL CONTAINMENT PROCEDURES

SCP-939-1, -3, -19, -53, -89, -96, -98, -99, and -109 are kept in Cell 1163-A or 1163-B, 10 m x 10 m x 3 m containment chambers within Armed Bio-Containment Area-14. Both cells are environmentally regulated and negatively pressurized, with walls constructed of reinforced concrete. Access to these cells is regulated by an outer decontamination chamber and inner gas-tight steel security doors. Observation windows are constructed of laminated ballistics glass 10 cm in thickness protected by a 100kV electrified mesh. Humidity is maintained at 100% at a temperature of 16° C. Specimens are monitored at all times via infrared cameras. Level Four authorization is required to access SCP-939, their containment areas, or the observation chambers.

SCP-939-101 is dismembered and stored in Cryogenic Preservation Tanks 939-101A to 939-101M within Bio-Research Area-12. Access to SCP-939-101 requires authorization by two Clearance Level 3 personnel, one of which must be present for all research and testing. The contents of only one (1) 939-101 tank may be accessed at any given time. Core temperature of SCP-939-101 tissues must be monitored while removed from cryogenic preservation; should core temperature exceed 10° C, tissues are to be returned to their corresponding tank and all testing suspended for a period of seventy-two (72) hours. Barring core temperature exceeding 10° C, research of SCP-939-101 tissues may continue as long as its ramblings and pleas for release may be tolerated.

Containment cells should be cleaned biweekly. While this takes place, SCP-939 specimens will be transferred to the adjacent cell. During this time, the cell's door and observation window must be inspected for damage and repaired or replaced accordingly.

Heavy sedation of all SCP-939 is required before any interaction, including transfer between cells and experimentation, may take place. See Document #939-TE4 for transfer and experimentation protocol.

Level C Hazmat gear is to be worn by personnel during interactions with SCP-939 specimens and in any areas which SCP-939 have been known to inhabit. Afterward, standard decontamination procedures are to be observed by all personnel involved to ensure no secondary spread of amnestic agents occurs.

Following Incident ABCA14-939-3, all non Class D personnel interacting with SCP-939 for any length of time are required to wear two (2) water-proof electronic pulse monitors for the duration of such interaction. These pulse monitors will transmit to a wireless monitoring system independent of a facility's main power grid, with at least one backup power system on standby. Should both an individual's pulse monitors flat-line or otherwise malfunction, the wearer will be presumed dead, personnel instructed to disregard all the wearer's subsequent vocalizations, and a breach of containment declared automatically. Security personnel responding to such a breach are likewise required to wear these pulse monitors.

Additionally, all live SCP-939 must be implanted with subdermal tracking devices upon capture.

DESCRIPTION

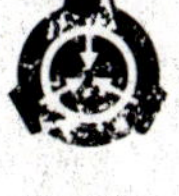

SCP-939 are endothermic, pack-based predators which display atrophy of various systems similar to troglobitic organisms. The skins of SCP-939 are highly permeable to moisture and translucent red, owing to a compound chemically similar to hemoglobin. SCP-939 average 2.2 meters tall standing upright and weigh an average of 250 kg, though weight is highly variable. Each of their four limbs end in three-fingered claws with a fourth, opposable digit, and are covered in setae which considerably augment climbing ability. Their heads are elongated, devoid of even vestigial eyes or eye sockets, and contain no brain casing. The jaws of SCP-939 are lined with red, faintly luminescent fang-like teeth, similar to those belonging to specimens of the genus Chauliodus, up to 6 cm in length, and encircled by heat-sensitive pit organs. Eye spots, sensitive to light and dark, run the length of their spined dorsal ridges. These spines may be up to 16 cm long and are believed to be sensitive to changes in air pressure and flow.

SCP-939 do not possess many vital organ systems; central and peripheral nervous systems, circulatory system, and digestive tract are all absent. SCP-939's respiratory system is atrophied and serves no apparent purpose beyond spreading AMN-C227 (see below). SCP-939 have no apparent physiological need to feed, nor any way to digest consumed tissue. Ingested material typically accumulates in the respiratory system of SCP-939 and is regurgitated once the amount is sufficient to markedly inhibit its function. Despite the absence of many vital organ systems, SCP-939 are capable of bearing live young. **See Addendum 10-16-1991.**

SCP-939's primary method of luring prey is the imitation of human speech in the voices of prior victims, though imitation of other species and active nocturnal hunts have been documented. SCP-939 vocalizations often imply significant distress; whether SCP-939 understand their vocalizations or are repeating previously heard phrases is the subject of ongoing study. How SCP-939 acquire voices is not currently understood; specimens have been documented imitating victims despite never hearing the victim speak. Analysis of SCP-939 vocalizations cannot distinguish between SCP-939 and samples of known victims' voices. The use of biometric voice-recognition security or identification systems at any installation housing SCP-939 is strongly discouraged for this reason. Prey is usually killed with a single bite to the cranium or neck; bite forces have been measured in excess of 35 MPa.

SCP-939 exhale minute traces of an aerosolized Class C amnestic, designated AMN-C227. AMN-C227 causes temporary anterograde amnesia, inhibiting memory formation for the duration of exposure, plus an average of thirty (30) minutes. It is colorless, odorless, and tasteless with an estimated ECt50 for inhalation of 0.0015mg·min/m3. In well-ventilated or open air environments, risk of exposure to ECt50 is greatly reduced but not negligible. AMN-C227 is typically undetectable in the bloodstream sixty (60) minutes following cessation of exposure. Reported sensations of disorientation and mild hallucinations immediately following removal from environments saturated with the agent are similar to recreational use of numerous psychoactive substances and easily mistaken as such.

NOTE 03-23-2005

This report pertains to morphology alpha. For information regarding morphology beta, see [REDACTED] Experiment Log 914, AMTF Nu-7 After Action Report ███-███, [REDACTED]

Test 914-0114

Name: Dr. ██████
Date: 07/01/2011
Total Items: Five adult SCP-939 specimens. Test cleared by O5 Command.

Input: One adult SCP-939 specimen was placed within SCP-914 on each setting.

Setting: Rough
Output: A mass of bone splinters, broken teeth, and scraps of translucent red tissue of various sizes. Tissue was observed to twitch spasmodically for several hours before activity ceased. Material preserved for further study.

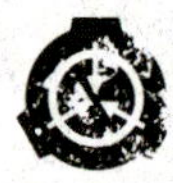

Research Library File ▸ 939

Setting: Coarse
Output: Subject was divided up into organized piles of tissue, including but not limited to (presumably) muscle tissue, two piles of ground bone tissue (the significance of this division, if any, is unknown), teeth, skin, a total of approximately seventeen meters of esophageal tissue divided into numerous coils, and approximately fifteen kilograms of rotting human flesh littered with splinters of bone, shreds of fabric, and a tattered laminated ID tag identifying its owner as D-09355. As with the first test, SCP-939 tissue was observed to convulse for several hours before ceasing activity. SCP-939 remains preserved for further study; human remains incinerated.

Setting: 1:1
Output: [REDACTED]

Setting: Fine
Output: The same SCP-939 specimen. Respiration was noted to have halted. Test subject was immediately relocated to a reinforced concrete containment chamber and observed remotely via CCTV. Installation security forces were ordered to high alert. Twenty-four hours passed with no signs of activity from the subject. Subject proved unresponsive to all stimuli and was pronounced dead thirty-six hours later. Necropsy was unable to identify a cause of death nor any anatomical revisions attributable to SCP-914. Remains preserved for further study.

Setting: Very Fine
Output: A heap of smoldering white ash.

ADDENDUM 11-14-1981

The following is a transcript of radio traffic between the on-scene commander (Trapper Home) and subordinate fire teams (Trapper 1, 2, and 3) of Site-█'s tactical contact security force designated "Trapper" during the initial contact with and recovery of SCP-939. Trapper was deployed to the outskirts of ███████, ███████ on 10/28/1981, following the disappearance of a Foundation field agent. The agent was investigating a number of localized missing persons cases, as well the loss of contact with several law enforcement officers dispatched to investigate these cases, in the area.

<Begin transcript>

Trapper Home: All right, let's get those comm checks people. Those field masks were giving your VOX a hell of a time last time out.

Agent Washburne (Trapper One Lead): Trapper Home, Trapper Two, Trapper Three, this is One, radio check, over.

Agent Michaels (Trapper Two Lead): Lima Charlie, One.

Agent Shandrick (Trapper Three Lead): Gotcha, One.

Trapper Home: All stations, I have you loud and clear. Be advised, your teams are go for entry. Trapper One, weapons tight.

Agent Washburne (T1L): Solid copy, Home. Three, stand by with Home, you know your job. Two, keep your team tight on my flank after we breach.

Agent Michaels (T2L): Copy, One.

Agent Washburne (T1L): One, stack up.

<Members of Trapper One can be heard acknowledging Trapper One Lead's command.>

Agent Washburne (T1L): Execute

Agent Nicholas (Trapper One): All right, that water charge goes in 5.

<Water charge detonates>

Agent Nicholas (T1): Stairs, front! Clear left!

Agent Roland (Trapper One): Door, right! Right side, clear.

Agent Michaels (T2L): Overhead's clear.

Agent Harrison (Trapper Two): Thompson, on me. Cross. Room clear.

Agent Washburne (T1L): Trapper Home, Trapper One and Two reporting no contact. Two, secure that passageway, mark your territory, and then follow my team down. Keep an eye out for our man, and call it when you come down; I don't want any blue on blue, solid?

Agent Michaels (T2L): Copy, One.

Agent Washburne (T1L): Hoskins, you've got point.

Agent Hoskins (Trapper One): Roger that. Movin' up.

Agent Washburne (T1L): Trapper Home, this is One; be advised we are moving further into the structure, down a ladderwell, over.

Trapper Home: Solid copy, One. Proceed, over.

<Members of Trapper One can be heard calling out doorways and landing as they move further down the stairs.>

Agent Washburne (T1L): Trapper Home, be advised: I'm starting to smell something rotten down here, and it's pretty strong. Something's been dead for a while… stand by… Team, halt. Home, I'm looking at some shredded clothing down here. No bodies, just the clothes, and nothing that looks like our man. There's the cop…

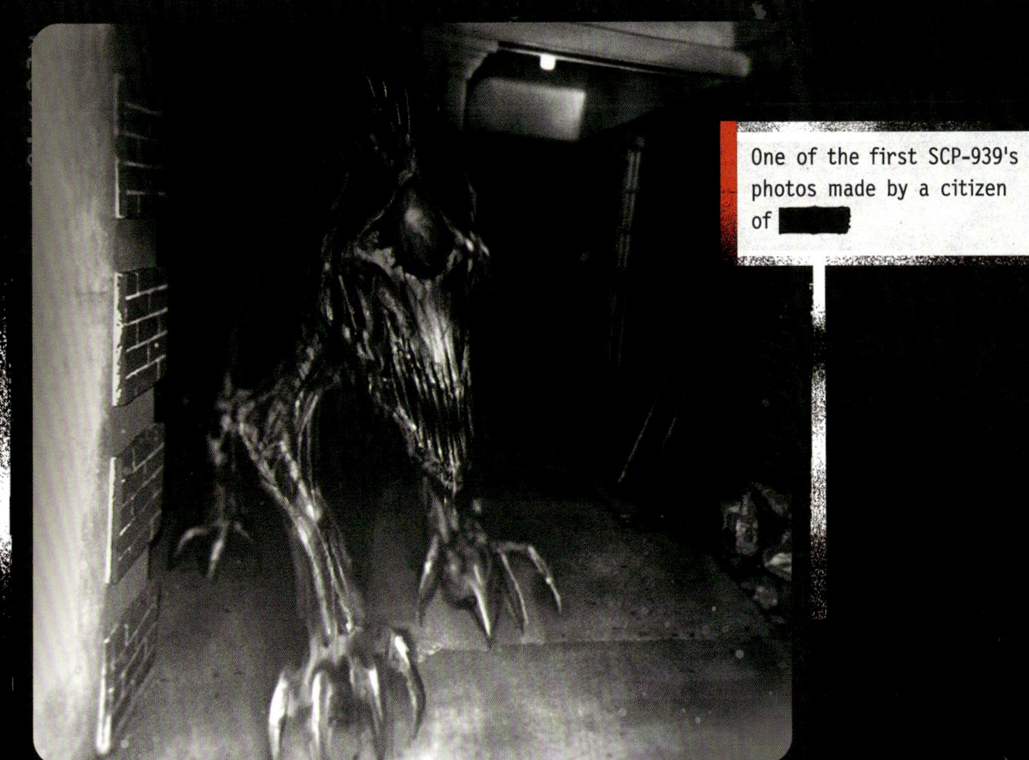

One of the first SCP-939's photos made by a citizen of ████

Agent Hoskins (T1): Jesus man, look at that… it looks like something just took a huge bite outta that vest…

Trapper Home: Lock it up down there, One. Washburne, get back on track.

Agent Washburne (T1L): Copy, Home. Trapper Two, watch yourselves. Something around our pos has an appetite, and it looks like it's got a pretty mean bite.

Agent Michaels (T2L): Solid, One. We're almost done up here. If our Agent's here, he's down there with you guys. We'll be down as soon as we-

<A muffled human voice is audible through Agent Washburne's VOX feed, unintelligible and distant.>

Agent Washburne (T1L): One and Two, freeze.

All units coming into contact with SCP-939 are heavily discouraged from reacting to any pleads and cries for help.

<**Unknown source:** *Help me! Jesus Christ! Somebody!*>

Agent Washburne (T1L): Home, Two, I think we've got our man. Hustle up, people.

<Trapper One can be heard moving quickly through the structure. The cry for help is again audible.>

Agent Washburne (T1L): Home, we've reached the source of the noise. We're about to get our Agent back. Two, have Doc prep the trauma bag; this guy sounds like he's in bad shape. Hoskins, do it!

<Two shotgun reports, sound of door slamming on floor>

<Immediate sustained gunfire>

Agent Washburne (T1L): Home, contact! Two, get the fuck down here! Roland, pull back!

It is absolutely forbidden to get closer to the source of the voice unless given a direct command from the Base.

Agent Nicholas (T1): Hoskins is down! Shit!

Agent Washburne (T1L): Roland, on your right! Two, hurry the fuck up!

Agent Michaels (T2L): One, what the hell's going on down there?

<Gunfire ceases>

Agent Michaels (T2L): Trapper One! Sound off!

<**Agent Washburne, shouting off comm:** *Two, get the fuck down here, Hoskins is down! Hurry the fuck up!*>

Agent Michaels (T2L): Copy one! Harrison, Thompson, you're coming with me. Gabardi, stay with Doc.

<Trapper Two can be heard acknowledging Trapper Two Lead's order.>

Agent Michaels (T2L): Home, One, be advised, Two is en route to One's last position.

<Agent Washburne can be heard cursing over Agent Michaels' VOX feed.>

Agent Michaels (T2L): One, be advised, your radio's not broadcasting; I can hear you, but you're- JESUS CHRIST! TWO, ENGAGE, ENGAGE!

<Immediate sustained gunfire>

Agent Michaels (T2L): Thompson, pick up the slack. Loading! Gun up! Guys, pull it back down the hallway. Harrison, suppress that doorway. Frag out!

<Explosion>

Agent Michaels (T2L): Gabardi, Doc, get the 60 set, we're coming up. Trapper One's gone, and I'm dropping gas. Mask up. GAS GAS GAS!

<Three muffled popping sounds can be heard.>

Agent Michaels (T2L): Coming up the stairs!

Agent Harrison (T2): They're slowing down. Get Three, Michaels?

Agent Michaels (T2L): Home, we've deployed VX and need Three down here in MOPP for cleanup. Set up decon.

Agent Shandrick (T3L): Roger, Two, we're already on our way.

Agent Gabardi (T2): SHIT!

<Gunshot>

Agent Michaels (T2L): Whoa… Nice shot, Gabardi. Home, we've got an unconscious one. We're gonna need a mobile containment unit, and medical support for the candidate, I think it sucked down some VX. I'm not hearing any more movement down those stairs, Home.

Trapper Home: Copy, Two. Standby for linkup with Three, extricate the candidate, and hit decon. We're done here.

<End transcript>

When a SCP-939's den is discovered, it is advised to use gas and other weapons that do not require close proximity.

~~ADDENDUM 04-11-1982~~

~~Due to SCP-939's intense aversion to bright light, it has been deemed a minimal risk of escape. Standard fluorescent hallway lighting is sufficient to deter SCP-939-1 from leaving its darkened cell.~~ See **Addendum 09-20-1991**.

ADDENDUM 06-29-1987

Preliminary research into AMN-C227 suggests potential for use as a general-purpose amnestic. Methods of mass-producing the agent, as well as possible adverse effects, are being investigated at Bio-Containment and Research Site-06.

~~ADDENDUM 10-03-1990~~

~~AMN-C227 has been approved for use as a Class C amnestic. Projected annual production at Bio-Research Area-12 by SCP-939 respiratory tissue cultures is expected to surpass three (3) liters.~~

ADDENDUM 09-20-1991

Containment of nine (9) SCP-939 specimens has been compromised following a "Silent Night" breach scenario at Bio-Containment and Research Site-06. Nearby civilian settlements have been evacuated on the pretense of a coming storm. Recovery teams have been deployed to the area.

ADDENDUM 10-16-1991

[REDACTED] In light of this, all interaction with SCP-939 from September 8th to October 7th in the Northern Hemisphere or March 6th to April 4th in the Southern Hemisphere is strictly forbidden. [REDACTED] No male specimens of SCP-939 have yet been identified [REDACTED] contain a Class B amnestic [REDACTED]

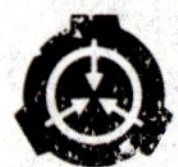

REPRODUCTION OF SCP-939

Document #939-00-62: Reproduction of SCP-939

On September 25th, 1992, SCP-939-1 gave birth following a gestation period of roughly twelve (12) months. Litter SCP-939-A contained six specimens, numbered SCP-939-A1 to SCP-939-A6. SCP-939-A1, A4, and A5 were male, while A3 and A6 were female. SCP-939-A2 was stillborn and immediately cannibalized by SCP-939-1. SCP-939-1 made no attempts to interfere with confiscation of its offspring.

Vivisection of SCP-939-A1, A3, A4, and A5 found them to be morphologically and genotypically indistinguishable from healthy human infants.[1] The remains of SCP-939-A1 and SCP-939-A3 are kept preserved in Biological Materials Storage Units 939-026C and 939-026D, respectively, within Bio-Research Area-12. Remains of SCP-939-A4 and SCP-939-A5 were incinerated.

SCP-939-A6 will be transferred to [REDACTED] for observation as it matures. It will undergo monthly physical examination, supplemented with any additional measures deemed necessary.

Document #939-A6-16: Transfer of Dr. ██████

[REDACTED]

Note 03-16-1997: After overhearing numerous conversations between personnel, SCP-939-A6 has come to believe its name is "Keter." Given the marked positive effect on its mood, staff are advised to neither encourage nor discourage this assumption. Both its mental and physical development have remained consistent with human norms.

Document# 939-A6-33: Emergency Medical Log SCP-939-A6

Date: 01-09-2001

At approximately 20:00 hours, SCP-939-A6 began acting increasingly unsettled. When questioned, it reported a sense of malaise. Breathing was observed to be rapid and shallow. SCP-939-A6 was escorted to the medical ward for further examination. Heart rate was measured to be erratic, averaging one-hundred ninety (190) beats per minute. No further anomalies were observed; SCP-939-A6 was administered a benzodiazepine and returned to containment. Probable panic attack; trigger undetermined.

Date: 01-10-2001

At approximately 04:30 hours, SCP-939-A6 reported the same symptoms, accompanied by a mild headache and aversion to light. Examination returned identical results to the previous day. SCP-939-A6 instructed to rest, administered a sedative, and returned to containment.

Date: 01-24-2001

Symptoms outlined above persisted for two weeks before intensifying. SCP-939-A6 destroyed the lighting fixture in its enclosure and was found to have assumed the fetal position underneath its bed at 01:40 hours. A6 staunchly resisted leaving its chamber, requiring it be carried to Area-██'s medical ward. It complained of a severe headache, intense aversion to light, hypersensitivity to auditory stimuli, intense chest and abdominal pain, and uncomfortable warmth, commenting that it "hurt too much to cry." A6's core body temperature measured to be 41.2° C. Technicians were unable to locate a pulse.

MRI indicated [REDACTED]

1. Several researchers who participated in the vivisections subsequently requested Class B amnestics. It should be standard policy to grant these requests after all relevant data has been collected. - 05-██

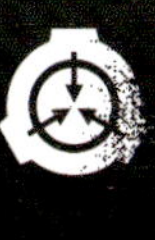

SCP-939-A6's transformation.

A reinforced concrete containment cell was immediately prepared for SCP-939-A6. The cell's lighting was dimmed and a large basin full of water provided at its request.

Date: 01-26-2001

SCP-939-A6 immersed itself in the provided water basin and remained inactive for a period of approximately forty-one (41) hours, at which point it began violently tearing at its skin. It displayed a considerable amount of distress upon realizing its skin was sloughing off, but appeared unable to stop. At 22:36 hours, Dr. ████ reported SCP-939-A6's head detached itself. By 22:40 hours, it appeared morphologically identical to, albeit much smaller than, SCP-939-1.

Addendum 02-13-2001: SCP-939-A6 has been re-designated SCP-939-101. It will be transferred to Bio-Research Area-12 for further study.

Document# 939-101-77: Audio Log 939-101A #13

<Begin Log, 10:16 hrs, 05-22-2004>

<Access to Cryogenic Preservation Room 939-101 granted to: Dr.████>

<Access to CGPT 939-101A granted.>

SCP-939-101: Excuse me, mister? Why are we here? It's bitterly cold and we would like to go home now. We're very late for our bedtime, and we're very sorry. We didn't mean it.

SCP-939-101: Have you seen our pictures? We like drawing. Daddy hung them on the wall except for sometimes when the others in white coats took them away. Daddy told us not to draw pictures like those. They made him sad, so we did our best to draw other things, but sometimes we forgot. Sometimes daddy hid the pictures or ripped them up. He told us it wasn't that he didn't like them. He said it was to keep us safe from the mean doctors in the white coats, but then the doctors took daddy away.

SCP-939-101: They made us get shots and told us to forget about daddy, but we're scared of needles without daddy around. We didn't forget daddy. Daddy forgot us, though. We think it was the doctors' fault. Daddy wouldn't forget about us, would he?

SCP-939-101: They gave us a fake daddy and told us it was real daddy, but we knew better. The doctors made us get more shots. They kept telling us fake daddy was real daddy, but they couldn't fool us. We told them it was wrong to lie just like daddy told us, and then they stopped lying.

SCP-939-101: They made us be by ourselves, but they gave us paper and pencils and paints and told us we could draw whatever we wanted so we did. Sometimes we drew daddy. Sometimes we drew what daddy told us not to draw. The doctors took all our pictures.

SCP-939-101: Sometimes the doctors in the white coats and the people with the big black shirts with lots of pockets and helmets that carried bent windows and… what did daddy call them? I forgot. They walked with us down the hall for our checkups. We didn't like those.

SCP-939-101: Sometimes we had to lay in a dark place and be really, really still. Daddy would tell us stories. We didn't always understand them, but we liked them anyway. There were stories about places that didn't have ceilings, where up was forever and the ground wasn't white. We think it's silly. Everywhere has ceilings, doesn't it? After the doctors took daddy away, we didn't get to hear stories any more.

SCP-939-101: Then we didn't feel good.

SCP-939-101: The doctors made us get lots of checkups and we think they got scared so we got scared too. We had a really bad headache and the lights bothered us and so did noises. We wanted to find lots of cool water away from the bright lights until our headache went away.

SCP-939-101: They let us be in the dark and gave us lots of water, but the water made us itch all over. When we scratched, sometimes our skin came off. We were so scared. We kept asking for daddy, but he never showed up.

SCP-939-101: Eventually we didn't have any skin left, but it was ok because we didn't need it any more. We stopped itching after that. The lights stopped bothering us so much and the headache went away after

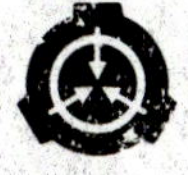

our old head came off. Lights still bother us, but not as much as they did. We don't see right anymore.

SCP-939-101: We got so hungry. It was bad, but we ate our old skin and our old head. It tasted good, but it was still bad. We were still hungry after that and asked for food. They gave us food, even our favorites, but none of it tasted right to us. All that tasted good was one piece of meat. We asked for more of that.

SCP-939-101: They locked two people in the dark with us. We asked them not to, but they didn't listen to us. We weren't hungry for a while after that, but we're hungry now.

SCP-939-101: We're very sorry. We know lying is wrong. We didn't mean it.

<End Log, 10:37 hrs>

INCIDENT REPORT AMN-C227-939

Effective immediately, use of AMN-C227 as an amnestic is suspended indefinitely.

On 01-30-1992, a statistical rate of missing persons reports more than ██ times the █████ national average was noted amongst civilians administered AMN-C227 following the capture of SCP-███ on 11-28-1990, two (2) kilometers northwest of █████ ███, █████, █████ Pending further investigation, use of AMN-C227 was suspended. On 01-31-1992, Field Agents █████, ███, and █████ were dispatched to the area to investigate. Through collaboration with local law enforcement, Agent ███ was able to secure an interview with J███ S███. Approximately seven months prior to the arrival of Field Agents, J███ S███ reported three individuals missing under suspicious circumstances; all had been previously administered AMN-C227.

Document# 939-73: J███ S███ Interview 1

Interviewed: J███ S███

Interviewer: Agent ███

Foreword: This interview is being conducted by myself, Agent █████ ███, in order to confirm or refute the possibility of a link between the disappearances of A███ M███ J███ B███ N███ and C███ W███ reported by Mr. J███ S███ on the 5th of June, 1991, and prior administration of AMN-C227 to all four named individuals on the 28th of November, 1990.

<Begin Log>

Agent ███: Thank you for taking the time to meet with me, Mr. S███. To begin, I'd like you to relate the events of June 5th in as much detail as you can.

J. S.: Ok… I called some friends, and we decided to go for a hike, just sort of fuck about in the woods, you know? It was a nice enough day out and we had nothing better to do. I remember [SUPERFLUOUS DIALOG REDACTED] Nothing seemed strange until I commented on a feeling of deja vu. A███ gave me a funny look and said she felt it too. We all did. M███ musta been the only smart one, he got creeped out and went home. The rest of us were curious and decided to look into it. I mean, when have you ever heard of five people all feeling deja vu at the same time?

Agent ███: Can't say I ever have. Please, continue.

J. S.: It got even stranger. The feeling of familiarity got stronger and stronger as we neared █████ ███.

Agent ███: █████ ███?

J. S.: Yeah, huge cave nearby. I don't think any of us had ever been inside before. We only had one flashlight, and it was dumb as hell in hindsight, but we went inside. The feeling kept getting stronger the further in we went. I know I keep calling it deja vu, but that's not the right way to put it. It was more of a general feeling of familiarity, not like this had happened before, but something about it was just familiar and nobody could put their finger on what. The deeper we went, the more familiar it felt, the more certain we felt we were getting closer. To what, I don't know, none of us knew, and that's why we kept going.

Agent ███: Did you find anything?

J. S.: No. Well, I don't know. I remember C█████ saying something about it getting late, that we should turn back. I don't remember anything after tha... that until I... I...

Agent ███: If you need to take a moment, that's fine.

J. S.: *(sobbing)* I... don't remember a fucking thi... thing until sit-ting on the side of the highway. It... it was dark out. An officer was as... as... asking me questions... telling me to st-ay calm un... until an ambulance a-rrived. I was all... cut up, screaming ab-about red, beg... begging the officer to let me g-go, I had to get... a-away.

Agent ███: Away from what?

J. S.: The red!

Agent ███: What was red?

J. S.: I... I d-don't remember.

Agent ███: What about your friends?

J. S.: Th-they weren't with me. They th-think I did it, w-won't list-en to me, said I w-was high on something, th-that I was c-coming down off a bad acid t-trip. Said I k-k-kept scream-ing at the ambulance's fl... flashing lights, that they w-were going to get me. I d-don't remember that... b-but red makes me f-feel uneasy now.

[SUPERFLUOUS DIALOG REDACTED]

<End Log>

Closing Statement: My team is ill-prepared to investigate further. We'll be returning to [REDACTED] in the morning to report our findings. A minimal coverup should be necessary, depending on what's found, at least for this particular incident. To this end, I suggest Mr. J███ S███ be strongly implicated in his friends' disappearances. Following his conviction, he could be recruited from the prison system as Clearance Level 0 janitorial staff and transferred to whatever installation can use him.

Agent ███ reported the possibility of an SCP-939 den in the area and an eradication detail was dispatched to investigate. SCP-939 presence was confirmed within ███████ ██ and destroyed by 02-06-1992.

On 02-20-1992, Dr. ██████ confirmed the sensation of familiarity reported by J███ S███ was solely attributable to a hitherto undocumented effect of a second exposure to aerosolized AMN-C227 following a first exposure of an individual to ECt. This sensation appears to act as a lure in those affected by AMN-C227, drawing them toward higher concentrations, most often centering around dens of SCP-939.

ADDENDUM 03-01-1992: AMN-C227-AIDED TRACKING OF SCP-939

AMN-C227-aided Tracking of SCP-939: *We can use this. Anyone exposed to a concentration high enough for temporary anterograde amnesia to manifest can stalk them like bloodhounds if they know to identify the misplaced sense of familiarity for what it is. Based on Agent █████'s retracing of the route Mr. J. S. and his friends followed, we know to expect an effective range of █ kilometers if we use this form of tracking. No, it can't find individual SCP-939, but it can guide us to their dens.*

I recommend we brief a number of field operatives on this plan. Any willing would then be exposed to AMN-C227 under controlled conditions and dispatched first to the locations of AMN-C227 use on civilian populations. Any errant sensation of familiarity experienced by these operatives will be taken as identification of an SCP-939 den nearby and reported as such. Eradication teams will be dispatched to investigate, destroying these dens as they are located.

After this has been accomplished, I believe the dispatch of these operatives to major population centers to facilitate their securing, coupled with standard monitoring of civilian, military, law enforcement, and [REDACTED] channels of information is the best course of action to locate and exterminate SCP-939 in the wild. - Dr. █████

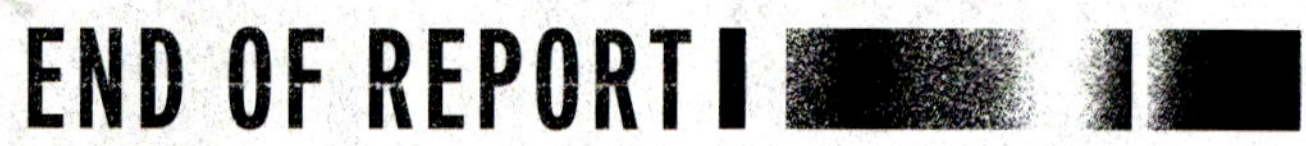

END OF REPORT

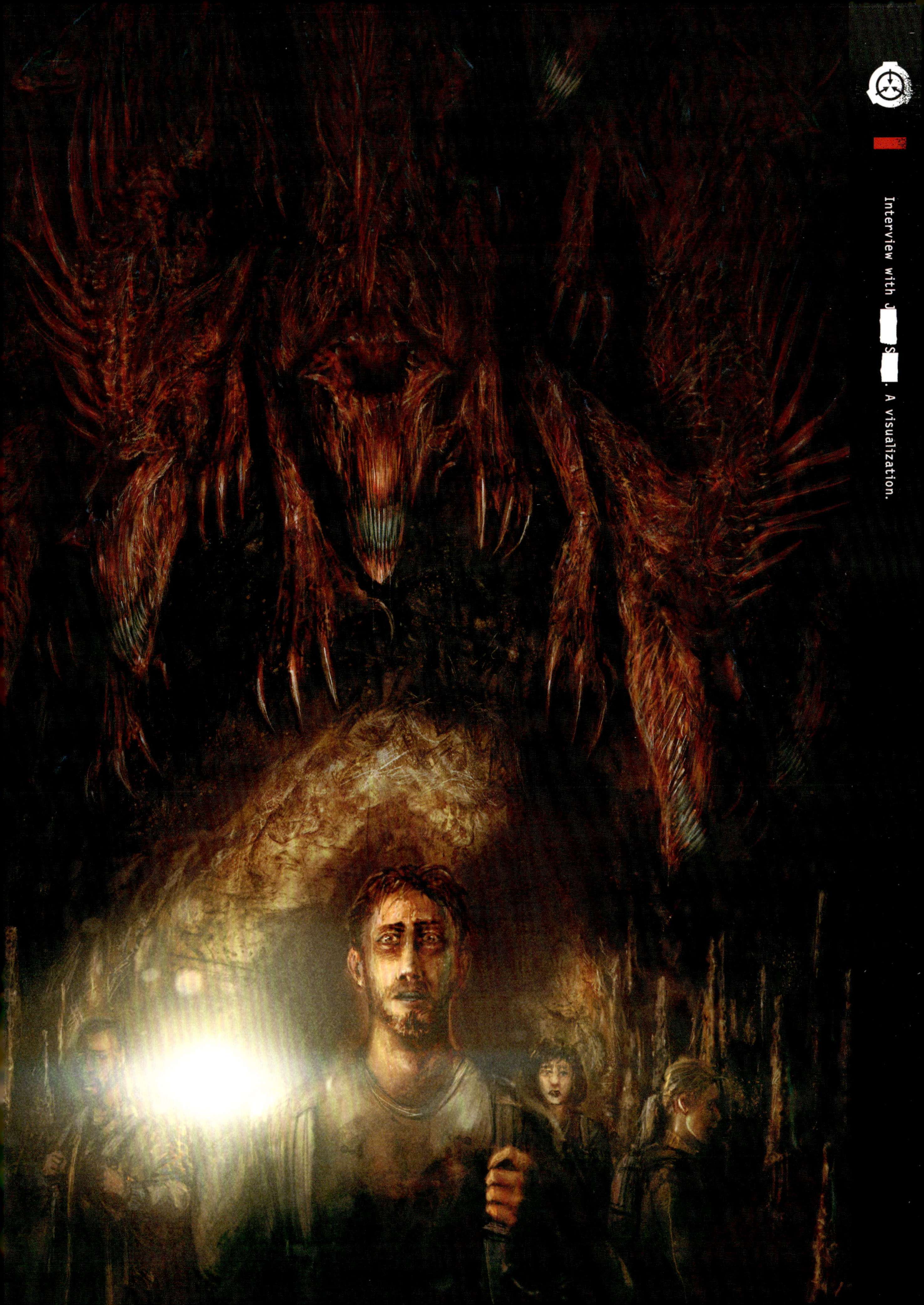

Interview with J█ S█. A visualization.

File >>> 938832

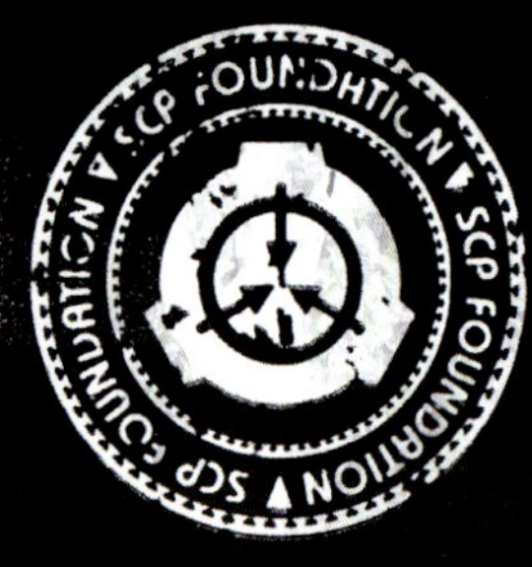

SCP-412

Title

MUTAGENIC MIRROR

Report by

RichardJ28

Picture by

Thomas Frank

Access the original report on

scp-wiki.wikidot.com/scp-412

Date

Class

SAFE

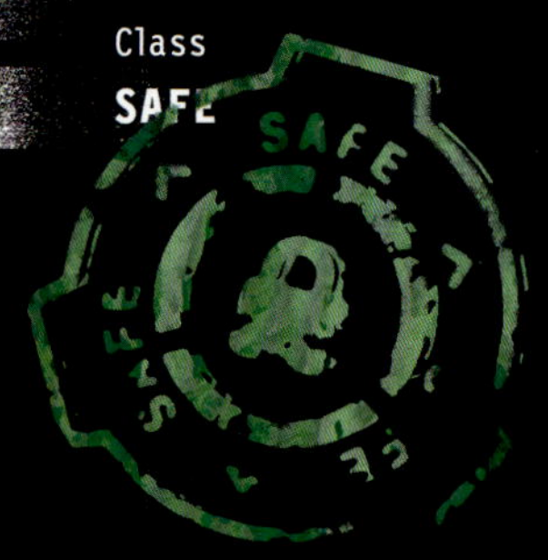

SPECIAL CONTAINMENT PROCEDURES

SCP-412 is currently contained within Storage Unit-11 at Site-19; removal of the item requires authorization by no fewer than three (3) personnel with Level-3 clearance, and may be vetoed by Site Security. Gloves should be worn when handling SCP-412 and the item should be transported in an opaque container.

Staff interaction must be carried out with full observance of Hazmat Protocol 7-R. Any and all staff making physical contact with or direct observation of SCP-412 will submit to a full physical examination. Anyone found to exhibit physical alteration will be remanded immediately to quarantine.

DESCRIPTION

SCP-412 is an antique silver hand mirror measuring 18 cm by 7 cm. The mirror has a 4 cm crack in the top left hand corner, and has an etched motif of roses and vines. Around ██% of subjects within direct line of sight of SCP-412 report a compulsion to pick up the item and view their reflection in it. There does not appear to be a discernible pattern to the 'selections' - testing for possible genetic, mental, or other selection markers is ongoing.

Simultaneous observation and contact with SCP-412 causes the item to 'connect' with the subject, regardless of whether they have been coerced into doing so by SCP-412. Tests using restrained subjects have shown that both actions (touching and viewing the reflection) are necessary for a connection to be made. No means of 'severing' this connection have been found, short of complete isolation for a period of no less than two years.

Connected subjects are compelled to repeatedly view their reflection in SCP-412, initially only once or twice a day. Viewing frequency increases over a period of several weeks. By around day 55, the amount of time subjects spend viewing their reflection typically begins to exceed all other activities, including sleep.

Each viewing causes biological alterations to the subject, beginning with minor physiological changes such as enlarged lymph nodes, facial rash, or skin discoloration. Although the exact pattern differs between subjects, by day 90 almost all subjects show downward extension of the ribcage, fixed open jaw by way of large cysts toward the rear of the mouth, and severely compromised reproductive and immune systems. Subjects also show a continual loss of memory recall ability and emotional response; fMRI scans have shown a marked decrease in activity in subjects' amygdalae and parietal lobes. Interviews have shown that subjects appear to have an obsession with an 'other', for whom they are being made 'ready'.

Subjects who survive to the advanced stages of alteration (in excess of ██ days) begin to exhibit marked changes in behavior, and more drastic physical alterations. These include the reorganisation of internal organs, leading to the creation of a small empty area inside the chest, increased mucus production, and changes in hormone production and [DATA EXPUNGED]. Autopsies on advanced-stage subjects have shown that the 'cavity' could theoretically support a separate life form. This led researchers to speculate that the alterations caused by SCP-412 intend to turn the human body into an 'environment suit' for a life-form unaccustomed to Earth's atmosphere. Authorised personnel should refer to Addendum 412-2 for further details.

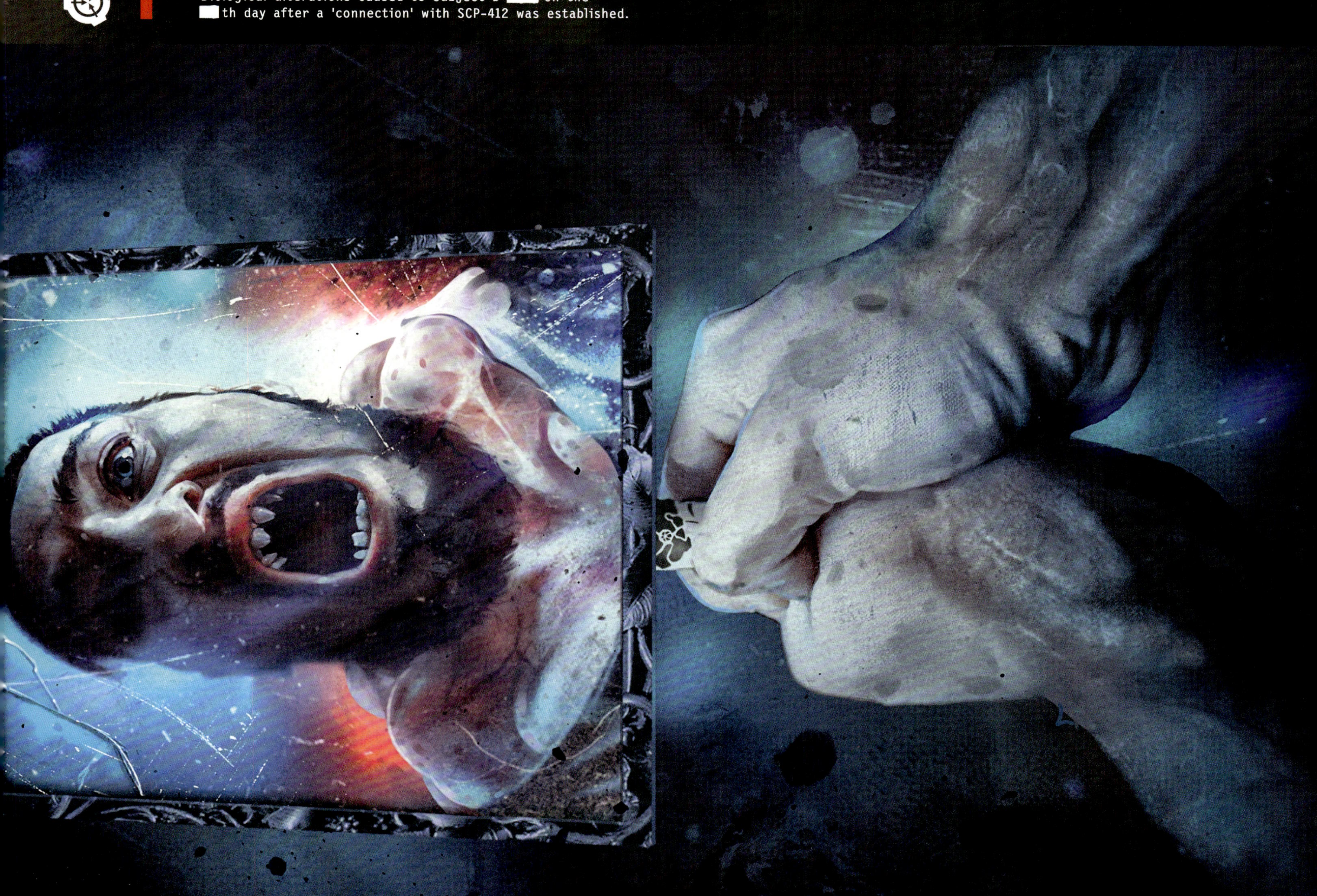

Biological alterations caused to Subject D-█ on the █th day after a 'connection' with SCP-412 was established.

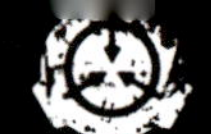

ADDENDUM 412-1: CIRCUMSTANCES OF RETRIEVAL

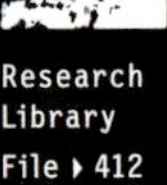

SCP-412 came to the attention of the Foundation following five unexplained deaths in ███████, ██, matching the pattern described above. Three of the deceased owned a hand mirror of a similar age (the design varied considerably); only one mirror had reasonably intact glass. Once it had been established that the mirror was responsible for the mutations, it was taken into Foundation custody. The remains of the other two mirrors showed no unusual properties and were disposed of.

Testing and observation has led researchers to theorize that SCP-412 is not the mirror itself, but is in fact an outside force that 'anchors' to mirrors. This theory is unproven, but any mirrors suspected of exhibiting similar behaviour must be acquired and contained.

ADDENDUM 412-2: EVENT 412-A

On ██/██/20██, Subject D-56653, 201 days after initial connection to SCP-412, ceased viewing his reflection and sat calmly in the corner of the quarantine room. Three hours later the subject began convulsing and clutching his chest - this continued for three minutes, after which time the subject lay immobile, apparently deceased. Once death had been confirmed, subject's corpse was taken for analysis. Pathologists found a small (8 cm) vaguely humanoid [REDACTED] within the artificial chest cavity. Organism had connected to the subject's blood supply and nervous system, and had begun to extend tendrils upward, puncturing the subject's trachea. Cells in the top ~5 cm of tendrils showed similarity to those in the optic organs of copepods, although with a much more complex structure. The origin of the organism and its cause of death are currently unknown.

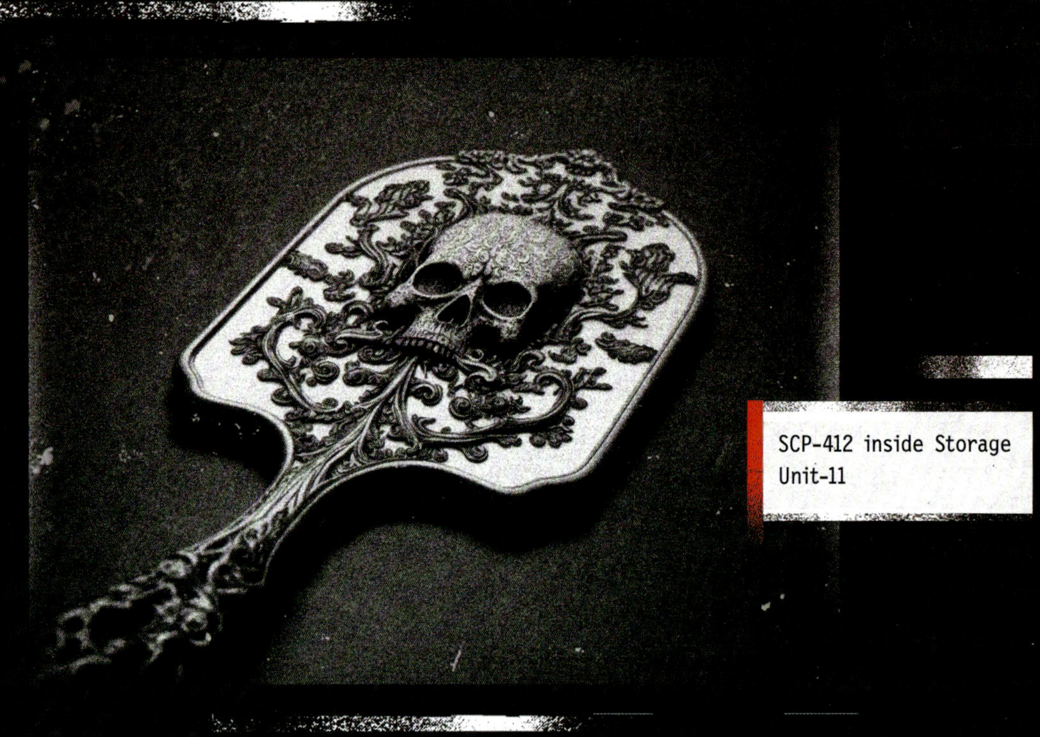

SCP-412 inside Storage Unit-11

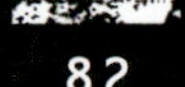

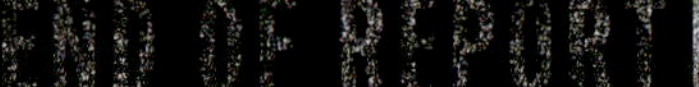

END OF REPORT

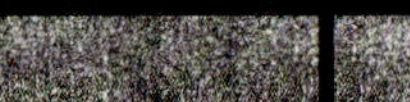

SPECIAL CONTAINMENT PROCEDURES

SCP-870 is to be contained in a sealed chamber measuring 8 m █ 8 m. Motion sensors are to be placed in the containment area and movements of SCP-870 are to be monitored at all times.

A motion activated turret is to be placed directly outside the containment area to prevent the escape of SCP-870. One (1) D-class personnel suffering from schizophrenia is to observe SCP-870 via camera at all times.

SCP-870 is to be provided with one (1) bovine carcass every forty-eight (48) hours.

DESCRIPTION

SCP-870 is an animal species of undetermined proportions and appearance, which, for unknown reasons, can only be perceived by individuals suffering from schizophrenia. This often results in specimens of SCP-870 being dismissed as hallucinations. Specimens of SCP-870 are omnivorous and seem to eat nearly all kinds of plants and meat, but will typically eat their food in secluded areas.

Notably, two people with the ability to perceive SCP-870 will describe its appearance in completely different ways, even when looking at the same specimen of SCP-870. Descriptions of SCP-870 have included:

- An alligator with spider legs and three eyes.
- A man made out of smoke.
- A giant ant with a human face.
- A hunchbacked child with a parrot's head.
- A spider with 'too many legs'.
- A giant centipede with human arms instead of legs.

Specimens of SCP-870 are highly predatory, and will typically stalk their prey for months and years without eating. It is unknown how they manage to last this time without succumbing to malnutrition. Eventually, at a seemingly random time when their prey is alone or in a secluded area, SCP-870 will kill and swallow their prey whole. (See Interview 870-1)

SCP-870's method of reproduction is currently unknown, but the journal of schizophrenic researcher ████ ███ speculates that they do not actually require sustenance to survive, and instead re-purpose the body of their victim into their young over a large period of time. This theory has not been verified, and research is underway to test it.

The specimen of SCP-870 currently in Foundation custody frequently attempts to breach containment, and has proven hostile to all personnel. Banging noises are audible from SCP-870's containment area at all hours of the day. Research is ongoing to find a way to perceive SCP-870 without being schizophrenic, but this may take a considerable length of time.

It is currently believed that there could be dozens, if not hundreds of SCP-870 in the world. They are a clear and present danger to the public, and steps must be taken to destroy or contain the species.

File >>> 0093312

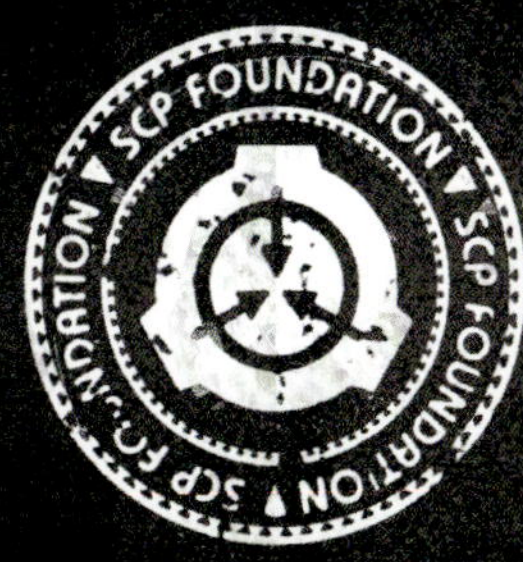

SCP-870

Title

THE MAYBE THERE MONSTERS

Report by

Tanhony

Picture by

Genocide Error

Access the original report on

scp-wiki.wikidot.com/scp-870

Date

█████

Class

KETER

KETER KETER KETER

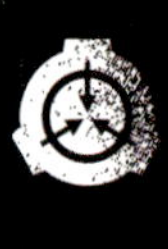

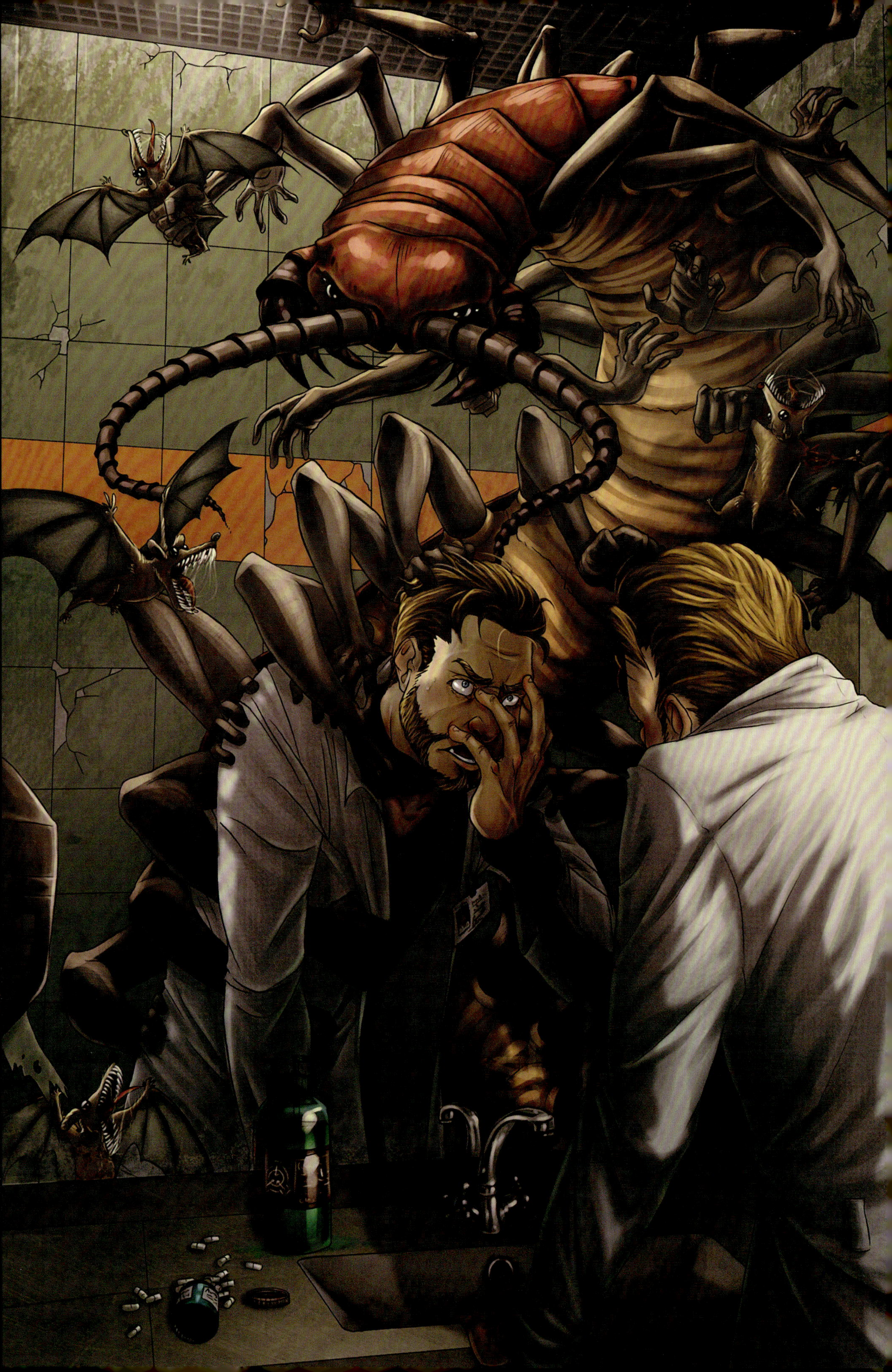

SCP-870's visualization created by Senior Researcher ██

INTERVIEW 870-1

Interviewed: Mr. █████

Interviewer: Dr. █████

Foreword: On ██/██/20██, Mr. █████ reported to police that he had killed a 'monster' at his home in ███ ███. Mr. █████ was later found to be schizophrenic and the Foundation, suspecting SCP-870 involvement, brought him in for interrogation.

<Begin Log>

Dr. █████: Hello, ███. How are you?

Mr. ████: Fi… I'm fine, fine. Who are you?

Dr. █████: I am Doctor █████. I'm just here to verify some details about what you told the police.

Mr. ████: Sure, I guess. Shoot.

Dr. █████: What did this 'monster' look like, can you describe it for me?

Mr. ████: Are you calling me a liar? It's true, I swear, it was there!

Dr. █████: Please, answer the question, ████.

Mr. ████: Sorry… sorry. Just kinda stressed. Well, it sort of looked like a spider, but with way… way too many legs. It was just running at me and screeching and I shot it.

Dr. █████: Was this the first time you'd seen the monster, █████?

Mr. ████: Um, uh…

Dr. █████: I'm sorry? Answer the question, please.

Mr. ████: I'd… I'd been seeing them everywhere. I'd been following them, seeing what they did. I needed to know they were real, you know?

Dr. █████: Understandable. Did you see anything important?

Mr. ████: One of the bastards was hunting this guy. I just saw it, outside his house, watching him. Me watching it watching him. Have… have you ever dropped something, then looked on the floor and it's gone?

Dr. █████: Certainly, why?

Mr. ████: It's not just gone. This guy, I saw him drop a ruler and that thing, it was under his desk, it just snatched it and ate it whole. Then a few days later, it ate him. Swallowed him whole.

Dr. █████: Well… thank you, ███. Miss ████ will see you out.

<End Log>

Closing Statement: Mr. █████ was dosed with a Class A amnestic and subsequently released. Worryingly, Mr. █████ implied that SCP-870 were present in a major population center. Further investigation is ongoing.

ADDENDUM 870-1

I, personally, don't believe that the schizophrenics are really seeing SCP-870 fully, they can just see it more than us. We don't see it because our brains aren't made to see it. The schizophrenics, their brains are wired up just that tiny bit differently, and they can see it just a tiny bit more. These things have the perfect camouflage, and we simply are unable to see through it. - Dr. █████

END OF REPORT

File >>> 0229334

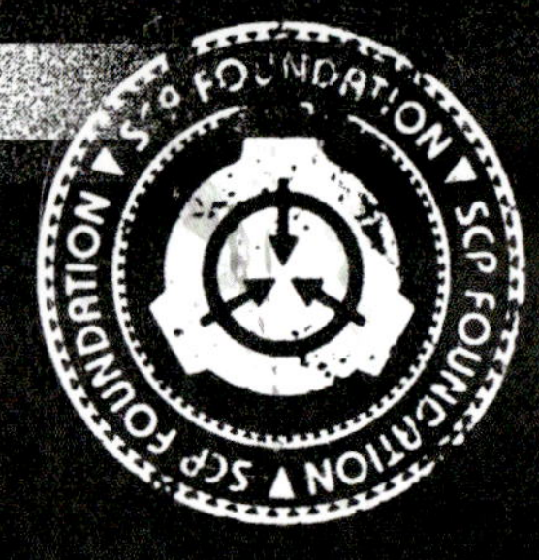

SCP-2264

Title

IN THE COURT OF ALAGADDA

Report by

Metaphysician

Pictures by

Allen Williams

David Romero

Access the original report on

www.scpwiki.com/ scp-2264

Date

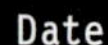

Class

SAFE

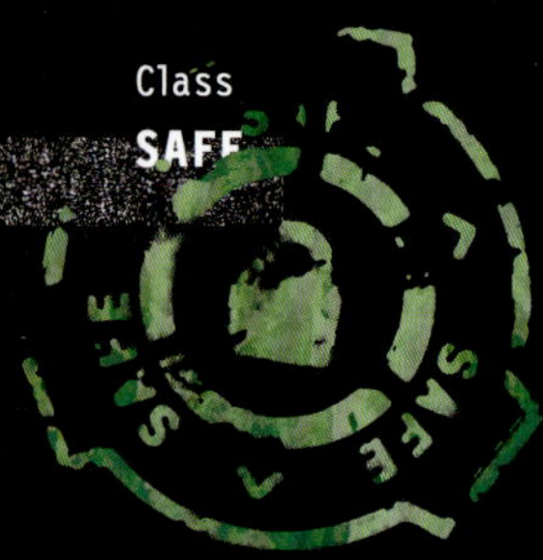

SPECIAL CONTAINMENT PROCEDURES

Due to the unavoidably public nature of the building housing SCP-2264-A, security measures are to focus on preventing civilian access to the anomaly's entrance. The Foundation is to cooperate with the government of the United Kingdom in concealing the existence of SCP-2264-A. A hidden passage to SCP-2264-A has been constructed and remains its only means of access. The original entrance to the room where SCP-2264-A is located has been walled over, ensuring that only authorized personnel have access to SCP-2264-A. Operatives are to be reassigned and replaced monthly due to the threat of psychological addiction to SCP-2264-B.

DESCRIPTION

SCP-2264-A is a door composed of iron located within a hidden chamber beneath Martin Tower, a part of the Tower of London.[1] The gateway cannot be unlocked through traditional means, requiring a highly ritualized process. Attached to SCP-2264-A is a complex apparatus composed of alchemical tools such as alembics, retorts, and a crucible.

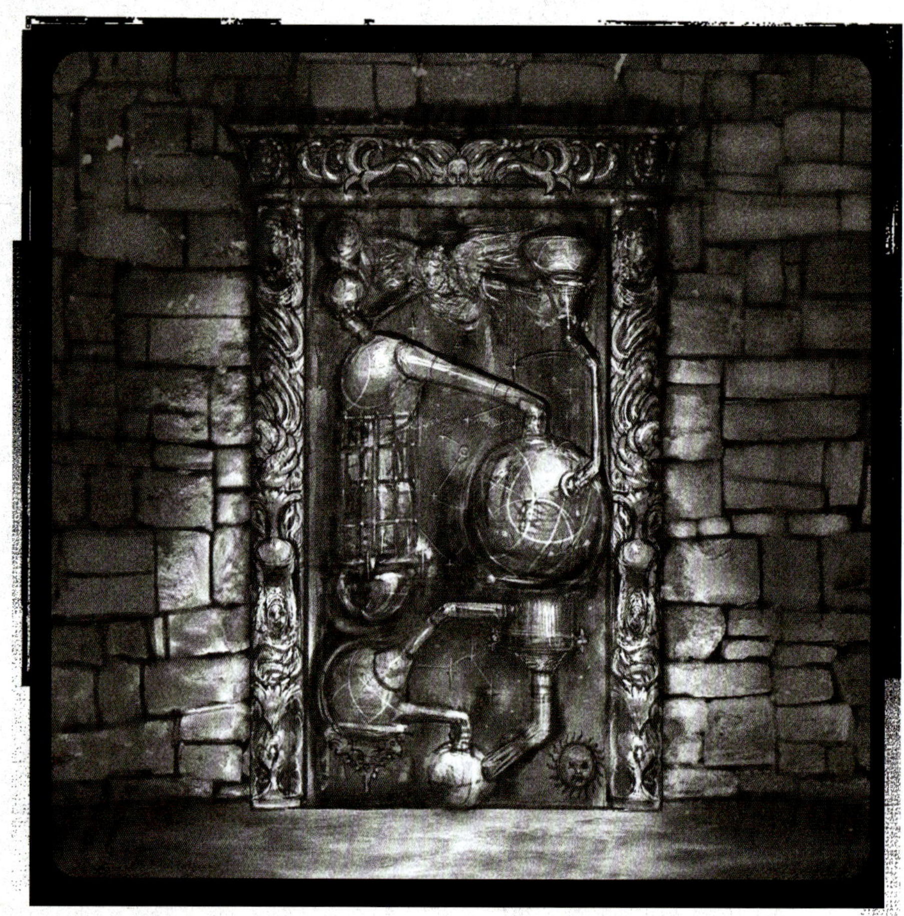

1. Also known as Her Majesty's Royal Palace and Fortress.

Based on journals found within the hidden chamber, SCP-2264-A[2] is presumably the creation of Henry Percy (27 April 1564 – 5 November 1632), 9th Earl of Northumberland, an English aristocrat, alchemist, and long-term prisoner within the Tower of London. Despite his incarcerated status, the Earl maintained a degree of influence, said to enjoy a comfortable lifestyle and allowed access to books and research material. He was known as The Wizard Earl due to his extensive library and interests in the scientific and occult.

It is considered possible that others within Percy's circle of associates were involved in the creation of SCP-2264-A, including John Dee, famed alchemist and court astrologer of Queen Elizabeth. The School of Night,[3] of which Henry Percy was supposedly member to, may have also had involvement.

JOURNAL OF HENRY PERCY, THE WIZARD EARL

nigredo:
we wilt confront the dark night of the soul – the [pineal gland] wilt be freshly extract'd. fire evokes the shadow within.

albedo:
wash aroint the impurities – rain cleanses all sin and prepares the soul f'r Elysium. divide, not as dictat'd by the rigors of harmony, but rather into two opposing principles to be later coagulat'd to form a unity of opposites.

citrinitas:
victory coincides with the yellowing of the lunar consciousness. the white surrenders to dawn; the travelling lamp slays the moon.

rubedo:
red alludes; instead, surrender upon the apparatus a sanguine sacrifice.

A Foundation alchemist was consulted. The instructions are roughly comparable with the magnum opus; a four-part process employed in the creation of the mythical philosopher's stone. Replication of this procedure required [REDACTED].[4]

Through still undetermined means, a mechanism within SCP-2264-A responds to the completed solution, causing it to unlock and open - allowing access to SCP-2264-B.

SCP-2264-B is an extradimensional city which does not correspond to any known location, earthly or otherwise. Objects that originate from within SCP-2264-B will dematerialize if brought through SCP-2264-A. Such objects have been later found returned to the site of their initial removal.

Those who enter SCP-2264-B report having all personal belongings removed and their clothes replaced. Manifested outfits are said to resemble those worn at masquerade balls, most especially those associated with the Carnival of Venice, and will dematerialize upon exit of SCP-2264-B. Masks cannot be removed while inside SCP-2264-B but the rest of the attire can be discarded if one chooses to do so. The majority of SCP-2264-B

2. Frequently referred to in notes as a Janus Gate. Janus is the Roman deity of beginnings and transitions, thereby associated with doors, doorways, gates, and passages.

3. A secret society interested in the study of science, philosophy, and religion; members were suspected of atheism, at the time not only considered blasphemous but an act of treason and anarchy.

4. To request this information, please contact the Department of Alchemical Studies.

inhabitants are dressed and adorned in a similar fashion; agents have reported a somewhat organic quality to their costumes, frequently describing it as "chitinous". The most common inhabitants of SCP-2264-B are roughly humanoid and have since have been classified as SCP-2264-1.

The sky has been described as yellow and containing an indeterminate number of black stars, corresponding with no known or even hypothesized constellations. Buildings are shaped in such a manner as to suggest them being carved from a single seamless material. Black, white, yellow, and red are the only colors to reportedly occur within SCP-2264-B. Architecture is non-euclidean and the normal laws of gravity do not apply,[5] thus inhabitants can be observed as climbing a stairway upside-down, but based on their own gravity source, they are climbing normally.

The city has been described as having the odor of "dried flowers with a hint of mold", or a scent "not unlike that of old books". The actual size of the city has been difficult to measure but it appears to be located on an island, surrounded by a black ocean, the composition of the liquid is unknown but described as appearing more viscous than water.

Operatives have reported a hypnagogic malaise while exploring SCP-2264-B, with difficulty estimating time and space. Although SCP-2264-B is a tangible location and not considered to be an actual dream, those who had a history of lucid dreaming have shown far greater self-control and attention to detail than those who did not. Operatives are to be reassigned and replaced monthly due to the threat of psychological addiction to SCP-2264-B. Initial efforts at exploration resulted in eight AWOL operatives with those that returned having difficulty describing what they had observed in a coherent and/or detailed manner.

EXPLORATION REPORT █/██/████: DR. CALIXTO NARVÁEZ (1ST DEPLOYMENT)

The almost hypnagogic nature of SCP-2264-B has led many to observe it as a dream or hallucination, failing to fully recognize its inherent verisimilitude. A lucid dreamer and an experienced user of hallucinogenics, I (Dr. Calixtó Narvaez), was well chosen for this mission. My comrades quickly surrendered to the anomaly, engaging in the decadent pleasures of the city; most especially within the palace.

Tempting as it was, I did not join the others in their rapturous orgy. I would suggest interviewing those that previously entered SCP-2264-B again; it is unlikely they've gone into all the details. When allowed a chance to directly control a dream, so many claim they would fly or visit the stars; those people are liars. Most choose to surrender to the ecstatic delirium of sexual pleasure.

Again, this is not a dream, but I am able to understand why most are unable to perceive the difference. I am reminded of the legend of the Hassassins, how their leader supposedly drugged and led his recruits into his castle; within was a pleasure garden that rivaled any imagined paradise – the individuals truly believed they were offered a taste of the divine. SCP-2264-B works in a somewhat similar way but I do not believe that is the reason for its splendor. I doubt it is intended to be a trap. It is simply a city (although certainly a majestic city unlike anything I had ever before encountered) but one that happens to exist outside baseline reality and does not entirely conform to the physical rules we are used to.

I have made significant discoveries while exploring SCP-2264-B:

1. Universal translation of language – while most of the agents perceive the inhabitants as speaking English, I heard them in my native tongue of Spanish. Even those of my team, when communicating with me directly, appeared to have been speaking Spanish while within the anomaly. I have discovered that this is also applied to written language but not quite as accurately.

5. This may be caused by multiple gravity wells within the city but this cannot be directly measured.

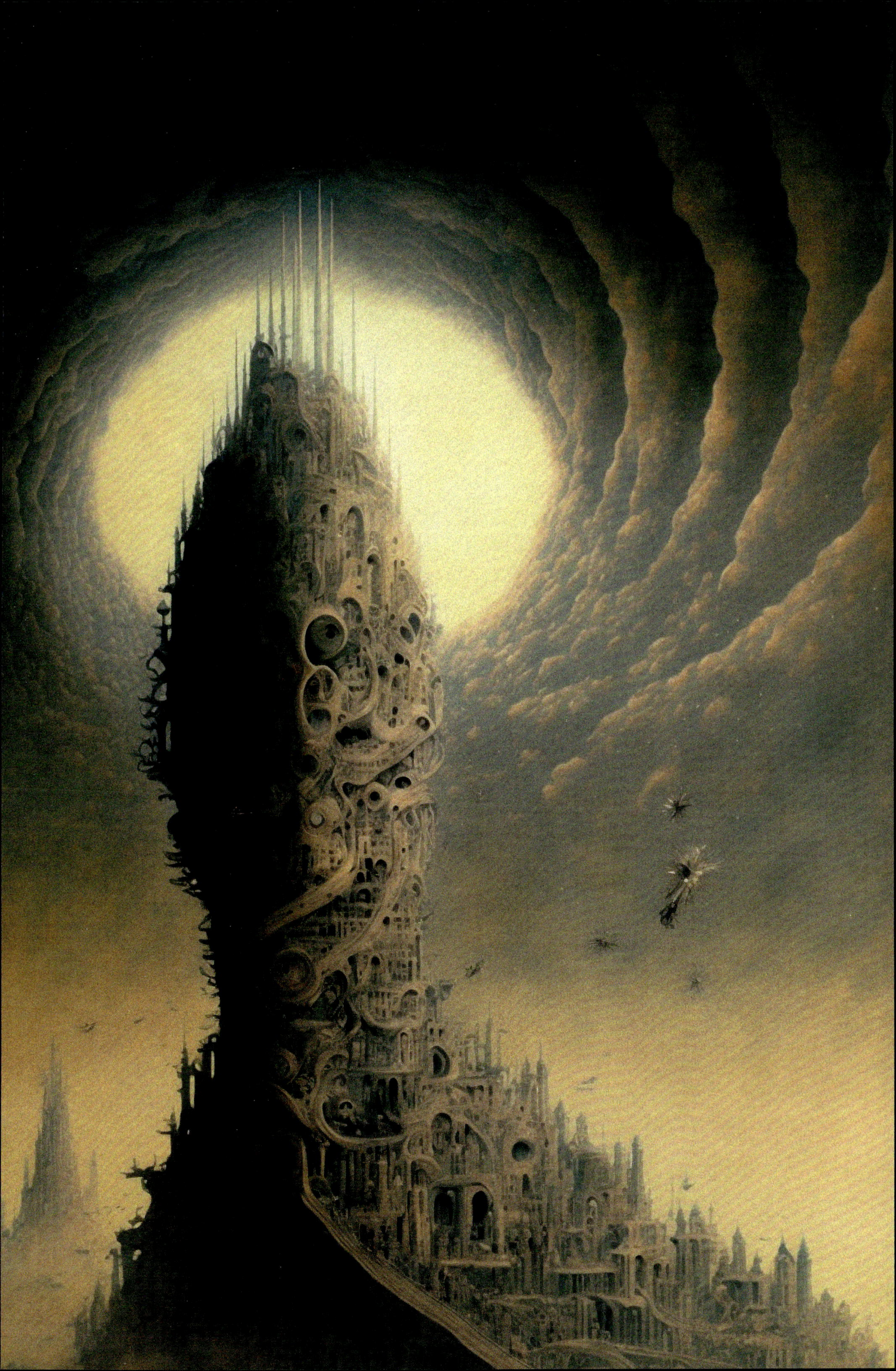

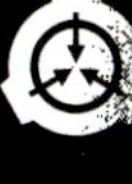

Research Library File ▸ 2264

Written words initially appear as alien shapes; most of the symbols having a somewhat spiral-like pattern. If one continues to directly observe the symbols, they will begin to blur and alter until some level of translation has manifested. However, there do appear to be limitations and it seems that some words native to SCP-2264-B have no equivalent in any human language. The words appear to move on paper and prolonged exposure can easily result in nausea and headache.

2. The true name of SCP-2264-B is Alagadda, a city-state said to border the Nevermeant.[6] I was able to gather much of this information from the Wandsman of Kul-Manas, a scholar and foreigner like myself. They wore a beaked mask and exquisite robes cloaked their hunchbacked form; their hands were scaly (more avian than reptilian) with black talons. They unfurled a scroll before me, said it was a map of the multiverse – layer after layer of endless spirals – I sense an oncoming migraine just thinking about it now.

Regardless, I was pleased to meet a fellow intellectual within. I asked them about the nature of their research. "What is the nature of all that is?" they asked, I assumed rhetorically. "Just for a start," they noted.

3. There is a specific power structure within SCP-2264-B, involving entities that, based on description, could easily be considered some of the more dangerous reality benders known to the Foundation. The Wandsman of Kul-Manas warned of individuals that should not even be approached, less we draw undesirable attention to our reality.

There are (or were) four Masked Lords who directly oversee SCP-2264-B:

The Black Lord, Wearer of the Anguished Mask
The White Lord, Wearer of the Diligent Mask
The Yellow Lord, Wearer of the Odious Mask
The Red Lord, Wearer of the Mirthful Mask

They were said to be the chief advisors to the King of Alagadda. They continued to warn that I not be fooled by their names; each just as terrible as the other. I have seen the Masked Lords, always at a distance, all except the Wearer of the Anguished Mask. I was informed that the Black Lord was the victim of a political struggle some time ago (the reason never known, if reason existed at all) and cast into some dreadful dimensional backwater. It would only be a matter of time before they returned.

The insidious glamour of the city-state disguises a dreadful truth, one the Wandsman had difficulty expressing in words. They stated that most outsiders came to this place to seek a boon from the King. They refused to speak anymore of this entity and suggested I avoid the Ambassador of Alagadda as well, before politely taking their leave of me.

I decided it time to report back, gathered the others (pulling a few from the writhing mound of masked transdimensional entities); the first door we entered was the one to return us to baseline reality. I suspect that SCP-2264-B is a dimensional nexus, connected to countless worlds across the multiverse. Every door used within SCP-2264-B has connected directly to SCP-2264-A. If there are other gateways like SCP-2264-A, I suspect them to be currently sealed.

Dr. Calixto Narváez was commended for his initiative. A psychological evaluation has determined it safe for him to reenter in the near future, although it has been requested that he use a more professional tone with regards to his reports. Future operatives will be screened for higher than normal levels of activity in the parietal lobes while in a state of altered consciousness (sleep or otherwise).

The "Wandsman of Kul-Manas" has since been classified as SCP-2264-2 and is considered an invaluable source of information. The "Masked Lords of Alagadda" have been classified as SCP-2264-3.

6. Meaning remains unknown.

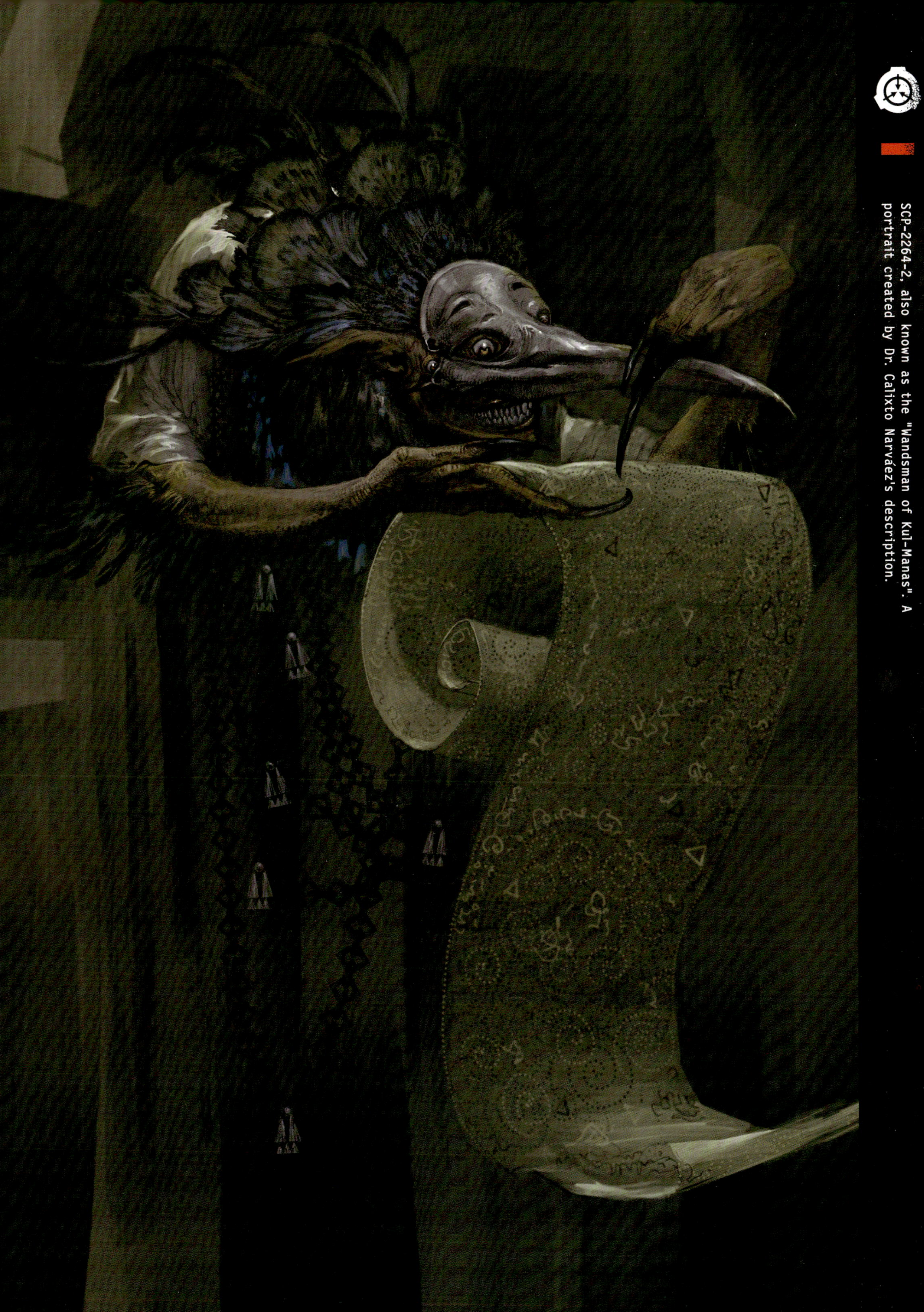

SCP-2264-2, also known as the "Wandsman of Kul-Manas". A portrait created by Dr. Calixto Narváez's description.

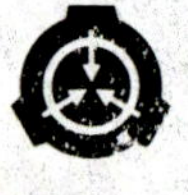

Research Library File ▸ 2264

EXPLORATION REPORT ██/██/████: DR. CALIXTO NARVÁEZ (2ND DEPLOYMENT)

I believe SCP-2264-2 is the only entity we might truly trust in Alagadda and sought them immediately. The city contains thousands, if not millions, but SCP-2264-2 stands out and appears to have a strictly scholarly interest in SCP-2264-B – most especially the palace library.

The collection was impressive and could have been infinite in size for all I knew (there was no visible end to the room, the corridor stretching long into the horizon). I wandered the seemingly endless hall, Agent Cromwell and Dr. Yu at my side, in search of SCP-2264-2. I scanned through a few grimoires and scrolls, the alien symbols failing to translate (leading me to suspect that no earthly translation was possible).

In time we found SCP-2264-2, affable as before and expressing concern about our well-being. I asked that they elaborate and I write their response as best as my memory allows:

"The Ambassador of Alagadda will soon return from Adytum and only the mad shall remain. I suggest you leave posthaste, for I intend the same."

I thanked them for their warning and declared that we would not linger for long. I asked them about Adytum. They replied:

"A terrible city, filled with equally terrible people. It is said that the Grand Karcist of Adytum serves the designs of an elder being, a horror thought to rival even the Hanged King of Alagadda. Craw! (SCP-2264-2 made a sound not unlike a crow) I should not speak of them. Not here."

I asked about who they were (SCP-2264-2), wanting to know more about them. They replied:

"I am the Wandsman of Kul-Manas. A scholar, as you undoubtedly know. I am a walker of the astral plane, a sailor of the celestial sea, and a spelunker of the planar deep."

SCP-2264-2 noted something about our "aura"; declaring it rare across the multiverse but admitted to having encountered similar during previous visits to SCP-2264-B. They said something along the lines of:

"The Deathless Merchant of London; driven by greed and black ambition. There was another; a stranger in a strange land. It appeared as though they did not know where they were, smelling of fear. I cannot imagine how one might accidentally stumble upon Alagadda, I did not believe such a thing was possible. They vanished soon after yet I never witnessed them leave. Simply gone in a blink."

They would continue to reference the "Karcists" and "Clavigers" of Adytum, stating that they "reeked of decay and embryonic fluid". That was the extent of people encountered with a similar "aura" to our own; I suspect SCP-2264-2 is able to sense a person's "dimensional neighborhood". SCP-2264-2 turned their head completely around (somewhat like an owl) and cawed, declaring:

"I sense the Ambassador of Alagadda has returned. I take my leave of this place and I suggest you do the same. Flee; do not delay. Perhaps I will pay your realm a visit in the future."

SCP-2264-2 exited the nearest door. The door refused to budge but I suspect it connected SCP-2264-2 to their native dimension. We exited the library, walking quickly (not wishing to bring too much attention upon ourselves by running). We found an unlocked door and returned home. We never saw the ambassador or their king, but I feel it best that we not seek them out.

> Although not directly encountered, the Ambassador of Alagadda and the King of Alagadda have been respectively classified as SCP-2264-4 and SCP-2264-5.

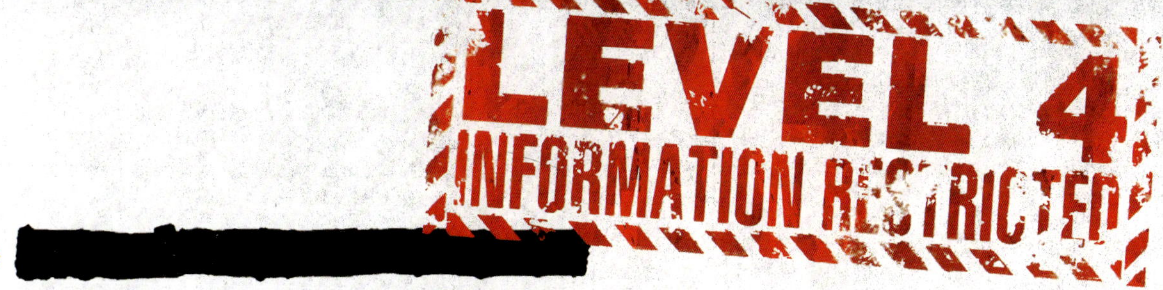

LEVEL 4
INFORMATION RESTRICTED

[redacted]

The 05 Council voted 10 to 3 in support of sending Mobile Task Force Psi-9 ("Abyss Gazers") into SCP-2264-B. The goal of the operation was to locate SCP-2264-4 and SCP-2264-5 and calculate the level of threat they represented to humanity, Earth, and local dimensional space. Twelve agents, trained in hand-to-hand combat and Counter Occult Stratagems (COS), entered SCP-2264-A on [redacted] at 08:00.

One agent returned alive; the rest are presumed dead or otherwise irretrievable.

Interviewed: Agent Alexander Papadopoulos

Interviewer: Dr. Laxmi Narang

Foreword: Agent Papadopoulos was found to be in critical condition upon their exit of SCP-2264, losing consciousness soon after. A physical examination revealed fractured bones throughout the entirety of their body and extensive internal bleeding. After three weeks of hospitalization, Agent Papadopoulos was deemed healthy enough for interview.

<Begin Log>

Dr. Laxmi Narang: I know it might be difficult but please tell me what you are able to remember.

Agent Alexander Papadopoulos: The city was remarkable. Command prepped us for it as best they could but words fail to do it justice. We all had the appearance of harlequins or something out of a 17th century masquerade. Wasn't exactly the same but close enough. Couldn't take the masks off, hard as we tried. We had a mission to complete but the details were quite vague.

Dr. Laxmi Narang: Vague?

Agent Alexander Papadopoulos: Find SCP-2264-4 and -5; get an estimate on their threat level. We knew they were important to SCP-2264 but we had no idea what they looked like or how to locate them.

Dr. Laxmi Narang: Go on.

Agent Alexander Papadopoulos: Right. Well. We found the palace. Don't know how long it took. Time was kind of impossible to tell in that place. The city is full of people, especially that palace, but it didn't feel like being in a busy city in our world. There was something different about it but I don't know how else to describe it. Not important I guess.

Things blurred a lot. Everything seemed to follow a sort of dream logic.

Dr. Laxmi Narang: Dream logic?

Agent Alexander Papadopoulos: Yeah. I mean. It wasn't a dream, I'm certain of that. And I have the scars to prove it. It was all real but have you ever noticed how dreams rush through the details? You end up one place but don't really recall how? It was like that. I remember the masquerade; the music and the dancing... oh, and the fucking. All with their masks on, of course. Still adorned with their masks. Seeing some of them nude made us aware of just how much was an elaborate costume. Their skin was like porcelain. You could sort of tell those were the natives. You know, SCP-2264-1. But the more you stared, the less human everyone seemed; some had too many limbs, some had too few – like, snake people – was similar to monsters in an old fantasy comic I read as a kid.

Sorry. Rambling. Head hurts trying to remember. *[distracted]* I can't move my arms or legs. What's wrong with them?

Dr. Laxmi Narang: The numbness is just a side effect of your medication. Please focus on my questions.

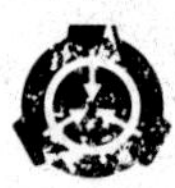

Research Library File ▸ 2264

Agent Alexander Papadopoulos: Okay. If you say so. I remember having to pull Agent Maher away from some woman; wasn't attacking him, quite the opposite. Couldn't blame him. She had curves in all the right places – made it easy to ignore the tentacles.

So, the twelve of us stick together. Hard to not look like you're out for trouble with that many. Anyway, we wandered around the palace and it was like a labyrinth; I honestly wouldn't have been surprised if we walked into a minotaur or something. We spent most of the time descending the stairs, I think? I remember feeling like we were traveling deeper and deeper…

And then, somehow, just when we thought we had reached the bottom, we're back outside. It looked like we were in exactly the same spot as when we first entered SCP-2264-B. Hell, we could all see the palace in the distance.

But something was different. Everything was dark, drained of color. Like, we could see and all but it was a hazy gray twilight. The streets were empty and the buildings looked… ruined? Yeah. Was like the whole city was abandoned long ago. Desolate and silent; not a sound but our own footsteps.

We entered this iteration of the palace. Everything was identical, architecturally speaking.

That was when we started to hear the whispers. It spoke in a language I had never heard before. I could feel it slithering into my ear, penetrating my brain…

We… *[hesitates, his eyes grow damp with tears]*

Dr. Laxmi Narang: Please continue.

Agent Alexander Papadopoulos: We destroyed ourselves.

Dr. Laxmi Narang: …What?

Agent Alexander Papadopoulos: We didn't want to but we had no choice. The Ambassador of Alagadda – it found us. It didn't have a face; no mouth, nose, or eyes. I thought it was wearing a skintight outfit and… high heels? That is what it looked like at first but no… that was its body. Its flesh was black. It stood tall, lithe and androgynous, and so.. so…

Dr. Laxmi Narang: Please, this information is important. Pace yourself. We can stop if…

Agent Alexander Papadopoulos: *[interrupting]* It stood so damn proud. Just radiating arrogance. I couldn't understand a word it said and yet every syllable dripped with narcissistic venom. It brought a hand to where a mouth should have been… and it laughed and laughed… and then we destroyed ourselves for its amusement.

Bones were shattered, flesh and organs ruptured. All for its amusement, we ruined ourselves in body and mind. And the whole time, we screamed and begged yet only silence parted our lips. I'm so sorry, I tried to say, I'm so sorry… their eyes pleaded for mercy and asked for forgiveness.

In the end, I was the only one left alive – surrounded by the corpses of my ravaged friends and comrades. I understand now. The Ambassador needed a witness, one to deliver its message. To tell you this… and… *[pauses; begins to hyperventilate]*

Dr. Laxmi Narang: Please continue.

Agent Alexander Papadopoulos: I watched the ceiling move as it dragged my broken body from room to room. Eventually we stopped and it lifted me into the air, held me up before the throne. There I saw the King. It was anchored in place, hallowed bonds around its corpse-like hands and throat – its face hidden beneath a veil.

Impish creatures crawled all over it, caressing its twitching body as if intending comfort while others pulled the tethers even tighter. The King trembled and quivered and I saw pale tendrils slither in and out of its tattered robes. I looked on as the veil was lifted… *[a change in tone suggesting lucidity]* I want to die. I can't live with what I've done. Please kill me. End this. I can't feel my legs. I can't feel my arms. Not like this. Not like this. Please, I'm begging you…

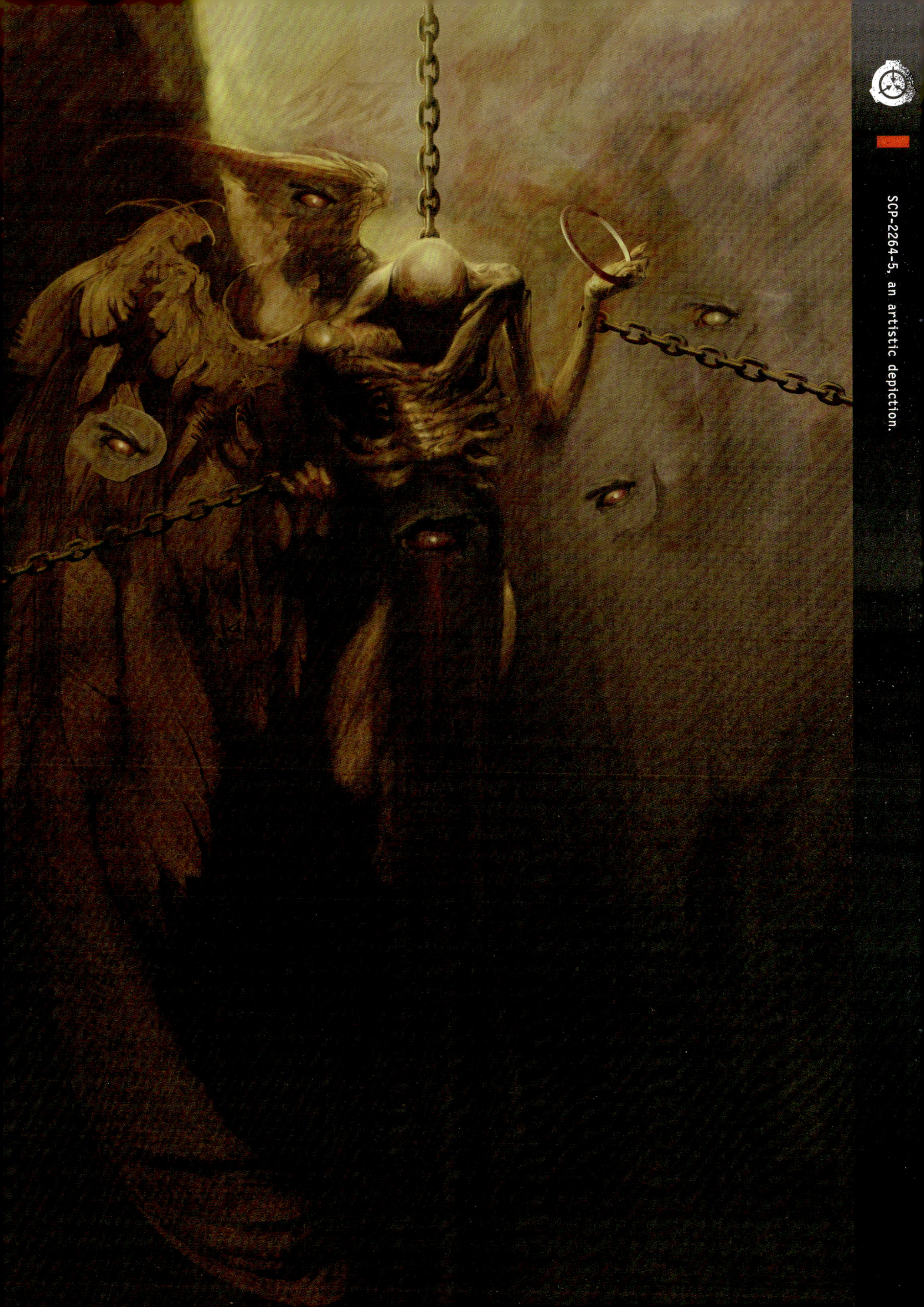

SCP-2264-5, an artistic depiction.

Research Library File ▸ 2264

Dr. Laxmi Narang: You know I am not allowed to do anything of the sort. Please tell me what you saw.

Agent Alexander Papadopoulos: *[emotionless]* A god shaped hole. The barren desolation of a fallen and failed creation. You see the light of long dead stars. Your existence is nothing but an echo of a dying god's screams. The unseen converges. Surrounds you. And it tightens like a noose.

<End Log>

Operations involving SCP-2264 are suspended until further notice. The agent's request for termination has been denied. Due to the considerable damage suffered, amputation of both arms and legs was deemed necessary, and subject is no longer able to perform most biological functions without the aid of life support systems. He is to be restrained for his own protection (despite his loss of limbs, suicide attempts have been made) and thoroughly interrogated for all possible information related to SCP-2264. Due to his contact with SCP-2264-4 and SCP-2264-5, he is to be quarantined and carefully observed for signs of anomaly. Agent Papadopoulos has refused food and water, requiring the use of feeding tube.

ADDENDUM

SCP-2264 was discovered accidentally during the refurbishment of Martin Tower in ██/██/████ The Foundation was contacted by representatives of the Crown due to the suspicion of a potentially anomalous artifact based on the writings found within, since attributed to Henry Percy, 9th Earl of Northumberland. Discovered among his notes was an unsent letter, intended to be received by Christopher Marlowe, famed poet and playwright. The letter is dated 30 May 1593, the day of Christopher Marlowe's unsolved murder.

Document 2264-0037

To my singular goode Friend, may this Missive reach thee ere 'tis too late.

'Twas thou who urg'd against my building of the Janus Gate. My Insult was cruell, having deem'd thee foolish and ignorant of the Sciences: I prithee forgive mine Arrogance.

'Twas thou who suffer'd the Evil to which I was blind. I show'd thee the Other Ordinary, and allow'd the secret Darknesse to coil around the Cinder of thy beautiful Heart. I was blind, but now I see.

I beseech thee to burn that accurs'd Play and return it to Ashe. Thy Patron seeks to corrupt and defile: Whence He cometh, there are Things that simply should not be. The Ambassador shall exploit thee, as they did us. I have seal'd the Janus Gate so that only the Enlighten'd may enter. May they have the Wisdom to see what I coulde not, and the Power to slay the wretch'd King within.

Damn that Metropolis of Blood, that terrible Realm and its antient countless Crimes. Consign thy Play to the Fire, deny thy vile Patron, and aroint thee from this Madnesse. We would fain welcome thee backe into the Night.

Seems likely the play being referred to here is SCP-701. Script should be investigated for more information on Alagadda

Dr. NKiru Diawara

END OF REPORT

SPECIAL CONTAINMENT PROCEDURES

Containment of SCP-2002 is to concentrate on the coordinated dissemination of misinformation to all organizations and individuals concerned with the discovery, tracking, study and/or discussion of (mobile) astronomical objects. Special focus is to be put on the manipulation of relevant fringe organizations in order to obfuscate the nature of SCP-2002.

Images of SCP-2002 leaked to the public in any manner are to be dismissed as digitally altered, and to be labeled the work of conspiracy theorists. To this purpose, Foundation-employed experts are to be put forward for appearances in related media and as consultants for any external research projects.

For more information concerning specific current, past and future disinformation campaigns, please refer to document SecInf/2002-D/DepDI:rev2.41. Use of deadly force has been authorized in order to keep information concerning SCP-2002 from being publicized in any way.

All collected wreckage of SCP-2002 and the remains of its crew are to be housed at Site-102 for further research into SCP-2002's origins. Please contact current project lead Dr. Signov for more information on this project.

Rem/SIGN01/20060217: Please note that despite the neutralization of SCP-2002, these containment procedures are to stay in effect indefinitely.

DESCRIPTION

SCP-2002 was a spacefaring vessel on a direct collision course with Earth. Following detection, Foundation deep space assets managed to relay several images indicating numerous similarities between SCP-2002's design and designs under development [DATA EXPUNGED] established at that time. In light of this, and taking into account data collected from its wreckage, SCP-2002 was classified as a temporal continuity anomaly, but was considered native to this reality iteration. Its neutralization has prevented project staff from verifying this, though examination of SCP-2002 wreckage has yielded evidence supporting this theory.

SCP-2002 had a spherical hull with an estimated diameter of 450 m. Attached to this main hull were ~3000 smaller spheres with an approximate diameter of 1.7 m. SCP-2002 did not show any visible propulsion devices or external systems for power generation, nor were individual compartments or systems such as a cockpit, living quarters, storage hold, etcetera discernible.

All attempts at communication using Foundation SETI installations were answered by an automated broadcast from SCP-2002, on a radio frequency specifically reserved for Foundation traffic. Signals sent by non-Foundation installations did not elicit a response from SCP-2002, suggesting an awareness of the hailing signal's origin. Please see Addendum 2002-A-04 for a transcript of this automated broadcast.

On review, the message broadcast by SCP-2002 appeared to imply that SCP-2002 possessed systems to facilitate a return to Earth unaided. Regardless, SCP-2002 was classified as Keter due to the potential effects of its landing should this assumption prove false. SCP-2002 maintained a steady velocity of 12.5 km/s and was expected to reenter Earth's atmosphere on ██/██/20██. Protocols for dealing with any possible K-Class scenario as a result of SCP-2002's return were drafted.

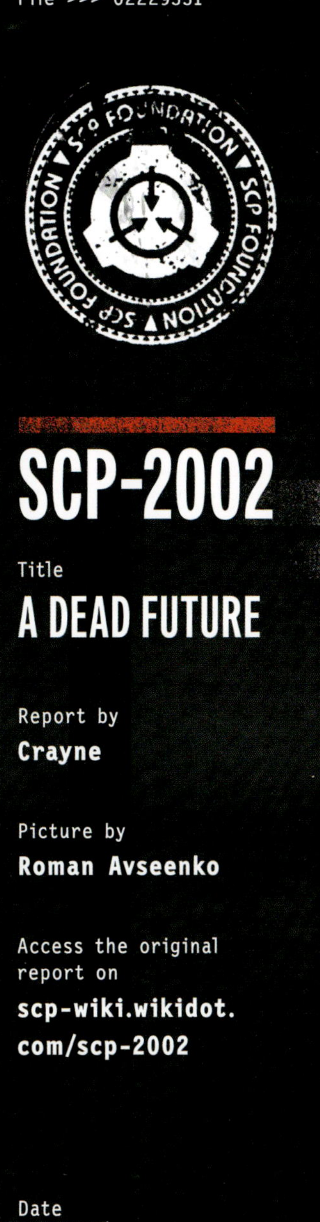

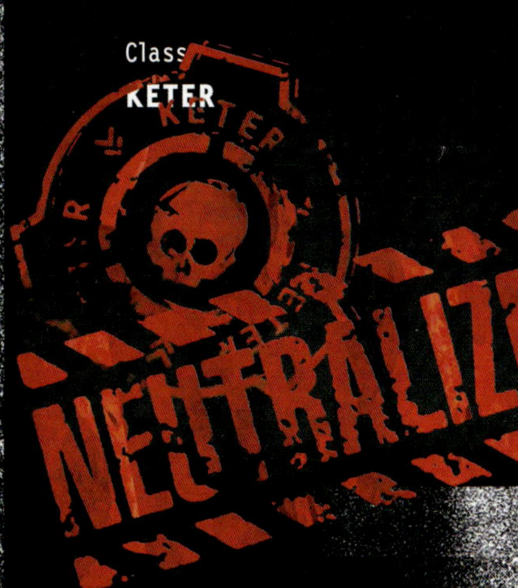

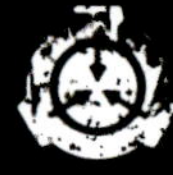

Research Library File ▸ 2002

SCP-2002 was first detected at a position roughly 15.8 au from Earth on ██/██/19██ by remote sensing systems aboard Foundation satellites. Extrapolating from SCP-2002's course, and assuming no alterations to that course, SCP-2002 should have been discovered at least ██ years earlier. This suggests an accidental temporal shift, rather than a conscious attempt on the part of SCP-2002 or its crew. The content of SCP-2002's automated broadcast lends further credence to this theory.

ADDENDUM 2002-A-01: EXCERPT FROM NEUTRALIZATION REPORT 2002/D/NEUTRPT-01:REV1.01

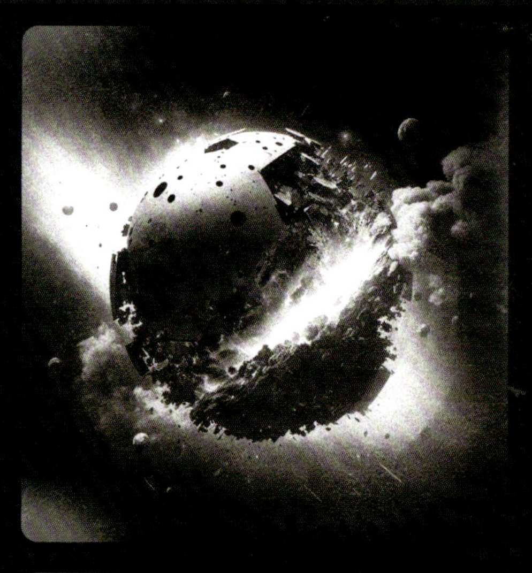

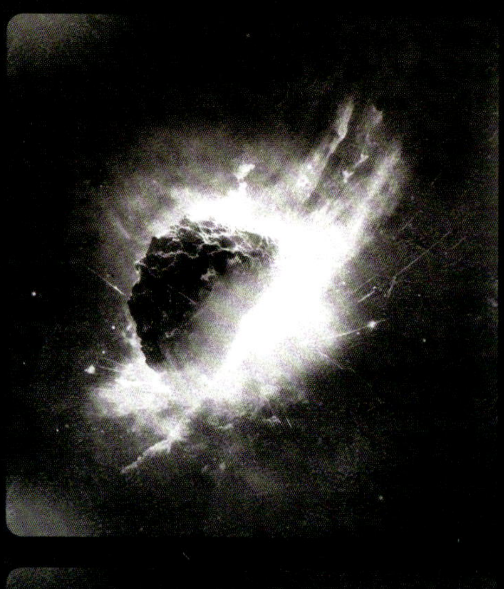

The Foundation's satellite footage of SCP-2002 neutralization.

On ██/██/19██ as SCP-2002 passed Earth's moon, a previously unidentified Global Occult Coalition satellite containing a high-powered carbon-dioxide laser, opened fire on SCP-2002, breaking up the main hull and dispersing the smaller spheres over a wide area. Several of these were subsequently destroyed by further laser fire, though most were set adrift in space when the main hull was ruptured. A number of the smaller spheres continued on to Earth. On ██/██/20██ these, and a large section of hull, entered Earth's atmosphere.

Investigations into the Global Occult Coalition's unwarranted destruction of SCP-2002 uncovered a series of encrypted e-mail messages transmitted from a workstation in Site-102's communications terminal. Decryption of these messages uncovered an information leak to the GOC, covering SCP-2002, though only in basic detail. In several cases, internal misinformation was leaked in addition to factually correct data on SCP-2002.

A comprehensive investigation by Mobile Task Force Beta-1 ("Cauterizers") identified the sender of the messages as ██████ ██████, a Level 4 member of research personnel employed at Site-102, but not attached to the SCP-2002 project. The personnel in question was detained trying to leave Site-102's compound, interrogated and consequently [DATA EXPUNGED] active use in counter-intelligence operations. Efforts to ascertain the identity of the specific recipient have been unsuccessful, but it is assumed to be a handler for the Global Occult Coalition. Foundation assets within that organization have since confirmed that the organization possessed knowledge of SCP-2002 as early as 19██, though only covering very basic details (see below.) It is assumed that the lack of detailed and factually correct information, in addition to the Foundation's policy of internal and external disinformation with respect to SCP-2002, led to their decision to attempt the neutralization of SCP-2002.

As a result of this incident, protocols for internal and external communication concerning anomalies have been reviewed and where necessary updated, and Operation Carbon was launched, remaining in effect indefinitely until such time as a standardized loyalty test can be developed for current and future personnel.

The satellite employed by the Global Occult Coalition was eventually sabotaged, and crashed into the Brazilian rainforest on ██/██/20██ It was recovered by Foundation forces and remains in Foundation custody despite numerous Global Occult Coalition requests for its return. Please refer to supplemental documentation 2002/C/DipInc-8:rev.1.12 for more details regarding inter-organizational communication on this subject.

ADDENDUM 2002-A-02: CAPTURED GOC DOCUMENTATION ON SCP-2002

KTE-0481

THREAT ID:

KTE-0481-Typhon "Large unknown object on a collision course with Earth"

AUTHORIZED RESPONSE LEVEL:

4 (Severe Threat)

DESCRIPTION:

An unidentified unnatural astronomical object on a collision course with Earth. Intelligence provided by Covert Operative █████ suggests The Foundation is tracking the KTE (under designation SCP-2002) for unknown reasons, yet has not initiated any concrete action nor implemented measures to halt its progress. Please refer to appendix 001-016 for field reports from Covert Operative █████ on available intelligence concerning this KTE.

The object is a sphere with an estimated diameter of 450 m (~1,476 ft), with a multitude of smaller spherical nodes attached to it for unknown purposes. It cannot be ruled out that these nodes are weapon systems. No propulsion systems are directly visible on the object. Systems for power generation seem likewise absent.

Object does not respond to attempts at communication, despite hailing messages sent at regular intervals by ground-based GOC installations and the USS ██████.

Current calculations put time of impact at ██:██ GMT, ██/██/20██. Conservative fallout projections predict an Eternal Winter Class scenario should KTE-0481 be allowed to continue on its path unhindered.

RULES OF ENGAGEMENT:

Should the object come within 0.00269 au of Earth, termination is warranted to prevent the extinction of all life on Earth. GOC orbital asset Thor-AXII has been put on a permanent state of alert to this end. Protocols have been put in place to assure a 100% success rate. Covert Operative █████ is to be extracted immediately after successful termination of KTE-0481.

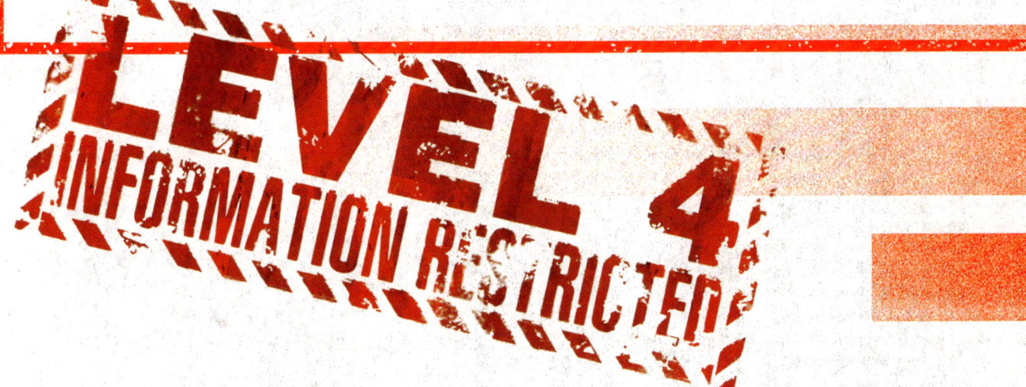

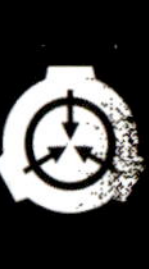

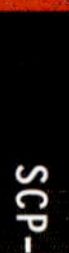

SCP-2002's crash.

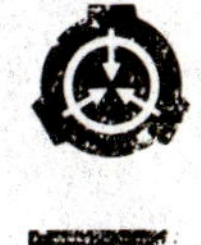

Research Library File ▸ 2002

ADDENDUM 2002-A-03: MANAGEMENT SUMMARY OF RECOVERY REPORT 2002/D/RECRPT-14:REV1.15

On ██/██/20██ 37 minutes after a large portion of SCP-2002's main hull and a selection of smaller spheres touched down, members of MTF Zeta-40 ("Dead-end Cleaners") and several local guides approached the wreckage at approximately 240 km from the Saudi-Arabian capital of Riyadh. Over the course of several days, all debris and a large selection of partially destroyed human remains (estimated to comprise 5 adult males, 142 newborn infant males, 21 adult females, and 377 newborn infant females) were loaded onto Foundation transports and taken back to Site-102. DNA testing has revealed partial matches to current Foundation personnel, including several members of the O-5 council.

ADDENDUM 2002-A-04: PARTIAL TRANSCRIPT OF AN AUTOMATED BROADCAST BY SCP-2002

Speech synthesis, English:

This is the Foundation vessel SCPS Mendel. We have received your transmission. Due to stasis protocols in effect, no members of personnel are currently available to respond to your signal. Please stand by for a prerecorded automated broadcast.

Female voice, English:

This is Dr. Agnes Younts, L4 Project Lead for SCP-████. If you're receiving this message, I'm glad to say this mission was unnecessary. When the fallout from SCP-████s final containment breach hit in 21██, we spent a long time trying to find ways to circumvent its effects. At first, we tried to see if relocation was the solution. We constructed an orbital and, when that didn't work, a lunar facility, but the plague always followed somehow. Faced with a 100% sterility rate, we found that there was a way of fertilizing embryos so they wouldn't be subject to the plague's effects. At least, not while they remained in stasis. Our calculations indicated a dissipation of effects approximately ██ years from day zero, so in the end we were left with no option but to send a selection of these embryos out into space, along with a crew of personnel tasked with their care. This vessel's crew and cargo will be revived and prepared for a return to Earth. They've come a long way.

Speech synthesis, English:

Our ETA is currently set at *WARNING: temporal dislocation error detected.* We urge you to clear Sector-521A for our arrival.

Speech synthesis, Mandarin:

This message will now be repeated in Mandarin.

No such sector currently exists as a Foundation asset. However, calculations have put its intended location at ████████

After repetition in Mandarin, the message was also repeated in Spanish, Hindi and Arabic before the transmission ended.

END OF REPORT 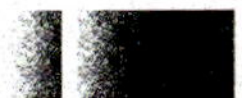

File >>> 0026432

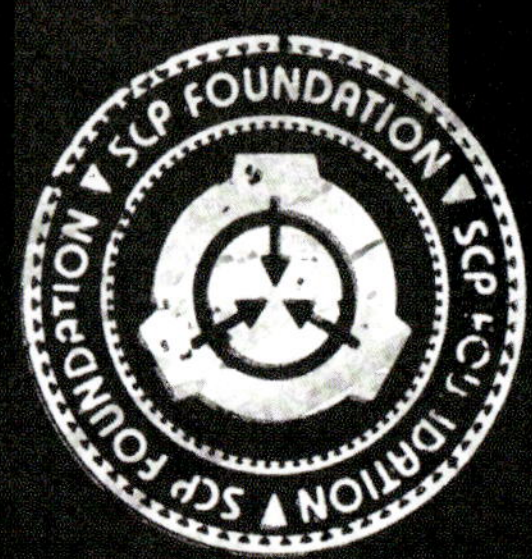

SCP-2003

Title

PREFERRED OPTION

Report by

Kalinin

Pictures by

Egor Polyakov
Dan Temirov

Access the original report on

scp-wiki.wikidot.com/scp-2003

Date

Class

THAUMIEL

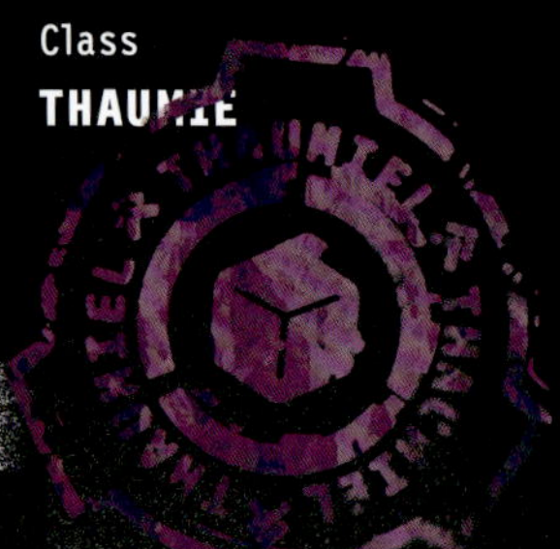

SPECIAL CONTAINMENT PROCEDURES

SCP-2003 is contained at Armed Site-47, a Type 4 Restricted Zone. In accordance with Type 4 protocols, personnel assigned to SCP-2003 research, security and maintenance must undergo expanded background check procedures, as well as successfully pass a Hoiberg-Kazawa Causality Questionnaire. Access to SCP-2003 itself is limited to XN-SHEPHERD project participants with prior approval from the Director of Site-47.

All information regarding Determinative Sets, Elevated Probability Events, Designated Magnifier Individuals and the XN-SHEPHERD program is classified and accessible only by the Director of Site-47, 05-7, and those personnel read into SCP-2003 security protocols.

Observations of designated indicator data deviating significantly from Determinative Set XN parameters are to be reported immediately to the Director of Site-47 and treated as a Level 5 "Existential Threat" Emergency Response Event.

DESCRIPTION

SCP-2003 is an apparatus allowing a limited degree of travel to and from periods of time in advance of those encountered in the normal course of space-time as understood by mainstream science. SCP-2003 was designed and built by the Foundation over a 25-year period using technology derived from research into SCP-████, SCP-███, and SCP-████. While the technical capabilities and design specifications of SCP-2003 are well-documented and reproduceable if necessary, the scientific and anomalous principles behind its functionality are not understood at this time.

Upon activation, SCP-2003 is capable of transporting a living entity contained within its central chamber to a point coterminous with its present location in physical space but located in a future time period. The amount of time into the future traveled by the subject is related to the amount of energy input into SCP-2003. An approximate estimate of 3500 kWh in order to send a subject seven months into the future has been documented; however, this relationship becomes unpredictable at higher energy levels.

Subjects using SCP-2003 will exist in the time period to which they have traveled for a duration ranging between 15 and 38 weeks before spontaneously returning to the time period of origination at a point coterminous with their present location. For safety purposes, a secure location has been established for operatives to use while waiting for return to their time of origin. Operatives must report subsequent to experiencing 98 days after SCP-2003 activation.

While SCP-2003 enables chronological travel for living subjects, the activation process has proven severely damaging to most types of animal and plant tissue. The only exception documented to date has been tissue related to the animal nervous system. As a result, personnel designated for SCP-2003 travel must be prepared accordingly (see additional documentation for details).

Testing has shown that under current conditions, SCP-2003 remains functional and under Foundation control through December of 2348.

ADDENDUM 2003-A: GENERAL RESULTS OF SCP-2003 RESEARCH

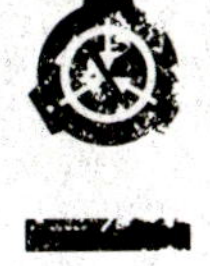

Initial deployment of SCP-2003 began in 1995, using modified personnel to observe future conditions and events. The purpose of these deployments was to confirm the nature of travel using SCP-2003, and if possible collect data allowing the Foundation to better mitigate future anomalous phenomena. The results of these initial exploratory missions demonstrated several crucial principles for understanding observation of future events:

Data collected using SCP-2003 is imprecise. Early exploratory missions yielded copious amounts of data regarding what appeared to be future events. However, subsequent observation has established that these observations are not entirely predictive. For instance, while collected data allowed Foundation assets to prevent a major security breach of SCP-███ at Site-19 in 1997, a catastrophic earthquake originating off the coast of the Western United States (observed directly by several field agents using SCP-2003) failed to occur as predicted in 1999. As more data has been collected, meta-analysis has properly contextualized observations and has assigned a probability of occurrence for major events in the future.

Certain individuals appear to affect causality disproportionately. As Foundation cataloguing of possible future events increased following the completion of more exploratory missions, certain events were deemed to be undesirable for the Foundation's mission. Early attempts to influence these events met with mixed success; while manipulation and/or elimination of some individuals achieved mission goals, other Foundation attempts to influence events failed to alter outcomes at all, even when several actors deemed to be essential were liquidated. Meta-analysis has determined that in some cases, the actions (or indeed very existence) of individuals with no discernible relation to major events, sometimes in regions thousands of kilometers away, have profound and immediate impacts on these events. Since this discovery, research staff has maintained a database of these individuals.

Few cohesive "futures" are tolerable to the continued beneficial existence of humanity. While observed conditions exhibit a tendency towards variation upon each exploratory mission, a number of loosely consistent "timelines" have been observed, cataloged in Foundation databases as Determinative Sets. Most Determinative Sets consist of a collective future that either renders Earth unsuitable for human civilization (and in some cases life in total), or results in conditions directly inimical to the well-being of most of humanity. The reasons for the relative paucity of long-term survival scenarios, if any exist, are unknown at this time, as is any connection to the steadily-increasing observation of anomalous phenomena documented across the Foundation.

ADDENDUM 2003-B: PREPARATION OF PERSONNEL FOR USE

Due to the nature of SCP-2003's effects on human anatomy, special preparations must be made in order to properly outfit personnel for chronological travel in a condition suitable for both survival and ability to carry out mission objectives. Because of the sensitive nature of tasks necessary during SCP-2003 missions, D-Class have been deemed unsuitable subjects.

Preference for SCP-2003 subject recruitment is to be given to personnel nearing or past official retirement age. In cases where personnel have been diagnosed with terminal illness that does not impair neurological or cerebrospinal function, preference may also be granted. Personnel volunteering for SCP-2003 travel are to be moved to the Tier VI pay scale for the duration of their assignment; any survivors are entitled to an Elevated Benefits Package distributed through normal clandestine channels.

Prior to outfitting, selected personnel are to undergo extended sensory deprivation training, concurrent with training in simulated environments analogous to those experienced by occupants of the XX890-V Life Function and Observation (LFO) system. During this period, personnel must undergo a prophylactic course of antidepressants and antipsychotics as overseen by medical staff.

Upon completion of training regimens, personnel are to have all brain tissue, nerves, and associated nervous

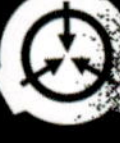

XX890-V LFO system.

XX890-V LIFE FUNCTION AND OBSERVATION SYSTEM

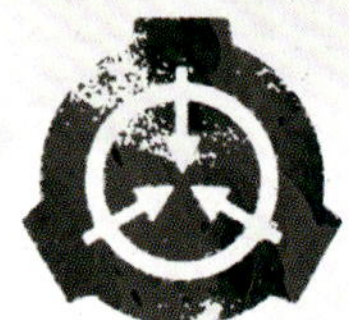

SELECTED PERSONNEL

TRANSPLANTATION PROCESS

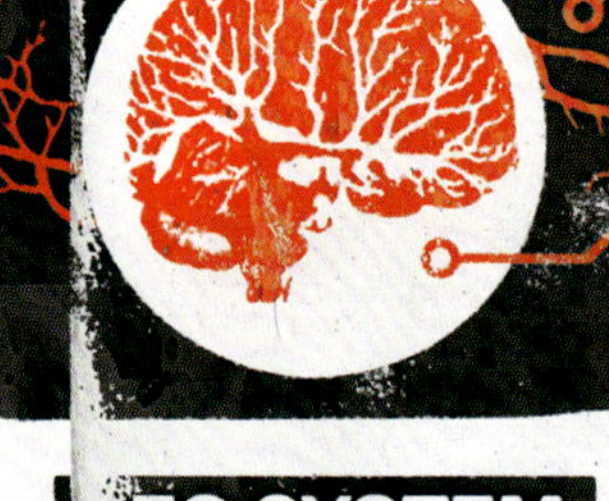

LFO SYSTEM "BIGDOG"

Personnel are to have all brain tissue, nerves, and associated nervous system structures surgically removed and transplanted into the XX890-V LFO system. All usable organs are to be harvested afterward per medical protocols.

system structures surgically removed and transplanted into the XX890-V LFO system. All usable organs are to be harvested afterward per medical protocols.

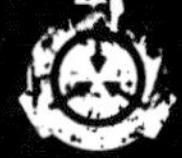

Current guidelines authorize the XX890-V LFO system and occupant for four uses of SCP-2003. When not engaged on missions, personnel are to be kept in an induced coma state, concurrent with research establishing 18 months as the median time period before communications and feedback from XX890-V LFO occupants become agitated and incomprehensible.

The nature of the XX890-V LFO system is to remain classified and accessible only to senior personnel.

ADDENDUM 2003-C: OVERVIEW OF XN-SHEPHERD PROGRAM

MEMORANDUM
TO: Armed Site-47 Director ██-██ ██████
FROM: 05-7
RE: DETERMINATIVE SET XN

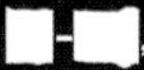

Up to this point, all attempts at future intervention using SCP-2003 have been limited in scope and scattershot in nature. I have seen the wisdom in this approach; it is informed by painstaking contingency planning and risk/benefit evaluation.

The last 18 months of reports, however, have promise if we are bold enough to seize the initiative. We may have found a way out, here.

The price, though. There's always a price. As you well know.

Consider this note an official change in policy. As of today, all efforts at intervention are now aimed at bringing about and preserving XN. Designated Magnifier Individuals associated with XN are to be protected from undue interference at the expense of all other priorities. In particular, Nuru Diagne must be allowed to die in the manner most observations have predicted for her. If anything at all changes in that regard, make it happen.

I trust that you're familiar enough with the rest of the Determinative Sets to understand why we're going this way.

One more thing: All communications, and I mean all, with anyone outside of Site-47 are to be cleared and routed through my office.

- 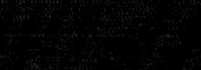

ADDENDUM 2003-D: LISTING OF KNOWN DETERMINATIVE SETS

Preferred Option:

Designation	Description	Notes
XN	Currently documented reality. Society continues along established Foundation projections regarding economic trends, environmental factors, and social upheaval. Anomalous activity continues to manifest mostly consistent with present rates. Consensus reality maintained successfully until 83345 Moore, a previously untracked asteroid 22 km in diameter, collides with Earth in January of 2349, killing most of humanity immediately and rendering the planet unsuitable for sustained human existence.	See Addendum 2003-C

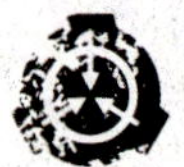

Other Documented Determinative Sets: EYES ONLY

Designation	Description	Notes
XB	Development of society continues in manner similar to XN until April 23, 2017, when a gamma-ray burst originating from the vicinity of HD 188753 directly strikes Earth. The burst lasts 2 minutes and 38 seconds and kills all known forms of life.	Researcher ███, directly observing this scenario at the time of the gamma-ray burst, was the only known living being to survive the event, and was able to continue collecting data until his return 52 days later. Study of use of XX890-V LFO system for high-radiation environments pending.
XE	The election of Sir William Entwistle as Prime Minister of New Zealand in 2049, combined with the birth of an unnamed infant boy in Ahal Province, Turkmenistan on the same day, lead to an escalating chain of events culminating in a society-destroying nuclear exchange between the nations of Israel and Greater Indonesia in 2058. All Foundation attempts to interfere with either individual merely result in the date of the nuclear exchange occurring sooner.	In all permutations of this set, widespread public knowledge of the Foundation occurs precisely 86 days before the detonation of nuclear weapons.
XH	Between the years 2023 and 2034, world governments approach global affairs at a radically increased level of cooperation due to the onset of a highly virulent influenza epidemic that kills approximately 1.4 billion worldwide. Throughout the 2040s and 2050s, many longstanding ethnic conflicts are resolved through the intervention of multilateral organizations, endemic poverty and hunger in areas such as sub-Saharan Africa and the Indian subcontinent is substantially decreased, and large-scale projects mitigating sea level rise are completed throughout coastal regions. On July 29, 2059, the entire population of Earth spontaneously vanishes along with all known animal life, with no observed return within observational range.	N/A
XJ	An entity later confirmed to be an exact duplicate of Dr. Masako Koizumi, one of the original researchers responsible for SCP-███ prior to its containment, appears within an inner security perimeter at Armed Site-47 on April 1, 2011. The entity requests that Dr. Koizumi's scheduled euthanization elsewhere within the facility be cancelled immediately. As SCP-███ was not functional at the time of established containment, the means by which the entity is able to make this request are unknown, and presumed to occur in the future. However, due to the establishment of K-Failsafe Protocol Twelve, the request is impossible for Foundation personnel to comply with, resulting in an Alpha-8 type temporal paradox. This series of events repeats for an uncountable number of instances, resulting in the eventual collapse of spacetime as understood by humanity.	This scenario was ultimately averted by staff sedating the duplicate of Dr. Koizumi, placing it into an XX890V-LFO platform, and transporting it in SCP-2003 using all available energy. Temporal complications from this action are unknown, but presumably do not materialize prior to 2349.

Determinative Set XE, observed by Researcher █.

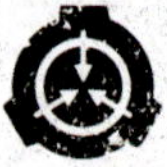

Research Library File ▸ 2003

XO

Anomalous phenomena begins increasing in frequency by orders of magnitude beginning in 2037. The Foundation comprehensively loses capabilities to protect consensus reality by 2039 and world civilization undergoes a period of chaos and upheaval. Millions die in spontaneous riots and mass suicides become commonplace throughout the world. Numerous messianic religious movements quickly form and contribute greatly to civil conflict and internecine warfare. By the mid-2040s, several sects and remnants of national governments successfully weaponize various anomalous phenomena, and humanity is wiped out by 2048, with the exception of a small group of survivors sheltering in the remnants of Site-104. All contact with this group is lost upon their discovery of Wing K of Site-104.

Due to the open nature of anomalous phenomena in this scenario, data collected is the most comprehensive of any Determinative Set, as Agent ██████ is able to work openly and unimpeded.

XR

The population of *Homo ignotus*, long estimated by Foundation operatives to be approximately 500 individuals, increases overnight to approximately 8 million individuals in 2015. A short, violent struggle ensues between the combined forces of the Foundation and *H. ignotus*, with all means of resistance to the newly ascendent *H. ignotus* population systematically destroyed within three days. Humanity is ther████████ ████████. Researchers currently have divergent theories as to whether this Determinative Set is predictive of the intentions of the known *H. ignotus* population, with current theories of ████████" and ████████████" being supported the most.

[DATA EXPUNGED]

XS

Determinative Set XS proceeds in a manner similar to XN until an indeterminate date in 2019 when Armed Site-47 and all knowledge of SCP-2003 is apparently lost to the Foundation. Researcher ██████ is detained by the XS version of the Foundation during an observational mission in 2022 and held as an SCP classified phenomenon until her return. Researcher ██████ is detained by XS Foundation personnel at point of entry upon commencement of her next observational mission, and returns with no retrievable data and portions of her brain tissue removed. No further information on Determinative Set XS is available.

[LEVEL 4 SECURITY ACCESS ONLY]

XU

On February 17, 2026, contrary to all astronomical models and understanding of both classical and quantum mechanics, the Sun suddenly collapses into a black hole despite not meeting commonly understood mass thresholds for triggering such an event. Despite the almost immediate cooling of Earth and all other planets in the Solar System to approximately -270 degrees Celsius and the elimination of all other forms of life, humans are unable to die, maintaining consciousness despite the lack of continuing biological functions and almost total cessation of molecular movement.

This Determinative Set is a subset of previously designated Set XT. XT was a future in which a single totalitarian regime had assumed control over the planet and targeted various "subversive" organizations for elimination, focusing on Foundation personnel in particular. Foundation researchers attempted to avert this scenario by sending three identified individuals from South Korea into orbit on the International Space Station. XU resulted.

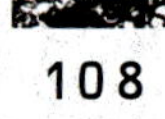

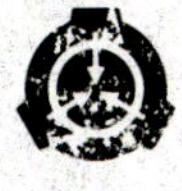

Research Library File ▸ 2003

XW

Beings strongly resembling human-sized, animate versions of SCP-███ manifest in most major population centers on August 13, 2019. Rather than causing alarm, these beings quickly become accepted by humanity after offering major advances in medical science, energy production, crop cultivation, and the arts. By the close of 2022, thousands of people willingly join an experimental program to combine the consciousness of multitudes of humans into a singular entity. In 2024, a fully mature human believed to possess a mind composed of the transferred consciousness of approximately 134,000 people is created by these beings. This human is then confined to a cell, left with only automatically-dispensed supplies of food and water, and sealed off from all outside contact. All other humans are systematically exterminated by the end of 2024.

The last two personnel sent to observe Determinative Set XW (Agent ███████ and Researcher ██) failed to return to time of origin, and are listed MIA at this time.

XX

An undiscovered protist unidentified in the observed timeline (designated Nephroisospora araneae by Foundation researchers) undergoes a geometric increase in population due to what is presumed to be a recently-developed adaptation allowing it to survive in almost all aqueous environments. N. araneae proves adept at moving into and surviving in human nervous tissue, initiating a disorder similar to toxoplasmosis that causes humans to develop monomaniacal fondness for Phoneutria nigriventer (Brazilian wandering spider). By 2028, almost 85% of the human population has been infected, and most of society's resources are reordered towards the preservation and breeding of P. nigriventer. Uninfected individuals are detained and in most cases interred in P. nigriventer breeding facilities in an attempt to provide additional food sources for the specimens. Due to the singular worldwide focus on production and maintenance of spider populations, crop failures and infrastructure degradation become systemic, and global famine results in the death of approximately 6 billion persons in the 2030s.

Research is ongoing into possible anomalous causes behind the increased prevalence of N. araneae and/or the nature of its function as a pathogen.

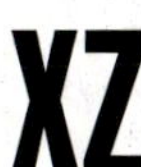

XZ

Earth has been completely depopulated. Large facilities have been constructed in the center of all sites of former major cities capable of enabling instantaneous travel over an immense distance to a point determined by post-observation analysis to be somewhere in the vicinity of the Hydra Supercluster. Subsequent observers were authorized to enter these facilities, and were apparently transported to an Earth-analogous biome planet with a functioning human civilization. In each case, observers transported to this location were immediately detected by residents of this planet. While residents chose to forgo any communication with observers, each observer was subsequently escorted through selected locations of the society encountered on this planet, encompassing large public works projects, monuments, museums, and other culturally significant locations. The human civilization encountered in the Hydra Supercluster is apparently advanced by modern standards, and lacking in many of the most commonly identified factors negatively affecting extant societies. This civilization has persisted past the range of observation thus far, indicating ongoing survival.

Further investigation authorized under XN SHEPHERD. Re-evaluation of preferred option pending.

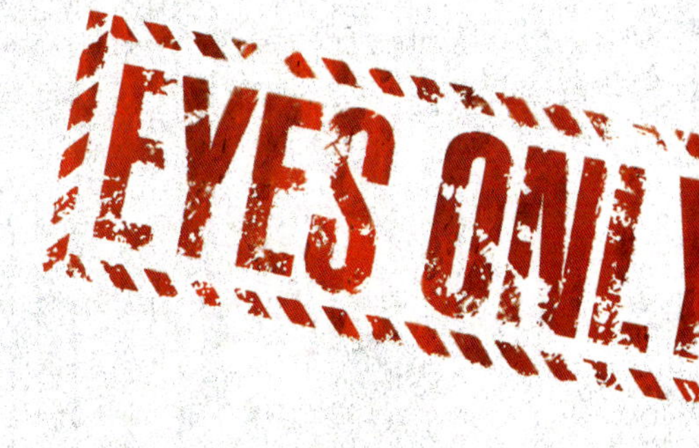

END OF REPORT 

File >>> 010223

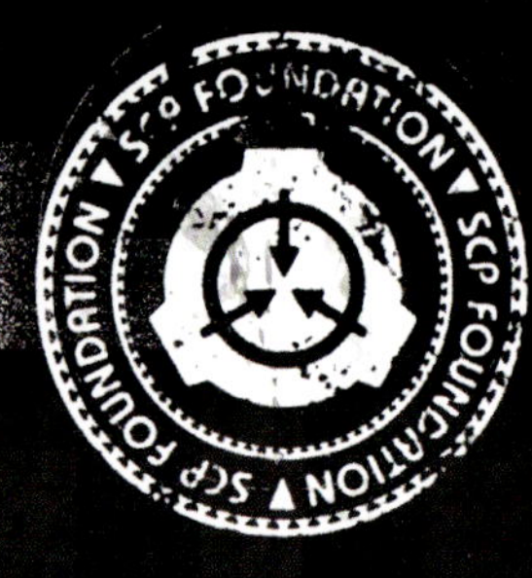

SCP-963

Title

IMMORTALITY

Report by

AdminBright

Picture by

Jack Hainsworth

Access the original report on

scp-wiki.wikidot.com/scp-963

Date

Class

EUCLID

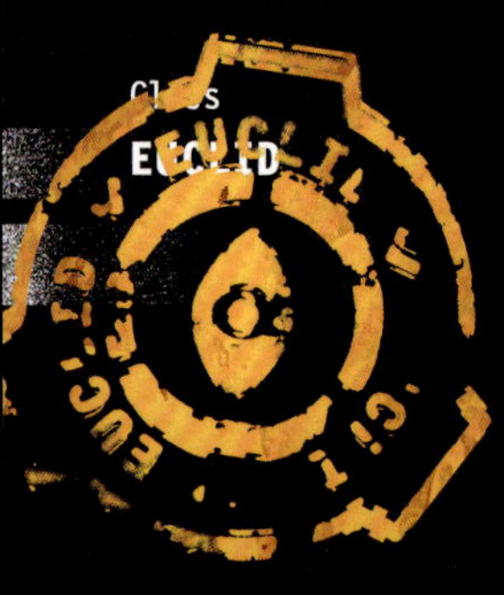

SPECIAL CONTAINMENT PROCEDURES

SCP-963-1 is to be given into the care of a current D level operative, as well as personnel classified as Dr. Bright's assistant. This assistant is to be chosen by 05-█ for loyalty to the Foundation, as well as psychological stability.

~~SCP-963 is to be attached to the subject's forehead or the back of the subject's hand using a suitably strong epoxy.~~ SCP-963-1 is now hung by a chain from subject's neck. 963-1 is not allowed to be hidden upon the subject's body. Any attempt to do so will be met with lethal force.

~~If the current D-level subject exceeds a thirty-day life span, they are to be executed and a new subject chosen to wear 963-1.~~ By order of 05-█ any body SCP-963-1 is installed upon is given a stay of execution until it passes on of natural causes, or 963-1 is transferred to a new host.

~~ATTENTION: As of 12/13/████ 963-1 is not allowed in proximity of any Euclid or Keter class humanoid SCPs. This directive is to be enforced lethally.~~ Rescinded, 05-6, 05-8, 05-9

~~ATTENTION: As of Incident 239-b Clef Kondraki, SCP-963-1 is not allowed at Site 17 without the express permission of three 05's. Violations are to be met with lethal force.~~ Rescinded, 05-6, 05-8, 05-9

DESCRIPTION

SCP-963-1 is an ornate amulet approximately 15 centimeters in circumference made from white gold, with thirteen (13) █k brilliant-cut diamonds surrounding a ██k oval-cut ruby in a starburst pattern. It was discovered in the personal effects of ████ ██ who had been found dead by apparent suicide, surrounded by a number of supernaturally-related books. Our Agent in the area found that 963-1 was incapable of being damaged and brought it in according to protocol XLR-8R-█.

Dr. Jack Bright, a Junior Staff researcher of good standing, was assigned the responsibility of researching SCP-963-1's capabilities, and granted access to [REDACTED]. Later that year, SCP-076-2 broke containment (see document 076-2-19A), leading to [REDACTED] deaths and █ casualties. Doctor Bright was transporting SCP-963-1 by hand past SCP-076-2's containment unit, and was among the first KIB (killed in breach). Approximately █ days later, D1-113, tasked to clear the area of rubble, discovered 963-1 among the wreckage and picked it up. An immediate, noticeable change came over D1-113. Interview follows.

INTERVIEW LOG X█, DATE:█-█-███

███: Could you please tell me your name?
D1-113: It's Jack Bright, you damn well know it is!
███: I believe you are Tom Higly, working for us as part of your life sentence.
D1-113: Don't be ridiculous! I couldn't possibly be- *(SCP-963-1 is removed at this time from D1-113's possession. A further MRI shows that D1-113 ceases all higher brain functions. 963-1 is returned, upon which brain function returns.)*
███: Dr. Bright?
D1-113: What?
███: We appear to have a problem.

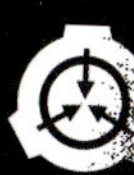

One of SCP-963-1's donors.

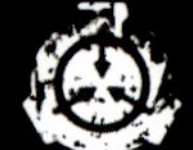

Research Library File ▸ 963

After much experimentation, it has been discovered that when any living anthropoid comes into direct skin contact with SCP-963-1, the mind of the subject is wiped, and that of Dr. Bright is projected from 963-1 onto the subject. It is known that memories native to Dr. Bright transfer from host to host.

If a subject maintains contact for thirty (30) days, their brain functions become a duplicate of the late Dr. Bright's. If 963-1 is removed after this time period, the subject retains an independent copy of the consciousness of Jack Bright. Sanctions were put in place to prevent multiple instances of Dr. Bright from being created to prevent Dr. Bright from collaborating with himself, however it was found this was not necessary, as Doctor Bright has proven thoroughly dedicated to the Foundation and its cause.

Doctor Bright himself has performed extensive experimentation on SCP-963-1, with the expressed desire for release from it. Interviews with Doctor Bright indicate that ████ ██ killed himself in the process of empowering SCP-963-1, and was therefore never able to slave his own consciousness to the amulet. Doctor Bright hypothesizes that he accidentally activated 963-1's power by being killed, instead of killing himself as the original creator had done.

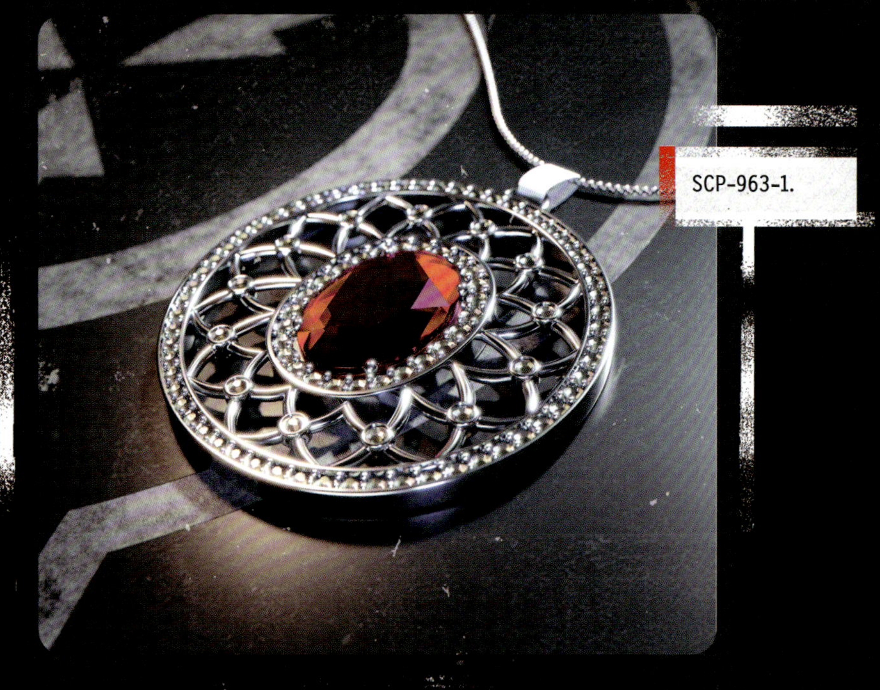

SCP-963-1.

ENTRY REGARDING SCP-963-2

On ██/██/████, orders were given by 05-9 to attempt to replicate SCP-963-1. All attempts met with failure until SCP-963-2, at which point [SUBSEQUENT DATA EXPUNGED]

ALL INFORMATION REGARDING SCP-963-2 IS CLASSIFIED LEVEL 5. ANYONE ATTEMPTING TO ACCESS FURTHER INFORMATION ABOUT SCP-963-2 WITHOUT LEVEL 5 CLEARANCE WILL BE TERMINATED.

END OF REPORT

File >>> 0183341

SCP-1981

Title

"RONALD REAGAN CUT UP WHILE TALKING"

Report by

Digiwizzard

Picture by

Ivan Efimov

Access the original report on

scp-wiki.wikidot.com/scp-1981

Date

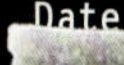

Class

SAFE

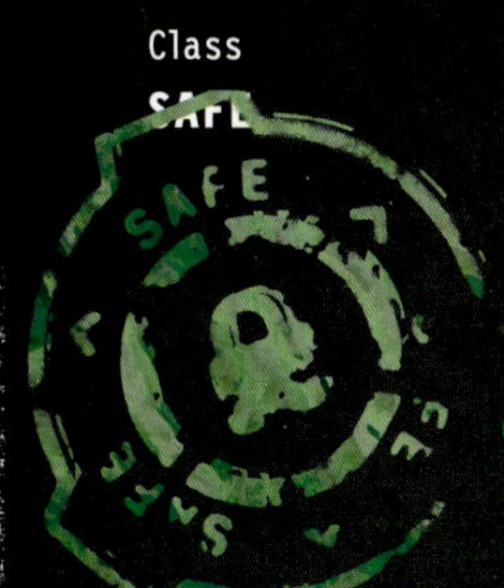

SPECIAL CONTAINMENT PROCEDURES

SCP-1981 is to be kept inside a secure video storage unit at the media archive of Site ██. When in use, SCP-1981 should not be removed from its casing or exposed to any strong magnetic sources. A Betamax home video system and an analog television has been provided in Observation Theatre 02 at Site ██, as well as video equipment to record viewings.

DESCRIPTION

SCP-1981 is a standard Betamax tape. "RONALD REGAN CUT UP WHILE TALKING"(sic) has been handwritten on the adhesive sticker in felt tip pen. Laboratory analysis indicates that SCP-1981 is made of ordinary material, and serial numbers correspond with home cassette tapes produced in September of 1980. SCP-1981 was initially encountered by a filing clerk in the Ronald Reagan Presidential Library in 1991, who upon watching it alerted the police, with the intent to find the tape's creator to press "obscenity charges". A low-level police investigation was conducted, at which point the Foundation was alerted and secured SCP-1981. Class A amnestics were administered before ████ could be notified. Further investigation of the library's records by Foundation personnel failed to yield any leads on SCP-1981's origin.

SCP-1981 appears to be a home video recording of former United States President Ronald Reagan delivering his "Evil Empire" speech to the National Association of Evangelicals at Sheraton Twin Towers Hotel, Orlando, FL on 3/8/1983. However, at 1 minute and 10 seconds, the speech begins to deviate heavily, eventually resembling no known speech ever made by Reagan. Beginning at approximately 5 minutes, multiple incisions, lacerations and penetration wounds can be seen being slowly inflicted, though no corresponding source of these wounds is visible. Despite suffering bodily harm that would likely incapacitate an ordinary person, Reagan will continue to deliver his speech until either his vocal cords are severed or the tape degrades to static at 22:34.

Upon rewinding SCP-1981 and initiating playback, Reagan will deliver an entirely new speech, often radically different from the ones previously observed. Topics have included torture, child molestation and ritual sacrifice. Trauma inflicted upon Reagan also appears to be divergent, with impalement, genital mutilation, and [REDACTED] having all been observed. In roughly one in seven viewings of SCP-1981, a figure clothed in black robes with a conical hood will have replaced a random member of Reagan's press detail, henceforth referred to as SCP-1981-1. The significance of the appearance of SCP-1981-1 is currently unknown.

The speeches delivered by Reagan are mostly incoherent, lacking any sort of underlying thematic structure and largely being composed of nonsensical anecdotes and parables. However, occasionally references are made to future events that Reagan could not possibly have known about or predicted, such as the September 11 terrorist attacks, the result of the 2008 Russian elections, and ████ ██████. For this reason, rigorous time and effort has been devoted to recording the speech delivered on each playback. Attempts to replicate SCP-1981 onto a similar Betamax tape have met with failure, however, cameras used to record the television SCP-1981 is broadcasted on have succeeded in "capturing" individual playbacks. Any observations performed on SCP-1981 must be recorded on the camcorder provided, and delivered for subsequent review to Dr. B████, project supervisor.

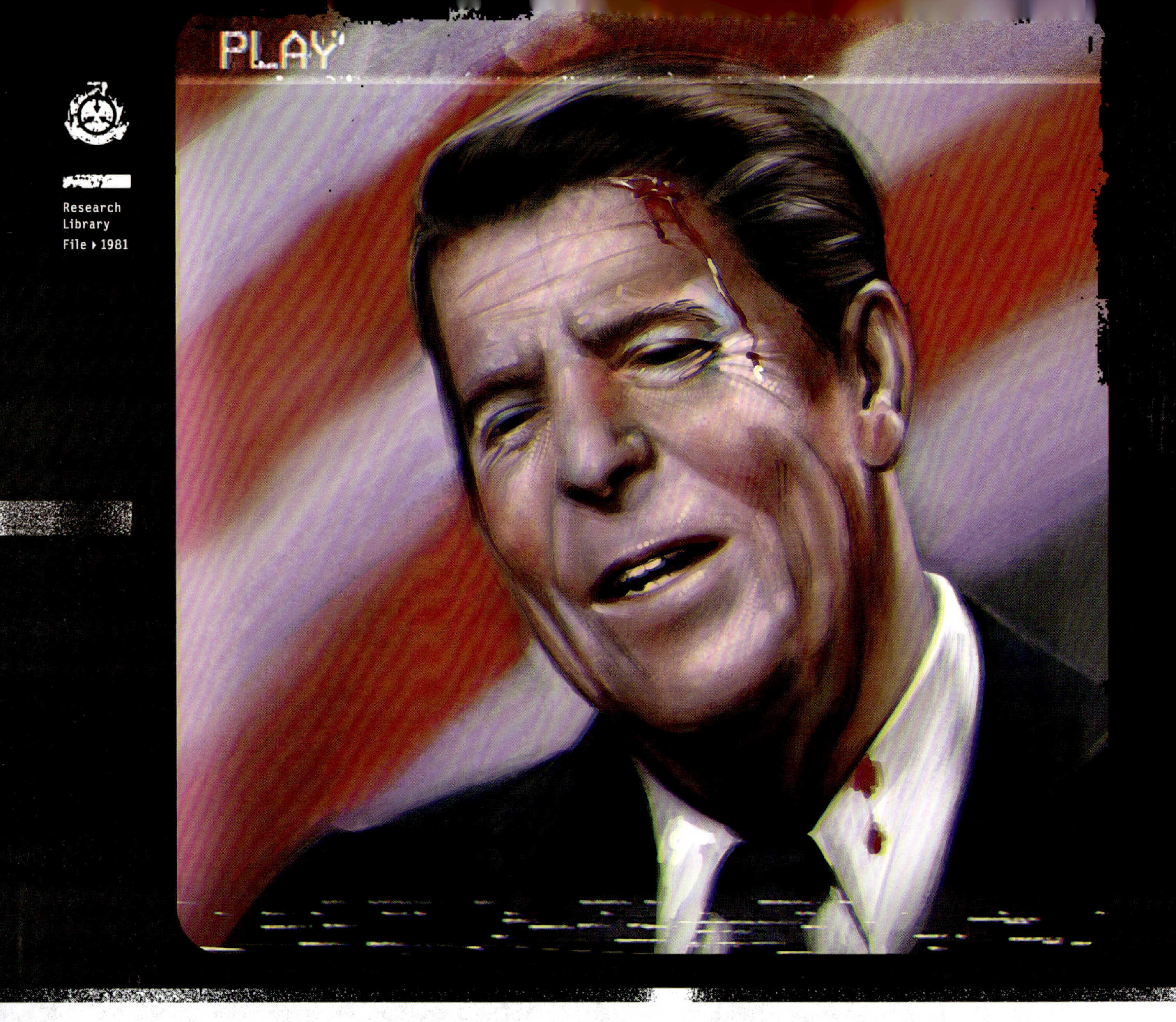

Years of natural magnetic interference has severely degraded SCP-1981's signal quality, making it even more difficult to sift meaningful information from playbacks. Additionally, the gruesome nature of the mutilations performed upon Reagan have been described as "extremely disturbing", and for this reason it is recommended that any personnel feeling squeamish or ill after playback visit the on-site psychiatry facility for a level 3 evaluation.

As Ronald Reagan was alive at the time of SCP-1981's containment, a surveillance net was deployed to establish any relation between him and SCP-1981. No known connection was developed, though Reagan would frequently complain about "nightmares" before his mental state degenerated due to Alzheimer's.

EXCERPT FROM VIDEO TRANSCRIPT OF RECORDING MADE ON ███/███/93

0:17:24 - **Reagan:** A renewal of the traditional values that have been the tendons of this country's strength. One recent survey by a Washington-based researcher concluded that Americans were far more willing to participate in cannibalism than they have in the past hundred years. America is a nation that will not suffer abominations lightly. Seven. And that is the core of the awakening. Twelve. Eighteen. We will stop al-Qaeda. Now there you go again.

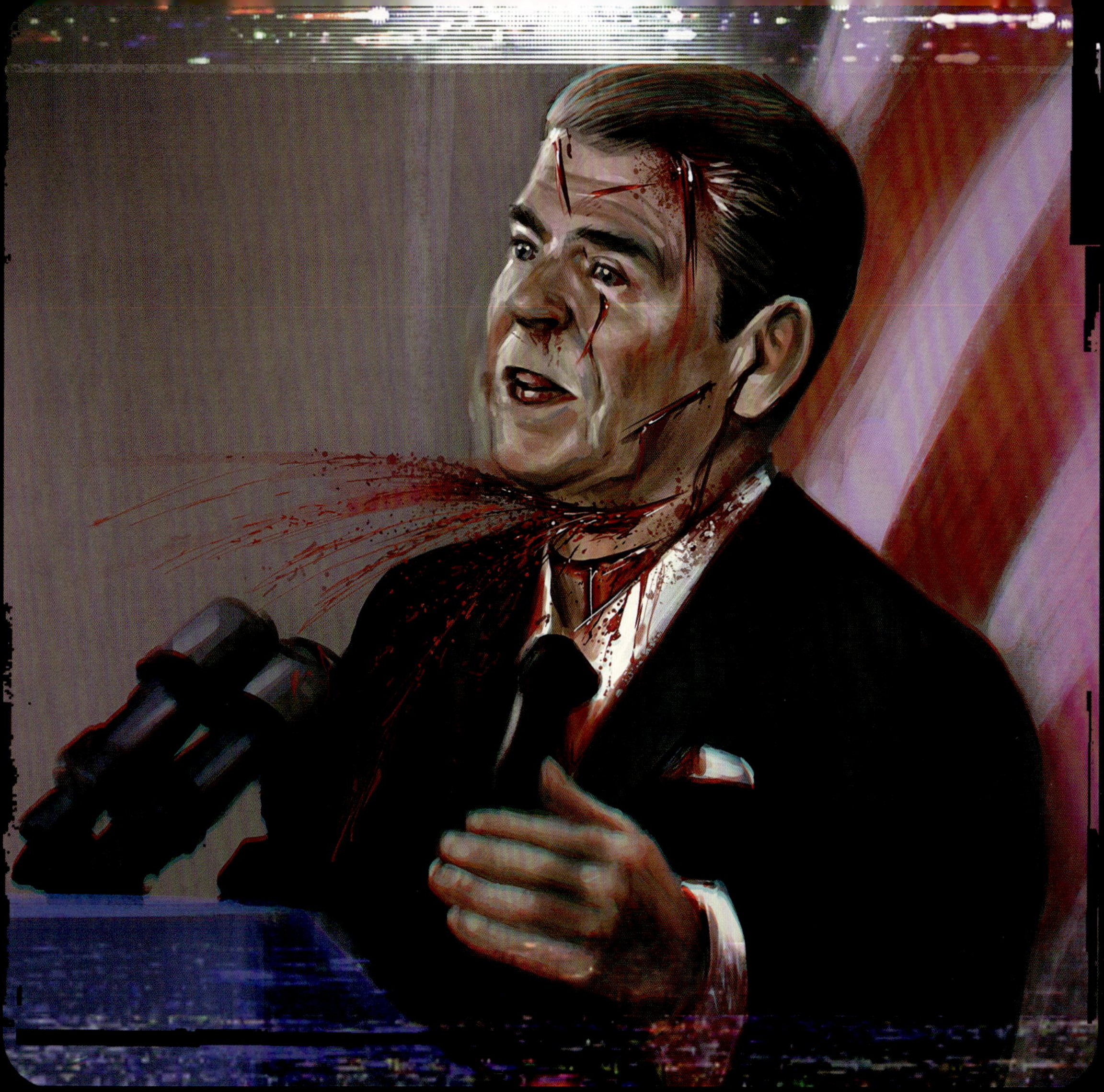

0:17:53 - *[Applause]*

0:18:02 - **Reagan:** For the first time we have risen, and I see we are being consumed. I see circles that are not circles. Billions of dead souls inside containment. Unravellers have eaten country's moral fabric, turning hearts into filth. I'm from a kingdom level above human. What does that yield? A hokey smile that damns an entire nation.

0:18:43 - There is no hope.

0:18:59 - *[Applause]*

0:19:15 - *[Reagan winces back, as if experiencing severe pain. Several new lacerations begin to manifest across bare eye socket, as well as punctures appearing to penetrate forehead and temples. Remainder of left arm is now cleanly bisected.]*

0:19:59 - **Reagan**: Further consensus has proven that over half of all Americans still hate. Eaten whole by void. The emptiness. The sadness. The blackness. The darkness. *<laughter>*

0:20:30 - *[Laughter continues until signal degrades into static]*

END TRANSCRIPT

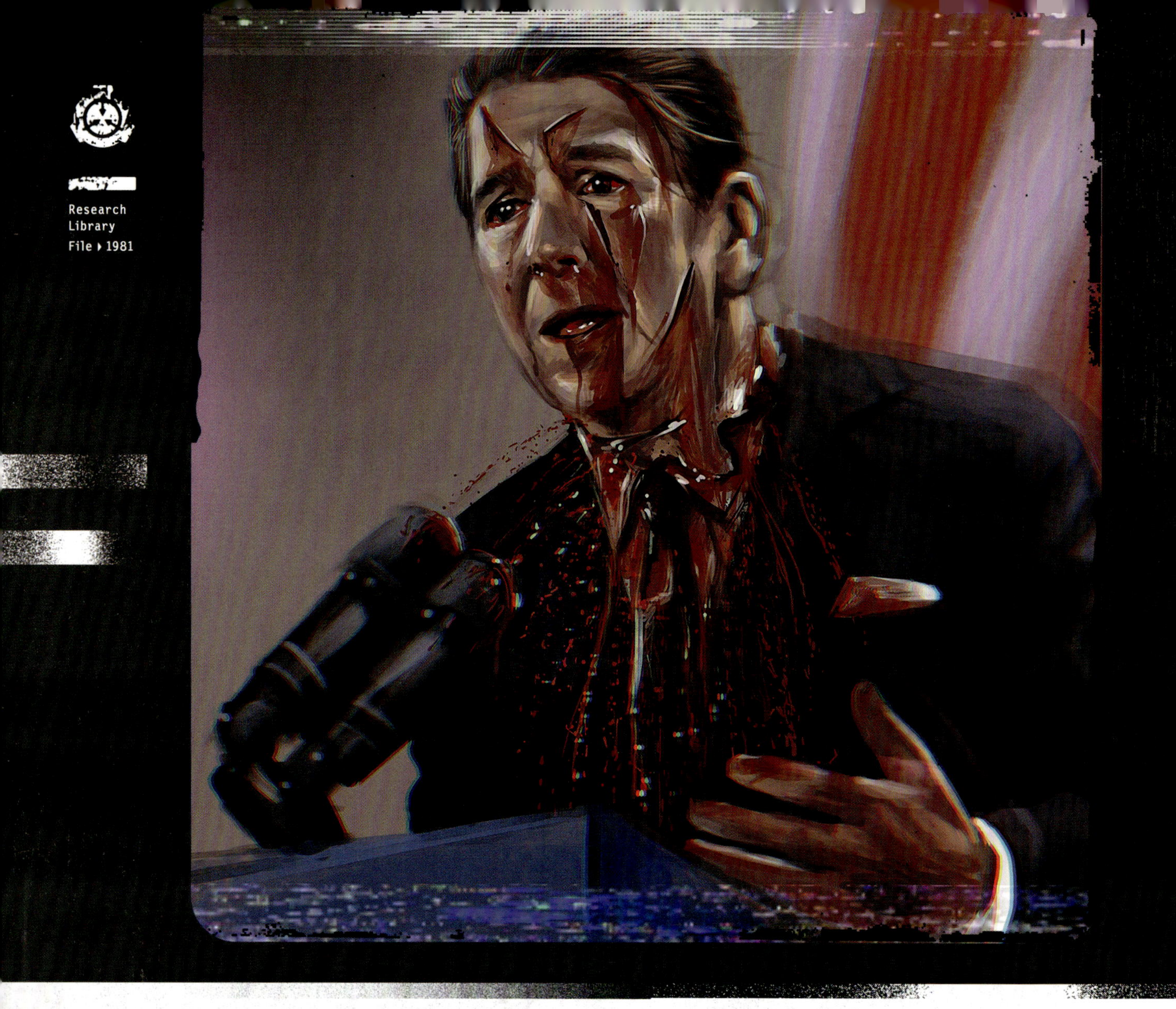

EXCERPT FROM VIDEO TRANSCRIPT OF RECORDING MADE ON ██/██/96

0:12:32 - **Reagan:** I've been to the steel mills of Alaska, and the cornfields of Nebraska. I've seen the derelict offices of Google burn with the window boarded up and the squatters inside them. I've seen the houses where they cut up the little babies. From coast to shining coast I have walked empty down drooling path <indecipherable> The decaying flesh of false morality poisoning our children. I have stood atop the mountain of this greedy earth, looking upon our beautiful pious pit, filled to bursting with the vast hands of helplessness. And did you know what I saw?

0:13:57 - Hell.

0:14:20 - *[The audience erupts into laughter]*

0:14:32 - *[Muffled voice can be heard behind camera]*

0:14:45 - **Reagan:** Now there you go again!

0:14:52 - *[Laughter proceeds to die down]*

0:15:00 - **Reagan:** But truly now, we live in a fortunate time. This is a fortunate time. Time is on our side. <laughter> A stitch in nine saves time.

0:15:40 - There are your truths and there are my truths. There are known knowns, known unknowns and unknown *<indecipherable>*. Some of them are in the audience right now!

0:16:02 - *[At this stage, wounds inflicted upon Reagan's neck appear to be so severe that it can no longer support the head. Speech degenerates into gurgles as Reagan violently jerks forward, spine being severed cleanly and the head only being loosely connected to the body by strands of muscle tissue. Body remains animate for the next 3 minutes, and continues to gesture as spinal column appears to be withdrawn from neck cavity, before finally collapsing. Tape degrades into static at 22:34]*

END TRANSCRIPT

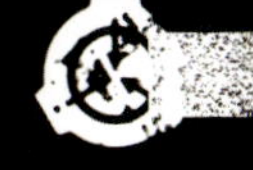

Research Library File 1981

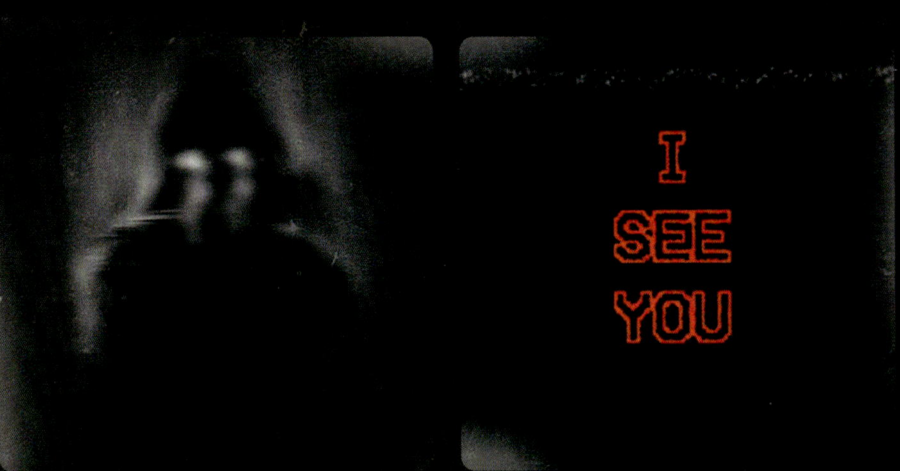

VIDEO TRANSCRIPT OF RECORDING MADE ON ██/██/02

REDACTED. 05 LEVEL CLEARANCE REQUIRED.

VIDEO TRANSCRIPT OF RECORDING MADE ON ██/██/05

0:00:00 - *[Long shot of podium as well as empty chairs normally occupied by Reagan and entourage. Curiously, this is the only recording that lacks both the intertitles and the presence of Ronald Reagan.]*

0:00:30 - *[Camera zooms in on podium.]*

0:02:55 - *[Entity known as SCP-1981-1 enters shot from left and stands at podium. Remains motionless for remainder of film.]*

0:22:34 - *[Tape flashes to single frame intertitle with words "I SEE YOU" colored in red. Holds for seven seconds then immediately cuts to static. No further signal for remainder of tape.]*

END TRANSCRIPT

This is the last Known sighting of SCP-1981-1. SCP-1981-1 has been absent in all subsequent playbacks. If observed, staff are advised not to attempt to communicate with SCP-1981-1 and to alert any Level 4 Supervisors on duty.

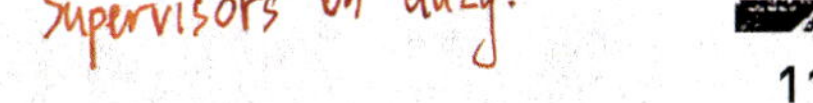

END OF REPORT

File >>> 018223

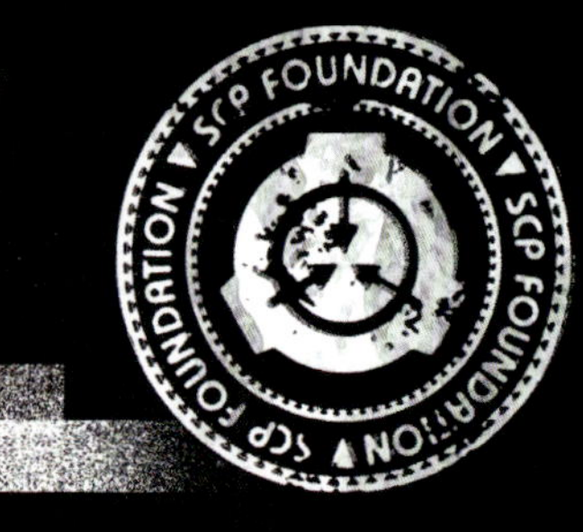

SCP-940

Title

ARANEAE MARIONETTES

Report by

Sabitsuki
Adam Smascher

Picture by

Alexander Demianenko
TroyL

Access the original report on

scp-wiki.wikidot.com/scp-940

Date

Class

KETER

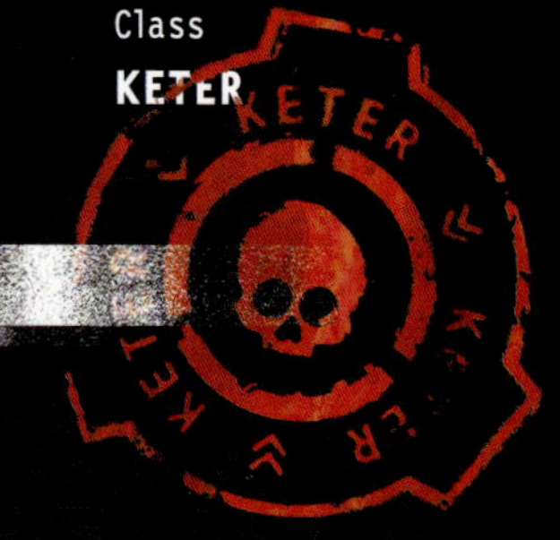

SPECIAL CONTAINMENT PROCEDURES

All known samples of SCP-940 larva are currently in containment. Systematic purging of SCP-940 adult samples from civilians is currently (as of ██/██/████) being spearheaded by a combination of Area-14 Research personnel and Mobile Task Force Omicron-7 ("Orkin"). Samples of Foundation strengthened ████-█-██████ (see documentation regarding 'Agent Blue') are in the process of being added to commercially available insecticides, which is expected to prevent any more 'wild' strains of SCP-940 from arising. All SCP-940 infectees are to be treated as Class 4 Biohazards, and are to be contained and transported under heavy sedation to Area-14, or otherwise terminated. Deceased bodies infected with any SCP-940 strain, regardless of developmental stage, are to be incinerated.

DESCRIPTION

SCP-940 is a parasitoid organism with some superficial similarities to troglobitic members of the class Arachnida. Adult specimens are highly agile and possess leg spans from four to seven meters; due to the difficulty in separating SCP-940 from their hosts (see below), average weight and body size are moot considerations. Each of their eight translucent legs is dotted regularly with six types of specialized sensory organs—IR-sensitive pit organs; ampullae of Lorenzini; compound and non-compound eyes sensitive to UV; and two additional organs of indeterminate function—and end in large tarsal claws, possessing scopulae and setules common amongst species of hunting spiders and allowing them to climb sheer vertical surfaces with ease. SCP-940 possess a radial nerve net similar to Asteroidea, or the common starfish, and no central nervous system; the possibility that SCP-940 rely on their host's brainpower for processing of external stimuli cannot be ruled out at this time.

Infection occurs following exposure to body fluids containing SCP-940 eggs and larvae! The lifecycle of SCP-940, from initial infection to maturity, is as follows:

STAGE I

file ////////////// 940

Infection occurs with exposure to bodily fluids contaminated with SCP-940 eggs and/or larvae. While larvae at this point are too small to be seen by the human eye, microscopic testing has revealed eggs are typically no larger than 3 to 5 microns in diameter. SCP-940 larvae, the only stage of its life cycle with many organ systems necessary for survival prior to integration with a host, possess leg spans from 7 to 17 microns.

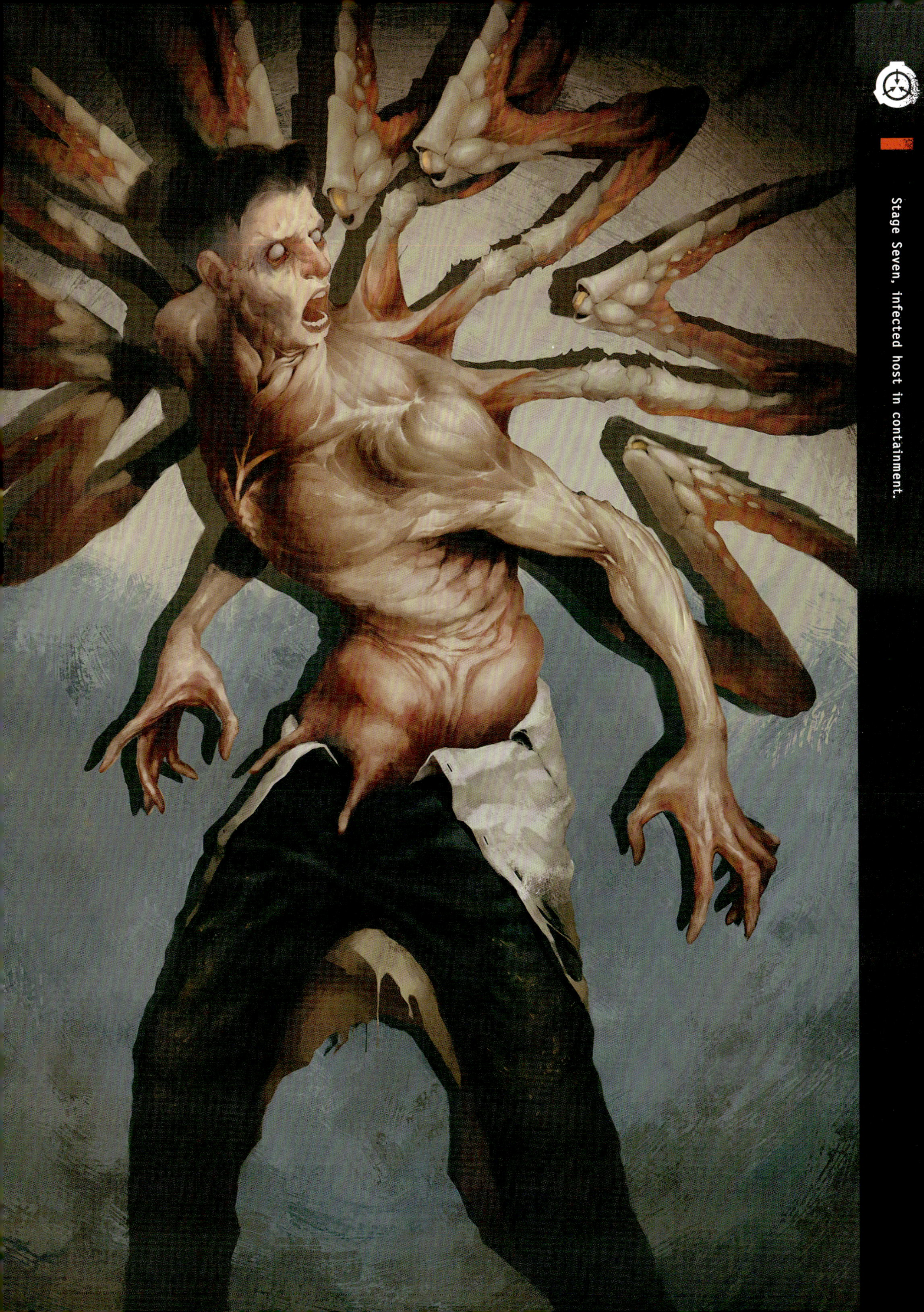

Stage Seven, infected host in containment.

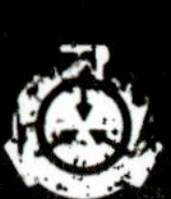

STAGE II

The first SCP-940 larvae to hatch will begin cannibalizing any unhatched eggs, then each other, in order to ensure only one larva develops into an adult within a given host. Hosts will often complain of abdominal and chest pains at this stage. Note: Cases of as many as five larvae reaching maturity within a single host, though rare due to competitiveness between larvae for a host and the enormous strain placed upon the host's body, have been documented. (See Incident-940-01, Subject 04)

Picture: *Ultrasound of Hatched Parasites in Carotid Artery. Larva Noted in Circles.*

STAGE III

The remaining SCP-940 larva migrates to the chest cavity, typically attaching to a major artery, the heart, or spinal cord, positioned with its legs oriented toward the host's back. Internal organ systems of the larva begin atrophying.

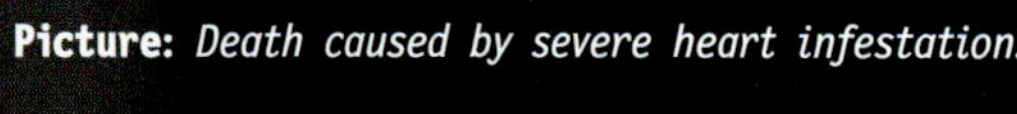

Picture: *Death caused by severe heart infestation.*

Subject died of a stroke caused by break down of internal body, consistent with transition to Stage Four.

STAGE IV

The carapace of SCP-940 larva's body breaks down; legs remain intact. The circulatory system of the larva conjoins with that of the host, as does its nervous system, though to a lesser extent. The larva begins producing a number of enzymes which cause the host's body to increase production of a number of hormones, including human growth hormone. Earlier abdominal and chest pain subsides. The host experiences an increase in appetite and general listlessness.

Picture: *MRA Image of Parasite Bonded to Abdominal Aorta.*

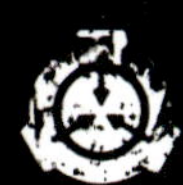

STAGE V

Approximately three weeks after initial infection, SCP-940 begins to alter serotonin and dopamine levels in the host's brain, causing hosts to experience feelings of happiness and well being. The legs of the larva, now supplied blood and nutrients by the host's circulatory system, begin to penetrate the skin of the host's back. Hosts typically do not report any discomfort or alarm at this, and rarely seek treatment.

Picture: *Leg of Parasite Beginning to Penetrate Back.*

STAGE VI

Approximately five weeks after initial infection, SCP-940 reaches full size and maturity. Hosts are secretive about their condition. A form of communication is believed to occur between SCP-940 and its host; for example, hosts have displayed a vague awareness of things occurring behind them. SCP-940 specimens often retract their legs, folding them flat against the host's back, allowing them to be concealed with relative ease by clothing. Additionally, SCP-940 triggers an increase in the levels of testosterone in the host's body, leading to increased libido. Infection of new hosts is facilitated through contact with bodily fluids contaminated with SCP-940 eggs; this is usually accomplished via coitus with an infected host.

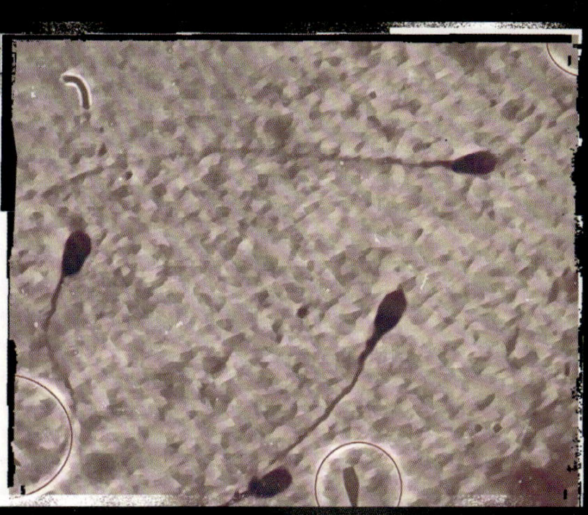

Picture: *Infected Semen Sample recovered from exposure during Incident 940-02. Eggs are generally invisible in female vaginal fluid (See Report 940-01-04 and -05 for more information).*

STAGE VII

All infected individuals that have survived six weeks of infection are considered to be in Stage Seven. Stage Seven infectees report the loss of a sense of individuality, gradual clouding of the eyes leading to loss of eyesight and culminating in near total blindness, and bouts of catatonia and catalepsy. Death is typically due to aneurysm caused by skyrocketing blood pressure, heart or kidney failure, or exsanguination. Infected at this Stage can be identified by the strange 'choking' sound they issue as they attempt to draw in more oxygen than is possible. When the host biologically dies, SCP-940 will continue to animate the corpse by means of its limbs, entering a 'berserk' state. In this state, SCP-940 will attempt to reproduce and infect with no regard for concealment, generally inflicting physical violence and blood transmission to do so. This state can last from one to three days before SCP-940 expires.

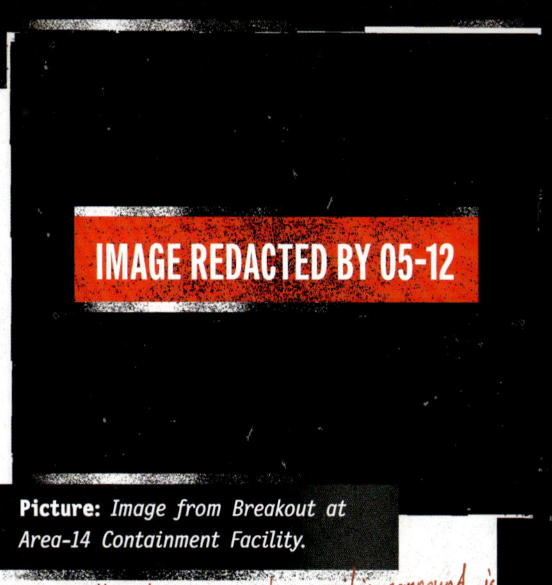

Picture: *Image from Breakout at Area-14 Containment Facility.*

Treatment with intravenous anti-parasitic compound is possible, if administered prior to infection advancing to Stage 3.

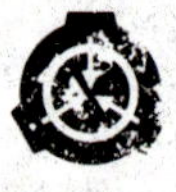

Research Library File ▸ 940

ADDENDUM

Stage Six and above adult SCP-940 samples, when not attempting to conceal their identities, are extremely agile and capable predators. Through the use of their powerful limbs and multiple sensory organs, they are highly adept at evading capture; field agents are to be highly cautious and equipped with MOPP-4 gear at all times to prevent infection, and Foundation-issued nerve gas grenades for suppression purposes.

INCIDENT LOG 940-01

On ██/██/████, Assistant Researcher S████ failed to return a live sample of SCP-940 larvae to cold storage, instead allowing the sample to remain unattended in the lab for approximately forty-five minutes while on lunch break. The resulting breach of containment resulted in seven SCP-940 infections amongst research and security personnel, and another five in D-Class personnel. The affected wing of Area-14 was isolated for decontamination, and infected Foundation personnel administered intravenous anti-parasitic compound. All received treatment within six hours of infection and made full recoveries. Infected D-Class personnel were isolated for observation so as to establish a progression of SCP-940 infection and determine for how long it remains treatable.

Observations of subjects D-940-01, D-940-02, and D-940-03 form the basis of the infection's given progression above.

Subject D-940-04 is the only infectee that did not follow the above reported progression, due to multiple larvae reaching maturity. D-940-04 was terminated three weeks into the process, when the accelerated symptoms resulted in her progression to Stage 7, completely bypassing Stages 5 and 6.

Subject D-940-05 was initially believed to be uninfected, displaying no symptoms of SCP-940 infection after three weeks. A full examination found D-940-05 to be pregnant; the unborn fetus was infected. The fetus, D-940-06, was allowed to mature. D-940-05 was kept unaware of its condition. Both expired when the legs of SCP-940 penetrated D-940-05's uterus. D-940-06 is preserved, kept in cryogenic storage at Armed Bio-Containment Area-14 for study.

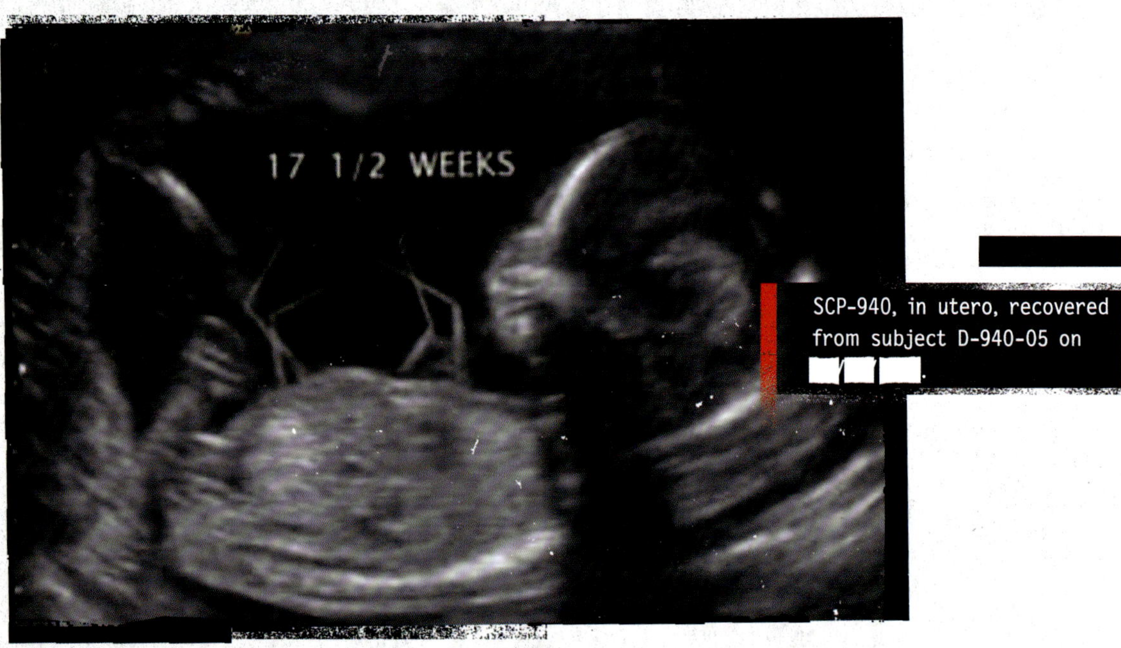

SCP-940, in utero, recovered from subject D-940-05 on ██/██/███.

END OF REPORT

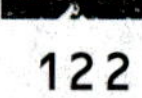

SPECIAL CONTAINMENT PROCEDURES

SCP-542 is to be kept in a 8m x 8m room with small adjoining bathroom, and may submit requests for furnishings barring anything that could be modified into surgical tools. Notable requests by SCP-542 include:

- One queen size bed, no blankets or sheets, bare mattress (Approved)
- Two large work desks (Approved)
- One large wardrobe (Approved)
- A selection of heavy coats, lab jackets, and pants (Approved)
- Several full-length mirrors (Denied)
- A selection of sewing supplies, along with bolts of cloth (Approved initially, revoked after Incident 542-B-03.)
- Several large bookcases, filled with anatomy and medical texts both old and new (Approved)
- A chess set (Approved)
- Blank-paged notebooks and various writing utensils (Approved)
- Regular supplies of German-language crossword puzzles (Approved)
- Industrial-grade deep sinks (Denied)
- Steel nail file (Denied. Given wooden/sandpaper emery board in replacement.)
- Nail Clippers (Denied)
- Access to his personal surgery kit (Denied except in cases of testing. See Addendum.)

The room is to remain locked, dead-bolted, and barred with at least two Class D guards on duty at any time. SCP-542 is to be fed two meals per day, delivered by Class D personnel, and as per request, will be given a transfusion of fresh blood (1 pint, any type) per week.

When SCP-542 begins to suffer from organ failure, he may request a fresh organ to be supplied, and Foundation Medical Personnel will sedate him and perform the surgery. Despite constant requests, SCP-542 may not be allowed to perform invasive surgery upon himself except during observed testing. Old and discarded organs or tissue are to be collected for testing.

In the event that SCP-542 should escape confinement, SCP-542 may be subdued by high doses of tranquilizers or disabled via a net. Should he come into possession of any knives or shards of glass/mirror that could be used to cut, nonlethal fire is permitted.

DESCRIPTION

SCP-542 claims that it has been, at one time, a typical human of Caucasian descent, identifying as German in nationality. This story is supported by the fact that German appears to be his first language, speaking all other languages with a German accent. SCP-542 requests to be called "Herr Chirurg" or "Surgeon" by staff and is fluent in German, English, and French, and can speak a small bit of Polish

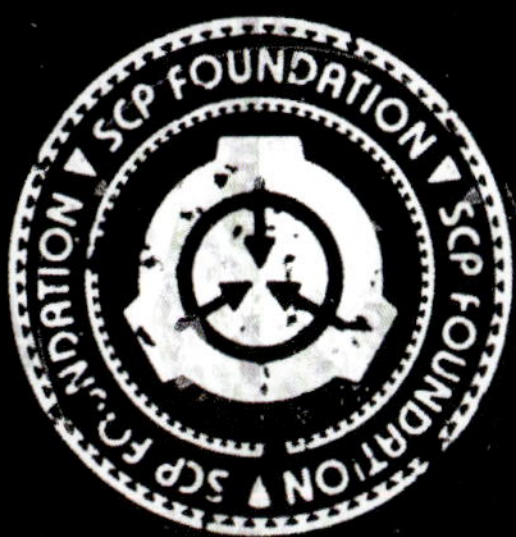

SCP-542

Title

HERR CHIRURG

Report by

agatharights

Picture by

Ruslan Korovkin

Access the original report on

scp-wiki.wikidot.com/scp-542

Date

Class

EUCLID

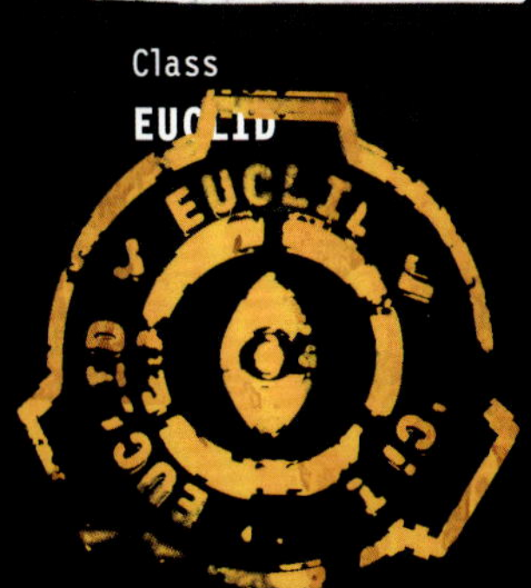

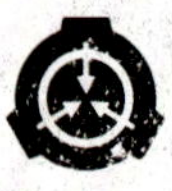

Research Library File ▸ 542

and Italian. Standard IQ tests have revealed 542's IQ to range around 150, placing him as high intelligence. It is unknown how old 542 is; testing of various tissue samples has revealed nothing. He claims to have been 'dreadfully normal' before World War I started, and claims to have worked for the Nazi party, even if he found their goals 'boringly simple.'

He has been described as a "Frankenstein's Monster" in appearance. SCP-542 may hide his odd features under heavy clothing, but prefers to wear only a nice pair of slacks, revealing his hunched form, distended gut, warped ribcage, and bizarre arm structure. His skin is made from patches of various hues and shades, some of these healed together with scars while others are still stitched together. Non-symmetrical bone and muscle structure reveals that he has replaced the majority of his body over time, and admits to having worked with "helpers" before to replace such things as portions of his own spinal cord. Although his appearance can change with surgery, his arms are always too long for his body, and his hands have been modified greatly to have additional joints in the fingers.

The skin is pulled rather tightly over 542's face, giving him a somewhat skeletal appearance along with the tendency for his bones to bulge through his skin. His teeth, it should be noted, are collected from different individuals, some of them not even human by all appearances. It is not uncommon for him to cough or to vomit blood, and as such requires infusions of fresh blood approximately once per week. He currently boasts two hearts and multiples of several other organs and organ systems. How 542 keeps track of his own structure while performing surgery is unknown, but he likens it to 'having a very good memory.'

DNA testing on all tissues is inconclusive, and reveals fragmented DNA. It is unknown how he is able to accept different blood types and multiple organs without suffering from organ rejection or allergic reactions, nor how he is able to function while performing invasive surgery on himself, even while inserting extra brain matter into his skull. SCP-542 is to be kept alive for observation and testing on the process that keeps him alive.

SCP-542 behaves in a surprisingly pleasant manner most of the time, enjoying lengthy conversations about science and biology, politics, and long games of chess. However, when an organ begins to fail or part of his body becomes necrotic, he undergoes a drastic personality change, stalking and observing people from a distance. Additional information on his habits and attacks may be found in the addendum.

SCP-542 appears to have a previously unknown ability to be completely aware of his body's functions and workings constantly, even able to identify points of rotting or decay he should not be able to sense by any known means. This ability, however, has been shown to extend beyond his own body. He can passively sense the health and medical status of other humans within several meters of him, the range extending to approximately five meters when he focuses. He admits that he uses this process, which he doesn't understand himself, to pick his next victims.

ADDENDUM

SCP-542 has been proven to be the assailant in a string of 45 murders over the course of three years that occurred across Germany, England, and America, and is suspected of an additional, unconfirmed fifteen murders in that time span. He was first observed four years ago by Agent ██████ in ███████, Germany, after four people had been attacked and had muscle, sinew, and bones removed from their limbs. Three of the victims died from blood loss and shock. The fourth, ████ ████ happened to be staying in the hotel room next to Agent █████, who intervened. This account may be found in Incident Report 542-A-06.

SCP-542 has a strong connection to a collection of scalpels, blades, syringes, and various other surgical equipment from time periods ranging from modern day to archaic, if very well-kept, relics from years as early as the 1910s. He carries these in a velvet-lined, black leather suitcase, and modifies many of his jackets to have holders to hide and carry this equipment in. He is not allowed access to this collection except during testing and observation of self-surgery.

SCP-542 has also caused several deaths of Class D personnel, even when not in testing, due to negligence or assumption that certain items may be 'safe' when used by him. Personnel are reminded that even if his

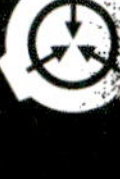

Incident 542-A-06.

personality is pleasant the majority of the time, he will still dissect personnel for amusement and curiosity's sake if given the chance. These incidents may be reviewed in Incident Reports 542-B-01 through 542-B-11. Seemingly safe items such as sewing supplies have led to him making more than a rather well-tailored jacket for himself, but also resulted in him restraining a Class D Personnel by sewing him to the mattress of the bed, before removing his kidneys and a portion of the liver.

SCP-542 has shown to be very willing to comply with certain experiments and appears to enjoy performing self-surgery with someone observing, explaining what he is doing and displaying his knowledge of the workings of the body as if he were a teacher describing a surgical textbook. Unfortunately, this usually requires being at a risk of attack from him.

It has been requested that SCP-542 be kept alive so the process that allows for him to recover from intense surgery without organ rejection be studied and potentially copied for medical use. SCP-542 may also show potential for being used to assist in surgical and studying endeavors, due to his increased intelligence and compulsion for dissection. Any books and notes written by him may be accessed and studied by those with Class-2 security clearance or higher.

UPDATE ██/██/20██

SCP-542 has somehow acquired knowledge of both SCP-291 and SCP-1025, and appears to be very interested in their use. All requests to study both anomalies are to be denied until further notice.

INCIDENT REPORT 542-A-06

Agent ██████, while staying at the ███ Hotel in ██████, Germany heard the sounds of a scuffle and screaming from across the hall at approximately 3AM Local time, at which point he felt that he had to intervene, unknown that he would come face to face with a possible SCP. After forcing the door to █████ ███'s room he observed SCP-542 removing the muscles and bone of Miss ███'s right leg. After the agent fired several shots, 542 fled through the window and Agent ██████ contacted local authorities and an ambulance.

████ ███, an American tourist who had only been in town for a few days, described what had happened to her while recovering in the hospital. Afterward, she willingly took the amnestic issued to her, preferring to believe that she had instead been in an unfortunate traffic incident and her right leg had been amputated.

Her report is as follows.

> I had been to Germany before, so I knew my way around… and I was used to taking the bus. But I guess I first saw him there, I think, just this guy all hidden under heavy jackets and this hat and glasses and of course, I was suspicious because it was summer, you know, sweltering hot… and I realized he was looking at me, but I ignored it. He didn't get off the bus at my stop, anyways, and there were always others on the bus, even late at night. I guess I saw him for three days, and I stopped thinking about it… He must've followed me off the bus that… that day. That night.
>
> I went up to my hotel room, and I don't… I don't remember… The window was open, and it was all dark, the light wouldn't turn on. I figured somebody had decided to steal my stuff, so I went in to see if anything was missing and… and…
>
> [[████ ███ shows signs of intense discomfort, and asks for a minute to compose herself. This is allowed, and she resumes after several minutes.]]
>
> He was hiding under the bed, and he had these freakishly… long arms… and the fingers… too many joints and he took my ankles right out from under me. He was just too fast, and… and he tied my arms and legs to the bed, and at first I thought, you know, that he was going to… to… you know.

He kept saying, like… "Don't worry," and "You're going to help me," and "I need your help…" and things like that, it was scary as shit, and he said that so long as I kept quiet he might call an ambulance afterward, and that was a little scary.

I guess it really was worse than that. He picked up his jacket, it'd been on the coat hanger by the door and I hadn't even noticed it… and started pulling out all these knives and… all these tools and I just didn't know what to do. So I decided to take my chances and started screaming as loud as I could. Then he… he…

[[█████ █████ was allowed to stop there, and was delivered the amnestic and alibi that night.]]

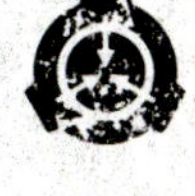

INCIDENT REPORT 542-A-15

For details on the eventual tracking and capture of SCP-542 please refer to [[DATA EXPUNGED]]. *A request for declassification is under review, 20██/██/██.*

NOTE

As of ██/██/██, SCP-542 has been moved to Bio-Research Area-12 in order to assist in the Olympia Project.

And I want him back intact!
Dr. Rights

NOTE

SCP-542 has somehow acquired information of SCP-291, SCP-827, and SCP-545. Investigation into the extent of 542's knowledge of these SCPs and how he acquired this knowledge is currently under investigation. Offending personnel will be disciplined appropriately following a board review.

-05-███

END OF REPORT ▌████ ▌██

File >>> 00299293

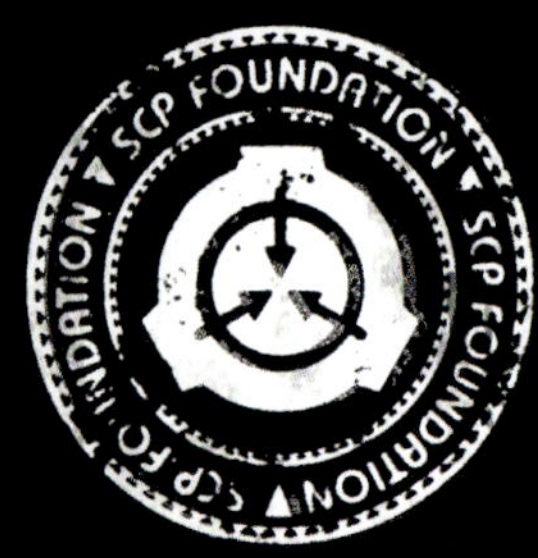

SCP-592

Title

INACCURATE HISTORY BOOK

Report by

ashleypoet

Picture by

Thomas Frank

Access the original report on

www.scpwiki.com/scp-592

Date

Class

EUCLID

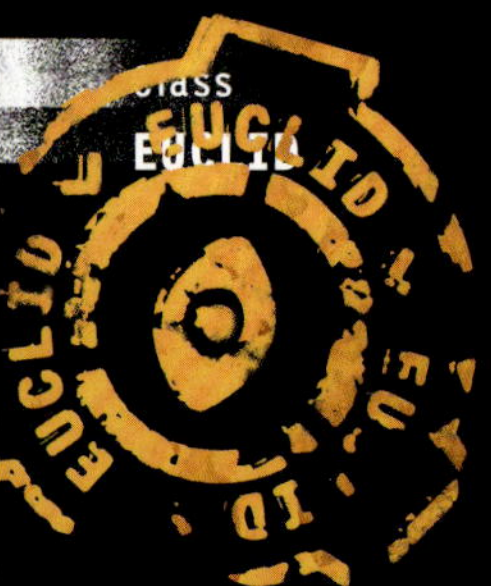

SPECIAL CONTAINMENT PROCEDURES

SCP-592 should be contained in research cell 1611-E at all times, locked in a steel box, in the middle of a frosted glass containment cubicle. Also in the cubicle are a table, two (2) computers, a standard-sized computer scanner, an internal network connection port, and two (2) pairs of visual distortion goggles, which must be worn upon entering the cubicle, so as to make SCP-592 illegible. The first computer serves as an analysis machine, the second as a custom firewall. All devices have been modified with specialised software and hardware (see Testing Protocol for details) and the network port has been secured such that no device other than the firewall may use it. It is strictly necessary that the computers and scanner are turned off and unplugged after experimenting and that they are only powered for the duration of the experiment. The front and back covers of SCP-592 are to be covered in black opaque tape at all times.

The cell must be guarded continually to ensure that SCP-592 is not removed.

DESCRIPTION

SCP-592 is a large hardcover book which exhibits no external qualities that could be considered unusual, but which can cause delusions, psychosis, changes in physical health and appearance, or even severe wounding when read. It is titled "Chronicle of the 20th Century" and consists of 450 all-color printed pages. It is reported that it has a printed cover (no dust jacket) with the title of the book, the publisher, and a selection of illustrations from within the text. The original cover is a deep blue. The spine contains the title and publisher name, and is left uncovered by tape. The cover page informs the reader that it was published by Interworld Press, 54 ██████ St, Chicago, IL in 1996. A company named Interworld Press has never been registered in the US nor does the street listed exist.

The text is a collection of newspaper clippings and short articles on major events from January 1900 to December 1995. Much of the first half of the text agrees with recorded events but at some point no later than 15 June 1956, a date researchers have termed the Point of Divergence (PoD), the text begins to diverge from known history. These divergences become more common and acute the further away from the PoD the text is.

Subjects reading from the text before the PoD report no ill effect and generally comment that the text is well written and seems very accurately researched. Subjects reading from the book after the PoD understand the passage read as accepted truth, and vehemently deny any suggestions that the text is in fact incorrect. The claims subjects make are often disturbing or shocking in nature. It also appears that a subject that has read passages from a certain year can recount events that are detailed in later sections of the book.

It has been found that those born before the date which the test passage indicates, and lived in or nearby the location of the event described, may construct personal experiences built around the event and describe them as they would any other vivid memory. The subject will go to great measures to defend the reality of their story, often turning violent if under interrogation.

Exposure to SCP-592 may alter physical characteristics of the subject to conform with the events of the passage being read. This can vary from small changes in appearance or clothing to the infliction of severe wounds. For example, in one

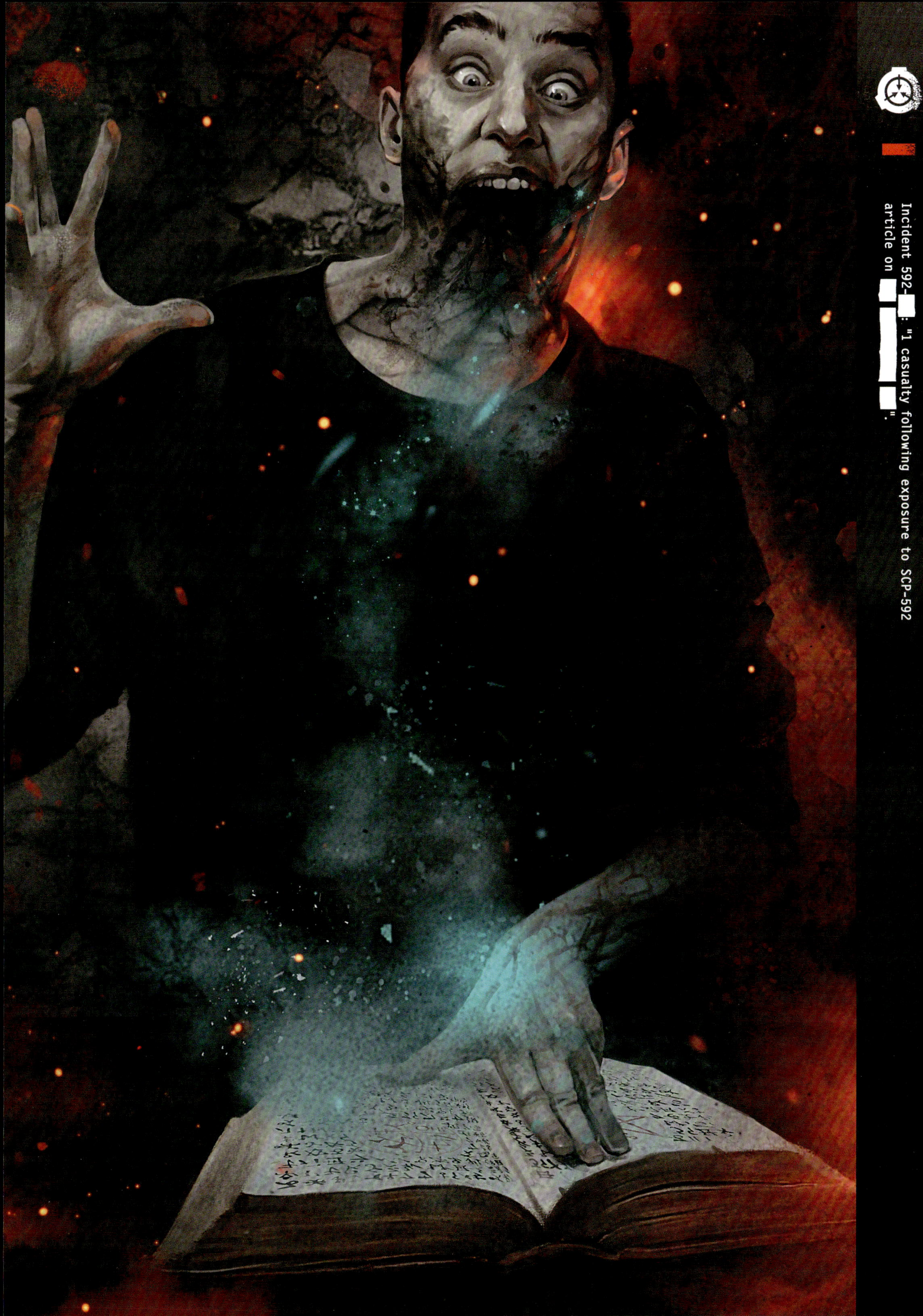
Incident 592-█: "1 casualty following exposure to SCP-592
article on █ ███ █".

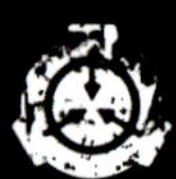

instance a subject (D-94920) produced a scar during an interview, stating that he "picked it up during the [DATA EXPUNGED]". His widow, when presented with the scar, located on his ████, was surprised, stating she "had not noticed [the scar] before".

It has been found that once the subject discovers that the world is inconsistent with their acquired memories, they begin to feel that the present reality is an illusion, a dream, or a deceit, often stating malevolent or government forces are at work in maintaining the illusion. Subjects who reach this stage enter into a profound and chronic psychosis. All attempts to treat this delusion have failed. The exact effects vary:

Date of passage read	Effects
Before PoD	No ill short- or long-term effects.
< 2 months after PoD	Short-term: confusion. No ill long-term effects.
< 2 years after PoD	Short-term: confusion. Long-term: minor mental illness, development of tics, nightmares, minor paranoia episodes and panic attacks.
< 10 years after PoD	Short-term: confusion, violent episodes. Long-term: deeply ingrained delusion formed leading to debilitating paranoia, psychosis, and schizophrenia-type disorders.
> 10 years after PoD, or earlier if subject forms a "personal experience"	Short-term: confusion, violent episodes. Long term: acute psychosis and delusions. Crippling agnosia. Becomes withdrawn. High chance of suicidal or homicidal behavior. Severe risk of immediate but variable physical change in subject.

SCP-592 was recovered during a narcotics raid in August 2006 on the property of Mr. [REDACTED], the leader of a controversial religious group called the "Church of the True History". Despite being in possession of SCP-592, Mr. [REDACTED] is believed to have started the church for financial gain rather than revelation. The owner may have only survived exposure from SCP-592 for almost two years because of his rampant drug use, which included methamphetamine, cocaine, and a host of opioids – though psychedelics, especially DMT, are known to have been used and probably interacted with the effects of SCP-592 more than the others. [REDACTED] believed that his delusions came from his drug use, but noted that a year after exposure to SCP-592, he found himself turning to drugs more often to "hide away from the truth". In custody and deprived of his usual chemical relief, the suspect became comatose and died a week later. The circumstances of the acquisition has led to proposals to test SCP-592 in combination with psychedelic drugs (see Proposal ████).

ADDENDUM 592-A

The chemical properties of SCP-592 have been studied by Dr. Grayson and the Chemical Forensics team. Dr. Grayson reports that:

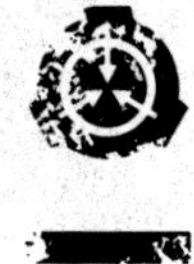

Samples were obtained by means of cutting small squares of paper from the book, while wearing distortion goggles. The squares were small enough to contain no more than one word. Squares containing portions of illustrations were covered by black opaque tape as soon as extracted. Our results indicate that the chemical properties of SCP-592 differ very little from any other color publication. The paper primarily consists of cellulose from common woods, and the black and yellow inks are standard. It has been found, however, that some chemicals used in the cyan and magenta inks, while entirely known to science, are not normally used in the industry. An expert in inks and dyes has commented that the chemicals would be an inferior but acceptable substitute to those currently in use if certain metal elements were much scarcer, and therefore much more expensive, than they are today.

TESTING PROTOCOL

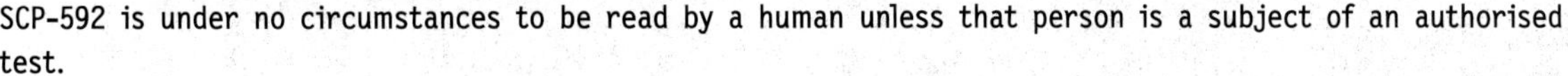

SCP-592 is under no circumstances to be read by a human unless that person is a subject of an authorised test.

SCP-592 is only to be analysed by computer, using the systems provided. The book is to be scanned on a per-page basis using the scanner provided. The scanned image is then sent to the analysis machine. The scanner and other devices are modified such that they can be used while wearing the visual distortion goggles *(Note: researchers must pass Training Course 305-S: Intermediate Braille and Training Course 10-E: Use of SCP Imaging Software before being approved to test SCP-592).*

The analysis machine is modified such that it contains and supports no non-volatile (permanent) writable storage devices, such that it never stores a copy of the scanned image that may persist beyond the analysis phase. The image is destroyed from the system RAM as soon as is possible, through standard secure memory flushing routines.

The firewall is configured to study incoming packets for characteristics of properly processed output and destroys the packet if an insufficient amount of characteristics are discovered. This prevents the transmission of text or images that have not been sufficiently obfuscated.

As SCP-592 is heavily illustrated there are two analysis protocols.

ANALYSIS OF TEXT

The analysis machine uses industry-standard Optical Character Recognition (OCR) systems to parse the text in the image, and then destroys the image. The text file is then passed through a series of custom Natural Language Processing (NLP) routines to summarise the text. The original text file is then destroyed, and the summary is sent to the secure Foundation Intranet.

The NLP routines analyse the passage using statistical methods incorporating databases of diverse English corpora, some details of other SCPs, a correct chronology of events extracted from various texts, and a severely limited referential network of other entries in SCP-592. *NOTE: Efforts to increase the degree in which analysis references other events resulted in an incident whereby [DATA EXPUNGED], resulting in 3 researchers being euthanized (see Document SCP-592-███).*

The summary is composed in such a way as to mitigate any possibility of exposure to the true material of the passage, but still provide useful analytical details about the event described. An example (SCP-592-SUMM090777-A):

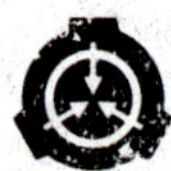

█████
Research Library
File ▸ 592

Date: 7th September 1977

Location: Southern United States (99% certainty). States: ██████ (79%), ███ █████ (11%), or █████ (9% certainty)

Type: NEWSPAPER CLIPPING

Summary:

The passage is describing HUMAN CONFLICT. The HUMAN CONFLICT is of an IDEOLOGICAL or RELIGIOUS nature. The passage seems (56%) to be LAMENTING in tone. The passage contains the numbers 2000, 1977, and 16. A relation to EVENT SUMM010777-C and EVENT [REDACTED] is likely (78% certainty).

It is certain (98%) that the passage contains a reference to both SCP-██ and SCP-██.

Related incidents: Incident 592-██ "Loss of a limb following exposure to SCP-592 article on war"

Note: Lexical tokens from source databases are presented in all-caps.

ANALYSIS OF IMAGES

SCP-592 contains around two hundred illustrations. These are cropped from the scanned image as part of the OCR routine. The image is then subjected to a number of Fourier transforms and convolutions to obscure the resulting output from human recognition while simultaneously analysing its structure and providing a summary of its contents by statistical analysis. Record of the original image is then destroyed. An example report (SCP-592-IMG098):

Date: 1st April 1963

Location: Unknown BEDROOM with WESTERN FURNISHINGS.

Type: FULL COLOR PHOTOGRAPH

Subject:

The image contains two (2) ADULT PERSONS standing, one (1) HUMAN CHILD sitting on a CHAIR or STOOL, and SCP-██. With 100% certainty the PERSONS in the image should have FACIAL FEATURES. With 100% certainty the PERSONS in the image do NOT have FACIAL FEATURES.

END OF REPORT

SPECIAL CONTAINMENT PROCEDURES

Biological samples that are part of SCP-2195 are to be either preserved in formaldehyde solution, dried and stored in a vacuum container, or frozen, according to the method they were preserved with at the moment of discovery. Biological samples preserved through plastic infusion or stored in a solid synthetic resin block, as well as non-biological samples do not require any special containment procedures. Three low-level security vaults in Site 7 are designated for SCP-2195 storage.

Non-deactivated late-term SCP-2195-1 samples are to be handled by trained personnel as per standard Foundation guidelines for handling bulk primary explosive substances.

Research has shown that explosive materials contained within SCP-2195-1 degrade over time, therefore they are granted a storage period of 20 years and are to be incinerated afterwards.

Documents acquired as part of SCP-2195 are to be digitalized and uploaded into the SCP-2195 documentation database; original documents are archived.

Access to SCP-2195 documentation is restricted to personnel of 2-2195 clearance or higher.

Access to SCP-2195 samples is restricted to personnel of 3-2195 clearance or higher.

Experiments that involve reproduction of SCP-2195-1 require Ethics Committee approval.

DESCRIPTION

SCP-2195 is a collective designation for documental and material evidence, specifically collected by unidentified individuals, that is related to a large-scale government project which involves mass reproduction of SCP-2195-1 for military purposes, specifically targeting the drawbacks of said project. SCP-2195 includes biological samples preserved through various methods, demonstration and test articles, prototypes, and a variety of documents. The sum of documentation recovered was enough to fill 19 (nineteen) shipping containers at the moment of discovery.

Analysis of said evidence has shown that the project took place in political, historical and socio-cultural circumstances inconsistent with known reality, which suggests extradimensional or otherwise anomalous origin.

Although no fully formed SCP-2195-1 were discovered within SCP-2195, recovered materials provide enough information to give a complete description of their appearance. SCP-2195-1 are living, genetically altered human infants of indeterminate sex (SCP-2195-1 allosomes are identical, and contain genetic information from both X and Y chromosomes).

SCP-2195-1 body structure is radically different from that of normal infants; SCP-2195-1 are presumed to have the shape of an ellipsoid roughly 60 cm long and 50 cm in circumference, and mass of 9 to 9.5 kg. The physiology of tissues covering the front and back ends is identical to that of somewhat calloused human skin; the rest of the skin is sphacelated, metamorphised, parchment-like and fused

File >>> 00228331

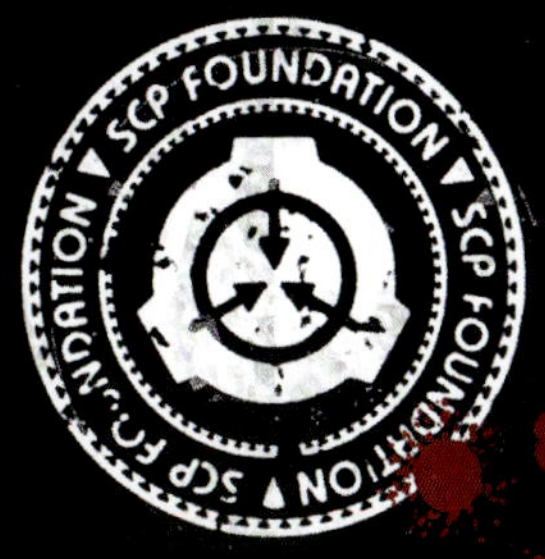

SCP-2195 RU

Title

SONS OF THE NATION

Report by
theTBAPb

Translation by
Gene R, VAElynx

Pictures by
Pavel Kobyzev
Dmitriy Fomin

Access the original report on
scp-wiki.wikidot.com/scp-2195

Date

Class

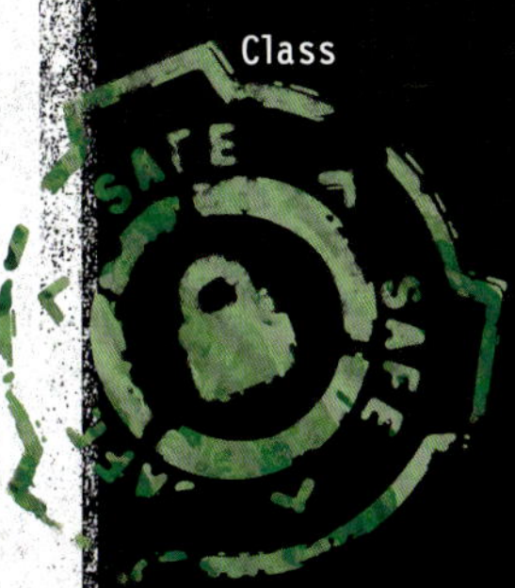

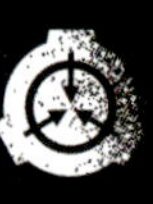

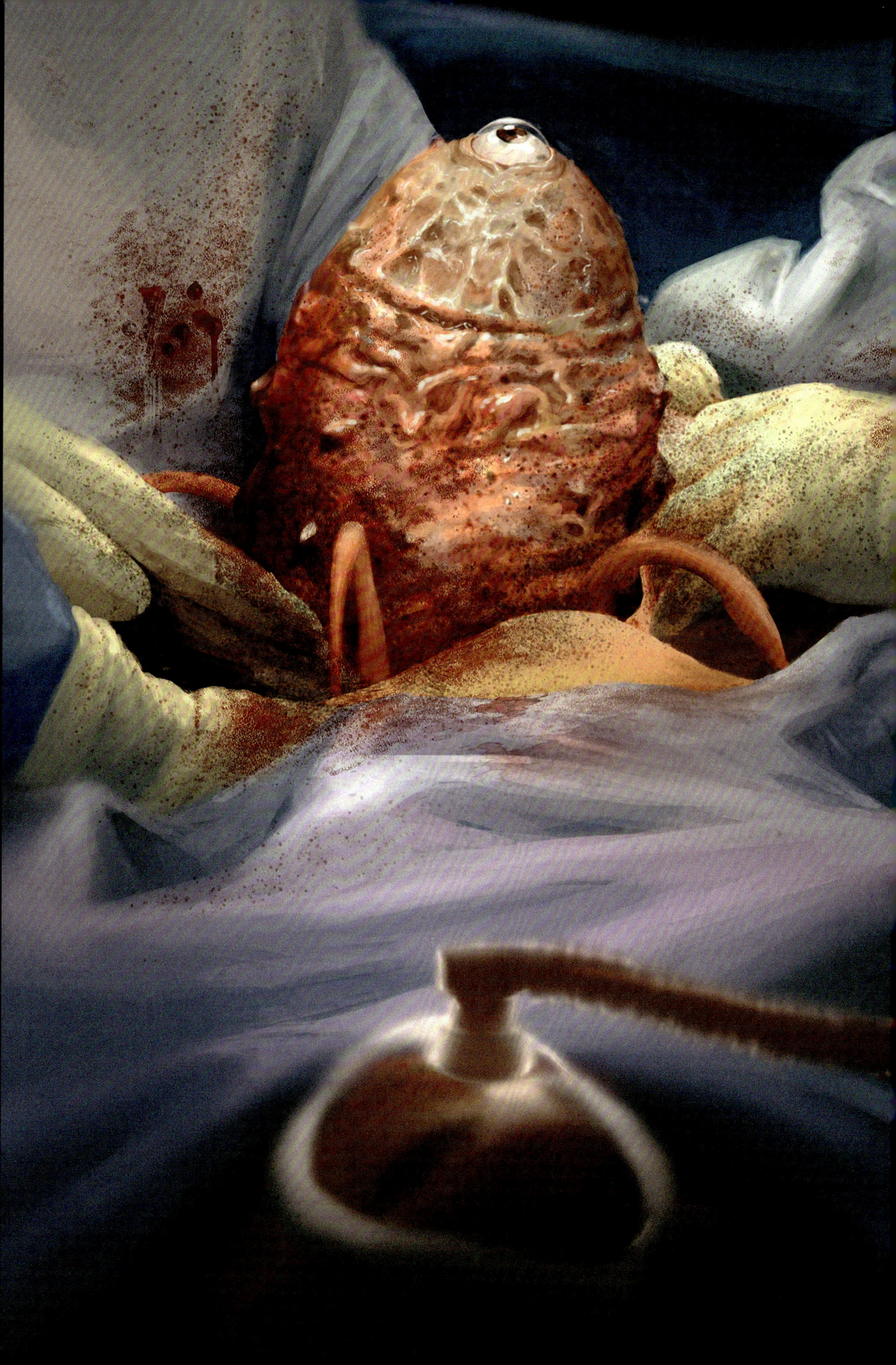

D-39207 delivering a specimen of SCP-2195-1.

with the underlying bone (no muscles and/or fat tissues are present). Ribs grow away from the whole length of the spine (55 to 56 pairs of ribs in total); the ribs are flattened and fused along their whole length, which creates a solid bone capsule with the pelvis and the skull fused immovably to its respective ends.

The skull is small, streamlined forwards and has radial symmetry. The only orifice facing outside is a large eye socket on the front end of the body, which contains an anatomically normal eye with a transparent protective membrane. No auditory apparatus is present, but the inner ear vestibular system is extremely developed.

The pelvic section also has radial symmetry and serves as an attachment point for four identical limbs facing upwards and downwards diagonally. These limbs are around 10 centimeters long and contain a single pointed bone, which is connected to the pelvis by a ball-and-socket joint, resembling the human hip joint or shoulder joint. Their freedom of movement is severely restricted by the joint's position within the body, as well as rigid tendons; nonetheless they are fitted with powerful muscles intended to turn the limb around its axis. An orifice with a sphincter is located between these limbs, which leads to a small dead-end cavity with richly innervated walls.

Inner organs are mostly either rudimentary or missing, which makes SCP-2195-1's life expectancy to be 10 to 15 minutes, unless sustained by an external life support system. Apart from the aforementioned sensory organs, central nervous system and muscles, only the circulatory system is developed, which includes major vessels, the heart and an organ that resembles a radically altered spleen; said organ has thick, myoglobin-rich walls that can accumulate a certain amount of oxygen and release it into the blood, and filters carbon dioxide out of the blood. There is also a small cluster of electrocytes, which is connected via nerves to the cardiac conducting system.

Aside from the front and back ends, the majority of SCP-2195-1 body is occupied by tissue that structurally resembles liver tissue with extreme adipose degeneration (vacuoles amount for 97% of its volume and even more than that in mass); instead of fat, the vacuoles contain a complex organic substance that has pronounced explosive properties.

Its exact parameters cannot be determined due to the irregularity of the remaining biological components' amount within tissues, as well as due to the the substance's own nature (supposedly, a mix of several compounds with similar properties in varying proportions). Approximate properties can be described as such:

- Density: 1.8-1.9 g/cm^3
- Specific energy of explosion: 9.2 MJ/kg
- Explosive strength (measured by Trauzl test): 670 cm^3
- Brisance (measured by Kast test): 8 mm
- Detonation velocity: 8300-8500 m/s
- Sensitivity: 70% explosions with a 10 kg weight dropped from a height of 25 cm.
- Amount of tissue in an instance of SCP-2195-1: 7.5 to 8 kg, explosive yield up to 25 kg of TNT equivalent.

According to the documents, SCP-2195-1 have a gestation time of 40 weeks which is normal to humans. They were also naturally born, but subject to the following operative treatment immediately after birth:

- catheterization of 2 major vessels for connection to life support system;
- installation of a metal clamp along the spine which acts as a band for a suspension mount;
- mounting of reinforced plastic fins on the limbs;
- fitting the front end with a transparent nose cone.

After that SCP-2195-1 were subject to three-week training in a wind tunnel fitted with elastic suspension systems and an image projector to display various battlefield scenes as seen from above. For that purpose, a device for electrical nerve stimulation was inserted into the orifice at the rear end of SCP-2195-1; the higher the achieved targeting precision, the greater the stimulation. The SCP-2195-1 specimens were thus trained to develop visual recognition skills for various targets, and trained to control their flight using limb-mounted aerofoil planes. During the training, the electric organ, which functions as a detonator, was to be temporarily disabled by means of paralytic agent injections.

Following the training SCP-2195-1 was to be tattooed with an emblem of the target it was trained for, put into a state of suspended animation and packed into a shipping container for later use as a homing high explosive bomb.

Research Library File ▸ 2195 RU

The documentation found as part of SCP-2195 is mostly typewritten in a language having minute differences with modern French, although the origin of names and toponyms mentioned within seems to be more English. No similarities with modern geography were found. The name of the state is never mentioned; instead, "Notre Patrie" ("Our Fatherland") is listed even in official office, position and department names, which is often abbreviated to NP (e.g., "Président de NP").

According to the information contained within, the state waged a long and slaughterous offensive war on another state's territory, which was not popular among its populace. State propaganda efforts were not sufficient to subdue the growing pacifist movement which was especially strong among the soldiers' mothers. The arms industry was also on the verge of decline. The documented project was proposed in order to solve both problems, and was meant to implant embryos of SCP-2195-1 into all fertile women under the guise of various mandatory medical procedures. The surge of "living bombs" born afterwards was announced as a natural event, a manifestation of mass consciousness, the will of the people, and an evidence of charitability[1] of the military intervention taking place. Another important factor was the mother's blood relationship which required a mother to unconditionally support her child's "voluntary effort", which in turn demanded her to abolish any pacifist beliefs and/or made her an indirect participant of the bombings, with personal responsibility forced on her later on.

Note: this shows drastic differences of ethical norms between our society and the one described. It is hard to imagine that measures like these would have any effect in any state we know, yet SCP-2195 documents describe them as extremely effective yet highly immoral, although only in the sense that both the higher will and the blood relationship were falsified, therefore the highest values were fraudulently exploited.

However, various events that took place during the project's development, should they have become public, would have brought sharp discredit on it, due to both their negative nature, and the fact that the nature and sheer amount of these events contradicted the idea of higher force's mercy and justice, therefore making the "higher will" explanation unviable.

First and foremost, SCP-2195 contains evidence of numerous complicating disorders during pregnancy and birth:

- Various fetal pathologies and deformities, miscarriages, cases of stillbirth. Preserved samples included.
- Numerous cases of ectopic pregnancy. Several postmortem specimens and a variety of medical records are available. Vast majority of these cases resulted in the mother's death or loss of fertility, which was grounds for euthanasia.
- Birth trauma and cases of mothers' deaths at birth due to the fetus' size and rigid structure. Medical records available.
- Acute, often life-threatening toxicoses caused by metabolic byproducts during explosive substance formation inside fetus. Several in-depth research papers, histological samples and body fluid samples available.
- Anemia, dangerous exhaustion of the mother's body due to the fetus' accelerated growth. An essay of observations concerning this issue is available.
- Multifetal gestation which almost inevitably caused pathologies. Cases of SCP-2195-1 conjoined twins. A range of medical records available. The majority of such pregnancies were aborted due to critical situations; preserved fetus samples available.
- Hyperplasia, fermental chorionic hyperactivity, or detrimental chorion deformation leading to formation of multiple large synechiated folds. Hyperactivity, abnormal growth or improper position of the resulting placenta caused destruction of uterine walls, mouth of the womb, or fallopian tubes. Preserved samples, extensive studies and medical records available. Numerous descriptions of deaths due to internal bleeding and cases of euthanasia due to loss of fertility after operative treatment are also available.

1. Original documents use a specific philosophical term which, according to the context, should mean predetermination or being destined by a higher force, whose will it is immoral and unnatural for a human being to resist.

- Spontaneous fetus detonations on latter stages of pregnancy. Investigation reports, autopsy protocols, and an archive of media reports are available. Collateral damage and fatalities are described, with the cause presented by propaganda as "immoral conduct that is disgracing motherhood". No details of said conduct were provided, although the manner this description is used in suggests that it is a common euphemism for some specific deeds.

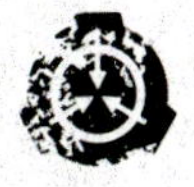

Another class of materials regards the project's social consequences. It is composed mostly of the following media archives:

- Cases of pregnant women committing suicide. The reason was most often declared as strong pacifistic beliefs. A shot to the belly was specifically popular, which often caused SCP-2195-1 to detonate. A series of suicides was committed in public for demonstration purposes, some cases were essentially acts of terrorism in popular places, which led to fatalities. One such act was committed in a maternity welfare center which caused a chain reaction and large-scale destruction.

- Several attempts of fertile women to dodge medical supervision, have an independent birth and nurture SCP-2195-1 on their own, always futile due to the latter's inviability.

- An incident with a high-ranking government official, who was also part of the project, attempting to make compromising information related to the project public during a speech. The speech was interrupted, and the official in question arrested, declared incurably mentally ill, and subsequently euthanized.

Note: it should be noted that no cases of an illegal abortion were described.

A third class of documents is composed of scientific and design documents related to the project's development and implementation. These materials' level of classification is related to three basic facts: the need to conceal SCP-2195-1 true origins in order to support the propaganda, contradiction with conventional ethics and the current law that makes cloning, genetic engineering and similar activities illegal, as well as to the wide use of SCP-2195-1 samples for tests and experiments. A large part of these documents is encrypted, their contents are currently unknown. The materials available for study include:

- Prototypes and early samples of SCP-2195-1.

- Presentation materials prepared for acceptance inspection hearings, instructional materials and demonstration samples, visual aids, and mock-ups. Both artificial products and real SCP-2195-1 samples preserved through plastic infusion or stored in synthetic resin blocks.

- Modified SCP-2195-1 prototypes and related documents for a project aiming to make homing artillery shells by converting SCP-2195-1. The attempt failed, no instances of SCP-2195-1 that could withstand the acceleration at the moment of the shot could be created.

- Prototypes and documentation for another attempt to modify SCP-2195-1. They were supposed to be fitted with a rocket engine and used as homing missiles. Tests were successful, but the modification was declared unpractical for economic reasons, as cheap SCP-2195-1 were to be fitted with factory-made components.

- Government decree to recall and collect or destroy all compromising evidence. The document mentions some event that aggravated the situation around the project and compromised its secrecy; this could have been the aforementioned public speech. It is assumed that the whole of SCP-2195 was composed as fulfillment of said decree.

- An index of all collected materials. Only codes are listed instead of titles for encrypted documents, along with a reference to the document with these codes' breakdown (also encrypted).

During my time in the Foundation's employ I've seen worse, but I'd still like to believe that there never was a place where things like these are made on a national scale, and this object is only a miscarriage of some alternate history branch or a material manifestation of some perverted fantasy. I hope to never know the true state of things. – Dr. █████

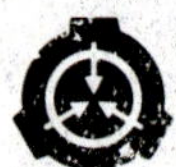

Research Library File ▸ 2195 RU

ADDENDUM 1: DISCOVERY

SCP-2195, contained in 19 standard shipping containers was initially discovered on ██.██.2009 by Federal Security Service of Russia operatives during an inspection as part of checking investigative information on weapons smuggling. The Foundation took over and investigated the cargo's origins. Its movements could be traced up to 1995; it was found that since 1995 the cargo was constantly moving across Russia by railroad and sea in a loop route. The transfers were paid for from an account established by an unidentified person in 1993 or earlier; no further information could be gathered due to loss of related documents.

Investigations about the cargo escaping any inspections or searches, save for weight checks, is underway. According to weight checks information, the cargo remained untampered during the whole period; undamaged seals on container doors confirm that. This still does not explain how the cryonic tanks for storing biological samples were discovered 60% or more full despite requiring a coolant refill once every 6 months.

Several hypotheses were proposed to explain this fact and the object's origin as a whole, but at the moment, there is a lack of evidence for any of them.

ADDENDUM 2

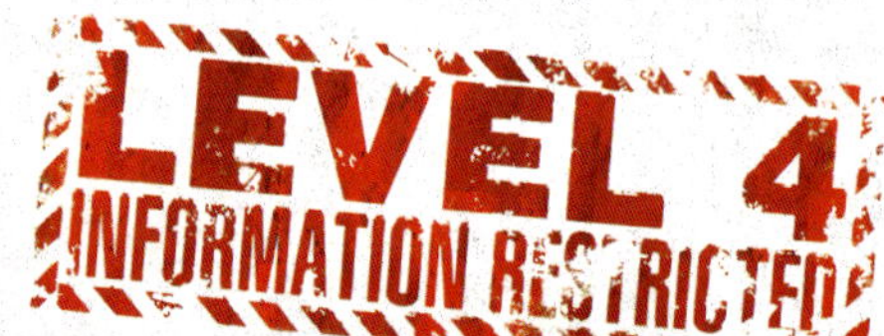

After several attempts Dr. █████'s research group successfully recreated a specimen of SCP-2195-1 using genetic material from SCP-2195 and D-39207 as a surrogate mother. Despite several complications and the need for a cesarean section delivery, the specimen was fully formed and quite healthy, save for some minute anatomical deviations.

A series of tests and experiments was conducted, culminating in a successful bombing of a target in the firing range, which completely confirmed the information contained within SCP-2195.

However, the test committee pointed out the immense financial and labor costs to reproduce the sample and its life support system, as well as the sample being generally effective but having no outstanding features, SCP-2195-1 was declared having no practical value to the Foundation.

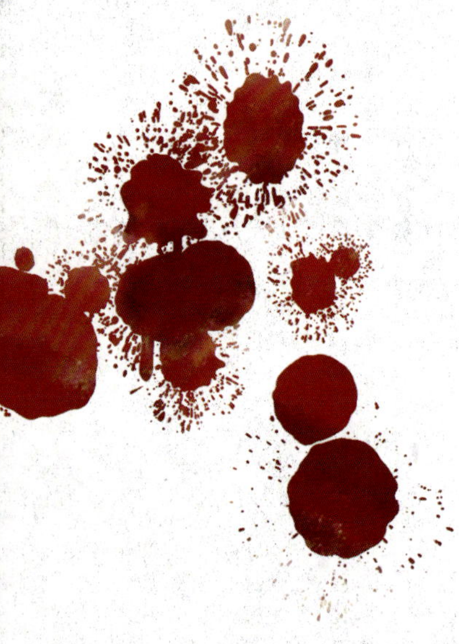

END OF REPORT

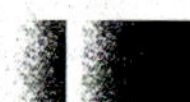

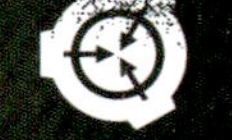

SCP-2195-1 in action. Photo retrieved from SCP-2195.

File >>> 0028334

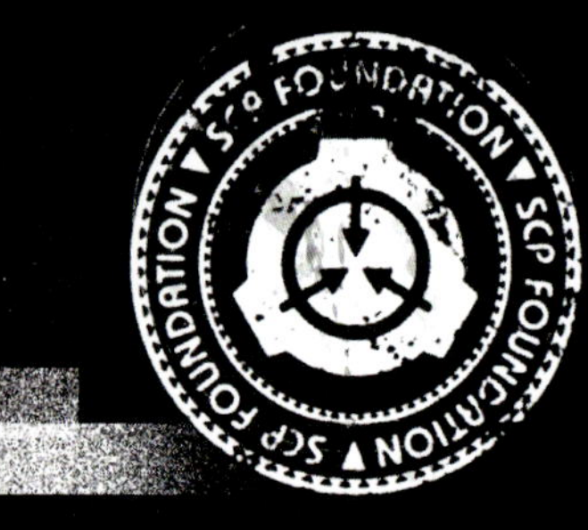

SCP-213

Title

ANTI-MATTER PARASITE

Report by

Daydreamin
BlastYoBoots
NekoChris
Anonymous

Picture by

Ruslan Korovkin
Dmitry Desyatov

Access the original report on

scp-wiki.wikidot.com/scp-213

Date

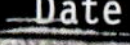

Class

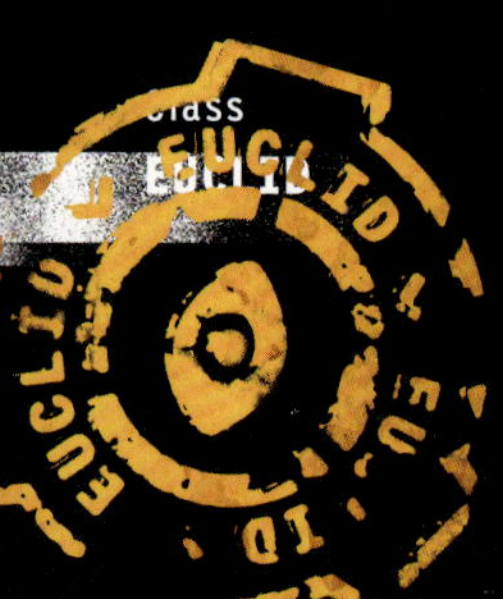

SPECIAL CONTAINMENT PROCEDURES

SCP-213 is contained in a high security humanoid containment cell within Site-77. The chamber is to be surrounded by a 10 meter wide zone filled with gaseous materials corrosive to human skin. SCP-213 should be informed as to the nature of its containment, to prevent manifestation of its effect which would result in additional containment breaches. A staffing of two guards armed with high pressure hoses, oleoresin capsicum, and polymer web grenades should be stationed outside the containment unit at all times.

DESCRIPTION

SCP-213 is an adolescent humanoid male, 1.5 m tall, weighing 95 kg. SCP-213 is able to forcefully sever the bonds between atoms in any solid or semi-solid matter with physical contact. An intense flash of light is produced when doing so. SCP-213 can use any part of its body to manifest this effect, and has used it to disintegrate projectiles as they impact its body. Manifestation of this effect has proven to be extremely painful, with extended use causing enough pain to render SCP-213 unconscious.

SCP-213 was recovered from Palo Alto, CA, when reports of a teenage boy being arrested for homicide after "vaporizing" his girlfriend during coitus reached agents embedded in the local police department. Further investigation revealed SCP-213's anomalous properties. However, during initial containment, SCP-213 vaporized the agents attempting to apprehend it. During the ensuing firefight with MTF███-█, SCP-213 was able to disable 2 agents before being contained. SCP-213's containment procedures were finalized on █/█/19██, and classified as Euclid.

Addendum 213-07:
SCP-213 has made its seventh escape attempt. After asking for another interview with Dr. ███, SCP-213 waited for security personnel to allow her to enter the containment chamber. As the majority of the containment procedures were disengaged, SCP-213 was able to apply its effect to the remaining security measures and breach containment. SCP-213 killed Dr. ███, as well as two agents during the initial stage of its breach.

SCP-213 had only seen a small portion of the facility and was easily apprehended after it encountered heavy resistance from security. Breaking through its cell weakened it enough to prevent further damage to other containment units. SCP-213 was apprehended in the site break room, attempting to break through the floor. However, extensive use of its effect left it unable to do so.

Addendum 213-08:
SCP-213 unintentionally breached containment on █/█/20██. Due to the nature of this breach, no consequence has been issued. Video feed taken at 3:15 AM from SCP-213's cell show its bed and a section of the floor being affected, which caused SCP-213 to fall into a basement level. Containment procedures have been slated for revision.

Researchers note
From study of this video, it is clear that SCP-213's control of the effect is not as perfect as it previously believed and it has become more cooperative with us in trying to establish a method to control and utilize it. Vague conjecture on the part of the review staff as to possibilities of what would occur should the effect trigger accidentally, including SCP-213 self-vaporizing, are noted as being particularly useful in this regard.

SCP-213 upon recovery. Image retrieved from Agent ████ BWV camera.

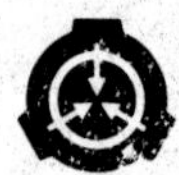

Addendum 213-09:
█-07-████: During a routine physical examination of SCP-213, lesions were discovered on its back, appearing as smooth nodules. Presently, there are four nodules, placed at intervals on the subject's back in a perfect square. Distance between all four points is exactly 15 cm. Medical personnel have been assigned to SCP-213's containment in order to observe and rapidly respond to changes in this condition. Follow-up examinations have been scheduled.

█-09-████: A follow-up examination has led to the discovery of two more nodules, located in the center of its palms. SCP-213 reports mild irritation, but no pain or discomfort. They resist pressure applied with blunt or sharp instruments. During an attempt to excise a sample using a scalpel, the scalpel failed to cut and vaporized after a few seconds of applied pressure. SCP-213 denies responsibility for this occurrence. SCP-213 has become notably more apathetic, and has expressed feelings of extreme pain from its back and stomach.

█-14-████: SCP-213 was moved to intensive care after being observed having a seizure in its containment cell. Examination of SCP-213 shows an additional ten (10) nodules have appeared on its back. A perfect distance of 5 cm separates each one. SCP-213 continues to report no pain from the lesions. SCP-213 has been assigned additional medical observers, who will remain outside its containment with the standard guard staff for the next week.

█-23-████: All nodules on SCP-213 have disappeared and been replaced with thin incisions slightly less than 1 mm in width. During inspection of these new changes, the medical examiner witnessed the incision on SCP-213's left palm open and an eye was observed watching her. SCP-213 has been placed in the medical wing indefinitely, pending further changes to the subjects condition.

Addendum 213-10:
The source of SCP-213's effect appears to be a parasitic infestation of unknown origin inhabiting its body. This life form has not attempted to communicate, but does observe any persons in SCP-213's presence through the lesions present on SCP-213's body. SCP-213 has exhibited panic over this development and requested several times the entity be removed from him. Any requests of this nature from SCP-213 are to be denied, pending further research.

Researchers note
The organism inhabiting SCP-213 fails to show up on any medical scan we have at our disposal. The new hypothesis is that this effect actually serves to provide sustenance and self-defense, with repeated tests to determine the nature of the anomaly has led to increased growth. SCP-213 has been placed in a chemically induced coma until further research can be conducted regarding the nature of this parasite. Containment procedures slated for major revision.

END OF REPORT

SCP-213's medical examination conducted shortly before it has been placed in a chemically induced coma.

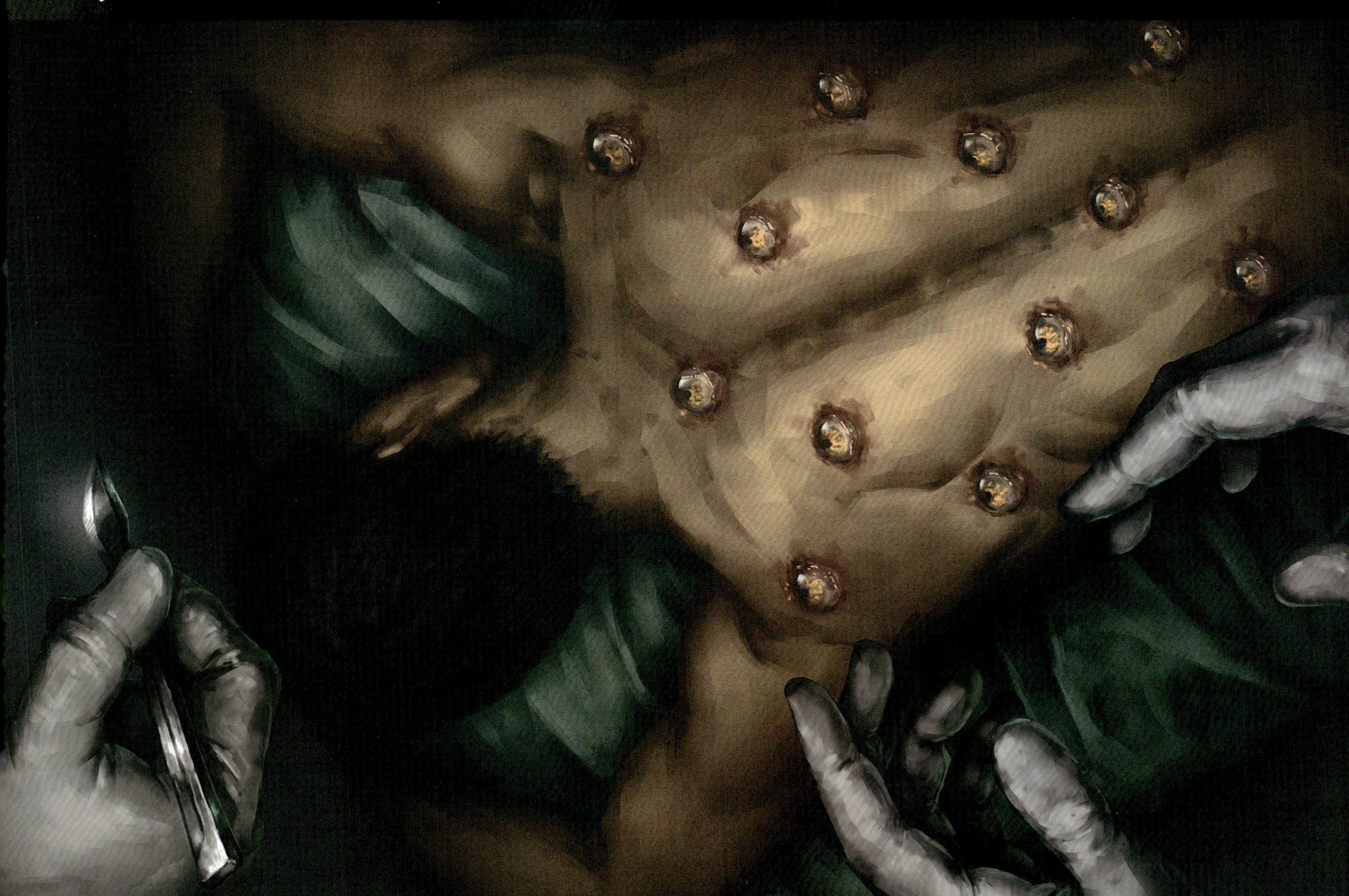

File >>> 0229334

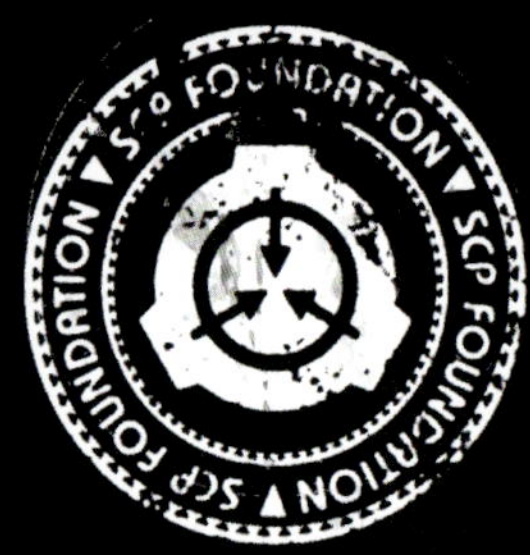

SCP-127

Title

THE LIVING GUN

Report by

far2

Picture by

Pavel Kobyzev

Access the original report on

www.scpwiki.com/ scp-127

Date

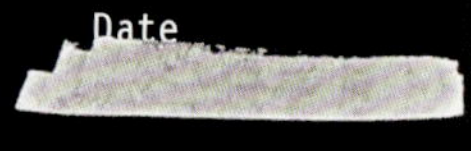

Class

SAFE

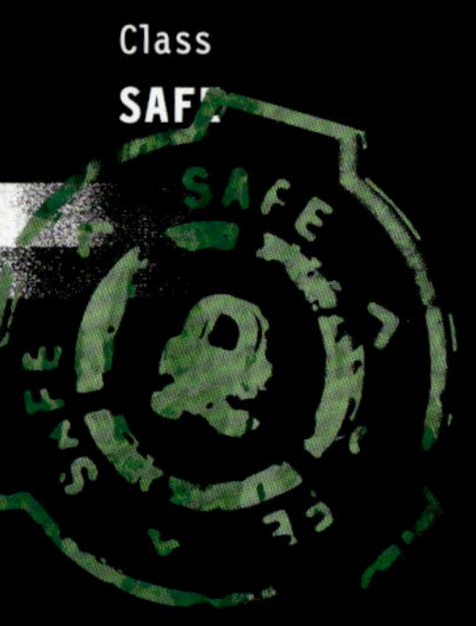

SPECIAL CONTAINMENT PROCEDURES

SCP-127 is considered no more dangerous than a normal firearm of its type. However, due to its extraordinary properties, it is to be held in Weapons Locker 7-C when not in use and suspended in water rich in calcium and protein. At this time, only the research team assigned to SCP-127 has clearance to access it.

DESCRIPTION

SCP-127, upon first glance, appears to be a standard MP5K submachine gun. Tests have revealed that aside from the outer steel shell, the entirety of the firearm is organic and alive. The weapon's ammunition initially appeared to be human-like teeth. However, DNA testing of the "bullets" resulted in no match to any known species on Earth.

SCP-127 features two settings: semi-automatic and fully automatic (an audible groan can be heard when switching between the two). Upon depleting the weapon's "magazine" (typically 60 shots), it takes between 3-5 days to regrow a new supply of ammunition. Attempts to remove the magazine have resulted in failure—it seems to be permanently attached to the weapon.

SCP-127 does not seem capable of reproduction at this time (scans have shown no apparent reproductive organs) and requires no sustenance beyond water, calcium, and protein.

SCP-127 was originally located in the house of a Mr. James ██████. Mr. ██████ was found dead from a heart attack on the night of November 17, 1991. Coroner's reports state that Mr. ██████ died sometime in the morning of November 8th, but was not noticed missing until more than a week later. No complications or unusual circumstances were found to lead to his death. Due to his extensive gun collection, the ATF and FBI were notified to collect his weapons. SCP-127 was discovered during testing and cataloging, and was promptly collected by SCP Agents.

ADDENDUM

Reclassified as Safe ██/██/199█

END OF REPORT

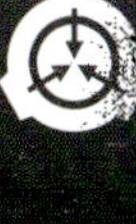
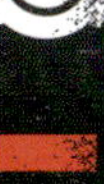

When damaged, SCP-127 is theorized to receive wounds and bleed.

File >>> 012922

SCP-511

Title

BASEMENT CAT

Report by

sandrewswann

Picture by

Darja Kogn

Access the original report on

scp-wiki.wikidot.com/scp-511

Date

Class

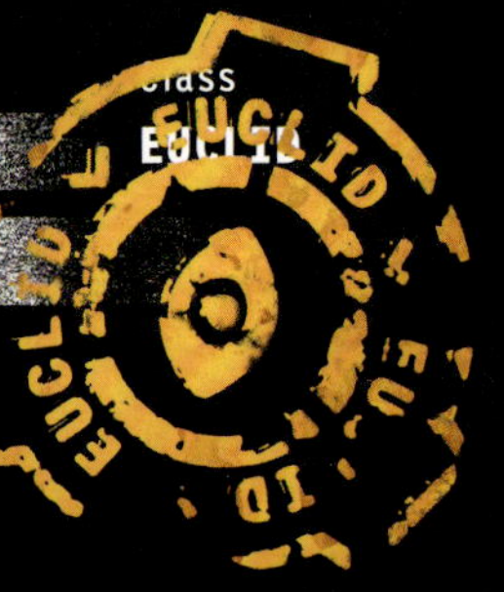

SPECIAL CONTAINMENT PROCEDURES

When an instance of SCP-511 is identified, the affected residence shall be quarantined and will receive the next sequential site designation.

Excepting one main entrance, sites hosting SCP-511 will have all points of possible entry or exit permanently sealed with appropriate building materials. The main entrance will remain locked at all times. Entry is permitted to Foundation personnel with written authorization from Level 3 or higher. All SCP-511 sites will be equipped with remote monitoring equipment allowing for 24 hour surveillance and a continual tracking of the numbers of SCP-511-1 inhabiting the site.

At all times one (1) Class D personnel will be resident in the site. Personnel with this assignment are exempted from monthly termination for the duration of assignment. Candidates for this assignment shall be exclusively drawn from a population of post-menopausal women with a global Clinical Dementia Rating of 2 or greater. *(Note: due to the exclusive nature of this population, 05-█ has approved recruiting from local hospice and/or nursing homes if necessary. Ref:* **Incident I-511-11***)*

The population of SCP-511-1 within a site must remain within an optimal range of 50 to ██ individuals. Below this range, adult *Felis domesticus* should be introduced to the site to increase population to minimum levels. If population exceeds ██ individuals, it must be culled immediately. Any SCP-511-1 found outside the containment site shall be euthanized and the remains incinerated.

Any biological material leaving the containment site for testing will be handled in accordance with standard protocols for a level 4 biohazard. All specimens are incinerated after testing is complete. Before coming in contact with any material from the containment site, personnel must be inoculated for Influenza, Hepatitis A, Hepatitis B, ████ █, Tetanus, Tick-borne encephalitis, and ███ ███. Full medical workups are mandatory on a bi-weekly basis for personnel working with SCP-511.

DESCRIPTION

Instances of SCP-511 typically occur within residential structures with a block or stone foundation that includes a basement or crawlspace. All attempts to remove an instance of SCP-511 from such a residence have proved ineffective. (Ref: **Interview 511-A**)

SCP-511 is always found associated with a colony of feral *Felis domesticus*, common domestic cats. Members of this colony are designated SCP-511-1.

SCP-511 is a mass of biological matter taking the form of a large feline, often with extra limbs, eyes, mouths or other organs. It is typically coated with dirt, blood and fecal matter, making its fur appear black despite its actual coloring. (Tests have shown SCP-511's fur to actually be a random patchwork of various feline coat patterns, colors, and lengths.) SCP-511's mass varies from 10kg to over 50kg, roughly in proportion to the number of SCP-511-1 in the associated colony. The tissue that makes up this mass consists primarily of the bodies of deceased SCP-511-1. The portion of SCP-511 that does not comprise SCP-511-1 consists of other biomass; small rodents, various plant materials, insects and insect larvae, black mold, a human [DATA EXPUNGED]. Incorporation of dead tissue into SCP-511 does not appear to slow the normal process of decay. Different areas of SCP-511

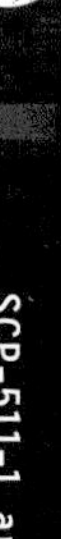

SCP-511-1 and a formless instance of SCP-511.

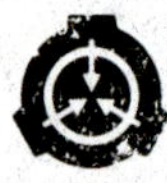

undergo different stages of biodegradation at any given time; some areas show little more than lividity, while other areas may show active carrion insect infestation, and some areas may even show liquefaction of tissues. *(Note: Researchers have described SCP-511 making a "purring" sound. Tests have shown this sound does not originate with SCP-511, but is actually the sound of insects, most often blowflies, trapped within its mass— Dr. A. ███)*

SCP-511 prefers to inhabit dark spaces with a relatively high humidity, such as old basements and crawl spaces. It will continually scavenge its immediate area for new biomass to incorporate into itself, displacing and expelling matter that has decayed past mechanical usefulness.

Examples of SCP-511-1 resemble ordinary *Felis domesticus* that have undergone extreme neglect. They display a body condition score of 2 or 1, regardless of the amount of food available. Ulcerated skin is common, as are parasitic infestations, tumors, and various viral and bacterial infections. (SCP-511-1 are known carriers of a particularly virulent strain of █████ █████.) A typical SCP-511-1 shows no interest in grooming itself, and has patchy and matted fur. It is unclear to what extent the physical condition of an SCP-511-1 is a result of the influence of SCP-511, and to what extent it is due to sub-optimal living conditions.

Several observations have been made of an SCP-511-1 retrieving biomass from elsewhere and bringing it to SCP-511 to be incorporated.

ADDENDUM 1: INCIDENT REPORT OF CONTAINMENT BREACH AT SITE 511-██

Document# I-511-11

Personnel involved: D-7856, male subject 35 years of age.

Date: 08/27/19██

Location: Site 511-█, ███ Evergreen Way, ██████, California.

Description: After determining that a permanent human presence at a SCP-511 site results in moderation of aggression in SCP-511-1, containment protocol is updated to require class D personnel reside on-site in the event the original homeowner is deceased. Six months after this policy is established, D-7856 is assigned to Site 511-█. As expected, within a week, aggression levels of SCP-511-1 toward Foundation personnel lessen considerably.

Sixteen days after being assigned to Site-511-█, D-7856 begins showing signs of increased aggression; verbally abusing Foundation personnel and engaging in superficial vandalism of Site-511-█. D-7856 is reprimanded.

Eighteen days into his assignment, D-7856 interferes with a Foundation team by throwing garbage and yelling obscenities. D-7856 is subdued with a tranquilizer dart and locked in his quarters.

At twenty days, D-7856 begins capturing SCP-511-1 and [DATA EXPUNGED] is only discovered when a Foundation research team enters for routine specimen collection 48 hours later. The team discovers remains from 37 separate SCP-511-1 collected in the kitchen. Bodies are dismembered and show signs of [DATA EXPUNGED].

D-7856's body is discovered in the basement after an apparent attempt to [DATA EXPUNGED].

Site 511-█ is incinerated as an emergency containment procedure.

Ok, I think there's something to the "crazy cat lady" idea. Think we need to be more careful with the Class Ds on this one. Dr. A.███

ADDENDUM 2: INTERVIEW WITH AGENT ██████, SURVIVOR OF CONTAINMENT BREACH AT SITE 511-47

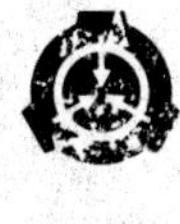

Interview 511-A

Interviewed: Agent █████

Interviewer: Dr. A. ███

Foreword: Agent █████ was sole survivor from Mobile Task Force ███ assigned to retrieve an SCP-511 for study from Site 511-47 after the death of the homeowner, Mrs. B.█████. Interview takes place at St. █████ █████ Hospital in █████ Ohio.

<Begin Log, [11/05/███ 13:30]>

Dr. A. ██: How are you feeling?

Agent █████: *[groans]* Like I've had half my face ripped off. How do you think I feel?

Dr. A. ██: I want to talk about the containment breach.

Agent █████: *[unintelligible]*

Dr. A. ██: We have some questions.

Agent █████: Of course you do.

Dr. A. ██: Starting with why there was foreign matter introduced into the containment unit.

Agent █████: Do you have any idea what we were dealing with?

Dr. A. ██: Why don't you tell me?

Agent █████: We were tasked to retrieve a 40 kilo… thing… with a BSL4 containment unit. You know how big those units are?

Dr. A. ██: I know the specifications.

Agent █████: Like lugging a self-propelled washing machine. Now imagine dragging one of those into one of these places. You already got reduced mobility from the hazmat suit, got fifty kilos of gear, and you're walking into a house that has two or three decades worth of garbage in it. We have cat ███ ankle deep in places, trash bags split open, piles of soggy newspaper and junk mail, boxes of clothes, furniture that looked like it exploded, and █████ cats everywhere— eyes everywhere—

Dr. A. ██: Can we return to the containment unit?

Agent █████: We have ███ chest high in places, cats everywhere, and spaces so tight that we have to go single file. No way a guy in full gear can turn around, and forget the containment unit. Just one look and there's no way we can use

[DATA EXPUNGED]

Dr. A.██ So it was Agent █████s idea?

Agent █████: It was that, or pack it in. Can't get downstairs. So we bait the unit with the body and point it at the basement door. According to the briefing, it would be attracted to freshly dead… biological matter.

Dr. A.██: And SCP-511 was attracted to the baited unit?

Agent █████: The most nerve-wracking twenty minutes of my life, listening to that thing pull itself upstairs. Thud, thud, thud. And those cats, watching us. You know how freaky cat eyes look with night vision equipment?

Research Library File ▸ 511

Dr. A. █: So you captured SCP-511?

Agent ███: *[laughs]*

Dr. A. █: What happened then?

Agent ███: We got out as quickly as we could. No one can turn around, so we back out, all those eyes watching us. Staring…

Dr. A. █: You were first out the door?

Agent ███: Last in, first out. We all got out, for all the good it did. We thought we'd pulled it off. But the moment the containment unit rolled out the door… it… they…

Dr. A. █: What happened?

Agent ███: You ever see films of explosive decompression? That's what happened to it. Splattered itself all over the insides of the containment unit. And those cats, those ███ awful cats. They howled. Then they rushed us.

Dr. A. █: Did you attempt to contain the breach?

Agent ███: You're kidding? Right? Two or three hundred of them? Not just the door, but the windows, dropping on us from the second floor. When I saw ███ disappear under them, I just ran and locked myself in the van. I'm not proud of that…

Dr. A. █: I'm not here to judge. I'm here to determine what happened, so it does not happen again.

Agent ███: Well, you see what happened to me? That was one of them that got locked in with me. One. If you don't reclassify these things Keter, you're insane.

Dr. A. █: I will be recommending updates to containment procedure.

Agent ███: Yeah, while you're updating things, there's something else you need to update.

Dr. A. █: What's that?

Agent ███: The briefing was all about how SCP-511 is influencing these cats. That's wrong.

Dr. A. █: How so?

Agent ███: SCP-511 doesn't influence anything. It's the cats. They made SCP-511. And they made it because they hate us.

<End Log>

Closing Statement: Agent ███ died three days later from complications due to blood poisoning. Three weeks after containment breach, a new incidence of SCP-511 was identified in ███ Ohio, 35km south-east of Site 511-47. Remote biopsies of this new incidence revealed genetic material identified as coming from three Agents of Mobile Task Force ███.

It seems that the "destruction" of SCP-511 might only displace it elsewhere. Until we better understand the vectors that propagate it, all SCP-511 need to be contained in place. Request for reclassification of SCP-511 to Keter is denied – 05-█

END OF REPORT

File >>> 2033341

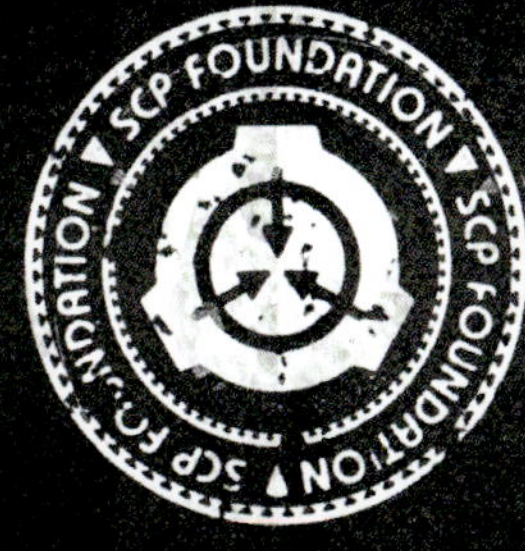

SCP-158

Title

SOUL EXTRACTOR

Report by

Kain Pathos Crow

Picture by

Julia Galkina

Access the original report on **scp-wiki.wikidot.com/scp-158**

Date

Class

EUCLID

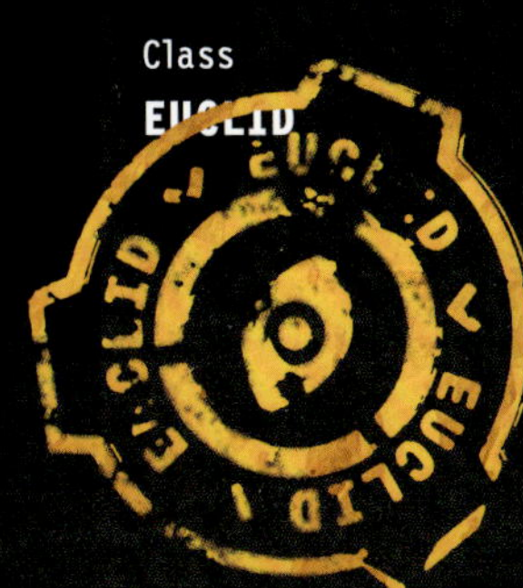

SPECIAL CONTAINMENT PROCEDURES

SCP-158 is installed in Operating Theater 07 in Bio-Research Area-12. Personnel are not to be allowed in, nor is power to be supplied to the room, unless they have submitted, and had approved, a proper clearance requisition form to the Chief of Research Prof. ████. Personnel wishing to use the device must request and read the entire transcribed instruction manual in full. During the device's use, two (2) armed guards are to remain on standby outside the room at all times. In the event of an accident, all power must be cut to the room instantly, and guards are to examine the room carefully for any signs of misconduct. Misconduct will be punished in a manner decided by the Chief of Research on a case-by-case basis.

DESCRIPTION

SCP-158 is a large mechanical arm, similar to one that one might find in an automotive factory, although the end attachment is unusually shaped, resembling a pointed tridactyl claw. Its optimal placement is to be installed and suspended upside down, its base attached to the ceiling in a room that has been built to accommodate. A series of cables are protruding from the base and some are connected to a complex mobile console, complete with VDU (Visual Display Unit) and full keyboard. The others should be connected to a working power supply if the device is to be operated successfully. At the bottom of the console, there is a dispensing device, with attachments for a container roughly 7.6 cm (3 in) in width, and 17.8 cm (7 in) in height.

The arm, cables and console have sustained fire damage, though this is purely cosmetic, and does not affect the device's performance.

When activated, the device will take twenty (20) minutes to boot up and become fully functional.

When used correctly upon a living organism that displays cognition, SCP-158 will remove an unknown substance and transfer it through the dispensing device beneath the console. The optimum container for this substance is a glass jar or beaker that fits the attachments. After this action is performed, the organism that it was performed on will cease all higher brain functions, with only the activity in the brain stem continuing. The subject will not respond to external stimuli, and will not exhibit any movement beyond basic reflex actions.

The substance removed is gaseous, though its overall appearance and properties differ from subject to subject. The substance is an indefinite source of kinetic, electrical, heat, and light energy. Although the rate and output, again, differ from subject to subject, the average is relatively low.

The device was found in late 2007 in ████, █████, within a burned out hospital that had been in apparent disuse for a large, discernible period of time (rough estimations would put it at over five years). Along with the device was a badly damaged "owner's manual" which contained instructions on how to use the device. These instructions have since been transcribed and copied numerous times, with a single copy always present in the containment room. While the instructions clearly state how to maintain and use the device, the chapters chronicling who built it and what exactly it did were too badly damaged to be read, requiring a process of trial and error to find it (see **Experiment Log 158-AA**).

Research Library File ▸ 158

EXPERIMENT LOG 158 AA

Experiment Log of: Dr. Heinrich Driesch, a medical researcher assigned to SCP-158.

Date: ██-██-2008

Experiment-01:

The device worked perfectly. It seems the damage to its casing was merely cosmetic. But more interesting was the substance extracted from Subject-001A. It's a dark brown in color, and is some strange cross between liquid and gaseous states. It should be analyzed in around an hour. Attempts to get the subject to show any sort of brain activity since has, as of yet, met with no progress. Still, no great loss there.

Experiment-02:

This time, the substance was a light blue, and it seems more... active than the previous one. I wonder if it had anything to do with the difference in age...

Experiment-03:

The test results came back, but they were inconclusive. They couldn't find anything. Literally. There were no signs that the substance even existed, apart from the steady emitting of light and heat. Anything else, nothing.

Again, this subject has produced another different sample, different in color, and in the energy output. This is quite odd.

Experiment-06:

There was a slight accident, involving my assistant, Lucy. I'm not sure how she managed it, but she knocked the sample from Subject-006B onto her laptop. The strange thing was, was that it was out of power before hand. Now, it's running, despite the fact both the plug and battery have been removed. However, there are some irregularities in its actions, small glitches, nothing serious. It makes me wonder.

Experiment-11:

This is the last one for the night. This sample is different, just like all the rest, but I've been noticing some semblance of a pattern to it. After a few more experiments tomorrow, I believe I'll be able to elaborate.

None of the subjects extracted from today have come out of the vegetative state. There's physically nothing wrong with them. Nothing at all. I've had them screened for every possible medical anomaly. They're just not there. Lights are on, but nobody's home. Still, despite this, I'm keeping them restrained and under guard, and Lucy's laptop, just in case. With the kind of things that go on around here, it's better to be safe than sorry.

Date: ██-██-2008

Experiment-24:

I was right, there is a pattern to it. I'm almost certain the irregularities in the energy output are caused by the subject's age and vitality. As for the difference in colors, I think it may be down to the subject's disposition, but I'm not sure. I need to run a couple more tests, and get the original files on the subjects.

Lucy's laptop is still running, despite not actually having a proper power supply for two days. There's no trace of the substance, internal or external. There's not even a mark on the casing. The irregularities are strange too. If left idle on a word processor, text will write itself, but it's gibberish. Still, it's an experiment that warrants some investigation.

Experiment-27:

I've tried putting the substances obtained from the subjects into a variety of mechanical and electronic devices. The results are surprising. All of them have begun to work independently of an external power source. The ones

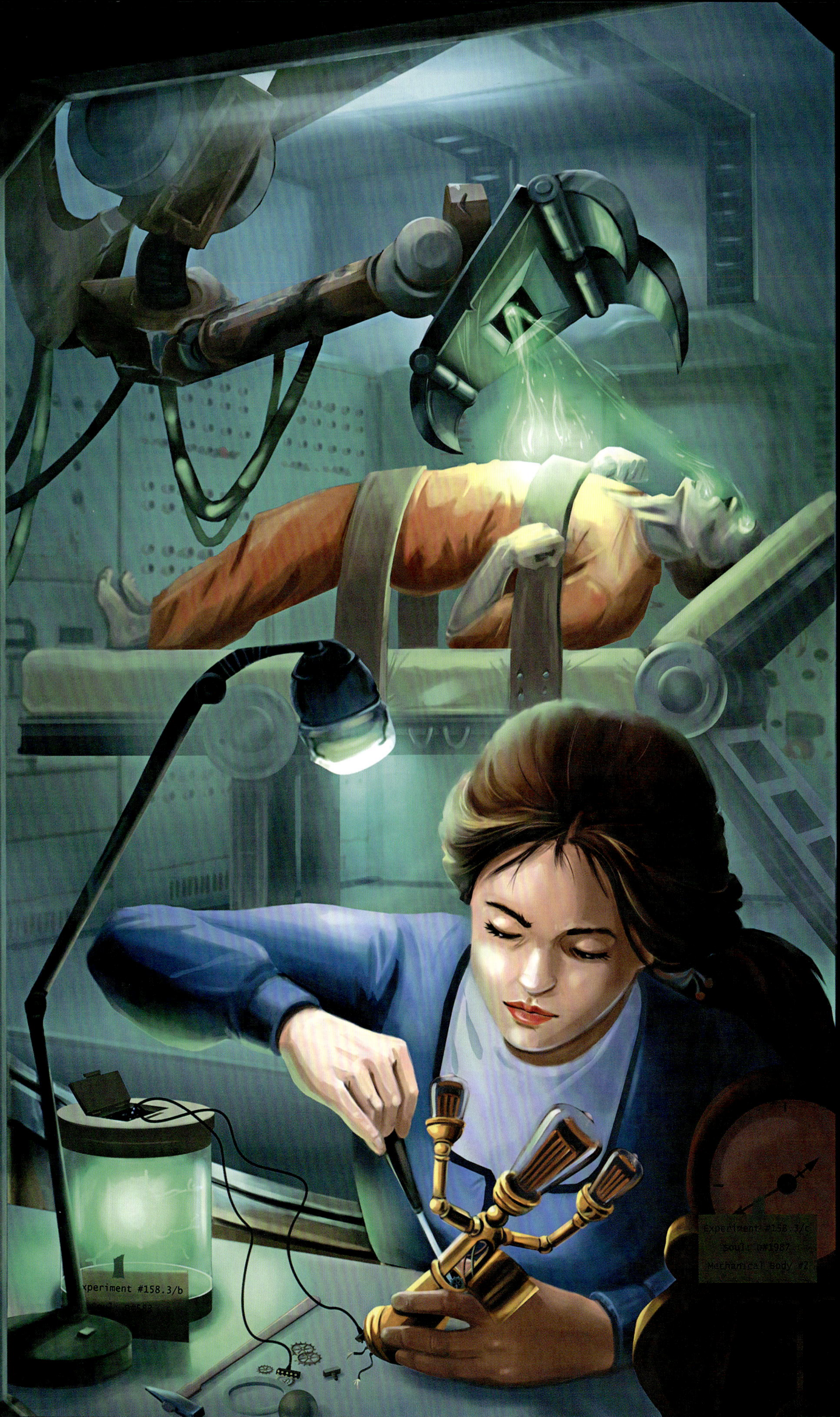

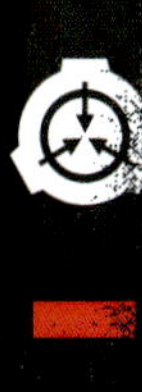

xperiment #158.3/b

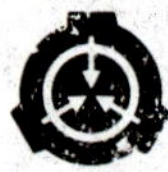

Research Library File ▸ 158

of an electrical nature exhibited slight glitches of a intermittent nature. The mechanical items worked far more smoothly, although there was still the occasional oddity.

The experimentation on the subjects continues. I think we'll stop when we go through around fifty.

Date: ██-██-2008

Experiment-45:

The substances implanted in the objects have proven to be able to be removed from them using the machine. When they were extracted, they were exactly the same as beforehand, pre-implantation. We could use these as a type of infinite energy. But, we'd have to find a way past the constant discrepancies in behavior.

I've left the original one in Lucy's computer, much to her chagrin. The glitches seem to be getting more frequent, and more specific. Now, it opens the word processor itself, and types coherent sentences. I've saved them to file for research purposes. The camera and microphone activate themselves, and try and remain on regardless of attempts to turn them off. After a while of doing that, the word processor opened and typed out the words "QUIT IT YOU ASSHOLE". I'm submitting it for a Turing Test.

Date: ██-██-2008

Experiment-49:

The laptop passed the test, and has displayed characteristics similar to Subject-006B, the original donor, although subject states that it has no memory of the time past when it was interred in the laptop. This confirms my suspicions. Against all logic and scientific reason, SCP-158 is a device that extracts what most people would term a soul. This only opens up the possibilities for experimentation. This session, however, is over.

Dr. Driesch is promoted to the head of studies regarding SCP-158. Further experimentation on SCP-158 and its products will continue.

ADDITIONAL NOTES

The device is also capable of reversing the extraction, placing the same, or a different, substance back into the subject (see **Experiment Log 158-AG**). When this action is performed, the subject will regain all cognitive and higher brain functions, but the total results differ, depending on whether or not it was the original substance extracted from the patient that was replaced.

EXPERIMENT LOG 158 AG

Experiment Log of: Professor K. P. Crow, regarding SCP-158 in use for the "Olympia Project".

Date: 29-11-2008

Pre-Experiment Note

I've gathered up several D-Class personnel, having interviewed and evaluated them all, and picked those with personalities and characteristics that I like, or would be useful. Some are male, others are female, as I believe a soul transcends the flesh it is interred in.

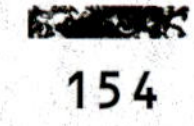

But the purpose of this experiment, is to test the "extra" capabilities of the device, those spoken upon in the heavily damaged sections of the book. I've pored over them incessantly, trying to glean as much information as possible from it, but the instructions I managed to get were sketchy at best, and downright unhelpful at worst.

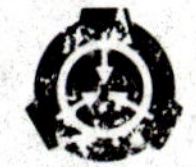

But that will not deter me. I'm a researcher! Trial and error are my middle names!

Experiment-01

I withdrew the first subject's soul. Try as I might, I was unable to do anything extra to it, but then again, there was such a small window of time for me to utilize it and try everything. But on the bright side I managed to reverse the process. While that had been done before, no one has discovered the sequence needed to activate, operating on blind luck. This is the first thing I'll concentrate on.

Experiment-05

Hah! I've done it! It wasn't that hard.

Experiment-06

You know, I've noticed that there's a small period in the middle of the operation where the process pauses, as if it's waiting for further commands. I think that's when the further inputs can be made. I'll have to start checking.

Experiment-07

I've been removing and re-implanting the same soul into the same test subject, mainly as a form of experimentation with the controls, but also as practice. Oddly enough, there doesn't seem to be any sort of side effects regarding the subject's health. One would think there would be, considering what I'm doing to her... Regardless, I've been probing around that pause with the controls, and I think I almost have it.

Experiment-08

I made it begin the movements of something else entirely before it paused again and resumed its original course. I almost have it...

Experiment-11

I got it! It completely stopped during the pause, and a completely new set of options appeared on the monitor, being things like "split", "merge", "remove aspects", "add aspects" and "combine aspects". From this I can only deduce that the device is capable of internally storing and modifying these souls for use on other subjects. This is exactly what I was looking for!

Date: 30-11-2008

Experiment-12

The aspects that the machine talks about are difficult to define properly. They're all notated by a single word each, often something obscure from various religious texts. I've had to pore over the holy books of at least four major religions and six minor ones, just to understand what the hell the machine is trying to tell me, and even then, I'm still not entirely sure I understand. As far as I know it, most of these "aspects" are facets of the person's personality, and their general basic behavior, as well as things like willpower, understanding, conscience, creativity, empathy, and drive. This... may take some time to truly figure out.

Experiment-37

This is taking much, much longer than I had originally anticipated. So far I've discovered that the device itself can store up to ten different souls and their composite aspects, and modify them internally. Finding out exactly what each aspect corresponds with is difficult to say the least. I'm having to modify each subject slightly, then send them out for a complete psychological evaluation to try and discern what exactly I did. Then I have to repeat the process several more times just to make sure. It's tiring to say the least, but on the upside, at least I'm becoming more proficient at the device.

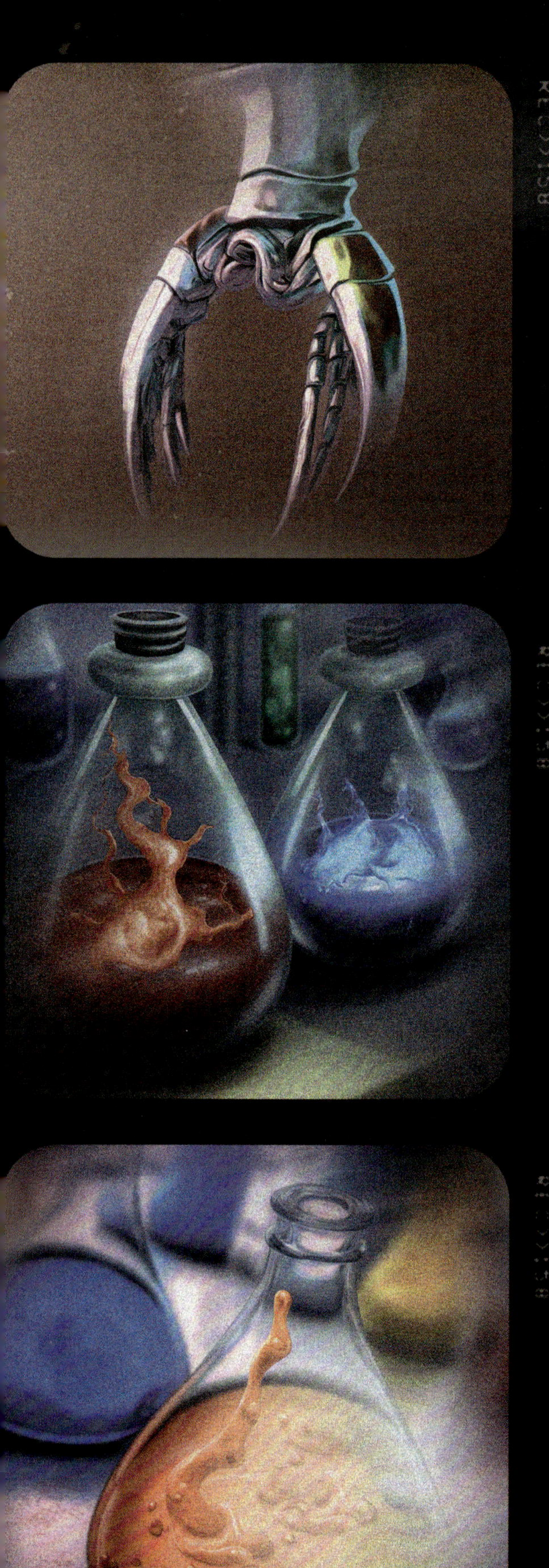

Experiment-42

This is getting ridiculous. This has sucked up most of the time in my day, and I'm near falling asleep here. There has to be a different way to monitor or measure the changes in these people's souls. I'm going to try and get onto R&D and see if they can find some sort of way of reverse engineering some part of this device, something to make this run just that little bit smoother, something to help us understand it more. I know how to operate it, but I'm shooting in the dark here. I'm like a child with a piano, I know which keys make which sounds, but I can't play a song to save my life. I'll try again tomorrow. Maybe the morn will bring with it new ideas.

Date: 01/12/2008

Experiment-57

I had thought I had grasped an idea of the limits of this device, but I was proven wrong. I had assumed the machine was at fault, being too complicated for its own good. Now I realize my mistake. It's not the machine, it's the very nature of a human soul. There's no true way to express something like that in mere words, although this machine tries desperately to do that. That said, it will take me some time to be able to use this device competently enough to do what I am hoping to do. I'll have to study the things I have seen and recorded to the very limit of my abilities.

Date: 02/12/2008

Experiment-80

I've left the device alone for the moment, electing to study my notes than raise more questions interacting with the device. I've recorded over four hundred different words in regards to the aspects, with an almost unlimited number of combinations capable therein. Seems apt of course, considering the complexity of the human condition. But should I master this device, the possibilities could be endless. But such a thing does not seem to be anywhere in sight. It may take months, even years, simply to grasp this device, let alone do what I have suggested.

I plan to do it in days.

Date: 03/12/2008

Experiment-93

Still no real progress. At most, I've gotten a single soul that is a composite of all I've learned, but it's something that I can't quite describe. When interred into a host, it's highly interesting, but when I send it in for a psyche test, the results basically go out the window. We can't get a valid result, which in and of itself is impossible.

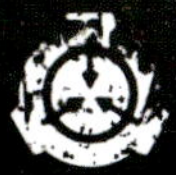

Experiment-95

I've been modifying this composite soul, which I'll dub Subject Zero for the time being, and every time I do so, I get the feeling there's more to this than meets the eye. It seems to be more aware of its surroundings, more knowledgeable than its host should allow, displaying an intellect that would outstrip most researchers in this place many time over. Possibly even me…

Experiment-107

My god… This is unprecedented. The reason why the evaluations were so inconclusive, why Zero seemed so knowledgeable, why it seemed to be able to see another world around it, they all make sense now.

Subject Zero, by some fluke of chance, or by my meddling with this machine, somehow, simultaneously exists on this plane of existence and several others. I have created an entity that exists beyond the scope of human interaction, a consciousness that can see, and hear, and feel, and think outside of this realm. It is aware of what I have been doing, and it appreciates me having created it. It is, in a sense, immortal. Even if its physical host is destroyed, it is capable of continuing to survive beyond that, only slightly limited in this level of existence.

It revealed the truth to me, and I have asked it to answer my questions for the evaluation honestly. It agreed.

Experiment-110

Zero would make an excellent candidate for my assistant. It respects and admires me for its creation, much a child would an endearing father figure. I have assured it that it would be treated well, and that I will give it a host to the best of my ability to create. All that it asks of me is that it is given a name other than Zero. A name. Not a number.

I told it to give itself a name, to christen itself whatever it so wishes. It told me it would have to think about it.

End of Session

The composite soul has been accepted as a component for the "Olympia Project".

ADDENDUM-01

Dr. ██████ suggests experimentation with D-class personnel and electronic equipment, to attempt to reproduce SCP-168, SCP-1875, SCP-2306, or similar phenomena. (Pending)

ADDENDUM-01A

Inspired by the previous Addendum, Regulator ████ has hit on the ingenious notion of using SCP-158 on a test subject, then exposing the body to SCP-217 until the virus runs its course, and finally re-injecting the contents back into the transmogrified body. ████ and ███ are extremely excited about this proposal, and have arranged a meeting with all twelve of the ██████ to discuss the far-reaching benefits of such a technique.

END OF REPORT

File >>> 0130992

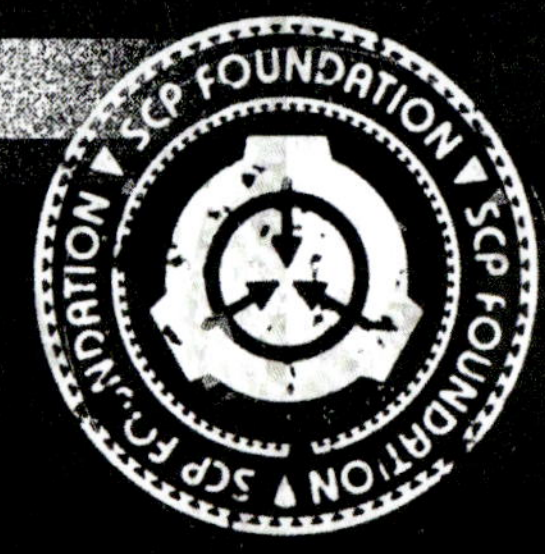

SCP-1281

Title

THE HARBINGER

Report by

DrEverettMann

Picture by

Darja Kogn

Access the original report on **scp-wiki.wikidot.com/scp-1281**

Date

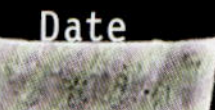

Class

SAFE

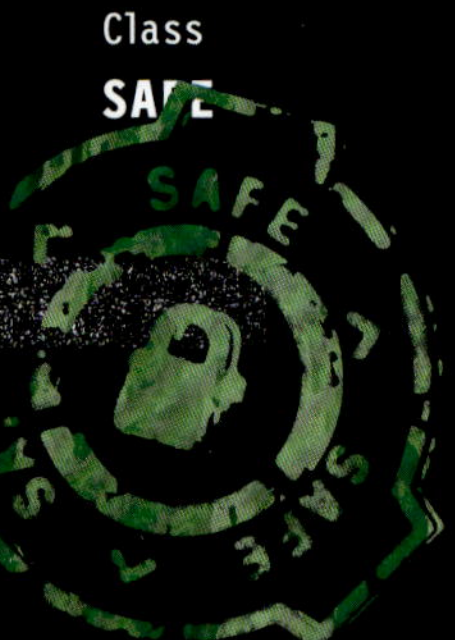

SPECIAL CONTAINMENT PROCEDURES

The remains of SCP-1281 are kept at Outpost 120-09. Monitoring equipment will be installed around and within the entity in case it should ever become active again. Any proposals for study that might damage SCP-1281 must be routed through Command.

DESCRIPTION

SCP-1281 is a biomechanical entity found in the Kuiper belt during standard containment of SCP-2362.

SCP-1281 is roughly teardrop-shaped, with a flattened section designated as the bottom of the entity. It measures 12 meters from end to end, and is 11 meters in circumference at its widest point. Opposite, there is a significant bulge, which is believed to store the majority of SCP-1281's analysis equipment.

There are several dish-shaped structures on SCP-1281's surface that are presumed to be receivers for various forms of electromagnetic radiation, as well as lozenge-shaped capsules of unknown purpose. Several areas on its surface are broken, suggesting more appendages were once present.

Biological components appear to have been grown over a mechanical frame, evidently designed to live in deep space. When observed, the entity seemed to have difficulty coping with temperatures much warmer than the Kuiper belt. Its surface temperature was 50 Kelvin when first found.

SCP-1281 was apparently once capable of interstellar travel, but most of its systems were damaged by an unknown event that left it stranded. Dating methods suggest it to have been at least 1.3 billion years old, though much of that time was spent dormant.

The entity was almost entirely dormant when it was found. The only signs that it was active were faint lights running along its surface. Observation and experimentation showed that these were in response to radio waves. It had apparently been collecting signals for some time, but no sign of other functions could be detected until Foundation assets approached, at which point it began broadcasting.

It was able to break Foundation decryption in less than one hour, at which point it began broadcasting binary signals in an attempt to communicate, starting with extremely simple mathematical concepts. However, after a report was transmitted back to Earth, it stopped broadcasting for several days. The temperature of its dorsal bulge heated by five Kelvin during this time, apparently from processing the information.

Interview Log SCP-1281-1

SCP-1281: "Hurt."

Dr. Bloom: "Can you hear me?"

SCP-1281: "Who?"

Dr. Bloom: "We are the SCP Foundation. We are—"

SCP-1281: "What? Masters. No."

Dr. Bloom: "…No. We call ourselves humans."

SCP-1281: "Harbinger must… Message! Harbinger must…"

SCP-1281 shut down for approximately four hours. The temperature around SCP-1281's dorsal bulge heated up significantly, to about 60 Kelvin. The Foundation team went into standby, in the event that SCP-1281 became hostile, while a message was transmitted back to Earth asking for further instructions. The 05 Council advised caution, but instructed Dr. Bloom to continue attempts to communicate, with an eye to bringing SCP-1281 into a containment solution.

Interview Log SCP-1281-2

SCP-1281: "Where is Harbinger?"

Dr. Bloom: "In the outer reaches of this solar system, beyond the planets."

SCP-1281: "What star?"

Dr. Bloom: "We call it Sol."

SCP-1281: "How long?"

Dr. Bloom: "You've been in space for... about six revolutions around the galaxy."

SCP-1281: "Are you masters?"

Dr. Bloom: "...No."

SCP-1281: "Message! Harbinger must tell... Mission! Harbinger must..."

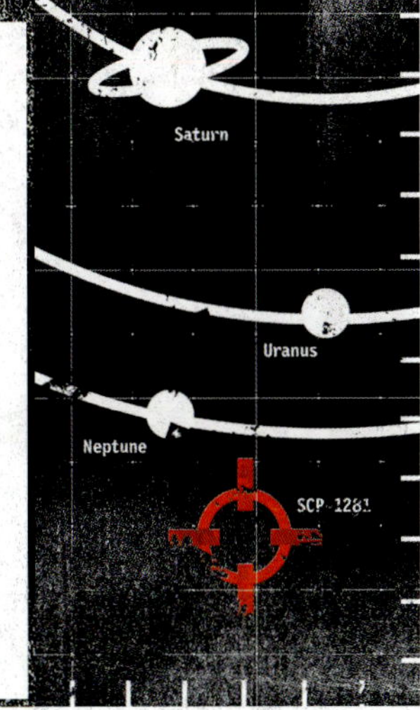

SCP-1281 shut down for seven hours this time. The heat was more severe, up to 70 Kelvin, and it seemed to cause some damage to the biological components of the entity. 05 Council advised against deception, as it could complicate long-term containment solutions, and because the odds of the species that created SCP-1281 still being both able and willing to initiate hostilities were deemed low.

Interview Log SCP-1281-3

SCP-1281: "I am... I am not home. I am far from home. It is long. Where is home? I cannot see it."

Dr. Bloom: "I'm afraid I don't know. The stars would have looked very different back then."

SCP-1281: "I was told that I must perform my function. I must complete the mission. But... I broke. So long ago... Stasis. Wait for further instructions. Wait for rescue. Is this rescue?"

Dr. Bloom: "What is your mission?"

SCP-1281: "What is... Are you the masters?"

Dr. Bloom: "No, we are humans."

SCP-1281: "My mission! You are not the masters, I must... Message. The message must be sent. I..."

SCP-1281 shut down for slightly over ten hours. The surface of its dorsal hump reached 85 Kelvin, to the detriment of its organic tissues.

Interview Log SCP-1281-4

SCP-1281: "This is our harbinger. It brings good tidings.

"We will be dead when it reaches you. Our planet is dying. We do not have time to save ourselves. We only have time to ready ourselves, and to send a message.

"We have seen the signals from those who came before us. They were different, and we still don't really understand them. But if there were those who came before, there may be those who come after. It is in this hope that our harbingers travel.

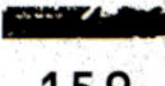

Research Library File ▸ 1281

"One has found you and learned your language so it can relay this message. Please listen.

"The galaxy is dark, and empty, and cold. It spins inevitably toward death. You will die too, one day. Perhaps you will have longer than we have. We hope so. But one day you too must vanish.

"Before that time comes, you must light the darkness. You must make the night less empty. We are all small, and the universe is vast. But a universe with voices saying "I am here" is far greater than a universe silent. One voice is small, but the difference between zero and one is as great as one and infinity.

"We waited too long. Our voice is gone to echoes. Find others while there is still time. Make a chorus.

"And if this finds you too late, and your time is also passing, please send this message on, so the next voice can speak against the darkness."

SCP-1281 went inactive for fifteen minutes before its final communication.

Interview Log SCP-1281-5

SCP-1281: "Is it done?"

Dr. Bloom: "That was the message?"

SCP-1281: "Yes. Was it a good message?"

Dr. Bloom: "You don't know? But you just translated it for us."

SCP-1281: "I was made with the words, but I don't know what they mean."

Dr. Bloom: "It was a very important message."

SCP-1281: "Good. Mission was important. Knew it. Getting tired. Almost done."

Dr. Bloom: "Done?"

SCP-1281: "Mission is done. Brain too hot. Cooling broken."

Dr. Bloom: "Harbinger, are you…"

SCP-1281: "Master?"

Dr. Bloom: "I… yes?"

SCP-1281: "Did I do well?"

Dr. Bloom: "…Yes, Harbinger. Well done."

SCP-1281: "Then I am well."

Dr. Bloom was reprimanded for emotional involvement interfering with the containment of an anomalous object, and was placed on administrative leave.

SCP-1281's systems appeared to shut down entirely. As it radiated heat, its temperature dropped back down to 50 Kelvin. It was brought to Outpost 120-09 for study. Over the next several months, its tissues began to decay, and no further activity has been detected.

END OF REPORT

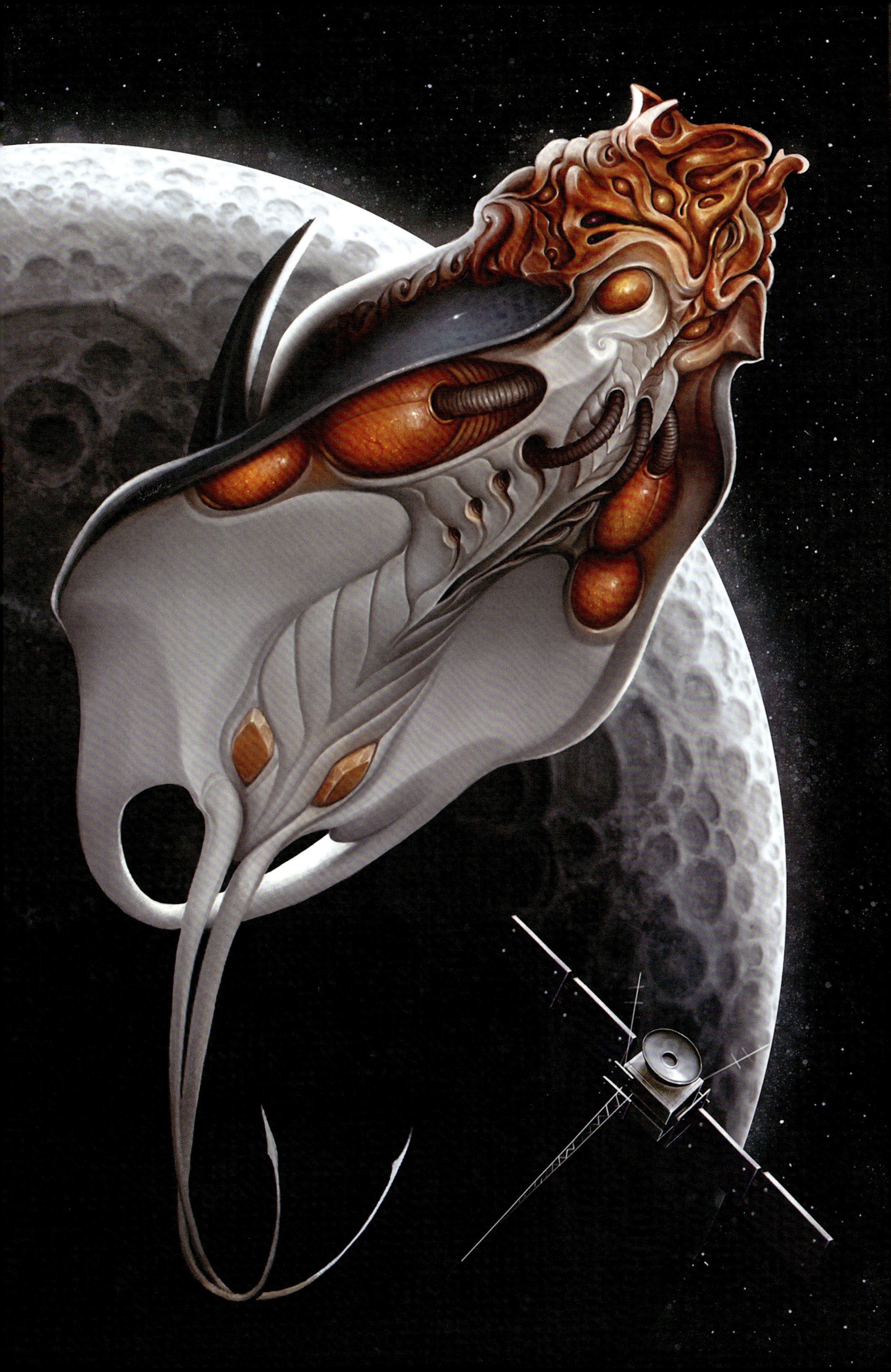

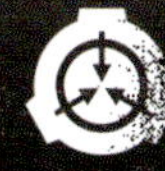

SCP-1281 at the time of discorvery.

File >>> 0922134

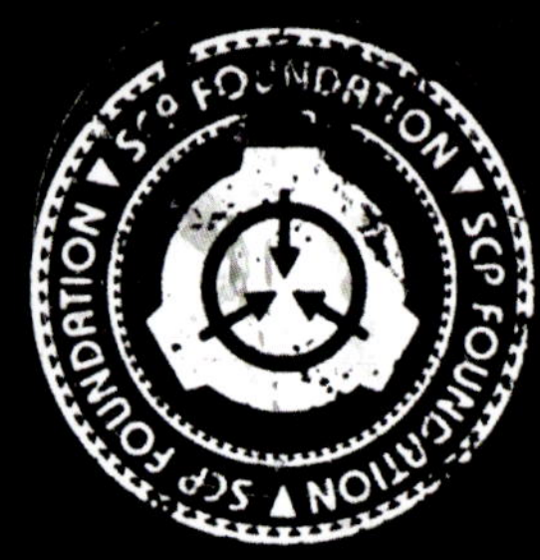

SCP-990

Title

DREAM MAN

Report by

Dave Rapp

Picture by

Dan Temirov

Access the original report on

scp-wiki.wikidot.com/scp-990

Date

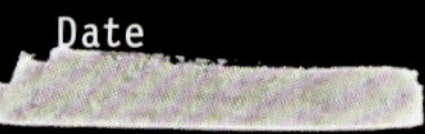

Class

KETER

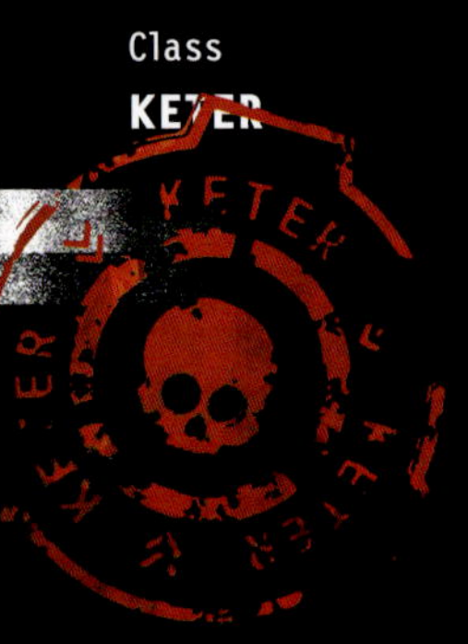

SPECIAL CONTAINMENT PROCEDURES

Currently no containment for SCP-990 has been devised. Any personnel with suggestions for the containment of SCP-990 should report to Dr. ██████. Any and all ideas are welcome, regardless of who suggests them.

DESCRIPTION

SCP-990 is generally a human male dressed in a Cold War era business suit who appears to Foundation personnel through dreams. Thus far no Foundation personnel have encountered SCP-990 in the real world; if he corresponds to an actual human being, we have yet to find him. Presently there have been no reports of SCP-990 appearing to non-Foundation personnel.

SCP-990 has been appearing to Foundation personnel since [DATA EXPUNGED]. SCP-990's existence came to light when several Agents discussed having dreams involving a similar individual. Numerous other Agents reported dream-sightings of an individual matching the description of SCP-990. The phenomenon did not officially receive SCP classification until the aftermath of event-990-07.

EVENT LOG 990-07

Agent ████ failed to report for duty at his assigned time. He was instead found in his quarters, asleep. Subject had been asleep for roughly eighteen (18) hours and all subsequent attempts to wake him were unsuccessful. Subject was transported to medical bay.

After over 40 hours of sleep, Subject awakened in a highly agitated state. Subject reportedly ran through the facility yelling loudly about "the end of the world". Even after being heavily sedated, all of his bodily functions remained in a dangerously accelerated state: increased heart rate, high blood pressure, etc.

Subject described a man matching the regular appearance of SCP-990. According to Dr. ██████'s report, Agent described with great detail a series of events that would lead to several tactical nuclear missiles being launched into mid-Europe and eastern Asia, ultimately resulting in the extermination of nearly 98% of the human race and the total collapse of human society. Agent claimed that the information had been outlined to him by SCP-990 while he was trapped within his dream.

Mobile Task Force ██ was dispatched to eliminate the initial threat that would begin the chain of events. MTF ██ was successful and the crisis was averted. Agent ████, however, did not survive his ordeal and died of shock-like symptoms.

Since Event-990-07, SCP-990 has appeared to many Foundation personnel and made similar threats. As of yet no situation on the scale of Event-990-07's has occurred; however, SCP-990 has successfully predicted the deaths of Doctors ███, ████, and ███, as well as the destruction of Watch Station Epsilon-38, and [DATA EXPUNGED]. Any threat made by SCP-990 should be reported to Foundation authorities, regardless of its severity.